the Leaving of Things

the Leaving of Things

Jay Antani

LAKE UNION
PUBLISHING

This is a work of fiction. Names, characters, organizations, places, events, and incidents are either products of the author's imagination or are used fictitiously.

Published by Lake Union Publishing, Seattle

www.apub.com

Amazon, the Amazon logo, and Lake Union Publishing are trademarks of Amazon.com, Inc., or its affiliates.

ISBN-13: 9781477826133
ISBN-10: 1477826130

Cover design by *theBookDesigners*

Library of Congress Control Number: 2014941171

Printed in the United States of America

Author's Note

As you read this story, you'll come across a variety of Indian words and phrases. You can probably guess what they mean, but if you want to know for sure, there's a glossary in the back. Enjoy!

Chapter

1

June 19, 1988

India wasted no time with me. Monsoonal air acrid with soot and sweat and something else—a densely Indian spice—slammed into my head, my lungs, my senses as I approached the door. I fell in behind my parents, a crowd of exiting passengers, and I felt every bit the prisoner as we trudged from the plane into a tunnel of dirty white light.

I wanted so badly to turn around and fly back home to America—to tell my parents, "*Stop!* This is a *huge* mistake." I didn't want to be here—certainly didn't want to *live* here—but life wasn't about choices. It was a sentence handed down to you.

From the mouth of the tunnel, we spilled out into the arrivals hall of the Bombay airport. The place echoed eerily with jostling bodies and announcements from an ancient PA system. I stared at the mishmash of Hindi and English: "Customs," "Immigration," "Baggage." But what the Hindi really said to me was *Kid, you're not in Wisconsin anymore.*

In one hand, I clutched the hard plastic case containing my video camera—a high school graduation present from my parents, and my proudest possession. In my backpack were a few prized

Rolling Stone issues, my music tapes, and books (Bradbury, Tolkien, Vonnegut) I needed near me at all times.

Two children and a woman in a sari rushed past me, knocking my video camera case out of my hand. It clattered wildly to the floor. Half-panicked, I grabbed the case and closed a tighter grip on it.

"Vikram, watch out," my father reprimanded in Gujarati, a few steps ahead, "or you'll lose or break that thing."

The gall of that guy, I thought. Dragging us from our home to this, and all he could say was "Watch out"? I glared at the back of his head. He was the reason we were here. He'd taken a fancy job at some astrophysics institute in Ahmedabad, a city in Gujarat about an hour's plane ride north of Bombay. It was the perfect opportunity for him to make good on his scheme to move my mother; my younger brother, Anand; and me back to what he called "the land of our roots." He'd given up his work visa—the one thing that kept us tethered to America—and uprooted us from everything that was and would be our lives.

India may have been the land of *his* roots, but it was the land of *my* exile.

Elbows and suitcases nudged and jabbed at me as we made our way down a set of steps to the immigration hall. A child stumbled over both my feet. A fat Sikh with an Air India shoulder bag pushed past me, bellowing instructions and waving wildly to someone in front of him.

To my left, Anand looked half-asleep. His face was drawn and his backpack slung low at his shoulder. He still wore his headphones. He'd kept them on most of the trip, while thumbing through his baseball magazine or one of his Choose Your Own Adventure paperbacks. I wondered if the headphones were his protection from all that was happening.

I glared again at my father. He seemed so focused, so *delighted* to be back in India. You see, he had grown up in Ahmedabad. In fact, we had lived in Ahmedabad before we'd left for America eleven years ago. And it was there that my father expected my brother and me to settle right back in—Anand into the eighth grade and me into my first year of college.

And my mother, you ask? She'd worn her favorite *salwaar kameez* today—so *tickled* she must've been to be back here! No doubt she was in league with my father. I decided I wanted nothing more to do with either of them.

A frowning immigration officer stamped our passports. We collected our things—two large and two small suitcases—and went inside the customs hall, packed with worn-out travelers and about the size of my high school gym. (It smelled like it too!) Inspectors on the far side of the hall picked through passports, paperwork, everybody's baggage like scavengers.

"Anand, what're you doing?" my father asked sharply. My brother had unbuckled his suitcase and was rooting through it.

"Not now, *beta*," my mother said.

But then, my brother found what he was looking for—his Brewers cap. He slid off his headphones and slipped it on.

"Why bother with that now?" My father shook his head, half-amused, half-irritated. He sized up the lines in the customs hall. "Forty-five minutes," he said.

"Forty-five?" my mother shot back. "This will take two hours minimum."

My father turned to her and scoffed. "You're sure of everything, aren't you?"

Our connection to Ahmedabad left in three hours from the domestic terminal. I asked how far that was.

"Far," my mother said.

My father pushed strands of thinning hair across his scalp and, with a long sigh, admitted, "Yes. It's far."

As long as we were waiting, I figured I'd better shoot some video. Since leaving Wisconsin (when was that—yesterday?), I'd been recording footage for a kind of video journal—my own first-hand reports on what it felt like to go from home-sweet-home America across Europe and on to the far Indian tropics. I planned on mailing the tapes to my best friends, Nate and Karl, and my girlfriend, Shannon, every month.

So I took the camera out of the case and panned across the hall, across the sea of faces, mostly brown faces, surrounding me: Some I recognized as tired fathers, much like my own father, in spectacles, short sleeves, and mustaches. I saw women who resembled my own mother, in their salwaar kameez, clutching purses and duffel bags. They all stood silently or in tense conversation, tending to their luggage and their children.

They all looked so miserable, and here I was, no different from them. *I was one of them.* That got me dreading my fate even more, so I put the camera away and sat next to Anand on one of the suitcases, hoping for conversation.

His headphones pulled over his Brewers cap, Anand bobbed his head, drumming his fingers on the suitcase and humming to the tune that filled his head. "Who're the Brewers playing this weekend?" I asked him as cheerfully as I could.

"White Sox," Anand said without even turning to me. "Last game of the series." He resumed his humming, his drumming. I left him to it. But I couldn't keep it bottled up like Anand; I needed to talk, to stay braced against my anxiety.

I glanced at my father again. There he stood, oblivious as ever to Anand and me, one hand at his hip and the other picking at his mustache, staring intently at the front of the line. I turned to my mother, who had propped herself atop a suitcase, tapping her chin.

"Are you happy?" I asked. "I mean, happy to be here?"

"Mm-hmm," she said absently, without looking at me. I didn't believe her, didn't *want* to.

Over the past few weeks, I'd been building a wall between me and the tide of fear, depression, and panic I could now sense rising. I knew it was there, filling up my heart. Keep it together, Vikram. Don't break.

So I thought of someone who calmed me—Shannon. Last I'd seen her was two nights ago. I thought of her hand reaching for mine across the table at Rocky's Pizza after spending our final evening wandering the record and clothes shops along State Street.

"Couldn't you stay?" were Shannon's words while she pressed my hand. "I'm staying in the dorms on campus this year. You could stay at my parents'. Work this year, go to school next year."

The thought of living at Shannon's parents' house made me laugh. There I'd be: the strange Indian kid, their daughter's boyfriend, holed up in their basement. I told her I'd feel like some goddamn refugee. "And I couldn't stay if I wanted to," I said. "And I do want to."

Even though I'd racked up straight A's over the spring and raised my GPA nearly a grade point, the odds were still against me. I hadn't bothered applying to a single school because my father had told me it was out of the question. He couldn't afford to send me to an American college. "You'd be on your own," he said and left it at that. So I tore up my college applications and shoved them into the wastebasket. It was upsetting as hell, but if India was inescapably my fate, I figured I'd better learn to live with it. Besides, there was still the matter of a student visa; I'd need one once my family left the country.

Shannon sighed. "A visa? But you're American; why would you need—"

"I'm not American," I said, shaking my head. "I was *never* American."

This was difficult (and awkward) terrain, having to explain to your American girlfriend the finer points of your immigration status. Then, almost for my own benefit, I added, "My dad couldn't turn down the offer in India. It's a big deal. Really exciting."

I held her arm, stroking the freckles there with my thumb. She didn't much like the freckles, but I loved them, loved how they burst into starry patterns below her eyes, on her shoulders, and above her breasts. She cried then, across from me, quietly. I saw the tears running down her face before she wiped them away and, more than anything, felt flattered that anyone would cry over me, let alone this girl—this American girl. Sitting with her, touching her, I felt like I had won her. And now, no sooner had she been won than I had to give her up.

I wished I could just snap my fingers right here in the middle of this horrible airport, make the whole world stop so I could collect my breath and get my bearings. And that's when something did it: my parents' and my brother's silences, the acrid and smothering air . . . whatever it was, the anxiety broke and burst over the wall.

Shit.

I stood up from the suitcase, said I'd be right back, and set off looking for the bathroom. I needed a minute to myself, to hold off the panic. Steady, Vikram; but no, there it was—throbbing in my ears, thudding in my chest. I saw a sign for the men's room and went in: a grimy cell with ancient sinks and urinals and stalls that looked like closets, everything reeking of mothballs. But I didn't care. It was empty in here; there was privacy. I tried to quiet myself, hold the anxiety back. Then I heard someone walking into the room behind me, so I hurried into one of the stalls and shut the door.

"Vikram?" It was my father. I didn't say a word. I heard him *humph* and then the shuffling of his feet as he left, and he was gone.

Next thing I knew the wall simply crumbled away and the tears filled my eyes. I stood there over the pit toilet, my hands braced against the door of the stall, and kept my eyes shut. Don't fight it, Vikram, no use now. So I let my feelings go. I saw the faces of all my friends, all the faces I might never see again. And I felt myself mourning—oh god, this was mourning! The feeling terrified me because mourning meant the end of something you loved. Was my soul acknowledging something I dared not admit to myself? I cried. It's okay, Vikram. It's no big deal. So you're mourning, it's okay. Sooner or later, you knew it would come to this.

Let it go.

I waited for the choking and tears to subside and for my breathing to even out. I wiped at my face, taking in the mothballed air. I stared down into the hole in the ground at a glint of water. I was breathing steadily now. The storm had passed. I opened the stall door and took a few deep breaths, readying myself to face my parents and get on with whatever this would have to be.

Chapter 2

They took my video camera.

"How long are they going to hold on to it?" I managed to blurt out as we hurried through the terminal's exit doors.

My father grabbed two luggage carts from a train of them. "Not long" was all he would say.

The customs officer—a sweaty, jowly bastard—had taken the video camera and, with it, all that I'd recorded on the two videotapes I'd stored inside the case.

Commotion had followed between my father and the officer about our not having a sales receipt for the camera, no proof of ownership. My father argued that the camera was our personal property, but the officer shook his head. "We detain item till you produce receipt," he kept insisting. Finally, the officer grabbed the camera case and waved us on, saying we were holding up the line.

"How do we settle this?" my father demanded. "Give me an address, phone."

The officer exhaled noisily and produced a business card out of his shirt pocket.

My father snatched it. "I'll be in touch."

"I thought I reminded you," my mother said now, a taste of scorn and defeat in her words. "'Put the camera receipt with all immigration forms.'" But my father was occupied with loading bags onto his cart. He was in no mood for this conversation. "I knew he was going to forget," she said to herself, hoisting a second suitcase onto a cart, its wheels wobbly, the whole thing tipsy.

"What good is screaming about it going to do now?" my father shot back. He checked his watch and said we'd better get a move on if we wanted to make the Ahmedabad connection.

That's right, I thought, think only of your connection. God forbid anything interfere with your precious plans.

We left the building and stepped into the subcontinental sauna of the June morning. I heard car horns—shrill and testy—as fleets of black-and-yellow Fiat taxis maneuvered like hyenas around the hippopotamus-sized Ambassador sedans. There was a wildness here, stewing in jungle heat.

We soon crammed into a taxi and sped off on our way to the domestic terminal.

It was eight p.m. back home, Madison steeped in beautiful summer twilight. And Shannon, I thought of her hair now, the apple-y fragrance of it, and the creamy skin of her arms, the adventure of her lips. Did she have that Smiths song on the stereo? It was one of her favorites. The one where the singer pleads with his lover to believe him—he meant to be with her, insists he still loves her, but he got drunk and was jumped by attackers who kicked his brains in, and he had to be rushed to the hospital. The lover doesn't believe him, but the singer pleads his case anyway. What I loved was that brief, beautiful guitar at the end—swaggering, bruised, and tragic (it spoke of me!). I could hear it now as we drove along, and, for a few seconds, I was with her, watching her dance to that song.

~ ~ ~

Ahmedabad.

Pigeons racketed in the rafters, their droppings decorating the cement floor of the airport. Trunks and suitcases were piled up like a haphazard barricade next to the baggage chute. Passengers filed through, picked up what was theirs, and proceeded to a barred gate behind which humans, pressed together several deep, waited with anxious faces. The air wasn't as muddy here as it was in Bombay, but I still had to work to breathe.

Right away, my father found what he was looking for. "Right there, right there," he said with a smile, and pressed past the crowd toward a familiar face: his younger brother, Hemant.

Hemant Uncle stood a couple of inches shorter than my father. Compactly built and copper skinned (after a lifetime spent on the cricket field) with graying, swept-back hair and a cheerful face, he sauntered toward us in that trademark unhurried manner I remembered from my childhood. Kamala Auntie, his wife, stood at his side in a purple sari with lilies on it. Her face looked lined and aged, I thought, by a combination of years, dust, and sun. The little girl with them was new. Anjali, their daughter, seven years old now. I'd seen her only in photographs, heard about her in letters. In a pink frock, her hair in pigtails, her complexion a shade darker than mine, she came forward with a bouquet of flowers in plastic wrapping.

Anand and I passed through an opening in the gate. We kept behind our parents now in the midst of a joyous reunion. My mother had tears in her eyes. So did Kamala Auntie. Hemant Uncle and my father threw arms around each other's shoulders, traded Gujarati familiarities, and began chatting as if they'd been apart only a couple of months, not eleven years.

"Go on, go on," Kamala Auntie said. Shyly, Anjali handed me the bouquet of flowers. I took it from her hands, smiling and thanking her as warmly as I could. Hemant Uncle, a pleased smile on his face, fixed his eyes on me as if he were trying to size me up, to see in me the six-year-old boy who lingered in his memories.

Kamala Auntie brushed my hair back, her eyes wet. Tentatively, in English, she began, "I saw you when—" and she held out her palm about waist high.

"Anand, you're very thin," Hemant Uncle said in a voice as deep as my father's but more booming, more theatrical. He wrapped one of his stout hands around Anand's shoulders. "I thought in America, everyone is big and very strong. No?" Anand chuckled, a little unsure, uncomfortable, and kept quiet.

"Vikram," Hemant Uncle said, turning back to me, "you too. Very thin. Here we'll give you proper food." He suggested an immediate diet of *dahi vada* and *bhelpuri*, which got him roaring with laughter before he walked off to fetch his car. I tried to laugh along like a good sport—these were smiling, unsuspecting, good-hearted relatives, after all—but felt only an intense loathing at being here and a powerful desire to escape. *Escape!*

In front of the airport, rickshaw drivers smoking *bidis* milled among khaki-clad policemen carrying wooden *lathis*. Motor rickshaws buzzed up and down like a swarm of yellow jackets, and I remembered them instantly from my childhood—three-wheeled canopied contraptions with narrow backseats where passengers bunched together and, up front, a seat for a driver who steered the rickshaw using a handlebar.

Hemant Uncle rolled up in a bottle-green Fiat, which Anjali and my parents piled into along with most of the luggage. Kamala Auntie climbed into a rickshaw, and Anand and I followed with backpacks, a suitcase, and the flowers Anjali had handed me.

Kamala Auntie instructed the driver to follow the Fiat in front of us. The rickshaw growled and shuddered to life, and we began motoring through the sensory assault of scooter, truck, bicycle, and bullock-cart traffic toward Ahmedabad.

The scrubland dotted with occasional apartment blocks was soon replaced with signs of the city: whitewashed storefronts open to the streets; signboards in Gujarati and English; men sitting in groups, smoking and talking, amid blocks of cement housing complexes. Bony cows lingered in corners, nosing through trash. And the trash—rotting food, plastic bags, and sodden newspaper—littered the roadside in abundance, scattered from waste bins by the animals. Kamala Auntie tapped my shoulder, and I turned to see enormous macaques that had overrun what looked like an abandoned bungalow girded with bamboo scaffolding. The profusion of wildlife in the middle of a city was too bizarre, too ridiculous. It was also oddly embarrassing; I didn't want to share any of this with my friends back home.

Anand and I exchanged looks of puzzlement, and that got Kamala Auntie emitting a kind of quick, high giggle. "It's like zoo, no?"

I tried to smile back warmly, nodded.

"You will get used to," she said.

I caught sight of a naked child—five or six years old—squatting over a dug-up hole in the ground. He squinted at me through the glare, his arms hanging off his knees, as he crouched there, shitting openly in the dirt. The child's eyes followed me as we passed, his expression completely innocent, without a trace of shame. For him, it was just another afternoon defecating in a hole on the side of the road.

Kamala Auntie's words came back to me: *You will get used to.* Used to?! *You don't seem to understand,* I wanted to shout. *I don't want to get* used to*!*

We joined streams of gathering traffic and began passing over a concrete bridge.

"Sabarmati River," Kamala Auntie said, pointing.

But the Sabarmati wasn't much of a river—more like an epic gash of cracked earth with a vein of brown coursing down the middle.

I wondered exactly where we were headed, how much farther we had to go. My father had mentioned something about a guesthouse, someplace we'd be staying until the bungalow in Ahmedabad was ready, but I knew nothing else. Never even wanted to ask.

Now, in Gujarati with a few English phrases thrown in, Kamala Auntie filled us in: Last night, she, Anjali, and Hemant Uncle had driven in from Baroda. They had already checked out the guesthouse (my father had arranged for the key to be sent to them weeks ago), bought groceries, and refrigerated several bottles of boiled water, and they had a meal cooked and waiting for us. They would stay with us for a couple of weeks while we settled in.

Wherever this guesthouse was, it was far—like, boonies far. We drove till the city became sparse again, and we were bumping along a potholed two-lane road bordered on both sides by dirt fields, food stalls, and hole-in-the-wall bazaars. Children played with kites; couples cut us off on scooters.

After a few minutes of lurching along this road, I noticed Hemant Uncle's Fiat ahead of us veer to the side and stop. We rolled up behind it, and the rickshaw gurgled and came to rest.

In that heavenly second of silence, I could hear myself breathe.

I checked my watch: the sun was up over Lake Monona now, clear and quiet, flickering through the elms in Shannon's backyard. I pictured Shannon in her bed: the green tank top, the freckled collarbone, the peek of her waist—

"*Chalo*," Kamala Auntie said, stepping out of the rickshaw. "We are here."

Next to the road was a red metal gate and, beyond it, a paved driveway. A row of trees overhung one side of the driveway and an apartment building stood on the other. Five or six apartments, steps leading up to each, lined the drive. From the Fiat, I saw my parents and Anjali emerge. Anand and I extricated ourselves from the rickshaw, hoisting up our backpacks, while Kamala Auntie paid the driver.

My father turned up the hasp on top of the red gate, and it squeaked open. Hemant Uncle pulled the Fiat into the driveway.

I approached my father and asked, "Where are we?"

"Ghatlodiya," my father replied, already walking back to the Fiat so he could begin to pull out suitcases.

Ghatlodiya. What an awful name. It spoke of all the backwater villages in this backwater country, far removed from the world.

The rickshaw that had brought us here fired up again. The driver wheeled it around, and soon he was puttering back the way we'd just come, toward the sun dropping now behind the sheds and shacks bordering the road.

Soon, he faded from view, lost in the orange scrim of dust and humanity and traffic. In a way, that rickshaw driver was my last link to America, the last piece of the journey that had brought me here. My heart ached to see him go.

I couldn't picture Shannon here, nor Nate or Karl, nor anyone from back home, for that matter. Again, the thought of sharing this with any of them—this *part* of me—embarrassed me.

Soon it would be my first night in India. And I was still having trouble breathing: smoky, muggy, dung-scented, this was the air I'd better get used to. I wanted to breathe in the fragrance of the flowers Anjali had given me, but realized I'd forgotten them in the rickshaw.

Chapter 3

Waking up was a nightmare. As if life had played the dirtiest of tricks on me. I'd be dreaming the same things I used to when I was in America, but then I'd wake and reality would hit me with a slow-motion blow to the head. I'd become aware of my soul caving and falling . . . and the bottom of that fall was my heart. It was like that for several weeks, but worst on those first days: that horrific sense of exile.

Anand and I would wake to a monsoon torpor, disoriented from jet lag, achy, and bleary-eyed, the heat slouching over everything like a swamp animal by eight a.m. We'd take a look around: the whitewashed cement walls; the pale, flecked tiles on the floor; the ceiling fan squeaking as it spun. From downstairs came the noise of kitchen utensils and raised voices: Hemant Uncle joking with Anjali or Kamala Auntie asking my mother a question. Who were these people? Through an open window, I would see an unfamiliar crumbled roadside, run-down storefronts, the sump behind the guesthouse, and a cow browsing for scraps. Everything seemed so unreal.

One morning, three days in, we heard a knock at the door of our room, a quick rap that I recognized as my father's. "Anand," he called, opening the door, "be ready, okay? We'll pay a visit to a couple of schools this afternoon."

Anand turned over and pulled a pillow over his head.

"Be ready, huh?" my father repeated, then, leaving the door open, walked back down the hall toward my parents' bedroom.

"I'm not going," Anand said in a muffled voice beneath the pillow. "I don't want to go."

I checked my watch, and, almost automatically, I began rolling the hours back in my head, trying to make the India-Madison time jump. But I stopped myself. I didn't feel like bumming myself out first thing in the morning. I crawled out of bed.

"I hate this place," I heard Anand say. "I'm not going."

Summer break had just started back home, but here schools were starting up again. Anand and I had a week to snap out of our jet-lagged funk and get into the swing of . . . whatever *this* was going to be.

"We'll figure something out," I said.

The guesthouse, thankfully, had Western-style toilets and sinks, one upstairs and one down. The bathrooms were Indian otherwise: no bathtub, just an undefined area marked by a drain, a spigot for running water, and, above that, a handheld showerhead attached to a tiny water heater. It made for a continuously wet floor that got dirty easily as people came and went, tracking their bare feet in and out. I picked my way to the sink and brushed my teeth.

My stomach hurt. I felt hopeless. No matter. Today I would write Shannon a letter. I would write it and get it mailed before the post office closed. And while I was at it, I'd get a bunch of postcards to send to Nate, Karl, and a few others to whom I'd made—and from whom I'd received—promises to stay in touch.

Downstairs consisted of the kitchen and one large room divided into dining and living spaces. Hemant Uncle sat on a sofa, focused on the Gujarati-language morning news on the TV while Anjali hunched over the dining table with the crayons and Disney coloring books my parents had given her. Perched over a book, her knees planted on the chair, she carefully worked in the colors that lay scattered next to her. Anjali also loved the chewing gum, the Bic pens, and the Jif peanut butter my parents had brought.

"So!" Hemant Uncle boomed from the sofa. "How is jet lag?"

I told him I was better, a bit better.

On the table, next to a container of spicy Indian snack mix, I noticed a toaster, a loaf of bread, and an opened carton of Amul butter. I put two slices of bread into the toaster.

"Vikram," my mother called from the kitchen, "is Anand awake?"

"Not really," I said.

"That boy," she groaned in Gujarati. "I'm going to have to go up there."

"Hemant Uncle," I asked, "is there a post office around here?"

"Post office?" he wondered aloud. He got up from the sofa, turned off the TV, and sauntered toward the dining table, his hands in his pockets. "Not familiar with this area."

"There is," said Anjali in a haughty voice, looking up from her drawing. "By the bus stand. I saw it when we went to the dispensary the other day."

Hemant Uncle's brows scrunched together. "Dispensary? Why the dispensary?"

Anjali shrugged. "I went with Mummi."

Just then, Kamala Auntie entered from the back door, through the kitchen, with an armful of line-dried clothes. "We went for *Bhabhi*," she said, meaning my mother. "She was having some pain that I knew some medicine for. It's nothing."

"Atch-cha." Hemant Uncle nodded thoughtfully.

The toaster clacked, and two half-jammed, half-burned slices of toast poked out. I pulled them out and spread Amul butter on both. The bread here was dense, coarse, as though sand grains had gotten mixed up with the flour, and the slices were only about half the size of the Wonder Bread I was used to.

The Amul butter made up for the bread, though. Fragrant with fresh cream, it tasted exactly as I remembered from Sunday mornings of childhood, when Hemant Uncle would bring home Amul butter and Italian bread from the specialty bakery.

My mother set a small steel cup of milk for me on the table and went upstairs to get Anand out of bed.

"How are things in Baroda?" I asked Hemant Uncle, taking a sip of the milk. "You're at the State Bank, right?"

"Hmm," he said, pushing away the coloring book he'd been absently flipping through. "State Bank since fifteen years. From Ahmedabad, I transferred to Baroda only five years back."

"Are you still playing cricket?"

He shook his head, laughing softly. "No. Now there is no time."

"You used to play a lot back in college, didn't you?"

"Right from my school days," he said, reaching for the snack mix. "Then played on college team, even on State Bank team." He ate the snack mix and wiped his hands free of crumbs. I couldn't help but notice he was heavier now than I remembered; there was a thickness to his face and around his middle.

"Your uncle is sportsman," came Kamala Auntie's voice from the living room. She was folding the laundry, stacking the clothes in neat rows on the sofa.

"Vikram *bhai*, watch this," Anjali said, leaping out of her chair. She asked her father if she could swing from his arm. Hemant Uncle obliged by extending an arm and letting his daughter swing from it with both hands. She giggled, and soon Hemant Uncle started laughing along with his daughter as he turned in half circles and she was lifted high on his arm, her legs swinging in midair.

I remembered how Hemant Uncle would play with me when I was a kid; he would let me swing from his arm and launch me onto the living room couch as I pretended to be Hanuman from the Ramayana, leaping the mythical archipelago from India to Ceylon.

"Ready, Hemant?" my father called, hurrying downstairs.

Hemant Uncle settled Anjali onto the sofa. "Chalo!" he said. "Just waiting."

"Where are you off to?" Kamala Auntie asked.

"To Institute," my father said. "Some paperwork there still to finish." He snatched up his briefcase from the floor beside the TV.

Kamala Auntie and Hemant Uncle shared a few quick words, and my father shouted up the stairs that he'd be back in a couple of hours. "And Anand," he ordered, "make sure you're up and ready by then." Then he and Hemant Uncle shuffled out the door and were gone.

"Would you mind showing me the way to the post office later?" I asked Anjali.

"Hmm," Anjali replied, taking up her position at the dining table with her coloring books. *"Chok-kus."*

Upstairs in our room, Anand lay curled up, his back turned to my mother, who sat at the edge of his bed. A tension hung in the room. I tried to steer clear of it as I stepped over to my bed and began straightening the sheets.

"If you really hate the idea of going to school, don't go," I heard my mother say. "Go and be like those rickshaw wallahs. Is that what you want?"

Not a word from Anand. No sound to be heard but the cawing of crows outside. Abruptly, he whipped off the sheet, rolled over, and got up. Eyes downcast, mouth in a frown, he began to shuffle away. "None of my friends have to do this," he said. "I hate this place." He walked out, and we heard him slam the bathroom door.

My mother grabbed the bedsheet from my hands. "I'm washing this today. I'll take care of it," she said sharply. She stripped the fitted sheet from the mattress and tossed the pile of sheets onto the floor. From the corner of my eye, I could see her shaking her head—out of what? frustration? guilt?—as she turned to Anand's bed and began pulling off the sheets.

"Do they have washing machines here?" I asked, if only to make conversation.

"Don't know." She gathered up all the sheets in her arms, adding, "I'm used to." She left the room, and her feet faded away down the steps. *Used to.* Those words again. But laced with a faint trace of cynicism, of the fatalism I'd heard in her voice many times over years and years.

I went to the desk in the corner of the room, opened the drawer, and took out the pad of paper I'd bought at the stationery shack down the road a day earlier. After a moment to collect my thoughts, I grabbed a pen and sat down.

To my love, I began, then crumpled up the paper and tossed it aside. *Dear Shannon*, I wrote on a new sheet. *Three days into the great adventure in the subcontinent, and I'm finally getting around to writing you.* I went on to write about the journey across the world that ended in Ghatlodiya, about the sights and sounds and smells of the streets and India's late-June heat and humidity. I wrote about meeting my family and about the video camera being confiscated in Bombay. Throughout, I tried to keep my tone casual, off-the-cuff; I threw in a wry, sarcastic joke, the kind I knew she would appreciate. But the more I wrote, the heavier my heart felt and the more badly I wanted to be with her. The feeling got worse till I was afraid my heart might burst, and I'd spill onto the page the truth about how much I missed her, how I wanted more than anything to be with her, in her room, under her posters of New Order and The Clash, while the sun went down over Lake Monona.

But then I imagined what her response would be: *You're really down right now, Vik, but it's just a phase. This is a big move for you, and I think the sooner you get into the spirit of this trip, the sooner you'll start enjoying it.* Such a reply might only drive me further away from her, and I didn't want to risk that. I was also afraid that spilling my guts might freak her out and she would break up with me immediately. So I cut things short and signed off with *Love, Vik.*

As I sealed the letter in the envelope, Anand came in, just bathed, indifferently toweling his wet, tangled hair. He wore a clean short-sleeved shirt and dark slacks—his school-visiting clothes, I presumed. My brother had conceded. I couldn't help but feel sorry for him.

"Got anything to mail out?" I asked. "I'm going to walk over to the post office with Anjali."

Anand scrubbed the towel against his head a few more times and threw it, bunched up, on his bed. "No." He dropped himself onto the edge of the bed, sighing deeply.

"Look," I said, turning to face him, "everything's going to be fine."

"How do you know?" Anand didn't look at me. He began biting his fingernails, picking at them—a longtime nervous habit.

"We missed out on summer vacation this year," I said, "but they get a lot of vacations here. A lot more than back home. Think Diwali comes up in four months, and that's a whole month off. The year will be over before we know it, and then we'll figure out a way to get back."

Anand mulled that over, glancing at the wall. Finally, he nodded. "What day is it?"

"Wednesday."

He sighed again. "No clue how the Brewers did in the Oakland series. Their last game was today."

"I'm sure they did great," I said, trying for encouragement. "Won every game."

Anand bent down, picked up a baseball magazine lying on the floor, and began poring through it. "Off tomorrow," he said to himself, "then the Angels."

"Coming with us to the post office?"

"I've got this school thing," he said. After a pause, he looked up at me. "You think the kids here know about baseball?"

"Doubt it," I said, trying a smile. "You'll have to teach them everything you know."

~ ~ ~

The post office was a drab room fermented in damp heat. It reeked of that mix of soot, sweat, and Indian spice that I was now getting used to, an acrid sweetness that was repulsive and intoxicating at once. The place hummed with the chatter of locals and the whir of an oscillating fan positioned on a counter next to jars caked with brown glue.

I wished I had my video camera with me, even though that might've attracted too much attention. I imagined running off a few shots of the moldy, peeling walls on which a "Don't Spit" sign was painted; the men in short sleeves clasping zippered satchels in their thin hands, a few of them with bidis poking out of wrinkled mouths. Stumps of bidis and bits of paper littered the room. The deeper I entered, the more out of place I felt.

My brown skin wasn't enough to ensure that I blended in; there was too much that gave me away as an outsider. I didn't have the bristly mustache, for one thing, that many of the young men here sported, and I didn't dress like the men here either, with their short sleeves, slacks, and slippers or loafers. I didn't pomade my hair and comb it in that severe part. (Top to toe, the men here were trapped in some 1950s time warp.) And as thin as I was, eleven years of pizzas and McDonald's had given my face a filled-out appearance, unlike the locals here, raised on *rotis*, rice, and lentils. Everywhere I went I stood out about as much as a white-skinned tourist who'd lost his way.

Anjali led me to a grilled window where a clerk weighed my mail and sold me stamps along with a dozen postcards. I put the postcards in the pocket of my shorts as Anjali guided me back to the counter, where I began fixing the stamps onto the envelope using the brush from the glue bottle. The bristles of the brush had hardened into a solid chunk, and it was like using a flat stick.

"Oh-ho, America!" came a voice behind me, and I became aware of a hand fingering the fabric of my shorts—a pair of white cottons with "Wisconsin" in large red letters along the side. "Hey!" I said, swiping the fingers away and stepping aside to find a boy, maybe eight or nine years old, backing away from me.

He grinned, a hand at his hip, and, in Gujarati, asked if I could spare him some money. But his tone wasn't pleading. It was wry, almost derisive, too much so for a kid his age. "How about it, boss? You got something extra for me?"

Then Anjali shouted at him, waving a finger toward the door. *"Jao! Hutt!"*

The kid, still grinning, gestured back at her with a flat, upturned palm. "*Wah-re-wah*," he chortled, "a little girl talking that way, you should get a good *phadda-phut*," and he mimed a slap and backslap, then took to his heels out the door. A few men glanced in our direction, indifferent.

"What was that about?" I asked Anjali.

"No school," she replied in Gujarati. "So they do that only, making mischief."

In bold letters, I wrote AIR MAIL on the envelope. The black ballpoint smudged and leaked, but the words were clear enough. I started to put the pen away, then hesitated. Turning over the envelope, I hastily scribbled on the seal: "Miss You," keeping my back turned so that Anjali wouldn't see. I handed the envelope to the clerk, who pounded dirty, illegible stamp marks all over it. And as he tossed it onto a pile of grubby aerograms, I got the same feeling as when I'd turned over my video camera to the customs agent in Bombay. It was this lonely, slightly terrified feeling, and I felt sorry for my letter, lying in that sad pile, left to the mercy of this miserable place.

The heat felt heavy on our heads as we walked back to the guesthouse, but then a breeze kicked up and the sun, for a moment, got clouded over as a rush of wind swooped in from behind us. Dust sailed across the road, and a paper kite that a group of kids had been struggling to lift suddenly took off. It rose as high as the upper stories of the apartment block to the cheering of the children who now ran along on bare feet, tugging and lifting at the line as the kite fluttered far above.

"Monsoon's here," Anjali said, squinting upward, shielding her eyes. Thunderheads had reared up in the western sky, a whole army of them. We picked up our pace. I didn't want to get the postcards soaked. More than that, though, I was beginning to feel naked out there in the open gaze: the outsider in his American clothes.

~ ~ ~

Back in my room, I sat at the desk and wrote out the postcards. Every now and then, I'd prop myself on my elbows and watch the frenzy of rain outside the window. Rapidly, over the course of the afternoon, rain clouds shrouded the sky, and the wind muted out the clank and clatter of the street. I noticed how still the world got just before the monsoon broke; the children had all run inside, the men disappeared into their shops or scootered off home.

The rain riddled the baked earth. I made a viewfinder of my hands—the thumbs and index fingers touching at right angles—and panned across all I saw. The muddied pockmarks of animal tracks. The corrugated rooftops of the shops peppered with raindrops, everything dripping and gleaming.

The downpour was interrupted only by the far-off thunder, like gunshots across a canyon, as I sat back down to my postcards. I wrote quickly to friends, starting with Nate and Karl—anxious to get these messages of my existence to the other side of the world. Throughout the postcards, I practiced the same easygoing attitude I'd tried for in my letter to Shannon: full of good humor, casual. I was the adventurer in India, after all; the last thing I wanted was to scare friends away with cries of confusion, loneliness.

I mentioned nothing of the dreadfulness of Ghatlodiya, Ahmedabad, of India, of the days passed in panic, boredom, fear, and the heat that hammered my brain. I did not mention the terrible chasm of distance I had felt the other day, lying in bed, staring up at the mindless circling of the ceiling fan. Nothing about the desperate yearning toward distant people in a distant place, nothing about the emptiness that now echoed within me or about a future that felt like a dark, forbidding road lit only by the faint, flickering hope that friendships would hold.

~ ~ ~

Over dinner that night, my father explained how he and Anand had visited three different private schools in Ahmedabad. At each one, the principal made the matter of enrolling Anand into a major hassle.

"'We can't accommodate transfer students,' they told me. But I knew what they were really getting at," he said, dipping a bit of roti into a small steel bowl of mango custard. "Baksheesh. What a shame."

"You didn't do anything that people here don't do already, all the time," my mother said.

"It's not a game I like to play," my father said.

But with schools starting next week, my father had given in: after being turned away at two schools, he gave the superintendent at the Gujarat Law Society Secondary School an extra thousand rupees to "expedite" Anand's enrollment.

Kamala Auntie said, "The bribe to get Anjali into the school we wanted was double that." It was not meant to be a boast, but it came out that way, an ironic boast. "Best to pay the *babus*," she said. "Otherwise your children get nowhere in India. If not school, then it's about getting your phone hooked up or electricity service, marriage, job. In everything, there is bribing." That made her laugh, wiping mango custard from the side of her mouth.

"That was your choice," Hemant Uncle said to her. "I wouldn't have paid such a bribe. But that school was *your* choice."

Confused, fidgety, Anjali spoke up, "Why is everyone mad? I got first class, didn't I?"

"Just barely," Kamala Auntie shot back. "And don't jump all over your chair." Kamala Auntie straightened Anjali's chair and went on to impress on her (and on Hemant Uncle) how she'd better raise her marks so they could transfer her to secondary school in Bombay when the time came. "Otherwise," she said, "how else you will become doctor?"

"I don't want to be doctor," Anjali muttered under her breath, kicking her legs under the table.

My father chewed, staring thoughtfully at his plate. "I hope there won't be such a problem getting *you* set up," he said, pointing at me.

"Where am I being sent off to?" I asked with an edge of sarcasm.

"St. Xavier's. Where we both went," my father said, indicating himself and Hemant Uncle. "I was science, and you were . . . what?"

"History. History major," Hemant Uncle said jokily, then turned to me, adding, "I was not good student. I liked to play cricket only. Your father was first class, but I 'cut class,' we used to say." He and my father shared a short laugh, nodding at the memory.

Anjali slunk in her chair. "Vacation goes by so fast."

"Sit up straight," Kamala Auntie said sharply. "And this year all first class, understood?"

Anjali made a supercilious grunting sound, puckered her mouth, and twisted it from side to side. "Can't wait for Diwali," she said under her breath.

"Fine," I told my father, "but first I need to make a quick trip to the post office."

"Another one? You were just there today."

"Few more things to send out."

"Girlfriends?" Kamala Auntie said wryly, a glint of mischief in her eyes.

"He already sent to girlfriend," Anjali announced. How she knew that I had no idea.

"Oh, Vikram has girlfriends," my mother said, "lots." I was beginning to feel uncomfortable. "Just show her your wallet," she went on. "He has pictures of all them. So many friends."

"No, I don't."

"Yes, show me," Kamala Auntie enthused, "after dinner."

~ ~ ~

I pulled open the Velcro flap of my wallet and handed it over to Kamala Auntie. She sat on the sofa next to Hemant Uncle with Anjali between them, leaning against Hemant Uncle's arm. My parents sat together on the other sofa, everyone watching a Hindi TV serial.

Kamala Auntie flipped through the pictures tucked into plastic sleeves inside the wallet and asked me the names of my friends. There was Nate, struggling to look natural, the studio lighting useless against the acne, his chin propped in one hand, affecting a thoughtful pose (it made me laugh every time I looked at it); and there was Karl, bushy haired, the bangs planing across the ridge of his eyebrows, lips pursed in a refusal to smile.

Kamala Auntie turned over to the next picture. Mine. It was the last copy I had. In that stiff gray suit—my father's—my hair feathered into a kind of Erik Estrada bouffant by the studio's makeup lady, my powdered nose bulbous in the lighting. I looked ridiculous. But Shannon had expressed a fondness for it. When I first showed it to her, she fawned over it. Then, I'll never forget, she kissed it. *She kissed it.* Never in all my days. It was why I'd held on to that picture—that memory.

"You are looking very smart," Kamala Auntie said.

"Thank you." But I was anticipating the next picture, the last one. Shannon's. I adored it. Her lips, the straightened line of her teeth smiling at the camera full on, her sparkling dark eyes, the dark-blond hair that fell to her shoulders. The lighting washed out her freckles. Her cheeks dimpled like a young girl's, but her jawline had the clean elegance of a sophisticated woman. It was that contradiction that drew me in. She gave me both.

"This is your girlfriend?"

I cleared my throat, my face starting to feel warm. "A friend."

Kamala Auntie looked up at me and back to the picture. "I think she is more than friend," she giggled. Then she handed me back my wallet.

As I sat there beside Kamala Auntie, Anjali, and Hemant Uncle, staring at the TV, I couldn't help but think of Shannon. Night here, day there. What was Shannon doing that minute? I pictured her sunning her back on the Union pier, her sunglasses on, watching the sailboats or reading a book of plays. In the back of her mind, did I still exist?

~ ~ ~

Upstairs in our room, as Anand slept, I lay in my bed and thumbed through my Bradbury book till I found the short story I hadn't been able to shake since I'd arrived in India: "Kaleidoscope."

It was the one about the astronauts. They're out there, the three of them, spacewalking, making repairs to their ship. Then a terrible malfunction, an explosion, and a blinding light. The explosion severs the lines anchoring the astronauts to the ship and launches them in three separate directions. Shock and terror fill the headsets as the astronauts drift deeper and deeper into space, farther and farther, trying to communicate through a weakening radio signal. Each man condemned to his end, however it comes, alone.

Chapter 4

I can pinpoint the exact epicenter of my catastrophe to one weekend the year before. It happened in October—about eight weeks into the start of my senior year. Without the disasters of that weekend, I would not be in India. I would be at home, in Madison, enjoying the summer with Shannon, Nate, and Karl before the start of college in August.

It was homecoming weekend. I'd made plans with Nate and Karl to get together after school that Friday. We were going to work on ideas for our next movie project.

Nate, Karl, and I made movies, ever since we'd met in film studies class in our sophomore year. Super 8s at first, then video once Karl got a secondhand camcorder. Mostly we made five-minute spy and zombie movie rip-offs, nothing fancy, just wild and hilarious. We had a blast making them.

Anyway, after school that Friday, Nate and I walked over to his place to start jotting down movie ideas. But then Karl called up to tell us he wouldn't be able to join us. We said not to worry, we would carry on without him. But deep down Nate and I both knew that without Karl around to crack the whip, we weren't much good.

To be fair, we did hit on a sweet idea, a cross between James Bond and Woody Allen set on a space station. But an hour or so later, our story session degenerated into jokes and watching Martha Quinn on MTV before Nate reached for the shoebox on the top shelf of his closet. The shoebox where he stashed his weed.

I knew Nate to partake of it now and then, though we didn't communicate that fact to Karl because we knew he wouldn't approve, and Karl was asthmatic anyway. I would take a hit, *just* a hit, to be companionable. This time, though, I took more than a hit, and before I knew it, we had cashed two joints. The walls soon pulled away, and we were laughing our asses off as we ate our Red Baron pizzas.

Some time later, it got dark out, and Nate's father came home. Nate suggested we clear out, take the bus back to school, and check out the homecoming game. Now, I hated football games, school spirit, and all that. Didn't care for it, didn't even get it, and neither did Nate. But we were too well baked by then to let the evening die out on us.

Shivering in our jackets at the top of the bleachers, we passed another joint between us. Nate offered to get us sodas and hot dogs. He handed me the rest of his stash wrapped in cellophane, to hold on to.

In our state, the game was a psychedelic blur—a carnival of helmets and bodies, pom-poms and miniskirts, a havoc of shouts and flailing arms and anxious, giddy faces. We won after a field goal late in the fourth quarter, and the whole place just erupted. Nate and I had even gotten into the spirit of things by then—cheering and clapping and stomping our feet.

As we left the field, walking toward the bus stop, we wondered in our giddy daze what to do next, and I told him we should hit the postgame party over at Emily Price's house. Emily Price was gorgeous. She was in my Spanish class, and for whatever reason, she had invited me.

It wouldn't be quite our crowd—all the popular, rich, and beautiful kids and whatnot—so I didn't think Nate would be up for it. But to my surprise, he actually said why the hell not. We agreed we wouldn't stay for long; the buses only ran till midnight anyway.

Emily Price lived in a brownstone off Monroe Street. Very leafy, very old-money. Intimidating. Nate and I knew no one there. Madonna, Journey, and Def Leppard blasted from the stereo while the popular kids packed the house wall to wall. There were liquor bottles everywhere and PBR cans stacked into a pyramid on the glass coffee table.

Emily said a few words to me, glassy-eyed and giddy, yet gorgeous the whole time, while Nate stood at the kitchen counter behind me. Over the noise, she chatted with me about our Spanish class and gushed on and on about how much funnier the class was with me in it. (I took it as a compliment.) I introduced her to Nate and started talking about the game (because what the hell else do I talk about with Emily Price?) when Emily began swaying a bit. Her eyes closed, and she uttered, "Whoa." She lifted a finger. "I drank waaaaay . . . excuse me." Then she turned, giggling with a girl next to her, and the two of them melted into the drunken uproar of the party.

Nate and I had just been blown off by Emily Price. No matter. There was drinking to do. We retreated to the plastic bottles of vodka and rum and the box of Gallo wine, all as bounteous as the harvest. Now, I'd had a beer or two in my time, but I had never drunk as much as I did that night. A switch had been thrown.

I lost track of how long Nate and I were at that party, partly because of the drinking and partly because of Shannon Halverson. Nate knew her from drama class, and he said, "Shannon, I'd like to introduce you to Vikram here."

"Vik," I corrected him and shook her hand. It was so delicate and elegant, like a princess's or a ballerina's hand. She said she remembered me from sophomore-year history, which was surprising because Shannon sat three rows away, and I sat toward the back. Now and then, I'd steal glances at her—chestnut-blond hair cropped short and brown eyes and nonlipsticked lips at once ordinary and sensuous, parting to reveal shimmering rows of braces. What a beautiful contradiction. A sign that she was beautifully imperfect and on the outer reaches of attainability.

The braces were gone now, and Shannon had grown her hair out below her shoulders. Lovely and silky and long. Sipping beer from a plastic cup, she leaned against the kitchen counter, talking to me in her brown denim jacket. More a woman now than ever.

I told Shannon what a great job she'd done in the fall play, *The Glass Menagerie.* I meant it too. In fact, I'd only gone to the play because she was in it—though I'd never told anyone that.

I asked if I could fix her a drink. She told me no thanks.

"That's good," I said, "'cause I'd have no idea how to fix you one." I regretted saying that—would it seem *un*cool?—but Shannon smiled and said she'd better be on her way. "Not really my scene," she said. From her jacket pocket, she took out a knit cap, tucked it over her gorgeous hair, and brushed strands of it away from her eyes.

What impressed me was how Shannon didn't sound the least bit embarrassed about saying something I wouldn't dare admit out loud: that this wasn't her thing at all. *Not her scene.* And she was happy to bail. I admired that.

"Maybe next time," I said as her shoes tip-tapped on the stone tiles of the floor toward the doorway.

She gathered a cream-colored scarf around her throat and said, "Don't wait too long." And that was all. She was gone, and I felt invincible.

By the time we left the party, the buses had stopped running. No choice but to hoof it home. It would do us good, we said to each other, a chance to sober up in the late-October air, so we made our way up Monroe Street out toward Odana Road, to the farther reaches of the west side. I had no idea what time it was—surely much later than I'd ever stayed out. I dreaded going home, sensing behind the stupor of booze the fear of seeing my mother still up, waiting for me, stewing with an Indian mother's shame and rage. But that night a reckless indifference had come over me, maybe the culmination of months or years of a pent-up defiance finally breaking through to roam free in the deep suburban night. The recklessness helped me to put the fear and dread out of my head and to enjoy its rewards, to be in the moment, as they say.

On our walk, Nate started on the subject of life after high school. He said he'd put in an application to Madison, expected he would get in. But it wasn't college he was excited about. No, he couldn't wait until August so he could move out of his parents' house and finally get a room of his own on campus. No longer would we have to sneak around if we wanted to get stoned or have a few beers.

We huddled in our jackets, walking under the scant streetlights that threw halos of orange on the thinning trees. The aftertaste of the booze hovered behind my eyes. Nate grunted and shivered, digging his hands deeper into his jeans pockets, hunching his shoulders.

"How great would it be to get out of this cold-ass place?" he said. "Florida or California or Arizona." He chuckled. "I'd probably spend all my time playing golf and lying out in the sun." He shivered again, we both did, and the wind cut through our jackets. "Screw it," Nate grunted. "You know, I should say the hell with my parents not paying out-of-state. I should pack the car and head out to LA. I wouldn't mind, Vik. I really wouldn't. Get high school over with, get in a car, and head out to California. You in? We can paint houses and make money all the way to LA, and the rest falls into place, you know?"

Falls into place? I wished I had Nate's faith. What a glorious future he seemed to have in store, but for me, things had never "fallen into place." Since the sixth grade, I'd moved around from school to school, state to state, almost every year. And getting through sophomore, junior, and senior years had felt like the last leg of a pointless, miserable marathon. All I wanted now was to graduate and put high school behind me. As for the future—I had no sense of one.

"Another thing about California is the film biz," Nate said. "You, me, Karl—we could totally write screenplays, you know, make films, start our own studio, man."

"Look, I just want to get through this high school thing, okay?"

"You've got to start dreaming big, man," he said, slapping his hands together. "Or your ass is never going to get out of here. Don't limit yourself to, like, today and tomorrow and whatever."

"Nate," I said, "get real."

"Real is what I make it, man," Nate said sharply under his breath.

Boy, Nate was getting *really* irritating. I wanted to take a swing at him.

"Gotta take a leak," Nate said, stopping in his tracks. For a couple of seconds, we stood there beside the grassy slope of the Dudgeon School campus, silent and dark. Then, just like that, he disappeared, trudging up the slope into the dark. He must've been making for the trees halfway up the slope, toward the school building.

I lay back on the slope. Looking upward, I was blinded by the glare of the streetlight for a second. I was feeling drunk again, very drunk, as I made out the silhouettes of the branches above. "'Real is what I make it,'" I muttered and chuckled, still tasting the anger and realizing it was, in part, directed at myself for not being able to share in Nate's grand plans, no matter how pie-in-the-sky. What a rotten feeling. Still, it wasn't his fault I envied him.

I lay there and let my anger subside, keeping my eyes on the streetlight, and listened to myself breathe. Then, slowly, crazily, the whole world began to tilt, and I was a ship leaning and pitching on storm waves. Up and down, side to side. My vision darkened as if an aperture were closing, and my throat suddenly clenched and my mouth wanted to vomit. On my feet now, I heard myself retch, and an unwholesome liquid came out, disappearing into the grass. More came out. I braced my hands against my knees. Worse than the vomit was the noise—ghastly, lacerating heaves from deep within the diaphragm that must've sent shudders through the entire neighborhood, out of proportion to the liquid trickling from my mouth. The sensation finally eased up, and, in relief, I dropped to the ground, coughing and trying to settle myself down.

And that's when, from the corner of my eye, I made out the sapphire-bright whirling of police lights. I turned to face the police cruiser, holding a hand up to shield my eyes from the glare. The cruiser, its headlamps spearing my eyes, prowled up to the curb like some predator. I saw the outline of an officer emerge and train a flashlight on me.

Nate's feet came scuffing against the grass behind me. "Oh, shit," I heard him groan.

"You boys want to step over here, please?" came the officer's voice, hard and authoritative.

As I stepped forward, I felt something, there in the front pocket of my jeans. I pressed my hand there, a bulge, and I made a realization that felt like one breathless leap into a deep hole: It was the weed. Nate's weed. Wrapped in the cellophane. I realized it about the same time the officer, his flashlight beam hitting us both in the face, asked if we'd been drinking. And what it was, son, I had in my front pocket.

~ ~ ~

A five a.m. phone call from the police had woken up my parents. My father told me they'd found me laid out on a cot in a holding cell, retching into a wastebasket placed next to me. He paid the fine—it wasn't cheap—and had to drag me from the station, into the car, and back into the house.

When I woke up a few hours later in my bed, in my room with no idea how I got there, I knew I was in deep shit. I had a throbbing headache, my mouth smelled toxic, and I found vomit stains all over my shirt. Yes. Very deep shit.

"I'm so ashamed. I'm so ashamed," my father said over and over again that evening as we faced each other. "You're a disgrace. Thank god they didn't file charges."

I stood there stoop-shouldered, my back aching from all the vomiting. He was right about the charges; a righteous shitstorm that would've been.

My father sat before me on the edge of the armchair, his shoulders rounded into a slump, as still as a practiced yogi. He rested his arms on his knees and kept his head lowered, but I could see his eyes were bloodshot behind his glasses, under his knotted brows.

From the kitchen, I could hear my mother cooking rotis and curried potatoes and *dal*. She was crying. Her sniffling could be heard over the fusillade hiss of the pressure cooker. It was rough hearing her cry, and my father's words that I was "a gone case." But trying to defend myself seemed a terrible strategy: anything I said would only rile things up further.

But I did *want* to say something, to apologize for the state in which they'd found me, laid out in jail like that. I told them I'd never been drunk before, and that was the truth. I told them another truth: the marijuana was not mine. But I said it wasn't Nate's either (in all this, I didn't want them questioning my choice of friends). So I told them a guy at the party gave us the marijuana, someone we didn't even know. And I'd simply forgotten it was there. Otherwise, I kept quiet. Obedient.

"I just don't know what to do with you," my father said wearily, taking off his glasses. He rubbed at his eyes, wiped at the bristles of his mustache. "You've got no future. I don't see it. This on top of your lousy grades."

My "lousy grades." I knew he'd bring it up sooner or later that weekend. You see, I'd been making straight C's since tenth grade, when we moved to Madison. And that fall, except for the A's in English and art history, it had been a trail of C's from first-period trig to last-period Spanish. My father, scanning my quarterly report cards, would bow his head, shaking it despondently like a priest who had failed his parish. He told me I'd never even make it as a junior clerk at the JCPenney and wanted nothing more to do with me.

I told him I was sorry. But what surprised me was the snide way it came out. See, I was angry—angry at being censured, judged, and criticized by a man who never seemed to care much what I was doing till a situation came along that demanded his attention. And then it was always a lot of moral lecturing, the Indian parent's weapon of choice. It could nuke almost any unruly behavior. But what really gnawed at me was the suspicion that I was being compared to the kids of all the other Indian families around town.

While he went on about how hard he'd studied in school, about getting into hoity-toity IIT–Bombay for his master's and earning a PhD fellowship so he could come over to the States (a story I'd heard a million times), my mind wouldn't budge from thinking of the other upstanding, straight-A Indian teenagers in town. How I resented them, those goody-goody conformists in their polo shirts and designer jeans, whispering privately to each other at all those Indian-American association dinners. All of them with their math clubs and sprawling west-side homes, their stably employed fathers and extravagant mothers encased in obscene amounts of makeup.

That's when my mother pounded in from the kitchen on her small feet, in her faded flower-print sari, clutching a rolling pin. The *bindi* on her forehead was smudged, and her hair looked barely held in place by bobby pins. Her eyes, her face looked ravaged by tears. "Do you know how hard your father worked?" She shook the rolling pin at me, then at my father. "Do you know what he went through?" I'd never seen my mother in such a state. "You'll never know, to finish his PhD? He worked like donkey all those years! One job here, one job there. And you pay him back this way?"

Then a strange impulse hit me by surprise. "You do everything for me," I shot back. "Everything—I get it. But I didn't ask for any of this. A year here, a year there. Stupid new school every year. No idea where we'll be the next year. You ever think what it's been like for me?"

It hadn't been easy. That was true. But, deep down, I knew my mother had a point too. My father had had a tough run from the very beginning. He'd come over from India a year ahead of us and weathered a difficult start at Cornell—broke, alone, and then, halfway into his first semester, finding out his father had suddenly died from a heart attack. By the time he finished his PhD, university posts for physicists had dried to a trickle, and it seemed my father was lucky to find a job at all. We began hopping around—from Ithaca to Plattsburgh, then on to Auburn, Los Angeles, and Madison—from one short-term teaching post to another. Then, when Madison fell through the summer after my junior year, my father took a last-minute teaching offer from a small engineering college in Syracuse. By taking the job, he became a transient, glimpsed for a few days on a visit home every couple of months.

Anxiety had always been an unwelcome guest in our home, but with my parents' finances cut to the bone from running two households on a teacher's salary, it had become a permanent squatter.

"You think he's there in Syracuse all by himself because that is his choice?" my mother shouted. She stepped closer, pointing the rolling pin at my chin. "He went there so *you* could finish your school here. So you and your brother would *not* have to move again. All for you, he did it."

"No one's life is easy," my father said to me. "Everyone does the best they can in their circumstances."

"But who lives like this?" I shot back. "No one at school lives like this." I lowered my head as more words poured out. "So he took the job in Syracuse. I didn't ask him to take it. Not my fault he can't find work. I just want to get out of this house!"

There was a silence after that I will never forget. It was the deepest silence, the lull before the storm rose again.

"How dare you?" my father said, shaking his head. The words hung like thunderclouds over me. "I would *never* have talked to my parents like that. Never." He didn't even look up. "I'm sorry, bhai." There was a long pause. "You need to learn discipline. You will learn it among your own people. This country has ruined you." Then, shaking his head, he stood up and withdrew to the kitchen.

I watched as he shuffled away, a hand over his scalp as if my presence—my *existence*—had bruised him there. What could I do? Apologize? No. I couldn't apologize for saying what I'd felt for years now. I'd meant those words.

I seethed when my parents blamed "this country" for every flaw they saw in their children. Why blame this country? I hated our life, but what did America have to do with anything? I liked it here. And what the hell did Indians ever do that was so right? They'd made a hopelessly poor and corrupt nation for themselves. Their caste system had allowed them to treat their own people lower than dirt for thousands of years. And they allowed animals to wander their streets—animals that in any other country would be found only on a farm or in a zoo or a cattle yard.

I could hear my parents in the kitchen, whispering to each

other above the clink of utensils, the running of the tap. It seemed my father was finished with me—for now. I turned and trudged back up the stairs to my room.

I lay down and tried to calm my thoughts. Unfortunately, something in my stomach wouldn't settle. It began to rise into my throat, right up the esophagus, and seemed like it would come exploding out. I sat up, and the stuff receded back into my stomach. I resolved to stay upright.

From downstairs, I heard my mother's voice raised once, then my father's raised in reply. The storm of statements and counter-statements boomed for a full hour. Then dead quiet. *You need to learn discipline* were my father's words. *You will learn it among your people.* What did that mean?

I stayed in my room most of that weekend, and my father and I didn't say a word to each other after our "chat" on Saturday. He went back to Syracuse on Monday.

That Monday, I still felt the effects of my hangover, but my shame and anger had settled down. It was in trig class that something suddenly clicked in my mind: I wasn't going to let anything get past me anymore. I was going to master every class, every lesson. Ask questions, get a tutor, stay after school, do the assignments, write the papers. I wanted to prove to my father that his son wasn't somebody to be ashamed of.

By the end of the fall semester, I was getting straight A's. What I discovered was that when I applied myself to my schoolwork and got rewarded with better grades, I started feeling more confident, and my social life got a boost. I became a better friend to Nate and Karl; I worked hard on our next film project together, which we shot and edited over Christmas break.

When the spring semester kicked off, people started inviting me—*me*—to parties. These were smart, bright people—yearbook editors, photographers, actors, people who could play instruments—in whose friend circle I'd imagined I could never belong. Shannon and I saw more of each other, and we started dating—something else foreign and delightful to me. Of course, I mentioned none of these extracurricular developments to my parents, whom I thought of as traditional Indians. When it came to Shannon—and the subject of girls in general—my policy was silence.

I actually began to contemplate a future beyond high school. I picked up applications from the counselor's office, started flipping through them in the evenings, whipped up a couple of entrance essays. By February, I'd boosted my GPA, but it was still a hair's-breadth short of the cutoff for Madison. I still had a shot at, say, Platteville or Whitewater. I could go there for a year, I thought, then transfer back to Madison, where Nate and Karl were both going.

Then, one night at the end of February, I answered a phone call from my father. It was unusually late for him to be calling. He asked to speak to my mother. She'd already gone to bed, so I had to wake her. It took her a while to pick up her bedroom phone, she was so discombobulated.

I was about to put my own phone down, but my father told me to stay on the line and then asked me to get my brother to pick up the extension downstairs in the kitchen.

With all of us now on the phone, my father told us he'd accepted a job, the project director position at some newly founded, big-deal national space and physics research lab in Ahmedabad, India. Ahmedabad. India. There was a charge to his voice.

"They offered it to you?" my mother asked, sounding elated. "I thought they weren't going to finalize anything for months."

"Funding clearance was fast-tracked," my father replied. "I just got off the phone with them. They offered me the job just now, officially."

He went on to tell us that, at the end of the school year, we'd be packing up and moving back to India. That it would do us all some good, reconnecting with family and with our roots, and that it was a high-level post he'd been offered. He sounded like this was his big break, the one he'd been after for years.

I tried to be glad for him; I'd never heard him so thrilled. But as for myself, I felt numb, shut down inside. From the familiar way my parents spoke about it, it was obvious that this job, the possibility of moving back to India, had been on their minds for a while now, the subject of many private conversations.

"How long?" I asked him.

"Long term," he told me. "It's a permanent post, Vikram. We wrap up everything at the end of the school year, and then you can start college in Ahmedabad."

"Long term," I heard myself say. "You mean we're not coming back?"

"When do we come back?" Anand asked, his voice distant, confused.

"In the future, Anand, you may decide to come back," my father said. "That's up to you. But this job is long term."

My mother said something. I wasn't paying attention. Then I heard my father say, "Vikram, I want to assure you and Anand on this point. Your education will not suffer. There are many good colleges there—science, commerce, even a design school that's one of the best, depending on what you want to study. And for Anand, very good private schools. I'll arrange everything."

"Did they say about housing?" my mother asked.

"Bungalow right there in Navarangpura, central Ahmedabad. Close to schools, market, and we should also have car and driver, everything provided."

A shadow fell over me as my father talked. It loomed over the months and the years ahead. It was as if someone had taken an oil painting, still unfinished, the artist still perfecting his brushstrokes, and dumped a can of black paint over it, smeared fingers across it.

While my parents' voices droned over the line, I put down the receiver and sat back at my desk. I had the feeling of being on the verge of something. A chasm.

And I felt sick staring down into it.

Chapter

5

Sooner or later, the moment had to come to sign up for college.

My father and I pulled up in a motor rickshaw in front of the drab, cement building with the words "St. Xavier's College"—written in English and Gujarati—across the front of it. Clusters of students milled about the college's front gate.

With a folder containing my high school transcript and grade reports in one hand, I followed my father out of the rickshaw, breathing in the smells of rain-washed asphalt and kerosene.

I took in the place I would have to call college from now on. It was a gray, moldering building edged with greenery, streaked with soot and mildew.

Off to one side of the building stood a large shed where bicycles and scooters hunched together, sheltered from the dark, brewing sky. Hero Honda motorcycles and Marutis—tiny hatchbacks I'd seen competing for road space around the city—clustered together in front of the shed.

We weaved past a few students through the front gate and followed a gravelly path toward the college building. Our feet crunched against the earth as we stepped carefully over tire tracks shining with brown water.

Boys in slacks and short-sleeved shirts lingered together, a few in flip-flops, their hair pomaded. The girls flowed by in twos and threes with long black hair ponytailed or braided, all chattering in their salwaar kameez, gold and purple. Long sheer scarves trailed like streamers from their shoulders. Would Nate or Karl think any of them were pretty?

Up a few steps, we entered the mouth of the building—an open entranceway leading into a lobby lit only by the inpouring daylight. It echoed with the sounds of students gathered in front of glassed-in cases on either side of the lobby. The cases contained message boards pinned up with various typed or handwritten lists and a shelf of plaques and trophies.

At the other end of the lobby, we climbed a wide set of steps up to the building's upper floor and made for a door with "College Office" printed on a shingle above it.

The college office was a large bullpen where clerks milled around aging furniture and filing cabinets piled high with paperwork, everything withered and flyblown. The scent of sandalwood and coconut oil laced with sweat wafted in lazy drafts under ceiling fans. In a meek, lilting voice, a student at the front counter was making an effort to explain something to a small clerk, fortyish, with graying, severely parted hair. Propped up on a stool, the clerk had a ferretlike face and wore oversize gold-rimmed glasses.

Along the nearest wall was a lineup of photographs—a kind of hall of fame of college principals. I scanned the photos till I came to the last one, a color photo of the current principal. The photo showed a pair of pig eyes obscured by dark spectacles; a downturned mouth tucked between thick jowls; the whole head topped by silvery hair, greased and groomed. "Father D'Souza" read the label below his picture.

As I stared into D'Souza's pig eyes, I heard the ferret-faced clerk shout at the student, "So tell your story to the principal, go on!" The clerks in the office froze and fell silent. "I asked if you have receipt, but you don't, so why are you here? Go on, go away!" The student turned, chastened, and slouched out of the office.

We stepped up to the counter, but Ferret Face didn't acknowledge us.

My father cleared his throat and said hello.

"*Bolo*!" said Ferret Face, rearranging papers on the counter.

"Vikram," my father said, pointing to the folder in my hand. I placed it on the counter. As my father explained our situation and that he wanted to get me registered at the college, Ferret Face thumbed through my grade reports, my transcript. His eyes peered beadily from behind his metal frames.

"What's all this?" Ferret Face muttered in Gujarati, examining a piece of paper. He asked if it was my transcript.

"Says so, doesn't it?" my father replied, pointing to the top of the page. "Grades and classes all listed."

I leaned over and pointed them out. "Right here—"

Ferret Face nodded, agitated. "But where is GPA?" he asked.

I pointed out my GPA on the transcript.

"This is not first class," he said and picked at his teeth with a finger. "This is below first class. It is second class. For Xavier's, all students must enter with first class."

Fumbling with Gujarati words, I told him to take a look at all the A's on my senior-year grade reports. Surely, those grades were not second class—

"But here it is saying less than first class." Ferret Face tapped the transcript with the back of his hand. "I cannot give admission. Unless," the clerk now lowered his voice, and his tone became as slithery as a basket of snakes, "you want to pay special enrollment fee, right now, to me. Cash only. Then, of course, I would consider—"

My father set his briefcase on the counter so that it thumped hard. "Listen, I have a history here and myself did my BSc here. I know Xavier's, and this boy's grades are absolutely fine." He propped an arm on the edge of the counter and leaned forward. "My company does business with the government, and I've got a meeting this afternoon at the education ministry. How would you like it if I told them about your suggestion?"

The clerk shot to his feet, snatching up the transcript, his jaw taut and his bony cheeks shining with sweat. His tone became defensive: "I am doing my job only. Where would Xavier's be if simply I let in every applicant, Mr. . . . uh . . ." He glanced down at the name on the transcript, then, after a pause, asked, "Mistry?" He peered back at my father. "Eh! You say you got your BSc here? I am BSc also. Sixty-eight!" After a pause, Ferret Face asked, "You're not Rahul Mistry, are you?"

"Do we know each other?"

"Harish Rajkumar," the clerk said cheerfully, extending his hand.

"Harish Rajkumar," my father repeated blankly.

"Harish, *yaar*. Third-year physics. I was playing on cricket team with your younger brother, Hemant bhai." He offered his hand again.

My father took it tentatively, smiled, and shook his hand. "Oh, Harish, right, right. That was a long time ago, yaar. Sure, now I remember. The cricket games, right here in the athletic field."

Harish Rajkumar grinned. His teeth were grimy brown nubs. "His brother was the real star player at Xavier's, huh?" he said to me, grinning even wider, as if he were relating a bit of folk myth. "How is Hemant bhai these days? We haven't met. He's at the State Bank, no?"

The two of them went on like that, catching up on old times.

I picked my folder up off the counter and wondered if my father was embarrassed having a son who was second class. He had to be. Even here, in Ahmedabad, India, I was still second class.

"Fill out and bring back to me," Rajkumar finally said, handing me two sheets of paper and a paperbound booklet whose cover read "St. Xavier's College of Arts & Science Syllabus" in crude typescript.

The syllabus seemed to have been written for a defunct boarding school from colonial times. There were courses in Victorian literature, Restoration comedy, romantic poetry, the sort of musty stuff I imagined ancient men in frock coats reading in front of ornate fireplaces.

I filled out the forms, picking English as my major, and handed them back to Rajkumar while my father counted out the cash for registration. Rajkumar scanned the form and passed it back to me. "You must put down foreign language."

"What are my choices?" I asked.

"Sanskrit."

He may as well have said Eskimo. I tried to explain to him that I'd never taken Sanskrit before, knew nothing of it, and asked if there might be a beginner's course in it or something else I could take instead.

Rajkumar shook his head ponderously. "If not Sanskrit, then Pali, Farsi, Hindi," he said, showing his teeth again. He took off his glasses and wiped them against his shirt. After he put them back on (they looked as dirty as before), he continued, "There is also French."

French? Did he say French? That I could handle. "French," I said.

Rajkumar shut his eyes and cocked his head, the way I'd seen Indians do to indicate acknowledgment. He scribbled "French" on the form.

My father handed over the cash, which Rajkumar tucked into a wooden drawer.

"Give my regards to Hemant bhai," he said.

My father smiled. "Of course, *dost*! Chok-kus." They shook hands.

"Oh, *bhaiya*," Rajkumar called to me, and in English he said, "About your French course. You must speak with Madame Varma about it. French professor. See if she will take you. She is just there in faculty room." He tilted his palm in the general direction of the way we had come. "If it is not okay, you must come back, and we must change to Sanskrit or somesuch."

His words sounded ominous. I braced myself for my meeting with the French professor.

"Okay, good, at least we've got you signed up," my father said once we were outside the office. He checked his wristwatch. I looked down the other end of the hallway and saw the shingle for "Faculty Lounge."

"It's a good thing you two knew each other," I told my father. "Might never have gotten in."

"I have no idea who that character was."

"But you acted like you did, told him your whole life story."

"He seemed interested," my father said, shrugging his shoulders, "so I just went along. It got you in, didn't it?" A quick laugh sounded in his throat. "What a character."

"And all that about your meeting at the education ministry," I said. "That was classic."

"That"—my father checked his watch again—"is actually true. I need to be in Gandhinagar in half an hour. So let's go talk to this French teacher, but then I'll really need to rush."

"I can talk to the teacher," I told him. "You go on ahead."

My father thought about this, his eyes popping behind his glasses, and he stroked his mustache. "You sure you know how to get back?"

I nodded. "Of course." After a few brief but emphatic directives from my father to "stay alert" and "be safe," he took the stairs, rounded the landing, and disappeared into the lobby.

I was on my own now. The hallway teemed with Indian faces, talking, laughing, gossiping. I tried to avoid the stares, the curious glances at my Levi's or my sneakers. I took the hallway as quietly, as confidently as I could.

You entered the faculty lounge through swinging saloon doors. It was a cavernous space, with a pair of French windows swung open to the monsoon breeze and the cool gray light. On the large table in the center of the room, where books and folders lay strewn, a copy of the *Times of India* rustled under ceiling fans.

At the far end of the room, a thin man in his fifties with frog-like eyes and wearing a starched white shirt—a faculty member, I guessed—was holding court before some teachers who sat at the table or on cane chairs against the far wall, some of them sipping from cups of chai. The man's neatly groomed silvery hair gave him a dandified look.

He was deep into his story, carrying on, arms fluttering dramatically: "And so," he said, "seeing the accident, I got off my scooter and went down to see how I could help. The poor chap on the motorbike was absolutely *beh-bhaan*, you see, unconscious, and the vegetable wallah had broken his arm. So just then, one cop shows up, and I told him, 'Thank god you've arrived. I've been waiting for the police.' Then he asks me if that's my scooter parked just there. I said, 'Yes, I came down to see if I could help these chaps.'" The man broke into a fit of laughter. "But that bloody cop tells me I've parked my scooter illegally, and he books me!" Scattered laughs erupted from a few teachers. Frog Eyes shook his head, pleased with himself, and hitched his pants up. "That's how it is," he said. "Whole country has gone like that, yaar."

I took a few steps into the room. A gaunt boy in short sleeves, gray slacks, and a pair of flip-flops went around with a wire basket that clinked with glasses of chai. He placed a glass next to a woman, her back to me, in a green paisley sari. She had black hair cut short and sleek. The woman didn't look up, just raised her palm to acknowledge the boy. She seemed engrossed in a book marked up with notes in the margins.

I approached the woman. The book she was reading—a thick paperback—was in French. The words looked dense, difficult, a thicket of unpronounceable vocabulary, conjugations, and accent marks.

"Excuse me," I said awkwardly. "I'm looking for Madame Varma."

She straightened and turned a stern face toward me as she took off a pair of reading glasses that hung from a chain. "What do you want?"

"I'm a new student here. I'm signed up to take French, and they told me in the office to talk to Madame Varma."

"Sit down," she said.

I slid into the chair beside hers, and she pushed her big French book at me.

"Translate that for me. Out loud."

I felt something give inside me. "Um, well," I said, "I've taken four years of Spanish, but never French."

"If you can translate this, I can take you. I don't have time for beginners."

I stared at the scramble of words. A few I could approximate the meanings of, but it was mostly a disaster, as if English and Spanish had collided on the page and this new language was the resulting wreck.

I began: "Field . . . bodies . . . dead . . . steal . . ."

Madame Varma closed the book. "Impossible."

A fist closed over my heart. "But I need this class."

After a brief pause, she told me, "Best if you sign up for a preparatory class at the Alliance Française. They've got a six-week certificate course in starter French. You take that and come to me afterwards."

I hauled myself up. So much for this.

"Thank you," I said politely. "Alliance Française, I'll do that." I made to leave, anxious to disappear through the swinging doors and into a hole in the ground. Take refuge there till I either died or got transported magically out of this country.

"One thing," Madame Varma said. I spun around to face her. "I believe they're signing up new students this week. Next session starts up in mid-July. Go straightaway."

I saw no choice but to do exactly what she said.

"Oh, um, where is the Alliance Française?"

"It's near Ellis Bridge."

"Ellis . . . ?"

"You don't know Ellis Bridge?"

"I just moved here a week ago. From the States."

"Just tell the rickshaw wallah you want to go to Alliance Française, near Ellis Bridge."

My folder tight in my hand, I left the lounge, took the stairs, and left the college past the echoing procession of students in the lobby. I wondered how far this Ellis Bridge was and when or if I'd be able to find my way back to Ghatlodiya when it was all over.

Students puttered in and out of the front gate on their scooters and bicycles, crunching and dusting along the gravel lane. Where the motorbikes and Marutis were parked, I noticed a girl—slender-legged, in a black T-shirt and Calvin Kleins, with thick black hair that spilled down to her upper back—sliding into the driver's seat of her white Maruti. Two other girls in salwaar kameez, clutching folders to their chests, got in with her.

I stepped out onto the dusty edge of the road. The buzzing of rickshaws—metallic, black-hooded hornets, fierce and angry—filled the road. Two of them were parked near the gate. I saw a pack of students pile into one of them, and the rickshaw tilted at a dangerous angle to the road. Didn't matter—the driver revved the thing up and off they went.

I steeled myself and walked over to the other rickshaw. I trained a sure, casual stare at the rickshaw wallah—he had pudgy, red-rimmed eyes and wore a dirty white shirt. "Ellis Bridge," I told him firmly, "Alliance Française."

He jerked his jowly face and rolled his red eyes toward the backseat. Before I got in, I remembered something my father did insistently each time he took a rickshaw anywhere. I took a look at the meter, fixed next to the handlebar, and made a circling motion with my finger. "Zero that out," I told him in Gujarati.

"*Haah-haah*," the rickshaw wallah said impatiently. "Have a seat, bhai," he said in Gujarati. He turned the dial on the meter to 0000. So far, so good.

As we started off, I saw the girl in the white Maruti pull out of the gate. She turned onto the road and zipped away in the opposite direction. I could see her as she passed, behind the wheel of the car, wearing sunglasses, her skin a medium bronze, talking to her companions, her teeth flashing. She pushed her hair back and sped off. From around here, I thought. Yet not quite.

~ ~ ~

The sun bore heavily through breaks in the clouds as we made our way to Ellis Bridge, past frantic roundabouts and the Law Garden—hidden by high hedgerows fronted by *pav-vada* and *bhajiya* stalls clamoring with noontime crowds. Ellis Bridge, the structure that gave the local neighborhood its name, was another in the series of concrete linkups between the old and new sides of this city divided by the Sabarmati River, now robust after all the rains. Commuter buses—red-painted, rusted, with fumes chugging from their tailpipes—came growling in from the old city, packed to bursting with passengers who would clamber on or hurl themselves off before their buses even came to a stop.

Compared to all this chaos, the Alliance Française was a sanctuary—a peaceful courtyard fringed with hedges and buildings. I paid the rickshaw wallah (though, having no clue how to read his mileage counter, I had to take him at his word) and proceeded through an opening in the front gate of the Alliance. It was the side gate, really, propped open wide enough to let visitors in. I went along the gravel walk, under the arcade that ran the length of the Alliance's redbrick compound.

A sign pointed me in the direction of the school, which lay at the end of a short, winding brick path on one side of the far building. There were roses, daisies, and marigolds here, and a pair of eucalyptus trees that gave shade as you approached the school's steel-mullioned glass doors. People passed politely in and out of the doors, carrying folders and forms, everything in French. A flyer advertising a Chopin recital was Scotch-taped to the glass paneling. I approached the door and could hear a swell of conversation from inside.

It was as if I had entered a parallel dimension. For a suspended moment in time, I was no longer in Ahmedabad, but hovering in some bizarre zone between India and Europe. Here was a cool, spacious lobby with French-language travel posters and books on shelves. A wrought-iron spiral staircase ran upward from the middle of the lobby.

At the small registration desk sat a severe-looking white woman, her face grooved with age, sacrificed to the hardships of Indian weather. She hand-stamped a form—*tap-tap-tap!*—and thrust it back into the hands of a twentysomething student. The student made that bell-like, side-to-side swing of his head and sauntered away.

"Yes?" the woman said to me sharply. I got the sense she was always pissed off around here. I felt intimidated, and that made me resent her—the irritable, high-and-mighty memsahib addressing her Indian coolies.

As calmly as I could, I explained how and why I needed to sign up for the beginner's French course.

Automatically, she handed me the registration form, and in her French accent—an accent I'd heard only in old Hollywood movies and Looney Tunes cartoons—she told me the fee would be six hundred rupees.

That caught me off guard. "Can I pay you next time?" I asked. "When the class starts up? I came here straight from college and didn't realize about the money. I'm sorry about that."

"Seven hundred in that case. You bring money with you on the first day." There was that accent again, so superior and European.

First it had been that customs agent who busted our chops before taking my camera away. Today it had been that ferret-faced clerk at the college office and that sourpuss lady professor. They'd all given me attitude. Now here was Madame Pissface pissing and huffing at me like I was her servant.

I signed the stupid form, pushed it in her direction, turned around, and stomped away without giving the old biddy another look. Two could play at this game.

"Monsieur?"

I kept on stomping.

"Monsieur?"

"What is it?" I shot her a look.

"Yours?" She was tapping my folder with her pen. The folder with all those second-class grades. I had left it back at her desk.

"Oh, uh, yes, thank you." I went back, snatched it, and hurried out. I hoped to god she wasn't going to be my French teacher.

~ ~ ~

It had gotten darker outside, the sky swollen and black now. As I walked back toward the front gate of the Alliance, splotches of rain began hitting the gravel path. The sky rumbled as if the monsoon gods were clearing their throats, warming up before the big show.

I hurried out through the side opening in the gate and hailed down a rickshaw. But when I told him I needed to get to Ghatlodiya, he shook his head, said he wouldn't go that far, citing the weather, and motored off. A second rickshaw wallah, though, after a pained and momentary scowl, gestured for me to get in.

Soon we were zipping along through a royal monsoon downpour. I held on tight, my grade-report folder tucked under my shirt, as the rickshaw's motor whined through rain-slashed roads, the rain swirling beneath us, the tires becoming pinwheels of rain. The rickshaw wallah hunched low over his handlebar to peer through the blurred, wiperless windshield. Black umbrellas mushroomed everywhere, and beneath them figures either rushed along or clustered together at bus stands. A goods truck roared past us, blowing its shrill electric horn, splashing water across the rickshaw's windshield, and almost throwing a man just ahead of us off his bicycle. As we passed him, I took a look at the man on the bicycle: thin-limbed, soaked through, pedaling hard. He pushed hair out of his eyes as we passed, and he squinted through the gray scrim veiling everything, the whole world around him. A cow, eyelids half-closed, hunkered beneath a vast, sagging tree in the middle of a roundabout.

In Ghatlodiya, the road got too narrow to contain the slog of bicycles, scooters, and rickshaws. A bus roared black fumes past us, passengers packed together, the opened windows and doorway a riot of limbs and torsos. The mildewed apartment blocks loomed on one side, with TV antennas like charcoal etchings against the rain, and telephone wires crisscrossed like vines off their parapets. There was no drainage here, and the waters had risen quickly to make an ankle-deep lake of Ghatlodiya. Without hesitating, the rickshaw wallah weaved straight into openings in the traffic, pitching the rickshaw so sharply a couple of times that I thought we would tip over. Wildness and strangeness all around me, I wanted my video camera, some way to record all of this—the commotion of traffic, rain, floodwaters, the honking of horns. A way to contain the disarray for myself and organize it so that my own mind could make sense of it. I wanted to share this with the people who now lived only in my mind, to share this with Shannon, Karl, and Nate.

Just then, the rickshaw wallah sped up hard, wanting to pull ahead of the bus that had now stopped to let off passengers. We swerved past them when I felt the rickshaw jerk violently to a halt, and I saw a small woman—sixtysomething, with a black umbrella and a plastic bag in one arm—stutter-step backward to avoid us, and saw her collide with a milkman on his bicycle. Next thing, all three—the woman, the milkman, and his bicycle—went clattering in a whirl of panic and shouting into the water. The woman was sunk up to her elbows, her umbrella rumpled and smashed in and her bag's contents of leafy greens, bananas, onions, and something wrapped in newspaper all thrown from her hands and scattered in the water. The milkman's bicycle had tin pots attached to the rear of the frame. Their lids had been knocked loose, and milk poured from them into rain puddles.

The rickshaw wallah cut the motor, and we both got out. Sloshing through the water, I went over to the woman and helped her to her feet. The milkman berated the woman for not watching where she was going, and the woman turned around and did the same to the rickshaw wallah.

I shoved the onions, bananas, and the newspapered package back into the bag—everything miserably wet—and handed it back to the woman. The rickshaw wallah got the bicycle upright on its kickstand while confused passersby all gathered to watch.

"Are you okay?" I asked the woman.

She turned from her berating and told me in a voice suddenly calm and collected, "I am fine."

The milkman and the rickshaw wallah were in a full-blown argument now, slinging names at each other. The milkman was complaining about all the milk he'd lost, gesturing madly at the nebula of pale white clouding the rainwater at their feet.

The woman checked her bag and then picked her way, soaked, from the uproar. That's when the milkman shoved the rickshaw wallah and the rickshaw wallah shoved the milkman. This wouldn't have mattered much were I not standing directly between the milkman and his bicycle. The bicycle and I went down together like clumsy dance partners. Gulps of water went down my throat, and I panicked, sputtering, coughing. I felt my back, my pants, my head, everything soaked through, and my arms caught between bicycle spokes. I tried to pry myself loose.

Immediately, others rushed up and pulled the men apart. I felt hands grab me by the armpits and haul me up. I shook water from my eyes and spat several times. The rickshaw wallah put his hand on my shoulder, called me "boss," asked me if I was all right. Feeling woozy, I nodded, and we sloshed back through the ankle-deep water to the rickshaw. The rickshaw wallah complained about the audacity of the milkman, whom I could still hear hollering as a couple of locals tried to calm him down and lead him away with his bicycle. One of his pots was missing its lid.

After that, the confusion of the rain-crazed world became strangely muted, as if I'd lowered the volume on everything with a remote control. I heard only the hornet-like buzzing of the rickshaw motor as we rode on, and the washing-over of the rain. From inside my shirt, I pulled out the folder with my transcripts and grade reports—all drenched now. I felt for my wallet—still there, thank god—and pulled it open: the pictures, tucked inside sleeves, were still dry, but the rupees were not.

The driver kept his gaze fixed on the road, hands gripping the handlebar tightly, revving the engine as we tore through the final stretch back to the guesthouse. Maybe he was pissed off, maybe he was ashamed of what had happened. Maybe both.

My mother, Anand, and Anjali were seated on the couch, and Hemant Uncle was at the dining table when I got in. The laugh track of a Gujarati sitcom blared from the TV. Dal and incense wafted in from the kitchen. I sloshed into the living room, feeling every bit like I was invading this quaint domesticity.

"I need cash for the rickshaw," I announced.

My mother got up from the couch, looked me up and down, and asked what had happened. I told the story, and that got Hemant Uncle chuckling as he sipped from a cup of tea. My mother tsked and shook her head before asking if I was all right.

I nodded and jerked my head toward the door. "Rickshaw's waiting downstairs."

"After what happened, he still expects to get paid?" my mother said, putting on her slippers and grabbing the umbrella leaning next to the door. "Anand, get him a towel." But before he even got to his feet, Anjali had darted off the couch and, in seconds, had a towel in my hands.

"It's okay, Bhabhi, I will go," Hemant Uncle said. He took the umbrella from my mother and went down the steps to speak with the rickshaw wallah.

“Go, Vikram,” my mother said, her tone calming down. “Go upstairs, change your clothes.”

~ ~ ~

As I pulled my suitcase out from under the bed and began picking out clothes, I thought over the events of the past few hours. And I realized that I didn’t feel depressed or resentful or angry or ashamed or anything—none of the feelings I’d gotten so used to over the past many months. Instead, I felt oddly energized, at peace with and proud of myself. Maybe it was my ego, or maybe it was my truest self calling out to me, I didn’t know. But in that moment, I felt like the man I wanted to be for Shannon, for all the friends I longed for: a man of action! What a rare feeling—I knew it wouldn’t last—but I was happy to know I could be that man, if I wanted to be.

Chapter 6

"Vikram, good morning," Hemant Uncle boomed as I shambled down the steps the following morning. "There's chai and food waiting."

A Hindi jingle played on the radio sitting next to the TV.

Everybody had gathered around snacks and cups of chai at the table. At the center of the table were opened wrappers seeped in grease and piled with savory bhajiyas—battered, crispy round fritters topped with cilantro, chilies, and diced onions. Judging from the Hindi-language newspapers the bhajiyas came wrapped in, they had to be from one of the snack stalls up the road. Next to the bhajiyas, I saw an opened wrapper of *fafadas*—savory fritters shaped like flutes and accompanied by the same condiments.

"College food," Hemant Uncle joked, chewing, wiping his hands. "You're in college, now, no? So sit down."

The radio advertisement switched to the deadpan monotone of a sports announcer calling the play-by-play at a cricket match.

"You're not looking so much wet this morning." Hemant Uncle laughed, sipping his chai.

"Luckily, you didn't get hurt," my father said. "Stay away from street fights."

"Did you get cut on anything?" Anand asked, looking up from a book in his hands, its covers freshly bound with laminated brown paper. "Because you could get tetanus."

"No one has tetanus," my mother said irritably, then to me, "Did you take your malaria pill?"

"No cuts," I said and went into the kitchen where we kept a bottle of malaria pills in the cabinet. These were gargantuan—horse pills—pink, the size of nickels. I choked one down with a swig from the water bottle on the dining table.

"Thanks, Vikram," my mother said. "Now if I could just get your father and brother to take."

"I took mine!" Anand snapped.

"Easy, easy," my father said. "After breakfast, I'll take the pill. It gives me nausea. After I eat, I'll take."

"You're going to cause problem by not taking those pills."

My father discarded the matter with a fanlike flip of his hand as he savored another bhajiya.

"Not so many, watch it," my mother warned.

"Don't worry, Bhabhi. We were the first customers at that stand this morning. This is good oil, it's fresh," Hemant Uncle assured her.

"Not just that," my mother replied, a note of tenderness in her voice. "He has a weak stomach."

"I've been eating this all my life," my father boasted, picking up another bhajiya. "Since I was a child."

"You're not a child now, are you?" my mother countered steadily, quietly.

I glanced at the book that Anand was flipping through. "What is that?" I leaned over him to take a look. "Holy crap, is that Sanskrit?"

"I have Gujarati, Hindi, and Sanskrit," my brother said glumly.

"Don't worry," my father said to Anand, "we'll get you a tutor."

"You will learn," Kamala Auntie said with a snap of her fingers, "very fast."

Anand groaned and picked through the book.

I examined the fafada, turning it over in my hands, sniffed it.

"What're you sniffing it for?" my mother scolded.

I took a bite. Like the bhajiyas, the fafada was redolent of corn flour, masala, and oil. Not bad, I thought, and finished it. I took another.

"When does your school start?" I asked Anand.

"Monday," he muttered, putting aside his book.

"Me too," I said. "Don't worry," and, in a lower tone, I added, "you'll be okay."

From the radio came the eruption of cheering crowds, and the announcer's voice lit up with enthusiasm—a jubilant tumbling of Hindi words poured from the radio, filling the room.

"This is Indian national team," Hemant Uncle said, glancing first at me, then at Anand. "They're playing match against England."

"You'll like this, Anand," my father urged. "Similar to baseball."

"Doubt it," Anand muttered and sipped from the cup of milk.

"How did everything at Xavier's go?" Kamala Auntie asked my parents hopefully.

"A bit of *dada-giri*, but he's all set now."

"You'll enjoy Xavier's," Hemant Uncle told me. "We had much fun during those days."

"Heard you kept getting in trouble with the principal," I said.

"Atch-cha," Hemant Uncle said. "That Father Prieto, I did not like him. He did not like me."

"That's what Pappa told me." I chuckled.

"Father Prieto, he was living in housing colony near Xavier's at that time. I used to make *mushkari* with my friends, and all the time getting into trouble for that. One time, we made this, uh, enormous *jaangiyo* . . . how you say . . . underwear . . . from dhoti fabric, and we hung on his clothesline. So that all the students passing his house, they'll see that only. So whenever someone would ask in which house is Father Prieto staying? You tell him look for the biggest jaangiyo. That's his house."

The thought of a humongous pair of underwear hanging outside the principal's front yard was enough to get Anand, Anjali, and me laughing pretty hard.

Hemant Uncle solemnly added, "But such mushkari got me suspended from cricket team. And also I got low marks on my exam." He smiled, taking a sip of the chai. "So now I'm in State Bank only."

I plucked up another fafada, ate it, and started into another, laughing in fits and starts the whole time. I wanted Nate and Karl there that instant to share in this; I wanted them to know I could still laugh at a joke. It was reassuring to know I still had it in me, this instinct to laugh.

The conversation at the table moved on, but by now my attention had turned to something else: a faint stirring in my gut. This twisting and churning, a kind of thudding. Pretty soon, it felt like there was a beast stamping its hooves around my insides.

It may have been the ditchwater I'd swallowed during my back-ass spill the day before or the *paan* I'd eaten days before that. In any case, sanitation was not exactly a priority in Ghatlodiya, with its pools of standing water along the road and out behind the guesthouse, where cows lingered and from where swarms of flies launched daily raids through the kitchen door. All those things might've had something to do with it.

All I knew was that the third fafada triggered a stampeding sensation from my chest down to my lower gut. There went the thudding, stamping hooves. My gut twisted, tightened. I backed away from the table, turned, aware only of a puzzled look from my mother and the sight of my father leaning in beside the radio so he could hear the sports announcer above Hemant Uncle's voice. And that was all. I was aware only of retreating to the toilet, hoping dimly for mercy.

~ ~ ~

All day Saturday, my head was a griddle—beaded with sweat, hot enough to cook rotis on. I spent the day in bed, in a moaning, gut-rotted malaise. Once my father came in and asked if I was feeling any better. I moaned for him to get out of the way as I pushed past him, clutching my gut, toward the bathroom. One bite of the rice and bland dal my mother later brought up to me, and I felt my insides caving. I pushed away the plate, turned over, and went to sleep. It was an underground kind of sleep, and by that night, I didn't care if I lived or not.

The following day wasn't much better, but I could rise from my coffin of bedsheets long enough to see Hemant Uncle, Kamala Auntie, and Anjali off. They had to drive back to Baroda that morning: Hemant Uncle had the State Bank to get back to on Monday, and Anjali was starting fourth standard.

Kamala Auntie and my mother insisted on a marathon of picture-taking. We felt like circus animals as they posed us individually, in pairs, and all together.

In one group picture, Hemant Uncle put an arm around me and drew me nearer on the sofa. "Come closer, Vikram. This is family picture," he said, and he kept his arm around me. Family picture. It was strange to think of myself as belonging to a larger family, bound by blood and shared history, and there was a warmth to the belonging, a comfort that was shockingly new to me. For eleven years, "family" had meant Anand and me and our parents—that's all. But this, I sensed, was a truer, more authentic feeling of family. Everyone in this picture belonged here, now, together. It made me even sadder about Hemant Uncle, Kamala Auntie, and Anjali having to leave. It would be lonely out here in Ghatlodiya without them.

~ ~ ~

The drumbeat of thunder sounded. Another downpour was imminent. In a hurry, Hemant Uncle finished loading up the Fiat, including the TV, which he shoved into the backseat. Anjali slid in next to the TV as the first sprinkles began to fall and the light shifted from a lighter to a darker gray.

"The boys will adjust," I heard Kamala Auntie say in Gujarati to my mother. They stood together at the bottom of the steps. "Just give it time. And they'll soon be local." She hugged my mother. "Come to Baroda. Come during Diwali."

"Chok-kus," my mother said, wiping her hand across her cheek.

Car doors slammed shut, the engine revved up, and calls of "*Aavjo*" were traded back and forth. Anjali opened the back window, leaned out, and waved good-bye. Soon, they'd backed out of the driveway and pulled away, motoring farther and farther down the ragged strip of road.

I told my father it was too bad we didn't have our video camera to record their going-away. My father agreed and let me know that he'd written to the customs office in Bombay. And if it came to it, he was willing to go down there personally and pry it away from them. "Let's give them a little more time. Then we'll see."

As I trudged back upstairs, I wasn't sure what bothered me more: that those criminal customs agents took my camera, or Kamala Auntie's talk about how I was going to "adjust" and be "local in no time." I flung myself back into bed, kicking the sheets off and resenting the damp heat. There was so much to resent.

~ ~ ~

The next morning marked the start of Anand's school year, and it was supposed to mark the start of mine. But I wasn't going anywhere: the fever still clung—as unbudgingly as that facehugger in *Alien*. I lay in bed, listening to the clink and clatter of my mother fixing breakfast. From my parents' bedroom came the chime and jingle of Hindi advertisements on the radio as my father dressed for work. Anand got into his school uniform—beige pants and a white short-sleeved shirt with the Gujarat Law Society emblem embroidered on the breast pocket—and packed his backpack with new schoolbooks. I noticed he stuffed his baseball magazine in with everything. Then he left the room and shuffled off downstairs in his school-regulation dress shoes.

I heard a rickshaw stuttering into the driveway, then a commotion of voices—my mother and father, and Anand—followed by much shuffling and the opening of the front door. "Bye, beta, have good day," my mother said.

"Be alert and careful," my father shouted from the front door. I heard Anand mumble a few words, and he was gone. The rickshaw faded on up the road.

Silence brooded. Nothing stirred. Not even the faintest breeze came through the window. The ceiling fan spun above me, offering nothing. I craved a signal. Something. Was I like those astronauts in Bradbury's story? I fished out my copy of *Rolling Stone* from my backpack, but all it did was deliver reminders. I put on my headphones and lay there listening to *Document*. R.E.M.'s last record. Transmissions. Twanging echoes, light-years old. Musical radio waves suffused with messages of America. After a while, the thought crept over me that no one back there gave a goddamn what happened to me. Not anyone. Friends can be such impostors.

My mother knocked at the door—two dainty knocks. "So?" she asked. "How do you feel?"

I took off my headphones. Pressed my abdomen. It made a noise like a toad.

"Maybe I should see a doctor."

The private clinic there in the boonies was a hole in the wall, with a dingy little waiting room crammed with sobbing infants, stick-thin mothers, and lethargic old men in dhotis, fanning themselves. The clinic's doctor—sleepy-eyed and soft-spoken—asked after my symptoms. Then he asked me to lie down on an exam table, tapped around my belly, and prodded about with a stethoscope. Throughout, his face remained calm, expressionless. Then he stepped away and produced a packet of pills out of a cabinet. He told me there was an epidemic of amebic dysentery going around Ghatlodiya; fecal contamination of the rainwater, he thought, and told me to avoid the water.

I remembered how I'd swallowed the water the other day, during my spill as the milkman and rickshaw wallah argued with each other in the rain. Fecal contamination. God, I wanted to vomit right there and then. "I see," I said, sliding off the exam table. I thanked him and took the packet of medicine.

The rest of the week, I kept to a strict diet of rice and yogurt, popped antibiotics twice a day, and slowly regained my strength. I also kept to my room, reading Bradbury, *Galapagos*, and *Rolling Stone*, till the pages were dog-eared, damp with sweat, Bruce Springsteen's face on the cover torn and creased. The afternoons ached, riddled with boredom and rain. Flies raged. Armies of them. I swatted as many as I could. When I was too exhausted to swat, I resorted to chasing them out through the kitchen door, back to the muck where they spawned. But they came back, always came back, filling up the kitchen and crawling all over the dining table.

"I've been chasing flies out that damn kitchen door all day," I told my father that evening.

"That won't do any good," he chuckled, after a day in his air-conditioned office.

"I'd like to keep from getting sick again," I countered.

"You look better." He untucked his dress shirt and drew up a chair to the dining table. "Good! That means you'll only miss your first week of classes." My mother set down a cup and saucer of chai in front of him, a couple of Parle-G biscuits tucked on the saucer against the cup.

My mother asked after my father's work, how things were shaping up. He said things were "very good," that they'd already landed a high-profile contract with the government to do some research ahead of the launch of a satellite the following year. "Quite exciting." They went back and forth like that, and I was startled by the matter-of-factness of what was happening. A new domesticity seemed to be taking shape here, my parents' chitchat unaffected by the changes around us.

But I was aware of an emptiness too, and new silences now that Hemant Uncle, Kamala Auntie, and Anjali were gone. Hemant Uncle's booming voice; Anjali humming to herself, busy with her coloring books; and Anand sneaking up behind her, pulling loose the ribbon tying her hair. And Kamala Auntie peeling mangoes to make custard in the afternoons.

After a few words were exchanged, the room fell quiet. My father sipped his chai and my mother sat with her arms crossed, a finger tapping at her chin. After a while, she glanced out the window, humming an old Hindi tune to herself, lost in her thoughts.

Chapter 7

My first day of college began with a walk to the bus stand, my backpack slung behind me. I'd loaded it up with a couple of notebooks, a battered hardcover Macmillan *History of English Literature* that looked like it had survived the London Blitz (all the copies at the bookshop looked like that), a small paperback of Restoration comedies, and another one of Victorian poetry I'd kept assiduously unopened. There was also a liter of water and enough room for a tiffin packed with a few rotis, dal, and vegetables—my sustenance for the length of the afternoon.

The walk took me along the road's baked-mud fringe of tin-roofed shanties, where men smoked and slept on *charpoys* and children ran barefoot and shat among chickens and dogs. The shanties abutted the now-familiar sight of paan sheds and snack vendors and other concrete shop fronts, painted over with Gujarati signs for shoes, umbrellas, and dentists.

You walked the length of this road till it ended at a junction with the main road—a slightly wider but much louder version of this one—took a left, and continued a few more blocks, hoping not to get knocked down by a bicycle or get your leg or arm clipped by a passing truck or rickshaw. The bus stand itself was a meager shelter—a red metal awning. It squatted there at the foot of a row of soot-stained, mildewed apartment blocks.

It was midmorning and hot already. There weren't too many others out, which surprised me. I was used to seeing Ahmedabad's bus stands crowded at all hours, but we were in the outermost reaches of the city where, perhaps, there were fewer commuters.

I stood under the awning, behind an elderly woman in horn-rimmed glasses—she could have been the same woman I had helped to her feet that day in the rain—with a tote bag full of newspapers and greens. I took out my wallet and removed from it a slip of paper. On it, I had jotted down a few Gujarati numerals, the numbers for the buses, along with the destinations of each. I would need to take the 43 to get to Xavier's, the 62 to get to the Alliance Française, and the 72 to get from the Alliance back to Ghatlodiya in the evening.

I put the list back into my wallet and, as I waited, began looking at the pictures in their plastic sleeves. Looking at Shannon still made me ache. She seemed farther away than ever. I thought of her now, her skin, her mouth, the pressing against and the pulling away, and the softnesses, everything now thousands of miles and half a world removed from my experience. The picture was the most beautiful thing I had brought with me, and it was all that mattered just then.

I heard kissing noises and taunting male voices behind me. I turned to find two shaggy-headed young men not much older than me, craning over my shoulder. The first leaned his elbows against the railing, and the second had his arm slung around the other. Around here, I had seen boys strolling the streets hand in hand or with arms around each other's shoulders, and I knew it for what it was—a friendly gesture—but it still made me uncomfortable and slightly embarrassed.

The boys started chuckling. "Girlfriend?" the first one said, cocking his chin in my direction and grinning. "American girlfriend?"

I smiled a neutral smile and turned back around. The boys began moving away.

"We find you nice Ahmedabadi, American," the second one said. "Much better than that one." They shambled away on their slippers, across the road, and became lost in the blur.

Then I realized something, and checked my watch to make sure. It was July 4. Fireworks day. Summer day. Barbecue day. Green backyards. The aroma of hamburgers. I stood there, dreaming of hamburgers. Melted cheddar and onions and ketchup. Potato salad. Potato chips. In my mind, I imagined a conversation with Shannon.

"Let's go to the lake today," I say to her. James Madison Park. Across the lake, we see downtown looming up on either side of the capitol, the dome and spire clear and sharp against peninsulas of summer clouds. We lie on blankets, then drive through town to Emily's—she has the pool. We swim and dive in the afternoon. I see Nate and Karl there, a whole congregation of friends. Afterward, Shannon ties her hair back (the way I like it), and the whole group treks off to Elver Park, into the wide open of its meadow. Shannon lies on my shoulder, and I clasp her hand. I hear Nate crack open a beer, offer it to Karl. But Karl doesn't want it. Not a good idea, anyway: he drove, after all. Nate makes jokes out of it. Then he passes the beer to me; I take it, sip it under the sky and the fireflies. A Frisbee whirs waywardly across our vision, a child scampers after it. Blooms of fireworks open up above us, vast as the heavens. And the dark field bursts with cheers and whistles.

"What'll we do with our lives?" says Shannon in my ear.

"We're going to do everything."

~ ~ ~

The bus was utterly empty when it arrived; this had to be the farthest stop on the route. I climbed on, took a seat in the back. The conductor—a thin man in khakis with gray bristles of hair—stepped up to me, very businesslike, and asked, "Bolo?"

When I told him my destination, he opened the lid of a metal box hung from his shoulder, pulled out a paper ticket, and punched a hole in it with a ticket-puncher. I paid him and took the ticket. He went on, and I was so glad that he paid me no more attention than if I were any other passenger.

The bus driver stood outside, a steel tumbler of water in his hand, eating a piece of fruit and chatting with a vegetable seller. Finally, he rinsed out his mouth, spat out the water, and handed the tumbler back to the seller. They said their good-byes, and the driver climbed back into his seat. When the passengers had all paid up, the conductor struck the overhead bar with his ticket-puncher: *Tink-tink! Tink-tink!*

With that, the red rusted beast of a bus growled to life, and we rolled out. From my seat in the back, I watched through the barred window as Ghatlodiya turned into Ahmedabad, going from the housing communities of drab apartment blocks to thickly crowded roundabouts and avenues. The bus bullied its way into the city, roaring and screeching, and heaved toward the side of the road, heedless of whoever or whatever was in its path, anytime it neared a bus stand. I watched the stands too—each one more crowded than the last, a gathering of determined and desperate faces.

I yearned for the video camera again, just to start shooting out the window and keep shooting as Ghatlodiya morphed into Ahmedabad—the satellite into the city. Right now, I'd settle for anything: a still camera, something I could use to frame the madness around and in my mind. I wanted the chaos outside contained, but, even more, the chaos inside contained, transfigured into something

I could touch, command, and concentrate. Maybe that way, my mind could cut the chaos into shapes I could understand.

When I left Ghatlodiya, there had been a dozen or so other passengers on the bus. Now, it was standing room only—elbows, torsos, and wild stares everywhere. Every few minutes, a few vacated the bus from the back doorway in a frenzy of hollers and shoving, but double that number piled on up front. At regular intervals, I heard the *tink-tink* of the ticket-puncher.

It had been more than a week since I'd sent off my first letters and postcards. I wondered if my transmissions had been received. Right then, it seemed so easy—so easy it terrified me—for a message to get lost out there in the wide, chaotic darkness.

~ ~ ~

The scent of sweat and coconut oil wafted through the college corridors and lecture halls swirling with Gujarati faces and voices. I had three lectures that day: Victorian Lit, General Psychology, and Intro to Economics. A feeling of death by boredom crept over me. I shook it off and pressed through the swaths of mingling, gossiping students.

I entered the already thrumming lecture hall in the wake of a stream of girls with ribbons in their hair and salwaar kameez ruffling in the breeze behind them. Three aisles of long wooden benches ran along the hall—the kind you saw in old English boarding schools. I noticed right away that the sexes did not mingle; the boys inhabited one half of the hall, the girls the other. It was a neat and disappointing division. The tube lights overhead were all turned off; no artificial light seemed necessary, as daylight flooded in from a row of windows along the far wall. It was shady in the hall, almost cool, with a pleasant brightness.

About halfway up the lecture hall, I took a seat at one end of a mostly empty bench and set my backpack at my feet. In the midst of the chattering and nervous energy in the hall, I just wanted to sit there quietly and not draw any attention. That's when a student in a cream-colored *kurta pyjama* strode up my side of the lecture hall, his books under his arm, and slid into the bench directly in front of me. His skin was mahogany-dark, and his looks were striking: gleaming, coal-dark eyes; thick, glossy hair combed smoothly back; and a handsome, chiseled jawline. He opened his notebook, and from the pocket of his kurta he produced an inkwell and a dip pen. I had never seen such writing utensils before. I wanted my video camera, any camera, some way to capture the details in his manner, his look, his antique accessories.

The teacher strutted in as quickly as a bird chasing crumbs, his willowy frame dressed in a starched white shirt and brown slacks. As soon as he appeared, the students all shot to their feet in a flurry of rustling and thumping, and calls of "Good morning, sir" erupted here and there. I made like everyone else and stood up—though the whole thing felt ingratiating and ridiculous.

The teacher sniffed at the air critically, waved everyone back down, and stepped onto the dais that separated him from the students. As he set his notes down at a wooden table in front of the chalkboard, it hit me that this was the same guy I'd seen when I'd stopped by the faculty lounge to speak with the French teacher the day of my registration. This was the guy blowing all that hot air about getting "booked" at the scene of a traffic accident. Old Frog Eyes.

Before the lecture started, I slid off the bench and went down to speak with him.

"Sir, I'm a new student," I said.

Frog Eyes looked up from his notes. "Just a minute," he said, and I saw that his small mouth was crowded with paan-stained, every-which-way teeth. Up close, his features looked softer, almost feminine, with delicate lines creasing both sides. But what gave him his regal bearing was the silvery hair, impeccably parted and combed. He opened a black-bound book. "Number?"

"Hmm?"

"Student number—" He leaned toward me over the table. "I see, this is your first day. You don't know your number."

"I've been ill. My name's Vikram. Mistry."

He slid his pencil down the roll call.

"One hundred eighty-four," he stated and put a tick mark next to the name. With that, I turned around to return to my seat when I bumped into the first blind person I had ever seen (apart from Patty Duke in *The Miracle Worker* and that blind girl from *Little House on the Prairie*).

"Oh, I'm sorry," I said.

Dark glasses covered his eyes, and he tapped a stick along as he went, feeling his way with his other hand. "S'okay, bhai," the blind student said affably, grinning, adding in Gujarati, "Usually I am the one bumping into others. So, don't worry. Who's this?"

"Vikram. Vik."

He took my hand with his free one. "Pradeep. Nice to meet you."

"You too," I said.

I shared a smile with him, then with the girl I saw behind him, in a skirt and a sleeveless blouse. She walked a step behind Pradeep with a hand at his elbow. She helped guide him to his seat, up front, center bench.

"Thank you," I heard Pradeep say, followed by a name.

"Sure."

It made me half stop in my tracks as I returned to my bench. *Sure?* It wasn't the word, but the accent she had said it in. American. Unmistakable. The breathy *s*, the lovely rounded *r*. It was a balm to my heart to hear it, for that one second.

I half turned in her direction and saw her take a seat on the opposite side of the hall—the girls' side.

She had to have heard me speak, heard my accent, that there was a coincidence here. But she never even glanced in my direction. Apparently never gave it a thought. She just fell into conversation with the girl beside her.

"Okay, okay, let us start," the teacher boomed.

PROF. SRIDHARAN, he wrote in large block letters on the chalkboard. "For those of you who are new to the class today. Or those who fell asleep at my first lecture—" He guffawed to himself, and polite, scattered laughter sounded around the hall. "Let us take up the rise of modernism in late nineteenth-century drama, shall we not?" And he put on a pair of black half-glasses and bent over his notes, which lay open on the table.

Sridharan stepped back and had opened his mouth to launch into his lecture when a lanky, shaggy-haired student loped in with a notebook in one hand and a pen dangling from his mouth. He wore a baggy black T-shirt emblazoned with a bold logo design. I leaned forward to get a better look as he passed the front of the lecture hall and saw, on the T-shirt, the red banner with "Harley-Davidson" in big white lettering and a bald eagle perched atop it with outspread wings. This sudden glimpse of American culture caught me off guard.

Sridharan, mouth still open, followed Harley with his eyes.

"Sorry, sir," Harley said dully. He slid in next to Pradeep on the front bench, throwing an arm along the back of it. Pradeep sensed him there, leaned toward him, smiled. He and Harley exchanged a few friendly words.

"Everyone has settled in?" Sridharan said brusquely. "Everyone is happy?"

Harley cleared his throat, straightened up. "Yes, sir. Sorry, sir."

Sridharan sighed and made a tick mark in his book. Then he took a breath and began. For the next fifty minutes, he rattled straight from his notes—an assembly line of authors, places, and dates—pausing only to chalk up names like Galsworthy and Ibsen and Shaw on the board, along with a year when some labor riots broke out.

The air, circulated gently by ceiling fans, filled with the scratching of pens and the rustle of turning pages. As he spoke, I scribbled a few notes, a peppering of facts I thought he might quiz us on, but I was stunned by the fury of note-taking going on around me. Everyone was hunched low over their notebooks and taking down, it seemed, every word that came out of Sridharan's mouth. The student in front of me filled up several pages quickly, pausing now and then to replenish his pen by dipping it into his inkwell. And his penmanship never flagged; it was always florid and impressive.

I glanced toward the front of the hall and a couple of rows over, to the girl who had walked in with Pradeep. There she was in profile, her black hair tied into a ponytail dropping to her upper back. She held a pen poised over an open notebook, but, unlike the rest of the students, she hadn't whipped herself into a spasm of scribbling. Instead, there was an air of cool disinterest about her as she stared ahead at Sridharan, occasionally turning her eyes to her notebook to jot something down. Then I remembered her from the day I'd come to college to sign up. She'd worn her hair loose that day, when she'd driven away in the white Maruti.

The moment the lecture wrapped up and Sridharan was tucking away his precious notes, I saw the girl get up and glide out along with a friend. She stopped only once, to say good-bye to Pradeep, and was gone, her friend at her heels.

I checked my schedule and noticed my next lecture didn't start for another hour. Racking my brain for ways to kill time, I found myself strolling around aimlessly. Soon, though, it occurred to me that I had to keep moving more intently, act like I had somewhere to go, never flagging or lingering. Otherwise I'd invite curious stares and attention.

From the first-floor veranda, I looked out onto the quad. For the most part, the men and women seemed willfully segregated here. The quieter females kept to their groups, and the gregarious males to theirs. They mingled somewhat outside lecture halls or in the bower that formed the quad's center or in the canteen on the opposite side of the quad, from which came the clink of soda bottles and waves of laughter. Students crossed the quad on paths bordered by patches of scant grass, marigold shrubs, and roses.

I was relieved to find the college library and eagerly took sanctuary there. The library was cool and quiet, as shady as the lecture halls. I made for the corner, where various newspapers were laid out on a pair of extra-wide reading stands pushed against each other. I scanned the papers—three across on each stand, with a bunch more on scrolls hung up on a rack nearby. *New York Times*? *Herald Tribune*? Not here. Not one newspaper from west of Ahmedabad. I saw newspapers in Hindi, Gujarati, and a half dozen other Indian languages. I did find the *Times of India*, in English. I began reading the English, and as I did, I could feel my brain relax, welcoming the words like old friends.

There were stories about Rajiv Gandhi mired in a Congress party scandal. There was a cricket column about the Indian team's series in England. A few pages in, I saw a small piece about the US presidential election, George Bush railing against Dukakis and his record in Massachusetts on the campaign trail. What struck me: Bush was in Wisconsin. In Madison! I could hear the cheers of the Republicans massed on Capitol Square. Shannon probably showed up and protested. But me, I didn't care what party was in town; in that momentary flash, I was home.

I heard a rustling next to me: someone turning the pages of a newspaper. I turned to the reader. It was that jet-eyed, mahogany-dark student with the fancy pen from my lecture. He glanced in my direction, a smile on his face, and returned to the paper.

"What language is that?" I asked, noticing the paper's doodle-like script.

"This is Tamil. From Tamil Nadu. Far south." His accent was typically Indian but not Gujarati. The *t*'s and *u*'s were more pronounced, and the words declarative, as if he had polished each syllable, speaking no more, no less than he intended.

"Are you also an English major?"

"Hmm." He shifted his feet to face me. "English. You are also?"

I nodded. "You were practically writing a book in that class. Does everyone take so many notes?"

"It is the only way to prepare for the essays, no? The exam essays."

"I don't know," I said. "I've never been to an Indian college before."

"Where you are from? London?"

"States." I explained about my father packing us up, our moving here.

"How long you are here?"

I shrugged. "Not sure. You?"

"I'm here for my BA. Three years. Then back to Madras for seminary studies." He turned to the Tamil paper and peered closely at something.

"Seminary? You want to be a priest?"

He didn't answer right away, didn't even look away from the newspaper. When he'd finished what he was reading, he straightened, faced me with a smile. "Priest. Yes."

"Is it far? I mean, where you're from?"

"Not so far as States, but, yes," he said. "It is far."

"I'm Vik," I said, glad to have met someone else far from home.

"Devasia." We shook hands.

~ ~ ~

The evening was so quiet. Anand and I hung out with our parents on the tiny balcony off their bedroom. Ghatlodiya settled down now, with the sun fading and the street cleared of all but a few rickshaws and bicycles. Children could be heard playing in nearby housing complexes and shanties. Pools of rainwater reflected the few streetlights.

Anand sat in a plastic chair, reading aloud the Gujarati alphabet and phrases from a schoolbook. My mother would correct him now and then, in between hearing my father update her on the goings-on at his work. I thought again of how he had a car to pick him up, drop him off, and now my brother too seemed to have door-to-door rickshaw service to and from school (along with a group of neighborhood schoolchildren). My mother, meanwhile, spent her days at home, sealed off from India's madness. Only I was foundering, on foot and in rust-bucket buses all day, all over this muck-filled city.

"Why don't we get Anand a proper tutor?" my father said, leaning his elbows against the railing. He turned to my mother, "He's not bad, though," he said, smiling. "In two weeks, he'll be a local."

"Let's wait till we're out of here, then we can make all arrangements," she said.

"There I've got news I've been waiting to tell you." He turned, shadowed in the twilight, and I had the momentary sensation he was pronouncing our fate. "We'll be out of here and in our bungalow by midmonth."

The hope in my mother's voice tensed with caution. "You *think* we will, or you were told for sure?"

My father nodded, laughing. "I got memo this morning. Bungalow will be ready by Sunday. From there, it'll all get easier."

"That we will see," my mother said plainly, then she turned to me. "How are you, beta?" Her voice calm and compassionate, like the cool of evening.

I shrugged. "Be all right."

By framing my thumbs and forefingers together at right angles, I made a movie screen out of them. I looked through them and followed flocks of swallows against the evening sky, racing together in fitful yet coordinated arcs.

"We'll get that camera back soon," my father said.

Anand closed his book and stood. He withdrew into the guesthouse, probably to comb through his baseball magazine again or listen to one of my R.E.M. tapes on his Walkman. My parents went back inside too.

I stayed out on the balcony as the evening darkened. The silence here was so primitive, as if I'd traveled not only thousands of miles but decades and decades into the past—a long way from the comfort of my American TV shows and phone calls to friends. Here, all I heard was the trill of a bicycle far up the road, a rickshaw sputtering off somewhere. Every once in a while came the faint voices of children and women, the clink of utensils and pots from the shanties. I could smell the cooking fires as the noises faded with the light. It was a primitive silence, a saddening silence, and I felt scared, alone in the sadness.

Chapter 8

A routine took shape. In the mornings, I trekked off to the Ghatlodiya bus stand with my backpack full of books and the tiffin of food, on my way to Xavier's. Classes lasted into the afternoon, till two o'clock—by which time a monsoon downpour would be lashing the city, and I would be famished.

Behind the college canteen, Devasia pointed out, was the hostel—a gray two-story building—where he stayed. After classes, Devasia would eat his lunch in the mess hall adjacent to the hostel. I would go with him, and we would eat together. With his Tamil appetite, Devasia would heap enough rice on his stainless steel plate to fill the underside of a Frisbee, while I'd sit down to my more modest Gujarati portions of roti and vegetables brought from home.

"Why you're not taking food here only?" he asked me the first time we were in the mess together, gesturing to the food being ladled out from pots by the serving boys.

I shook my head and smiled. "Dysentery isn't something I want twice."

My French classes started up the following week. After lunch, I took the bus, bumping and bashing my way to the Alliance

Française. On the first day, I paid the severe-looking French witch the seven hundred rupees I owed her. (Happily, I never saw her again during the six weeks I took that class.)

The class met in a small room—too small for the dozen of us enrolled, but it was equipped with an air conditioner. You walked up the narrow spiral staircase from the lobby of the Alliance and into a noisy whoosh of dreamy-cool air—sweaty, musty, but what a relief.

I kept to myself and my exercise book and wondered what it would be like to kiss our instructor, a round-faced, rosy-cheeked early-twentysomething from Kashmir who had spent two years living in Paris. Her French was efficient, not snotty the way I imagined all things French to be. The words came out of her like water down the stones of a happy brook. She spoke of writing postcards on sunny afternoons at café tables outside the Pompidou.

After two hours of French, I emerged dazed and dislocated. The gravel path of the Alliance, often drenched from the rains, gave way into late-afternoon Ahmedabad. Back to my own life. I staggered up the road and joined the commuters—the bankers, clerks, and housewives—who'd collected together, ready for the melee. When the bus arrived, this civic peace collapsed instantly and something just short of a riot broke out as everyone hurled themselves over each other to get aboard the bus.

It was no different on that day, my second day of French class. I managed to clamber on, shoved up by the velocity of onrushing passengers. The conductor squeezed through—always insisting on his fare—and I pulled out my wallet, paid for my ticket.

Tink-tink!

I hung on to the overhead bar, wedged into a sliver of space. I thought of how it had been two weeks since I sent my letters. Still no word from home. Had my letters gone missing, somewhere between here and America? All my transmissions scattered to the stars? The frightening thought occurred to me again that I had been forgotten. I could taste the bitterness rising up inside me and tried to shake it off. Stop panicking, I told myself. Write them again and use a post office in the city, not that miserable shack in Ghatlodiya. I resolved to do that. Just that.

The bus was packed shoulder-to-shoulder now. I held on to the bar and began to doze off, wedged between bodies, to the rocking motion of the bus. Once you got used to the smell, after a long day, it wasn't too hard to do.

I snapped out of my stupor as we entered the city's outer neighborhoods, Ghatlodiya the last stop, farthest out. As the bus ground to a halt, I anticipated the stampede to disembark. Bucking up my backpack, I pushed ahead and, in the tangle of legs and hands, shouts and sweat, I got one leg off the bus, then the other. *Ah! Free!* I separated from the mob and took a few steps. That's when I had the sensation of feeling lighter, of weightlessness, of something—a solid part of me—suddenly yanked from my body. I felt my back pocket—

My wallet!

It was gone. Lifted. Into thin air. Outer space.

Hysteria welled up. I flung myself around, searched for faces, for fleeing bodies. But everyone, men and women indifferent, dispersed where they willed. I found myself grabbing at arms, spinning around on my heels, roaming the crowds, looking for the slightest clue. I got a few looks but no sign of the thief. The pickpocket. The asshole who took my wallet. I couldn't care less about the money inside or the college ID—I wanted the photos.

My heart dropped several floors in my chest. Everyone cleared the bus stand, gone every which way, to the bazaars or to wherever they lived. The bus slumbered where it stood; this was the last stop on its route and the driver had stepped off for his break. I scrambled back on. I searched the seats, below the seats, the floor of the bus from front to back.

"Eh! *Abbay-oy*!" the driver shouted. He stepped back on the bus, a bulge of paan in his mouth. He immediately pegged me as someone "not from around here," so he quit shouting and just stared at me quizzically. Probably he thought I was some harmless lunatic.

"I'm looking for something!" I shouted in English.

But except for mud and scraps, nothing remained in the bus. It was gone. The wallet, the pictures, gone. I felt hate, a sudden impulse to rage, to weep. I staggered off the bus, my mind fuming. I couldn't speak, not even a swear word (nothing powerful and condemning enough came to my mind). It was minutes later before I regained my senses, became aware that I wasn't on the bus anymore but walking up the road, surrounded by strangers. Without my wallet. My photos. My last links to home. I was almost back at the guesthouse before I felt the rage cool off and the sadness begin to set in.

~ ~ ~

A letter from Shannon arrived—finally!

> *July 2, 1988*
>
> Dear Vik,
>
> Got your letter this afternoon and wanted to write you back right away. Emily wanted to go on one of her Saturday shopping sprees on State, and I had auditions at the Union, so we came down to campus together. I'm sitting on the terrace right now, and the sun's going down, and I wish you were here enjoying it with me. Maybe you could calm me down. I just finished trying out for the drama festival. They're doing two Tennessee Williams plays at the university theater

in August. I think it went well, but . . . As you know, I'm not the most confident about my auditions.

Vik, I really, really miss you. And as freaked out as you feel right now, I know that this is going to be the most amazing experience. Do you have any idea yet how long you'll be there? Is it really for good? Somehow, I think you'll be back, before you know it. And, to that end (drum roll, please!), I'm sending you an application for next fall. I know, I know. There's a lot to this—it won't be easy—you'll need your own visa, and I've heard about how hard it is to transfer to the UW from overseas, blah, blah, blah. But who knows? Maybe we'll be watching a sunset together this time next year . . . ?

I'll officially be moved into Sellery Hall at the end of the month. I cannot wait. Free at last! OK, sweetie, I'm thinking of you, so you can put your worries to rest. And, no, there are no hot new men in my life. Just you. Here comes Emily, and she's got three humongous bags in her hand, so I'm going to wrap this up and write you a proper letter as soon as I get a chance.

Miss you!

Love,
Shannon

P.S. Nate says hi. I've seen him and Karl a few times. They're writing a script or something together.

P.P.S. Don't you dare throw away the application.

~ ~ ~

I wrote back to Shannon immediately, telling her about the stolen wallet. I had a couple of pictures of us already, tucked between the pages of my yearbook, but asked for another of her senior photos anyway. Mostly, though, I was relieved that she was still thinking of me.

I thought about running the letter over to the Ghatlodiya post office but nixed the idea. I figured I'd better wait to mail anything till after we moved into the city, to that bungalow my father spoke about in a neighborhood called Navarangpura, and use one of the city post offices.

That Sunday, I packed up my suitcase and backpack. My mother wasn't feeling well—stomach pains, she said—so I told her to lie down. I took the clothes from the line, folded them, and packed them in my mother's suitcase. Anand had gone with my father in a rickshaw to the institute to fetch the company Ambassador that would drive us over to Navarangpura.

The car pulled up. Behind the wheel, his neck craning so he could see over it, was the same driver who took my father to and from work every day. Our personal chauffeur, making extra on a Sunday.

"They're here," I said, poking my head into my parents' bedroom. My mother was lying on her back, her palms crossed low over her abdomen. "How're you feeling?"

She took a deep breath. "Better," she answered.

Moments later, we were on the move again. The Ambassador banged and splashed its way through Ghatlodiya and into the busier neighborhoods of the city. The monsoon rains had left the roads potholed as if from weeks of artillery fire.

My father, sitting up front, spoke of hiring a cook and a maid right away to help my mother around the house. She would not have to deal with washing clothes, cleaning, or going to the market. Things would quickly fall into place, he said. He had already alerted the shipping company in Bombay, where the things we'd decided to bring with us—the TV, VCR, stereo, my father's home computer, kitchen things, and linens—had already arrived and were waiting.

In a few days, it would all be in Ahmedabad, and our lives would settle into a happy order.

If the need arose, like today, we would always have the car and driver at our disposal—and he patted the driver on the shoulder. The driver smiled back meekly. And, for me, he would buy a Kinetic Honda scooter, or whatever vehicle I wanted, so I could zoom around the city to my heart's content. He was way more enthusiastic than I could handle. I'm glad all of this is working out so well for you, I wanted to tell him.

"No cook," my mother said, her sunglasses on. She sat in the far corner of the backseat. I could tell she wasn't feeling well. I wondered if her eyes were closed behind her sunglasses. "I don't want someone else cooking for us. The Ahmedabadis always use too much oil, and that's the last thing you need."

"We can tell our cook to cook light."

"I can manage," my mother replied sternly.

My father looked at me, gesturing to a neighborhood of concrete apartment low-rises out beyond a shopping complex. Eucalyptus loomed up over it. "You were born just over there," he said, his voice muffled by the wind in the open window. "Behind this is Jainagar Complex. Back then, there was nothing here. Just fields." He shifted his look to my mother. "Remember that? Jainagar?" Then to me he said, "Your Hemant Uncle, Kamala Auntie, you, your mother, myself, and your grandparents, all under one roof. For only few years, then we left for America."

My mother said nothing.

My father faced the road ahead now and chuckled to himself. "Simpler days," he said, half in a dream.

The bungalow was in a row of them, just off a busy roundabout where four roads intersected. We crossed a wooden gate and a dirt driveway fringed by what had once been a garden, reduced now to briars, scrub, and weeds. The bungalow lay to one side of the drive, a two-story cement structure with a balcony overlooking these unruly grounds. We would occupy the top half while the bottom would remain shuttered.

It all seemed a repeat performance of our arrival a few weeks ago. Every suitcase, backpack, and handbag, everything lugged from the car. The driver, mild and solicitous, helped us, taking the suitcase from my mother's hands. Up the dirt path and around the corner of the bungalow, we came to the front doors.

My father unlocked them, pulled aside the bolt, and opened the doors to the entryway. Daylight leaked into a dark stairwell. The flip of a switch threw on a melancholy light from a single bulb somewhere above. Our steps echoed; the luggage knocked against the stairs. It was rather spooky. Up one flight, past the locked and empty first-floor bungalow, up another flight, and we arrived at our door. This was it. Our home.

The place had the musty lingering nostalgia of British officers billeted here during the last days of colonialism. There was an airiness too, an Old World spaciousness here. Whitewashed walls, high wooden ceilings, stone tiling on the floors.

In the kitchen, veined granite countertops and wooden cupboards. We were relieved to find there was a tiny Kelvinator fridge installed and copper pots already on the two-ring gas stove. The living room, the dining room, and the two bedrooms were all fully furnished. My parents had a small balcony off their bedroom. I felt a small victory in discovering that the other bedroom—the one Anand and I would be sharing—had the big balcony. We stepped out onto it and took a look: straight ahead was a view of the weed-choked garden and University Road, and beyond that, the athletic field fronting the H.L. College of Commerce. Another vantage gave on a muddy shopping plaza.

At least we were in the city now. Not in the boonies. The world seemed slightly more within reach.

"We can rent videos now," Anand observed, pointing toward the plaza. "Looks like there's a paan shop with videos there."

My father stepped out onto the balcony. "And your college is just there on the other side of that." He indicated the roundabout straight ahead. A sprawling peepal tree grew in a ringed plot of earth in the center of the roundabout, blocking the view beyond. "Maybe another mile. Just a straight shot."

I didn't care to listen, though; the last thing I wanted to hear was a pitch about how easy things would be, especially one coming from my father.

"And Anand," he added, "your school is just a bit farther from there. Everything nice and close, right?"

"Yeah," Anand said, "isn't it right down the same road? Right past the college."

"Exactly."

Anand was really getting into the swing of things, I thought. Traitor. Cooperator.

"Where is the post office?" I asked. "That's all I need to know."

My father looked off in one direction, then the other. "I am not sure. But it's here. Not far. This is Navarangpura, after all. Central Ahmedabad."

In the kitchen, my mother began steeping chai. With a pair of tongs, she lifted the steel pot from the flames, waiting for the roiling brew to settle a bit, swirling it, concentrating the masala, sugar, and tea grounds before setting it back on the burner.

"How did you get the tea already?" I asked her.

"Your father's surprise," she said, lifting the pot and pouring the chai through a small strainer into a ceramic teapot. As she poured, she nodded toward the pantry. "Look there." I checked it out: The shelves were already full of oil, sugar, flour, tea, spices, cornflakes, even Parle-G tea biscuits and Indian snacks, all in canisters arranged side by side, as if some magical delivery boy had showed up here in advance and set everything up. Shopping bags bulged with all kinds of produce. The fridge as well was stocked with sliced bread, eggs, butter, sealed plastic bags of pasteurized milk.

"When did you do all this?" I asked my father.

Seated at the dining table off the kitchen, he arched his brows and shrugged enigmatically.

"But when?"

"I've got my ways," he said coyly, nodding his head. "Your mother told me what all she needed, and I made the arrangements. Simple."

I slid into a chair at the table. Anand and my father munched on Parle-G biscuits straight out of their wrappers and bowls of *murmura*, seasoned puffed rice. My mother brought out the teapot and cups and poured steaming chai. She sat down, raising her cup with both hands.

"How do you feel, Ma?" I asked.

"Much better."

"It's going to get easier," my father said again. "Wait till everything arrives in a few days. Then we will really be cooking."

"We should give the driver some food," my mother said. She put together a plate of murmura and biscuits and poured a cup of chai and a steel tumbler of water.

"Vikram, would you mind going down and giving him?" my mother said.

The driver was reclining in the backseat of the Ambassador with a towel over his eyes, arms folded, when I found him.

I cleared my throat. "Hi," I said, hoping he wasn't sound asleep.

"Hmm?" The driver removed the towel from his eyes, squinted at the food I'd brought out, and smiled. He opened the passenger-side door and took the plate, cup, and tumbler I was balancing in my hands. He set the plate and chai on the seat beside him and tipped the tumbler toward his mouth, keeping it inches above his lips as he emptied it.

"Thank you." He sounded so grateful and sincere. It made me feel sad for some reason.

On either side of our bungalow stood identical bungalows, only with better-tended grounds. Peepal trees towered between them, their leaves lying everywhere. There was something ghostly about this place, a peace that felt out of time and at odds with the city outside its wooden gates.

I half expected to see a sahib in his jodhpurs reclining under a canopy, sipping whiskey and polishing his elephant gun while a turbaned servant fanned him. A shrill cawing cut the air, and I traced it to a peacock strutting across the roof of a storage shed next door. I'd never seen a peacock in real life before, and I marveled at his bearing, the royal blue of his neck and breast, the tiaralike crest, and the sweeping green of his tail. The peacock bobbed his head in my direction for a moment, then, fluttering his wings, dropped out of sight onto the far side of the shed.

I found a wooden box about the size of a birdhouse hung on a nail beside the bungalow's front doors. The box had a mail slot along the top, a see-through plastic panel on the front, and a tiny door that opened after you pulled a hasp on the side. Here it was. My mailbox. But more than that: my lifeline.

Chapter 9

Our things arrived from Bombay. We unloaded boxes from the truck's battered wood-framed bed and laid them out in heaps resembling barricades. Slowly we fell to the task of unpacking and organizing. My parents got their kitchen appliances set up, the Hindi movie collection arranged next to the TV, the VCR and stereo, all plugged into power transformers and ready to go.

Soon enough, the others' lives settled into a harmonious daily rhythm. Every morning, before I even dragged myself out of bed, Anand would be up and dressed in his school uniform. I could hear him and my mother in the kitchen before the putt-putting rickshaw pulled up in the drive—the one assigned to transport him to and from school, along with a few other classmates who lived in the area. That made it a kind of rickshaw pool. The babbling of my brother's rickshaw companions carried up over the balcony and into the bedroom. "Anand!" one of them shouted. "Chalo, yaar!" Then I heard Anand rushing out of the house, followed soon by the whirring away of the rickshaw. From my parents' bedroom across the hall, I could hear my father tap-tapping away at his computer and, above that, the booming announcements of All India Radio interrupted by jingles for Lifebuoy, Raymond shirts, or Thums Up cola. The same ones over and over again, every morning, every day.

My father hired a man to houseclean. Grizzled, gaunt, and wearing round Coke-bottle glasses, he showed up cheerfully each morning with his rags, brushes, brooms, and bottles of chemicals. Squatting on his haunches, he would move through the house, first with a short broom made up of thin, bunched-together shoots, next with a damp rag and bucket of water. He would clean the bathroom too, splashing water and solvents all over the floor, then scrubbing everything down with a hard brush and sweeping all the tracked-in dirt into the drain.

There was also a cleaning girl. She lived in the shantytown that sprawled along the road a few blocks west of us. She would come in the mornings, announcing herself with her bangles and her anklets, swishing by my room in her ankle-length skirt, her bright-colored, full-bosomed *choli*. Her nose and ears shimmered with jewelry. She would do the wash, hang it out on the line on the balcony, and, in the evenings, reappear to clean the dinner dishes. I couldn't help but steal glances at her as I sat on the balcony in the mornings before class, scanning the *Times of India* (for any item about or from America) as she leaned over the parapet to wring out the wash or as she hung clothes over the line. She couldn't be more than nineteen, I guessed, and she was scorched bronze by the Gujarat sun, and she smelled of the dust of the shantytown. When she spoke or smiled, her teeth shone stark white against her face.

"She's quite something," I told Pradeep, the blind student, one day before the start of Sridharan's lecture.

"Vikram bhai," he said, grinning mischievously, "I thought you were already having girlfriend, no?" He shifted on the bench, too giddy to sit still. "Now you must ask yourself"—he leaned toward me, his hand on my arm, a brotherly warmth between us—"is it worth to drop your American girl for this village beauty? If so, count on me, eh, bhai? I myself will sing at your marriage function!" He laughed convulsively, his shades nearly falling off his face.

"I just wanted to describe her to you."

"And you've done wonderful job, bhai."

"Because around here," I said, "it seems that men don't really chat up women, do they? I mean, the guys are happy to just stand around and stare at them."

"It is the great tragedy of our nation, Vikram bhai. See here in this lecture hall," he whispered. "Boys are on one side, girls on other side. You don't have to *see* to see that. We want to mingle, but it's the tragedy of our culture, you see. It forbids that."

"Why such a long face, Pradeep?" The American voice again, the words like waterfalls in paradise. I sat up. There she was, today in a brown kurta top and jeans, hair flowing to her shoulders. At her heels that tagalong friend of hers, with her overeager smile, dressed today in a lime-green salwaar kameez patterned with flowers.

"Priya, Priya, Priya," Pradeep said. "My dost Vik and I were only discussing you girls. That's why long face."

"So predictable." She took a step toward her side of the lecture hall, her notebook pressed to her chest. "That's all boys ever talk about, isn't it?" Her eyes moved from Pradeep to me.

"What else is there?" I said, smiling. Was that too forward? I hoped I hadn't embarrassed her. Feeling somewhat embarrassed myself, I extended my hand and gave her my name. Tentatively, shyly, she took my hand and asked me where in the States I'd moved from.

"The Midwest," I said. "Wisconsin."

She said she didn't know the Midwest too well. Her home had been in Massachusetts. "Boston. But I moved back three years ago."

"It doesn't sound like it's been three years," I said.

She smiled. "You don't lose the accent if you don't want to." As she turned to walk away, I noticed she wore a tiny gold stud in her nose—a traditional Indian touch—and the paradox of that and her American accent together in one package excited me. I watched her go, but I couldn't help noticing that her friend paid particular attention to me, unable to suppress her smile, holding her stare a second too long.

Priya was drifting away toward her side of the hall when, suddenly, she became obscured from my view by a black T-shirt. "Side, boss," came a gruff voice.

I looked up to discover Harley-Davidson in the aisle, wanting to slide in next to Pradeep and me on the bench.

Sridharan entered the classroom, and the whole class was on its feet. He leaped onto the dais. With his typical haughty disregard, he gestured for us to sit down—the emperor before his subjects—and went about arranging his things on the table.

I got up with the intention of moving back to my customary spot, behind Devasia a few rows back. Harley slid past me onto the bench, next to Pradeep. "Sit down, yaar," he whispered to me. "If you are Pradeep's friend, you are mine also."

I obliged and sat at the end of the bench, on the aisle. Harley leaned over—he smelled of cheap cologne—and stuck a hand in my face. "Vinod," he said. The mustache, the pompadour, the gold necklace. It was as if Travolta's and Pacino's DNA had been spliced together in some freak genetic experiment. We shook hands. "She's nice, no?" he said in a low, sly tone. He stared off in Priya's direction, then back at me, waiting for my response, so I humored him with a nod and a smile.

"She likes you," he said. The remark caught me off guard. I couldn't tell if he was putting me on, and I didn't like it. "I'm not kidding you, yaar. She and her girlfriends were discussing you in canteen. I think she is liking you—"

"Mr. Deshpande!" Sridharan stepped toward the front of the dais. "Unless you or Mr. Mistry have anything to add on the subject of realism in late Victorian drama, I advise you to keep your mouths shut."

"Yes, sir," Vinod muttered.

I shifted where I sat and straightened up. A low chuckling rippled across the hall.

By now I was used to the strenuous note-taking and would fill several pages, almost half my notebooks, trying to take down Sridharan's prattling word for word. My hand and wrist felt stiff and sore afterward.

Before wrapping up his lecture, Sridharan announced that our midterm exams had been scheduled for the week before Diwali, in the last week of October. "If I were you," he cautioned, "I would start practicing with your essays now."

Concerned murmurs filled the air above the shuffling of notebooks and the rising of feet. We made our way into the corridor—Pradeep tap-tapping with his stick and Vinod guiding him with a hand at his elbow.

Once outside, I wanted to say good-bye and head for the library (my usual retreat between classes, where I could sit in peace to browse the latest issue of *Time*), but then Priya and her friend happened by. Suddenly, her friend broke away and asked us, with dramatic effort, if we cared to go to the canteen for cold drinks with them. She beamed at me eagerly and with a palpable nervousness. Priya, on the other hand, seemed content to stand by, hardly looking my way, while we made up our minds.

Pradeep said no, that now was his rehearsal time. "I must go upstairs," he said. "We are using a vacant hall on top floor."

"Do you need someone to come with you, Pradeep?" Priya asked.

"I will be all right," Pradeep assured us.

"What do you rehearse?" I asked.

"I am singer," he told me. "Classical mostly, but also Hindi pop songs. *Filmi* music from fifties, sixties. At the moment, I am rehearsing for the big Diwali function. You *have* to attend, yaar."

"Uh," I mumbled, "sure."

Vinod threw an arm around Pradeep and gave him a good shaking. Pradeep flinched. "This guy is practicing like mad, yaar," Vinod said boastfully, as if he were a promoter talking up a prize-fighter.

"How is it going?" I asked.

"It is . . ." Pradeep searched for the word. "Satisfactory."

"Satisfactory nothing," Vinod boomed. "This guy is spectacular. He's going to be number one in whole India. Number-one playback singer in Bollywood. You wait for the Diwali talent show, Vikram bhai. Then you will see this *pandit*'s talent."

Pradeep chuckled, shy and flustered. "Maybe, maybe."

"Well." Priya seemed put off by Vinod. "We'll see you around."

"At canteen?" tried her friend again, a last plea before the two went their way.

We nodded and waved good-bye.

"Maybe, maybe. No maybe, yaar." Vinod's arm encircled Pradeep's neck like a yoke. "We have deal, no? We have deal!" He grinned at me and gave Pradeep another shaking. "I'm going to be this guy's manager."

Pradeep chuckled some more—"Sure, sure"—and separated himself from Vinod. He said good-bye, then slowly tap-tapped his way toward the end of the corridor.

Slowly, taking deliberate steps, Devasia appeared. I asked him if he cared to join us for a cold drink in the canteen. He wore a sour look that morning and the usual luster in his eyes had dimmed.

"I am going back to hostel." He shook his head and made circling motions over his stomach. "Canteen food is not agreeing."

"Ouch" was all I could think to say. For a moment, the pains of sympathy stirred in my own gut as Devasia shambled away across the quad to his room and, surely, to the sanctuaries of cot and toilet.

"Problem is they are not boiling the water in the mess hall," Vinod informed me as we crossed the courtyard. "So you are drinking filth along with the water. What do you expect in that case?"

"You don't have to tell me twice." But I was barely paying attention to him. All I could think of was Priya and the possibility that there was any hint of truth to what Vinod told me back in the lecture hall. I only wanted to speak to her, to speak with any girl I found halfway interesting and attractive who didn't keep to her own sex. The boys didn't talk to the girls here and vice versa, apart from fleeting conversations exchanged giddily here and there.

Vinod asked me the standard questions about America and why I had moved. Then he told me he used to live in America too.

"In Florida," he said with affected nonchalance. "Six months there, a year also in San Diego and after that NYU." He said he went over to get his BA, but he lost interest in his studies and decided to come back. "After I finish here, I'll push off again," he said. "London, New York. Not sure yet. I've got uncles in both places, waiting for me to come back. After graduation, I'm gone. I can't stay in this *kachurputti* place."

We entered the canteen—a small gray room with small tables and large windows that overlooked the quad—throbbing with students gossiping and laughing. Someone waved us over; it was Priya's friend, seated at a table with three others, including Priya. Cola bottles everywhere. I felt Vinod's hand at my back urging me forward, and we pushed on for the table.

I got the sense these were the popular kids at Xavier's, the rich kids. Besides Priya and her friend—who introduced herself as Manju—there was a fair-skinned girl, half-German, half-Indian, named Hannah; and Ashok, a stout-shouldered third-year guy seated next to her, who spoke of getting his MSc in computer science at this place in Delhi. He told Hannah that computers were the wave of the future. Indeed, Ashok fixed all his attentions on Hannah, and they spoke closely; truly, this was the first coed gathering I'd found here, and I felt strangely like a transgressor as I sat among them.

Ashok, Hannah, and particularly Manju fell over each other with questions about America, what brought me here, and how I was adjusting. Vinod interjected with his own impressions of life in the States, which, somehow, seemed culled from American movies and sitcoms.

Priya leaned forward, sipping from her bottle of Limca, her elbow on the table and her chin resting in one hand. Her skin was a shade darker than the typical Gujarati's, and her eyes glistened black. Her hands were slim, bare, the nails translucent with clear polish and the skin radiant with moisturizer. Except for the gold stud she wore in her nose, Priya seemed free of any ornamentation, while the lip gloss and the kohl accenting her eyes were her only touches of makeup. A bump high on the bridge of her nose and a slight prominence to her lower lip kept her features, thankfully, from reaching classical perfection, and I wondered if they didn't make her even prettier. I was desperate to ask Priya something, to hear her speak.

"What are you majoring in?" I blurted.

"Psych." She wiped at her mouth. "Not crazy about it, but I was even less crazy about English and econ."

"You could've gone to H.L. or some other school and majored in commerce, right?"

"I could've," she sighed, either weary or bored. Her voice was so quiet, by the noise of the café. "But a degree from Xavier's means more than one from almost any other college in the state. You know, you can go further with it."

I thought about that for a second, curious. "And where do you want to go?" I asked.

"Don't know," she said. "I've still got two years. Lots of time to decide."

"So, now I have to ask," I continued. "Why are you here? I mean, here in India?"

A measured pause, then, "My father's a lawyer. About three years ago, he decided to leave his firm in Boston and start his own practice here."

"Just decided to pack it up?"

"He wanted to raise my sister and me here, close to family, and . . ." Her sentence finished with a light toss of her head and the flick of an eyebrow.

"Wanted to keep an eye on you."

She laughed, tipping back a bit more of the Limca.

I had not expected to meet Priya, someone this close to my experience. I wondered if Shannon would be jealous if she saw me now and couldn't help but feel a twinge of guilt. Then again, after her lack of letter-writing, I hoped she *would* be jealous. And what would Nate and Karl think of Priya? They would agree: she was beautiful. "Bring that lovely thing back to America," I could hear Nate's voice now, "and give your boys back home a chance."

"Have you visited America at all since?" I asked.

"A couple times," she said. "I've got cousins there."

"Ever think about moving back?"

"I could," she said vaguely. "I was born there, so it's always an option."

That quickened my blood. "You were *born* there?" To be an American citizen: the ultimate blessing. "What are you doing here, then? If I were an American, I'd be in America right now."

She kept the Limca bottle tipped at her mouth, and I could tell I'd hit a nerve because her expression became serious. She lowered the bottle and spoke in a low, steady tone. "America isn't the Holy Grail. I mean, everyone around here thinks it is." She rolled her eyes toward Vinod, now in a heated discussion with Ashok about the relative merits of Harley-Davidsons versus the indigenous Enfields. "But whatever. I just don't get the America worship. There are plenty of places to live in this world. America isn't the be-all-end-all."

"This world is mostly shit," I snapped. "Maybe America doesn't matter to you because you can go back anytime you want."

Vinod's voice suddenly leaped above all others. "A Harley will leave it in the dust, yaar!" he said forcefully, his palm angled as if he were going to karate chop Ashok's neck.

"It's not just power," Ashok countered, sleepy-eyed and sure. "Enfield has certain class, you know, that Harley cannot match."

"To hell with class." Vinod pumped his fists. "What I want is power!"

Hannah laughed, covering her mouth.

"You should be wherever, do whatever you want, no matter who you are," Priya said defensively, almost smugly.

"Really? And you want to be in Ahmedabad, huh?" I hoped that hadn't come out snobby.

"What I want is no one's business," she said. "I'm here right now. And when I want to leave, I will."

I was not enjoying the direction this conversation was going. I wanted to like this girl and for her to like me. So far, neither was happening. What nerve had I struck?

"You're right," I managed to say. "It's your call. We should be and do whatever."

I was happy for the interruption when Manju leaned over the table to ask, "You are going to be in our French class, no?"

"French? Uh, yes, I am," I said. "But how did you know . . . ?"

Manju giggled. "Madame Varma told us we will be having one student joining class late. I thought it must be you, as you cannot take Farsi or Sanskrit or like that." She smiled and shrugged coyly. I told her and Priya about the class I was enrolled in at the Alliance Française.

"I was in that same class last year," Priya said.

"We both were," said Manju, all teeth and fluttering eyelashes.

"It's not so bad," I said.

"It's a breeze," Priya said. "But then you've got Madame Varma to deal with."

"She's tough, huh?"

"I hope you like *Les Misérables*," Priya said.

She finished her Limca, then slid her chair back to leave. Straightening the hem of her kurta and brushing her hair back over her shoulder, she said she'd see us all later, and that it was "nice" to meet me.

I told her good-bye as pleasantly as I could, but I still tasted a lingering bitterness from our conversation. In a flurry of good-byes around the table, she clipped away on heels that peeked beneath the cuffs of her jeans. Priya's exit was a cue for the rest of us to go our separate ways. I shook hands with Ashok and Vinod, waved to the girls, then turned and sped toward the college gate.

"Hey, take it easy, man," Vinod called out.

I spun around and found him following me, hand extended. I shook his hand again. This time, he grasped my hand three different ways, in that typically American switch-up handshake. "Whatever you need, man, I can arrange whatever, I'm here for you," he told me. "You want to get friendly with Priya?" he half whispered with mock sleaziness and slapped my shoulder, laughing.

"Ha." I played along like a goddamn good sport but felt the need to extricate myself, unsure whether I was angry at Vinod, at Priya, or at my whole goddamn life. I thought if I didn't leave, I might knock Vinod out cold or throw up on his shoes or start screaming obscenities right here in the quad—the new student gone insane!—and the school year barely started. I pulled away in a half-crazed, overeager daze with a wave good-bye, leaving him to join up with some other rambling gang of class ditchers.

I began the fifteen-minute walk from college back to the bungalow. The sky grumbled, and I noticed it had darkened since morning.

As I stepped past the college gate I felt the first drops of rain, and I picked up my pace. What was Vinod going on and on about? *Get friendly with Priya!* Did that mean what I thought it did? And what made him think he could make that happen? Priya had hardly given me the time of day, and she'd stung me with her words.

"Vikram! Vikram!" came a girl's voice about ten yards behind me. Oh, no! It was Manju. She held a black umbrella in her hand, stood at the college gate, and motioned toward the rickshaw she had just hailed. "Do you need a lift?"

"No, thanks." I shook my head. "I'm not that far. Bye!"

She may have said something else, but I didn't want to stick around. I just turned and walked as fast as I could, keeping my ear tuned for the motor of her rickshaw, assurance that she was going away. I did not fancy sharing a ride with Manju any more than I fancied stepping into warm cow shit.

As I walked home, Priya's words stuck like burrs in my brain: *be wherever, do whatever you want, no matter who you are.* Isn't that what she said? *When I want to leave, I will.*

What a fucking luxury, I thought to myself, feeling an envy and bitterness I'd never expected to feel toward her. The luxury of choice. Because being able to choose one thing over another—one place over another, one kind of life over another—that was something I could never imagine feeling. That must be true freedom.

By the splat of raindrops on the road and on my head, I knew we were in for a heavy rain shower; I'd be drenched by the time I reached the bungalow. I thought of the hours ahead: after lunch came the journey aboard the number 62 bus to the Alliance Française. Then back home for dinner, studying, and cramming for the midterms. I wondered, as I did each afternoon, if any letters might arrive for me that day.

None did.

~ ~ ~

My father offered to buy me a Kinetic Honda scooter, sleek and sturdy. I chose the Luna moped.

"The Kinetic will last longer," my father said.

He was right: compared to the Kinetic Honda, the Luna was a skin-and-bones machine—just sinews of cables running from a pair of handlebars and tires that looked hardly more durable than a bicycle's. The Luna was just the basics, the kind of vehicle that lurked along the edges and got where it needed to go without attracting attention. It was a machine meant for transience, and transience was my ally.

"The Luna will do," I said.

With the Luna, I no longer had to sweat and shove my way along on buses. It would zip me around wherever I needed to go, and that meant college, mostly, and the Alliance Française.

The French course went on for six weeks. It was set up to give students a practical knowledge of the language, but what it did, more than anything, was thoroughly dislocate me. Our lesson book contained short sketches—dramatic scenarios that we read along to cassettes in which actors voiced the lines, acted the parts, and the whole thing was done up like a mini French radio play. A broadcast from another world.

"*Je m'appelle* Jacques Martineau," said the disembodied Continental voice. *"Je suis pianiste. J'habite à Paris, place de la Contrescarpe."*

Color illustrations of the blond, urbane-looking Jacques Martineau accompanied the dialogue and the supple male voice on the cassette.

That's all it took for the boundaries in my mind to crack open. I imagined a world outside the immediacies of Ahmedabad, a clean and cosmopolitan Parisian universe in which this erudite musician, Jacques Martineau, lived (in a neighborhood called Place de la Contrescarpe, which had to be galaxies removed from anything I knew, might ever know) and conducted his affairs free of anxieties and despair. A part of me deeply wished to be this fictional French musician, far away from here, living another life entirely.

Another grammar lesson involved a carload of teenagers on a road trip through rural France. They suffered flat tires and encountered surly farmers (who eventually welcomed them into their home and served them delicious plum-dark wine). In the next lesson, the teenagers rolled into a cobblestoned village and danced to a bandstand concert during the Fête de la Musique. I imagined myself in each of these adventures, wishing I were out in the European country myself, with Shannon at my side.

In another, a father came home to announce to his children that he had been promoted and they would all be moving from Paris to a distant city called Montpellier. The children whined and stamped their feet, lamenting how they'd lose their friends and how their schooling would be disrupted. But nothing doing. Their father packed them up and off they moved. The kids' antics amused me. Parisian wimps. What they needed was to spend a few weeks in Ghatlodiya.

The course ended with an exam, which I passed, and on my way out, I picked up my certificate from the instructor. She was still sweet and pleasant but looked worn out after almost two months of vocabulary drills, conversation exercises, and pop quizzes.

I asked her if she planned to keep teaching at the Alliance. "No, this was it," she said with a warm, pert smile. "I'm getting married in the winter, and he is French." She and her fiancé had met while she was living in Paris the previous year.

"Congratulations," I said. A chorus of congratulations and surprised "Wow"s erupted among the few others lingering in the classroom.

"So"—she took a deep breath—"I'll wrap up here. Visit my family in Delhi for a few weeks. Then push off." She smiled modestly, casting her eyes about the room, lost in thought. She handed out the certificates, exchanging good-byes with her students, calm and cordial, but I could tell there was an eagerness in her heart, a happiness radiating from her center, just waiting to burst. I basked in it and could feel her joy for days afterward.

~ ~ ~

Letters from Nate and Karl arrived. They had indeed, as Shannon reported, worked on a script: a *Key Largo*–meets–*Night of the Living Dead* horror noir over the summer. Karl was quite serious about it, but for Nate, it was a lark. Otherwise, Nate had spent his summer the way he'd spent every summer since sophomore year in high school: painting houses. He said he'd raked in enough to cover tuition, books, and "recreational purposes" throughout the school year, which had just kicked off. (He'd celebrated with a kegger on his dorm-room floor.)

Madison was roasting through a drought, Nate wrote. "I don't think we've had weather like this since the dustbowl days, and it made the housepainting a real bitch!" He mentioned his father's yellowing lawn, the withering golf courses, and the refuge of the swimming pool and the multiplex. ("The movie to see, if and when it makes it to India, is *Who Framed Roger Rabbit*—even Karl liked it.") With the letter, he sent a clipping from *Rolling Stone* about R.E.M.'s next record, coming out on Election Day in November, and an article about Michelle Pfeiffer from the *New York Times* (Nate was a fan of hers and thought I was too). "I hope you're hanging in there, Vik," he wrote. "We could use some of that rain you're getting! Take comfort: new R.E.M. in only four months! Oh, I ran into Shannon on campus a couple of times now. I think she really misses you."

Two distinct reactions warred in my mind as I folded Nate's letter away: envy and disappointment. Envy that my own life wasn't as easy and relaxed as his clearly was: housepainting, golf, movies, and swimming pools. Not a bad summer, right? And disappointment that he expressed zero interest in how I was doing or feeling. What a shallow prick, I thought. Weeks without hearing from him and the best he can do is "hope you're hanging in there"? That doesn't cut it, Nate. But then I remembered our high school days: laughs over lunch hours, parties, weekend movies. Raucous and innocent times whose end had come too soon, but which were now among the best memories I had.

Karl's letter was typed and mentioned various writing projects besides the script—including a play and a novel—that he was taking stabs at. ("Since your leaving, Vik, I'm feeling less confident, less inspired, and it doesn't help that Nate doesn't feel as committed about the script as I do. I'd hate for the summer to end without finishing something.") He tentatively mentioned a girl, Bridget, whom he had met just before high school graduation: "We saw the new Louis Malle at the Majestic and some Buster Keaton shorts at the Civic Center the same week" and so forth. They had joined the programming committee of the campus film society together. He was expressing what I thought was a crush, though I believed Karl would never admit to such a vulnerability. But then he proved me wrong and confessed: "I really like her. I don't know how else to put it. I mean, romantically," followed by his characteristic backpedaling: "It's too early for words like 'romance,' and I would never presume."

Then he said:

> I'll be honest: I don't know how to approach this subject of your life in India. It's beyond me. You're going through changes I can't imagine. I'll need your help. Tell me how I can help you, Vik. We never got a chance to have a heart-to-heart before you left; that's fine, I know you wanted to spend as much time as you could with Shannon. Maybe these letters will help patch up the lost time.
>
> People will tell you that they care about you, and they want to hear from you. But people go on with their lives and just as soon forget. Know one thing: I'm not going anywhere.

I took the letter out to the balcony, the rain now settling, running off the eaves from the gutters, splattering onto the muddy drive. I read the letter over again. For the first time since I left, I felt the possibility of connection.

I'm not going anywhere.

It brought tears to my eyes. It did. I couldn't help it.

Chapter

10

Anand's school, Gujarat Law Society Secondary, was just a couple of miles farther down the road from St. Xavier's. He asked if I could pick him up after school so he wouldn't have to sit through the long rickshaw ride and wait as the driver dropped off students ahead of him on the route. I didn't mind doing it; it gave me extra time to tool around, to be on my own before setting off for home, and to see another stretch of the neighborhood.

So after finishing up my classes, I swung by on the Luna to pick him up. The road took me past the newer apartment high-rises. Their ground floors were taken up with shopping complexes—Xerox stores, photomats, medical clinics, and video stores. Each had a small plot of paved space where scooters huddled together. It was a far cry from the anarchic dilapidation I saw elsewhere in Ahmedabad, and I felt refreshed whenever I would see a sign, the faintest glimmer, of urban planning in this chaotic place.

On this day, I pulled up alongside a row of rickshaws and cars waiting in front of the school—a whitewashed cement monolith of a structure. Seconds after the bell, a flood of uniformed students poured out of every door, rushing toward the gates. Almost simultaneously, every vehicle outside the school building roared to life.

Out of the swirling sea of black hair, white shirts, and canvas book bags, Anand emerged, gabbing with classmates. He proceeded from the gate and waved good-bye to two boys—one a thin, large-browed specimen with buckteeth, the other a thatch-haired roly-poly—who both climbed aboard a rickshaw.

"Mayank's dad's getting him a Nintendo," Anand informed me glumly.

"That the fat kid or the skinny one?"

"The skinny one."

I cranked the pedal of the Luna, got its motor revved up, and climbed on. "Didn't know they had Nintendos here," I said.

Anand propped himself on the seat behind me—the Luna had a banana seat with room enough for two small-to-average humans.

"They call it something else here," he said. "Anyway, he's getting one, the lucky duck."

I pulled away into the dusty crosscurrent of students and vehicles. "Want to stop by the paan shop and rent a video?" I asked.

Anand mentioned that his (fat) friend Jyoti really enjoyed the last Schwarzenegger movie.

"*Red Heat*?" I scowled.

"They got it on video here already," Anand said.

"No thanks," I said. "I'm going to pass."

Indeed, *Red Heat* was the last movie I saw in America. Nate, Karl, and I had seen it the day it came out—the day before zero hour (my move)—because Nate had a hunch it would be the perfect Hollywood summer movie send-off. Karl and I couldn't argue with the promise of mindless action plus air-conditioning, so off we went in Nate's beat-up VW Rabbit for a noon show at Point Cinema.

It was a pathetic, god-awful travesty. Two hours gouged clean from my last day in America. As we staggered out into the stun of daylight, I worried it would be the last Hollywood movie I would see for a long, indefinitely long, time.

There we were: Karl and I pissed off at Nate, Nate pissed off at himself, and all three of us confused as to how best to redeem our last day together. So we went to Vitense Golfland on Whitney Way and played its rinky-dink nine-hole course. We rented irons and putters, no bags, and smacked scuffed-up golf balls along the drought-ridden fairways. We played dismally, but we didn't care; mostly, we made jokes about people we knew in school and mocked Nate as he hacked at the ball, digging ruts in the earth.

As we finished our game and tallied up our scores (Nate, believe it or not, won by five strokes), Nate and Karl began discussing their fall plans. Karl was considering a production assistant job at WHA, the public TV station that had its studio in the basement of the film department.

"I hear they're looking for more hands," he said. "So, who knows, it could lead to something. It'll be good to get some production experience."

"I prefer to work tax free," Nate said and spoke excitedly of how much money he would be raking in before the semester began. "I've got seven painting gigs lined up between now and August," he said. "Drought season is bad for the golf business but great for the housepainting business."

We left Vitense and got back into Nate's car. Karl complained, as always, about the legroom. He felt—and looked—like a human accordion, there in the front seat.

"I should be flush by the time summer's over," Nate said. "After that"—he held out his palm for emphasis—"don't talk to me about work."

"What about you, Vik?" Karl asked. "You got any idea where you'll be going to school out there?"

"Yeah, what's the deal, Vik? You haven't said anything."

I hated answering questions about India. I had kept myself in the dark about the details, half out of anger, half out of fear.

"Every place has a college, right? There's got to be like a . . . a . . . Calcutta Tech or something," Nate said.

That got Karl laughing.

"I mean, you gotta be able to major in, like, snake charming or sitar playing or whatever." Nate smiled, unaffected, serene at the wheel, his eyes hidden behind sunglasses.

"One thing I hate is an ignorant asshole," I snapped.

"Whoa! Whoa!" Karl said from the backseat.

"I didn't mean anything," Nate said, laughing under his breath. "Just asking."

"Yeah, Vik, he was just goofing around."

I didn't say anything for a while, just stared out the window. "I don't know where I'm going. I don't know a fucking thing."

Silence hung in the car, as stifling as the heat. The Rabbit had no air-conditioning. After a minute of nothing but the noise of the hatchback whining along Whitney Way, the sun daggering into our eyes, Nate spoke up.

"Vik"—his tone was solemn now—"do you want me to drop you off at Shannon's?"

I thought about that, checked my watch. Six p.m. My parents would want me home for dinner and possibly to help with any last-minute packing. I'd been gone all day. After I put in my quota of time at the house, I would sneak out and see her.

"Vik," I could hear my mother's voice, "there's so much to do. You can't spend one night at home?" And I could see my father rooting about the suitcases in the living room, urgently shouting questions that my mother complained she couldn't hear, barely bothering to look at me as I walked in. Their disapproval weighed on my chest. And I dreaded entering the house, dreaded that feeling of my heart caving in. Shannon already seemed a universe away.

"Just drop me off at home," I said.

~~~

Anand and I decided to skip renting a video at the paan shop and go straight home. He said he had the tutor that afternoon, anyway. My father had hired a language tutor to show up every other day to help Anand out with his Gujarati, Sanskrit, and Hindi lessons.

"How's that going?" I asked as we sped toward home.

"I already don't need him," Anand said, complaining how the tutor was wasting his time with lessons that didn't challenge him, covering things he'd already gone over on his own weeks ago.

Anand was really fitting in beautifully here, and it made me feel suddenly and momentarily alone.

We pulled through the gate and swung around the path to the front door. The anxiety always hit me at this point, as I steered the moped toward the door. My eyes not wanting to, but compelled to, check for any sign of an envelope in the mailbox. Seeing a hint of an envelope was like spying treasure.

There it was. A letter. A corner of it visible like a miracle shining through four square inches of clear plastic. It was a substantial envelope. From Shannon. I hadn't heard from her in weeks. She owed me a letter. No, two letters. I had waited and waited.

I plucked it out of the mailbox and wanted to rush upstairs into our place, into my room, fling off my backpack and float away in the river of her words. But I dared not seem too excited. That would only make me feel vulnerable. Compose yourself, Vikram, and walk quietly upstairs with your brother. Easy does it.

My mother opened the door. She looked tired, her eyes sleepless, told us lunch was ready on the stove, to help ourselves. She said she was going to lie down. Anand began serving himself—the
~~~

usual rotis, dal, vegetables. I forgot my appetite and tore into the letter instead.

~ ~ ~

September 3, 1988

Dear Vik,

I could say I've been too busy to write the past few weeks, but that wouldn't be a fair excuse to either of us. I've let two of your letters go by unanswered, not because it's been nuts around here (which it has!), but because I've been struggling with myself to actually say what I think I need to. In short—you were right. It just took me a couple of months to let it sink in. Life's pulling us in crazy new directions. You don't know where you're going to be—India, here, wherever—or for how long. Our relationship's been great, but what we had was also brief and not as intense as it might have gotten had you stayed. Given that, I don't think it's right that we emotionally tie each other down. This is not to say I don't care about you—I really do—or that we shouldn't keep in touch. I just don't think it's fair that we expect anything more from each other than distance would dictate (as harsh as that sounds). So there it is. It hurts to write these words (but you were always one for the direct approach, so I'm following your lead!). (I'm glad my roommate isn't here right now to see me crying . . .) I know you've been struggling. I can feel it in every line of your letters, and I want us to be there for each other, but as friends. I wanted to clear the air with this letter, take the weight off all that's been hanging between us since you left. I doubt any of this surprises you, Vik. They're pretty much the words you said to me the night before you left . . .

I skimmed the rest of her letter, a long ramble about life at her dormitory, her new classes, her show getting extended another two weeks, how excited she was to be auditioning for more shows in the fall. I folded the letter and tucked it neatly back in the envelope.

A lizard, like an elongated green gummy bear, had attached itself high on the wall. It raised itself on its webbed and sucker-tipped front feet, darted its head. A dark sliver of tongue shot in and out of it. How repulsive.

It was true: Shannon was repeating back to me the very words I'd once said to her. It was like hearing radio-wave feedback from outer space, a final signing-off before all was lost to static, silence, a severing before the eternal drift.

I grabbed a rolled-up *Times of India* off my desk and began thumping it against the wall in an effort to guide the lizard toward the window. It didn't budge. I fanned at it. No response. Finally, I folded the newspaper up into a sturdy square, got up on the bed, and took a swipe at it. The lizard dropped from the wall straight onto my head, and then scrabbled off me. I flipped out and dropped myself onto the bed, waving madly at the air, before I caught sight of the lizard skittering across the floor, escaping through the slit under the balcony door.

"Damn thing!"

My mother appeared at the door. "My god! Look at you. What happened?"

"Nothing." I exhaled. "It was nothing." I patted at my hair, swatted at my shirt, and tried to shake off my jitters. I hated lizards. And snakes. And frogs.

"I am leaving," my mother said. "I have appointment. But I'll be back before dinner."

"Are you all right?" I asked vaguely, noticing she was carrying her purse and had her sunglasses pulled over her head.

My mother moved off into the hallway. "Could be too much sun. I'll be back before your father comes home." Then I heard the bolt of the front door slide open and, a moment later, the echoing of the door as it shut.

~ ~ ~

I wrote a short letter back to Shannon saying, of course, I understood everything. She's got her life. And she should in no way feel "emotionally obligated" to whatever it was we had. No need to, and for the very reasons she had cited, etc. And that was it.

Only later that week, while I was at my desk prepping for midterms, did it hit me, the losing of her. I felt my chest cave in at the thought of it. Dropping my notes, I went out to the balcony to collect myself. I had tried so hard to keep my feelings to a minimum, telling myself things had ended exactly the way I knew they would and the only way they could.

It was all as I'd predicted. But just because you predict something will happen doesn't make it any easier when it actually does.

On my way back from posting my letter, I resolved not to write to Shannon anymore. We both needed to move on. But she must've been much farther down that road than I was, because I never got a letter from her again.

Still, I couldn't help stealing a glance in the mailbox whenever I pulled up on the Luna, home after my classes. Now and then, a letter would arrive—from Karl usually, though once or twice from Nate too. But more often than not, my hopes soured instantly because the mailbox would be empty. And my thoughts would darken into bitterness as I stomped up the stairwell, resigned to the long afternoon ahead.

The afternoons themselves blurred into a cloud of doldrums that spread over the rest of the monsoon and into October. I would leave college, pick up Anand, and head home, where my mother would have lunch ready. By then, the morning help would have finished the housework and be long gone; on the balcony, I would find the laundry drying on the lines, and the floors would always look swept and washed.

Sometimes, Anand and I would walk over to the paan shop tucked into a corner of the dusty shopping plaza across the road from our bungalow. The front of the counter was papered with Hindi movie posters splashed with sweaty and vengeful heroes glowering alongside honey-skinned, almond-eyed heroines whose crimson mouths were always parted in romantic rapture. From the counter, we could scan the shelves that lined three sides of the tiny shop. The labels were in various states of decomposition, and the tapes—some of them in cases, some not—looked in about the same miserable shape. If it wasn't a Hindi movie, it was a pirated Jackie Chan or Bruce Lee flick or some random Hollywood fare. We had watched *The Dirty Dozen*, *The Untouchables*, *Where Eagles Dare*, and *The Great Escape* several times each by October in our craving for American entertainment, a wisp of the culture to breathe in. Mostly, though, with homework and exams, we each retired to our respective corner of the room, our attention on our books.

Studying for midterms meant writing up dummy essays based on anticipated topics. Like the rest of my classmates, I found myself in a fury of memorizing and writing by rote: I devoured every word from the Macmillan *History of English Literature* and my poetry volumes, dredging up dates, names, titles, quotations, and lines of verse as I cobbled together one essay after another. It was unnerving, especially because the only way to ensure high marks, from what Devasia told me, was to pound out exhaustive, long-winded essays—six, seven, eight, nine pages at a stretch. If it wasn't English, then I was taking stabs at psychology or economics essays. But the subject didn't make a difference: after a couple of hours at it, with the sun throbbing at a steady wattage from the windows, I would be nodding off.

There were times I gave in to the drowsiness, slipped into the embryonic waters of an afternoon nap. I often woke to the hammering voice of Anand's tutor, enunciating the Hindi alphabet forcefully, repeatedly, in the living room.

Late one afternoon, the tutor already gone, I woke to my father's car pulling up the drive. My eyes opened to the Macmillan lying on my face. I got up, annoyed at myself for passing out again. From the kitchen, I heard my parents talking. I lingered in the hallway, listened into the dining room.

"How did the appointment go?" I heard my father ask in Gujarati.

"She thinks cell count was a little high, prescribed antibiotic," my mother replied, appearing from the kitchen, her hands gripping a pair of tongs that held a small wok full of vegetables. She set the wok down on the table. My father followed with cups and plates. "And she wants me back for X-ray."

"When?"

My mother noticed me.

"Soon," she said and clammed up.

There was nothing for it. I walked through the dining room, past both of them, into the kitchen. Pretending I was thirsty, I opened the fridge, got out the jug of water we kept there—boiled and filtered—and poured it into a steel cup.

"It's okay," my father muttered. He switched on the oscillating fan perched on a high shelf in one corner of the dining room. It whirred noisily, buffeting each of us with drafts of warm air. "It'll be okay."

"What will be okay?" I asked casually, sipping the water.

My father set the plates around the table. "Conference," he said. "Got a conference in Bombay in a couple of weeks."

"Chalo, Anand," my mother called into the living room, where Anand was watching our video copy of *Star Wars* again. "Dinner."

I washed up and joined my father at the table.

"I know Ma has been to see the doctor," I told him confidentially. "If there is anything—"

"If there is anything you need to know, we'll inform you." His voice was stern, officious. "Right now, keep to your studies. And that's it."

Anand entered the dining room and pulled up a chair. We passed around the container of rotis. My mother served us from the wok and the pot of dal.

"So I've got a conference coming up in Bombay," my father said again. "I'll be gone a week. Look after your mother."

"Maybe you could look into the video camera?" I asked.

He nodded, scooping the vegetables on his plate with a roti. "I'll do that. We'll get that back." Then he asked Anand how he was getting on with his schoolwork, about the tutor.

"I already know more than he does," Anand said.

"We'll see about that when your marks come in," my father replied, then added with a chuckle, "That's what I like to hear, though. We Mistrys are like that. Always ahead of the game, no?"

Was there a game here? If so, I felt miserably behind.

"Okay," my father consented, "we'll look into a new tutor for you."

"Can you also look into a Nintendo? Remember, you made me give up my old one—"

"Yes, yes! Nintendo, fine, but we'll look into that at Diwali only. Right now, we'll figure out a new tutor for you, and you continue with your schoolwork."

That must have been agreeable enough to Anand because he quieted down and picked at his plate. "Are we visiting Hemant Uncle over Diwali?" he asked, chewing.

"Maybe." My father looked at my mother. "And before I leave for Bombay," he added, "I'll get a new gardener. That front area looks rubbish. Then again, who knows, we may move into better quarters next year." His eyes lit up. "Probably in Gandhinagar, much cleaner than Ahmedabad or Ghatlodiya. And you can keep attending Xavier's." He waved his hand at me as if he were conferring divine privilege. "Or, if you like, you can try the National Institute of Design. Excellent school. They've got media and . . ."

He fumbled for the appropriate terms. "Video and all. And they're right here. Go check them out."

"Don't worry about me," I said, shifting in my chair, uncomfortable with him paving my future for me.

My mother, I noticed, ate quietly, keeping her thoughts to herself.

"In meantime," my father continued, turning to her, "we'll get gardener and new car by the end of year. Why not?"

"That would be awesome," Anand said.

"Why don't you get settled into your job first?" my mother said, summoning her strength. "You've only started there three, four months. Anything can happen. Who knows, they may cut you off, and we'll be left with nothing again, like two years ago."

"How did two years ago get into this?"

My mother lowered her tone, and her face assumed a false calm. "I just need some peace right now. Not another move or any big plans."

My father grunted. "This is not like two years ago, or three, or four, or whatever." Drafts blew uselessly and loudly from the fan up on its perch. "It's going to be different here. How do you still not understand that?"

They kept their gazes lowered. Anand and I stole glances at each other, then at our parents. The dining room's single tube light cast an eerie pall over us, and the blackness of night behind the screened-in windows offered nothing of the world. This room felt like a cell for condemned souls. How did we get here? Was there a way out?

Chapter 11

My writing hand achy, eyes bleary, brain sore, I retreated to the library in between my Victorian Lit and French midterms. I wanted to hide out there while I decompressed.

Devasia was on his way out as I walked in. He pointed to me and arched his eyebrows—his wordless way of asking how I thought the exam went. I made a "so-so" gesture with my palm then pointed back at him. He answered with a thumbs-up and a shrug. We shared weary smiles as he exited the library, and I stepped up to the counter.

I asked the librarian for the current issue of *Time*. He shook his head, waved his hand to the magazine rack behind the counter, and told me it was checked out. He'd let me know when it was back.

That was disappointing. I'd counted on spending a bit of my downtime before the French exam getting acquainted with the latest from America. I settled at a table with an exhausted sigh and hoped the wait wouldn't be long.

I flipped open my notebook and got out my copy of *Les Misérables*, using the automatic exam-time anxiety to brush up on my notes. Madame Varma had made us all get French-language editions of *Les Misérables*, and we were reading several chapters of it, discussing its finer points in class. Comprehension was a steep climb at first, but the Alliance course had gotten me up to speed well enough to get over the hump. I reread the opening passages of the novel—the same section that Madame Varma had made me translate when I'd approached her about joining the class at the beginning of the year. I had flunked her on-the-spot quiz that day, but since then, it was as if I'd drunk some magic potion. My brain had learned to decipher the language's squiggly, accented gobbledygook, the way your body learns to make antibodies against an invading virus and keeps you alive.

But instead of studying, I found myself doodling in the notebook. It loosened up my rigid fingers to doodle and let my brain relax. Odd protoplasmic shapes and squiggles, and pretty soon I was drawing heads and hands, eyes and faces.

I found myself drawing a series of storyboard frames on a page in my notebook. Now what to fill them with? I began doodling, and it became a rickshaw, splashing like mad through a monsoon downpour. I drew a harried, rain-slicked face in the passenger seat, a hand gripping a metal bar. In the following squares came shadowy figures scurrying in the gathering torrent, the rickshaw lurching to a stop behind the diagonal frenzy of rain, a woman crashing into a milkman on a bicycle. I drew in a delirium of recollection, as if I were revisiting a dream.

A hand entered my view and dropped a magazine onto the table. It was *Time* being set in front of me. "Thanks," I said to the librarian, who didn't turn around but continued his shuffle back to his post.

On the cover, the space shuttle Discovery blasted off from its Cape Canaveral launchpad in a wake of light and smoke that made the image look strangely celestial. I thumbed through the issue and my heart was invigorated by articles about the next Indiana Jones movie and one about U2's tour of the States (Nate had mentioned in a letter that he was seeing the show in Chicago). Here were messages from America. I brought the magazine to my face and took in the scent of the page.

"What's up in America?" a voice called out, and I jumped.

It was Priya. She came up behind me with a smile and sat down across from me at the table. I wondered if she'd seen me smelling the magazine. How embarrassing!

I had not spoken much with Priya since our conversation in the canteen, and that was three months ago. Since then, it had been polite hellos and brief bits of business about the French class.

She was plainly beautiful today. Her hair was gathered back in a ponytail, and a thin copper-colored necklace took the curve of her neck. The necklace had a gold pendant in which a tiny figure was embossed, worn over the front of a faded maroon T-shirt with "Boston College" on the breast pocket.

"What's up in America?" I said. "Lots that I'm missing."

Priya didn't respond, just opened her French notebook and her copy of *Les Misérables*. Of course, she didn't really care about what was happening in America, I thought. After all her smug talk in the canteen trying to put America in its place, she couldn't care less. My guard was up. Then she said, "You know what I'm missing? MTV."

It was a sincere remark and made me feel more at ease. "I know. There isn't much to TV here, is there? Except that one channel. It's like we're living in East Germany or China."

"*Love Boat*, oh my god, I watched every episode. *Dynasty* too." Priya's face lit up with recollection. "But I liked *Dallas* way more. I tell my cousins to tape episodes for me and send them over. I've got a whole shelf of American TV. You can borrow them whenever."

I'd never watched any of the shows she'd mentioned, but her conjuring up familiar names from far away, things only the two of us knew, somehow made me feel warm and connected to her.

"Do you still keep in touch with your friends there?" I asked.

"I've got one friend who still keeps in touch," she said. "But friends drop away after a year or so. It's too long a distance."

What a harsh thought, and probably true. I didn't want to consider just how true, so I changed the subject. "Music," I said. "Where do you get your rock and roll around here?"

"My cousins tape the Top Forty off the local station for me, so I keep current. Well, current, with a six-month delay." She laughed. "Same with TV, movies. Cousins bring them over, or I catch up when I visit."

"Top Forty?" I said teasingly. "I was afraid of that."

"What's wrong with Top Forty?"

"Nah," I countered, "you want the good shit, not Whitney Houston and Madonna. I'll make you a mix."

We were quiet for a few minutes after that, turning to our studies. I looked up from my notebook and watched her lips as she read the French sentences from *Les Misérables*. She paused and looked up to ask if I felt ready for the exam.

"I've no clue," I said. "French has been kind of a crash course. I still don't know whether I'm coming or going."

She glanced at me and shrugged lightly. *"Mais vous pouvez parler en français tres bien, je pense."*

"No, no," I said, flipping through the magazine. *"C'est un situation tragique."*

That got a quick laugh out of her before she asked, "So this is what you do between classes? Sit in here with your *Time* magazines and get your dose of America?"

I nodded vaguely, mentally scanning for sarcasm in her tone. Regardless, it was true. I couldn't deny it. My company consisted mostly of myself and occasionally Devasia and Pradeep. In fact, for Pradeep, I had begun dictating class notes into a tape recorder. After Sridharan's lectures, I would join Pradeep in his hostel room and read out the notes I had just taken, point by point, into his tape recorder. Devasia and I were his main sources for these audio notes, and Pradeep used them to study for the exams. Besides those guys, I didn't mingle with anyone.

And for whatever reason, I'd been oblivious to Priya. She kept to her group—Manju, Hannah, Ashok, and their clique: Ahmedabad's moneyed. The reverse-expatriates. Hers seemed a rarefied class that existed somewhere above the soot and misery and smoke of the rest of the city. Priya was out of bounds to me, in principle anyway.

In America, I had always felt hopelessly out of place, unaccepted by the popular kids in school. I felt classless and outcast, and I came to despise the snobby and rich kids—Indian, American, didn't matter. But here—the place of my roots, where my father suddenly had a steady and high-ranking job, where I was in social proximity to Priya—I could, theoretically, mix with those of her social class. I belonged to it. But the thought made me queasy. Mingling with Priya's friends, her too-cool-for-school clique, would've felt like a betrayal—of myself, my past, of everything I'd gone through. So, yes, I chose to sit here, in the library, a social and cultural neutral zone, and get my dose of America.

"And it's quiet in here," I said. "No one bothers you."

Priya said she felt even less ready for the exam than I did. She glanced through her notes, her attention flitting hummingbird-like up and down the pages. I kidded her about her nervousness; it had to be a put-on. In class, whenever Priya would read from the text, her pronunciation was flawless. It transfixed me. And her answers to Varma's questions, so easy, natural, I felt like she could teach this stuff herself. How could she *not* be ready?

Finally, her eyes lifted from her notes, and she said, "You know how we have to prepare essays for all these *possible* questions?" she asked.

"Yeah," I said, groaning.

"I've never gotten used to that," she said. "Makes me feel like the cows out on the street."

I gave her a questioning smirk.

"We're graded on how well we chew all this up, and then"—she mimicked throwing up—"regurgitate it all. It's sick." I was surprised to hear her then bring up how much happier she had been studying in America. She remembered school being fun, more imaginative, where it didn't feel like you were cattle forced up and down the chute, you were made to think for yourself.

"Let's go," I said, my heart leaping. "Chuck all this, and let's go there right now."

"Shh." The mousy-looking librarian glared at us.

We went back to our notes, but a minute later Priya leaned toward me. "Are you going to the Diwali show?"

I shrugged maybe. The show was tonight. Pradeep was competing in the talent contest. He'd been preparing for weeks. Sometimes when I would show up at his hostel door with my notes, ready to dictate them, I would hear him in his room practicing an Indian *ghazal*, his voice rising and falling gracefully to the sitar and tabla playing on the tape recorder. I knew nothing of Indian music, but there was no doubt that Pradeep had a beautiful singing voice. "I suppose I should go for Pradeep," I replied, but Priya's attention had turned back to her beat-up *Les Misérables* paperback.

"There are, like, pages missing from this," she said, pursing her lips. "I mean, we haven't gotten to these chapters yet, but . . ." She shut the book and slid out of her chair. "I'm going to go downstairs and see if I can replace this. Maybe they have another copy. Be right back."

"What do you mean, downstairs?" I asked.

She jerked a finger toward the floor. "That's where all the books are."

That's when I realized that all I had seen of this library was this room: the tables, the reading stands, the large cabinets along the walls housing Masterpieces of World Literature volumes and the like. I'd assumed this was all there was to the Xavier's library.

"Wish I'd known that before I spent two hundred fifty rupees on this." I waved my brand-new copy of *Les Misérables* in my hand. I thought I'd been so lucky when the Alliance Française had one copy of the French-language version of the book. But apparently Xavier's had copies of its own.

"At least yours is in one piece," Priya said, turning my book over in her hands, her lovely hands.

"Shh!" It was that librarian again.

"Sorry," I said. Then I got up to follow Priya, in her Boston College T-shirt and Calvin Kleins, through a door at the far end of the checkout desk.

We descended two short flights of stairs lit by a naked hanging bulb. At the foot of the stairs, an open doorway led into a kind of cellar. Visible in the dim incandescence, a musty, low-ceilinged room was filled with bookcases divided by a central aisle. I scanned the rows and rows of shelves, each receding into the dark. History, philosophy, physics, botany—the names of various fields were scrawled on yellowing labels on the sides of the shelves. It was as if Priya had led me to an ancient burial chamber, and except for us, it was empty. It smelled of slow attrition by termites and dust, but to me the place was thriving with life: the bookshelves were bursting with a mysterious, longed-for harvest.

I saw a shelf labeled "Visual Arts." The books there, for the most part, were moldy textbooks on Indian miniature painting. I riffled through them for images of Hindu erotica but found none, just words like millions of dead ants on the page. Then, on the tattered spine of one hardcover, I saw *American Photography to 1970.* The year I was born. I grabbed it, and the instant I opened it, it fell apart in a dozen pieces: pages fell from the binding and scattered on the floor, leaving fibers like nerve endings dangling from the spine.

"What happened?" It was Priya in the aisle. She had managed to find another copy of *Les Misérables*.

I gathered up the pages and shoved them back into the book.

"Looks like you picked up a dud," she said. "Be careful with the books down here. They're barely held together."

"Might be a dud," I said, tucking the book under my arm, "or it might not."

"Let's get this over with." She sighed, and we walked toward the stairs.

"And where are you off to for your Diwali holiday?" I asked her. "Don't tell me. Is it some fancy-pants hill station in Rajasthan? Or is it London this year?"

Priya shook her head, smiling. "What do you think we are? The leisure class?"

"Yes, actually." I smiled.

"I'll be right here in Ahmedabad the whole break." We took the stairs. "No hill stations, no London. Been there, done that. What about you?"

"Visiting my uncle in lovely Baroda," I said with a touch of sarcasm.

"You'll miss my birthday," she said. "It'll be quite the happening."

"I'm sorry," I said, feeling genuinely bummed I would miss the chance to see her. "Happy birthday."

We got to the landing, where she paused and began penning something down on the cover page of her *Les Misérables*. "If you get bored, here is my phone." She tore away a strip of paper and handed it to me. "I'm sure me and Manju and Ashok and all will be hanging out somewhere, sometime."

I said I'd do that—though I had no intention of mingling with the others she'd mentioned—and pocketed the number. Then I thought of how there, in the privacy of that tiny landing, we'd shared an intimate thing, this surreptitious passing of a phone number. A moment all our own, finally, outside the boundaries of life at St. Xavier's.

~ ~ ~

I found a camera sitting on my bed. A still camera. I found it as I entered my room after my last midterm, burned out and ready for the Diwali holiday. A month's break from insufferable Xavier's. All I could think of till then was lounging the afternoon away, looking at the Dorothea Lange and Walker Evans photographs in the book I had checked out. But here was a camera. Three rolls of film lay next to it.

I unsnapped the carrying case—MINOLTA studded across the front—and looked the camera over. I peered through the viewfinder; it beat framing shots by joining my thumbs and forefingers at right angles, something I caught myself doing all the time here, standing out on the balcony. A fixed lens, a focus ring, a frame-advance lever, and a tiny handle you turned to wind up the film. Very simple. But I had no recollection of this camera.

"Whose is this?" I asked my mother. She was in the kitchen, preparing rotis for lunch.

"Don't you remember?" Just as she said it, I did: Indian potluck parties in Ithaca when I was in sixth grade; the Grand Canyon on our drive out to Los Angeles; Anand's birthday party at the Chuck E. Cheese's. The camera was present on all these occasions, but it had fallen out of use after we'd moved to Madison. "Your father was sure he had that camera, and he was right. He found it while he was packing this morning."

As I was taking my last midterm, my father had left for his conference in Bombay, a day's train ride away.

"So we'll see him in Baroda?" I asked.

"That's the plan," my mother replied, using pincers to flip the roti over the flames so that it puffed up, a transformation I always thought magical. "Your Hemant Uncle expects us there in two days. Your father will come to Baroda after his conference."

"Let's hope he comes with the video camera," I said.

After lunch, I loaded the Minolta to test it out. The shutter release clicked just as surely as if the camera were brand new. I began by snapping photos from the balcony of all the things I'd been craving to capture: the sprawling peepal at the center of the crossroads, its upward-outward nimbus of green that could itself be a landscape against the blue-silver sky; the farmers reclining on their carts in the peepal's shade; the hard, soot-eaten angles of the shopping complex whose boxy corners fought with the sinuousness of the trees and telephone wires foregrounding it. The camera gave me the containment I'd craved ever since arriving in India. It gave me a way of trapping the world in a tiny box, impressing order where there was no order at all. Looking through the viewfinder, pressing the shutter release, hearing the click did something to my bloodstream, and I felt a bit like a junkie getting his fix after a long dry spell.

Chapter 12

I brought the camera along with me to the Diwali show that night. A soft late-October breeze carried the tempting sweet-and-savory aromas from the bhelpuri and *meethai* stalls that vendors had lined up outside the college grounds. The stalls' kerosene lamps speckled the road and illuminated the crowds of customers happily packed around them. I walked through the front gate under trees now strung up with Diwali lights, creating a constellation all their own. Tiny clay lamps arranged on ledges here and there gave the place a magical, mysterious illumination.

It seemed like every student and teacher from Xavier's was here and had brought their family tonight—the place was jam-packed, giddy with the anticipation of a holiday, more socially at ease than I'd yet known Xavier's to be. People milled together along the drive and the front entrance of the college or strolled the athletic grounds, sipping from bottles of Thums Up cola or eating bhelpuri from newspaper wrapping. A cacophony of cheering and *garba* music from loudspeakers radiated from the athletic field—I saw a stage had been set up there overhung with a battery of lights, and a garba was in progress before an audience of maybe three hundred, clapping along to the *dandiya* rhythm.

Dancers swirled together in a circle onstage—the women in brilliant red-and-gold saris, the men in orange turbans worn Gujarati-style, matching tunics, and white leggings—all striking their dandiya sticks together. They struck in time with the music being sung and played by a row of musicians seated on cushions behind the dancers. A male and a female singer performed at microphones, each chiming cymbals along with the harmonium player and two tabla players. The music bursting through the loudspeakers rose in pitch, quickened in tempo, and the dancers kept pace, bowing, whirling, dandiyas clashing, as the audience whooped, clapped, whistled more and more energetically. The music and dancers churned up together into a fury, till everything dropped in a final note, and a clash struck simultaneously onstage. The singers, musicians, dancers, everyone bowed with joined hands, and the crowd got to its feet in a fever pitch of applause. I found myself swept up too, breathless, clapping and cheering, and I hoped I hadn't missed Pradeep's performance. I looked around but couldn't find Devasia and decided to head over to the hostel.

Devasia was still in his room, and I was glad to have found a friend on a night teeming with strangers. He invited me in, said he was almost ready. He was dressed in his typical kurta pyjama, neatly pressed, and stood in front of a mirror, combing his glossy hair. He shared this room with another South Indian student either already gone for the Diwali holiday or at the festivities outside.

"Quite the party," I said. We could hear the crowds, an announcer through the loudspeaker introducing the next act.

"I also did not believe it would be such a big event," Devasia replied, putting the comb back into the top drawer of his desk.

I scanned the gray room, furnished with only two metal cabinets, two cots, and two desks. A wooden cross hung above Devasia's desk. Other than that, only a calendar picturing the actress Sridevi, belonging to Devasia's roommate, hung on the wall. I snapped a picture of him leaning over his desk with the cross behind him.

"You have got new camera?"

"Old camera," I said. "But it works. Thought I'd send some pictures home to friends."

He snapped into place the metal wristband of his watch. "You are going somewhere for Diwali?"

"Just Baroda. My uncle lives there. You, Madras?"

His head swung in that bell-like motion I was now used to. "My parents, they are expecting me, no?"

Parents, I thought, always expecting something. It made me wonder: "Devasia, if you didn't have to become a priest, what would you want to do?"

He turned to me with a puzzled look. "*Have* to, meaning?"

"Meaning most students study what their parents did, or what they're *told* to study by their parents. Seems that way a lot here."

Devasia cocked his head, not understanding. He checked his appearance one more time in the mirror mounted on the face of the metal cabinet, then turned to me. "See," he said, "my mother is teacher, my father works for Madras electricity board. They have not said to me I must go for this profession or that one, or get married or not. I have made my choices myself. Since I was six, seven, I was active in church, our charity work, so forth."

"So you've always wanted to be a saint?" I asked, more sarcastically than I meant to, as we made for the door.

Devasia chuckled under his breath. "But I enjoyed. Our minister encouraged me to begin seminary studies. And for that I am here."

"And after you're done with all your studies, you think you'll be a priest in India or, you know, join a mission somewhere else?"

"In India. Why not?" he said. "There are many churches in South India. Many Christians. I will do my work in Tamil Nadu only."

"What's it like there?"

Devasia fished out a key from the pocket of his kurta, and we stepped out of his room.

"It is not like this in South." With a faint air of disdain, he gestured with his hand to indicate the surrounding city. He turned the lock on the door, and we proceeded along the hostel corridor to the stairs. "So dirty here," he said confidentially. "People defecating on the road. It is disgusting."

I did not consider Ahmedabad my city, but somehow I took what he said personally and felt ashamed.

We could hear another music performance come booming through the loudspeakers over the hostel roof. A male-female duo sang a bubblegum Hindi pop song, accompanied by its backing disco melody blared through a boom box. I recognized it as "Ek Do Teen," a flashy number from a current Bollywood movie that I was beginning to hear incessantly from car radios and the chai cafes around college.

We decided to check Pradeep's room, and as we approached, we could hear Vinod's voice coming from inside. Gently, I pushed the door open to find Pradeep, in a dress shirt and dark shades, shifting from foot to foot impatiently, his stick in one hand. Vinod lay back on the edge of the bed, wearing his Harley T-shirt, laughing hysterically—face sweaty, mouth wide open so I could see a missing tooth in the upper corner.

"Chalo, Vinod, I must go," Pradeep said, at once agitated and nervous.

I knocked on the door.

"Who is there?" Pradeep turned, startled.

"It's Vik and Devasia."

"Ohhh," Pradeep said, relieved, as if we'd just saved his life. "Vik! Devasia! Help me to get Vinod from here. The show has already started. I'm now late."

Vinod sat up on the bed, his eyes distant and a smile skewed across his face, hair disheveled. He didn't reek of alcohol, but stepping into the room, I picked up the distinct whiff of marijuana.

"Hey, hey, American," Vinod yelled. He broke into a fit of laughter and raised his palm. "High five."

I humored him. "Vinod, we need to get out of here." I touched his shoulder and tugged at him lightly. "Pradeep's on in a few minutes."

Vinod raised his arm as if to swat mine away. He looked at his shoulder where I'd touched him, then at my hands as though I'd infected him with something. "Why don't you bugger off?" he said. "Go when I am ready, yaar." That familiar aroma of charred, pungent cannabis filled the space between us as he spoke.

I returned to Devasia, who stood at the door with Pradeep, and told him, "Why don't you take Pradeep where he needs to go. I'll get Vinod out of here."

"Thank you, yaar," Pradeep said. The two turned and left the room.

Vinod stood over Pradeep's desk, humming a Hindi tune and rolling himself a joint. When he finished, he toked deeply and sat down again.

"How long you been here, Vinod?"

Vinod held it in, then exhaled. "It's compulsory I am here," he droned. "I am Pradeep's manager." The smile from his face morphed into a scowl, and his eyes wandered to the door. "He is gone?"

"They left because Pradeep's about to sing," I said, "so let's join them."

"One minute." He held up an index finger, then two fingers. "No, two minutes, two minutes, two minutes . . ." He took another hit, then extended the joint to me.

I waved it away.

"It's good weed, yaar."

"You smoke a lot, Vinod?"

Curls of smoke rose from his mouth, and he settled back on the bed, propped on his elbows. "Only way to get through Xavier's," he said. He considered his joint up close and spoke to it. "Need to get high once in while when you're in such low place."

I could tell the performance of "Ek Do Teen" was in its final stretch, the synthesized tablas and keyboards from the boom box rising in a crescendo with the onstage vocals. The audience clapped along to the happy rhythm.

"I've never been in such boring place," Vinod muttered sleepily, then began laughing again. "We got to get Sridharan stoned, man. Can you see it?" He rolled onto his side, doubled over. "That damn class would actually—I would actually *want* to attend in that case."

The song finished onstage in a crescendo of tablas, and a round of applause rose up.

"I thought you were Pradeep's manager, Vinod," I said impatiently. "Come on. Let's get out of here." Vinod took another hit, then snuffed out the joint with his fingers and tucked it away in the front pocket of his jeans. "For you, American, there is no worry," he said wearily, somewhat acerbically. "For me," he waggled his thumb back and forth, "no chance."

He sat up and hunched there in silence at the edge of the cot. Then he slapped his knee. "Let's go," he mumbled, but instead of standing up, I could see his body was threatening to lie back down. So I leaped forward and pulled him back up. He began singing a song to himself, a whimsical old Kishore Kumar tune from the fifties that, suddenly, I remembered Hemant Uncle playing on the family stereo back when I was five or six. It was from a black-and-white comedy about auto mechanics, with Kishore Kumar playing the head mechanic, who romances a beautiful customer in the rain.

The rest escaped me. My father still sang that silly song now and then. He got a laugh out of it.

Vinod stood a head taller than me, and he was not small, so it took some work to get him to his feet and out the door. The stage was set up just around the corner, behind the hostel building, but Vinod was already dragging his feet halfway up the veranda.

We made it to the path that led from the main gate to the athletic field. I could see through the spangled trees, under the stage lights, that the announcer was back on, droning words through his microphone. Meanwhile, the wind brought the aromas from the gathering of vendors outside the gate. I could hear the vats of oil sizzling. Pungent, flavorful smoke rose in clouds, illuminated yellow by the kerosene lamps. We moved past the scooters rolling in and out through the gate, hardly noticed in the half darkness and the pell-mell of festivity.

Suddenly, Vinod stopped in his tracks. I asked him if something was wrong, but he only smiled and shook his head. Then he threw his arms around me, and I was steeped in the smell of sweat and cannabis. "I am gone," he groaned.

"You sure are."

He backed up on his heels, and a contented smile replaced the half-dazed, half-tired look on his face. "No," he said, pointing beyond the gate, "I am gone." He turned around and shuffled toward the gate, weaving past scooters and half-shadowy figures.

"But Pradeep is about to sing," I shouted. "Shouldn't the manager be there when his talent is about to go on?"

Vinod's shoulders shook, and he broke into laughs again. Jovially, he slapped a student on the back, startling him, and walked away. "Happy Diwali, American!" he shouted, raising his hand and disappearing into the busy road. I wondered where he was wandering off to.

I stood at the back of the audience, scanned the crowd sitting and standing in the aisles for Devasia. Everyone from college had to be here. The audience had swelled to four hundred or so—a sea of heads backlit by the stage lights, but no sign of Devasia. I looked up to see a canopy of eucalyptus leaves lit magically in the lights, glowing as if from within against the night. I snapped a quick series of shots of the crisscrossing leaves.

"Are you Xavier's resident photographer now?"

It was Priya walking by, joined by members of her clique. There was Manju beaming at me, and Hannah, Ashok, and a few other faces I didn't recognize.

Pradeep went on next, and he was the sensation of the night. He performed an extended ghazal—I'd known he had a nice voice, but tonight he sounded like a recording star. Mellow, nimble, untiring, and confident, his voice *owned* the ghazal, starting with a flamboyant up-and-down spiraling of notes, steadying out before the tabla player accompanying him struck the ghazal's rhythm. Pradeep had the crowd hypnotized, and we roared and cheered him on, and when he finished, everyone demanded an encore. He went on to sing three more songs—more popular tunes that I had heard my parents sing around the house at one time or another—that got the members of the audience singing along excitedly.

When Pradeep finished his performance, the announcer wasted no time declaring him the winner of the talent show. The audience got to its feet in a wave of whistling, stomping, and clapping. A pair of students rushed onto the stage to wrap a silk shawl around Pradeep's shoulders, the winner's shawl, and a female student in a lilac-blue salwaar kameez walked on to present him with a bouquet of roses. Pradeep stood there beaming, a bit embarrassed by the attention, shifting his walking stick in his hand and adjusting his shades nervously.

Afterward, I hung out with Pradeep and Devasia. I snapped pictures as Devasia congratulated Pradeep, of others surrounding and congratulating him. Priya left soon afterward, but I made sure to get her face as she clasped Pradeep's hand and told him how happy she was for him. I knew the pictures would all come out a blur of overlapping faces, mouths, and eyes, all awash in Diwali lights, and in fact I hoped they would—I thought how perfectly that would convey what I felt, giddy, on the eve of a hard-won holiday and a celebration of a friend's crowning victory.

~ ~ ~

Before leaving for Baroda the next day, I bought five more rolls of film. I kept snapping all the way to Baroda. The windshield of the rickshaw festooned with festive tassels; the picture of the baby Krishna, an angelic blue, tacked up above the rickshaw driver's seat; the electric lights decorating the facade of the train station, strung up to read "Happy New Year"; the cows maundering on stick-thin legs among the crowds; all the Diwali travelers elbowing past each other or else slumped on the floor awaiting their departures, babies, mothers, grizzled men with bidis wisping between thin lips. During the clattering ride, I stood at the train's door snapping what I could of forlorn fields and lantern-lit towns, phantasmagoric railroad signals, electricity pylons towering like exoskeletal giants against the violet-and-orange pulse of twilight.

In Baroda, Hemant Uncle came to pick us up in his Fiat. He lived not too far away from the station in a two-story bungalow in a housing colony. We passed a cricket field where a night game was in progress, pennants flapping in the evening wind, crowds in the benches cheering beneath bright lights. From speakers blared a commercial jingle for a laundry detergent, the voice high and chirrupy.

The roads in the colony had not yet been paved, so we bumped along on a dirt lane under scant streetlights. Firecrackers greeted us from all directions, snapping and popping, along with fountains spouting showers of red and yellow, starbursts of sparklers in children's hands. I heard the *tak-a-tak* of drumbeats sound from around a corner, raised shouting, whooping, boasting, and Hindi pop songs blared from nearby speakers.

As we approached Hemant Uncle's house, a servant boy in a short-sleeved shirt and shorts rushed out to open the swinging gate, and we pulled into the drive alongside the house. Kamala Auntie came out with a cheerful hello, hugged us all, and asked if we had adjusted yet to life in India. I shrugged, smiled, didn't know how to answer, but she was in such good spirits I decided to tell her, "Yes." Anjali appeared, back from watching the neighbors set off firecrackers, and wasted no time in asking her parents if we could start lighting off our own.

"Easy, easy," Hemant Uncle said.

We took our bags into the house, and I noticed a *rangoli* pattern on the floor of the patio.

"That's amazing," I said to Kamala Auntie. She said Anjali had helped her make it, and it had taken them all week to put it together, an intricate, dazzling sunburst of colored powders. The rangoli was shaped like a lotus blossom, with deep-orange petals filled in with ornate symmetrical lines of pink, yellow, and blue. Swastikas patterned the inside of each petal, and a golden om symbol occupied the center. I imagined my friends back home would've been startled by the sight of the swastikas, but here, you saw the swastika everywhere—an auspicious symbol almost as old as India itself.

Hemant Uncle had built this house three years ago, soon after he accepted his promotion at the State Bank and transfer to Baroda. It wasn't a large house, but it was charming—a bright, clean sanctuary with red-and-green tiled floors that looked freshly swept. The place seemed worlds away from the noise and crowds we'd just passed through. Copper-colored Diwali *diyas* glowed softly in the far corners of the living room beside the sofas. Incense sticks burned from a small, gold-lacquered Ganesh shrine installed on one wall of the dining room. Framed photographs of my paternal grandparents, both now dead, hung above the shrine. When I saw that, I bowed my head, closed my eyes, and said a quick prayer. I'm not sure why; it just felt right. I still had memories of them from before we left for the States, and I was surprised by the twinge of loss I felt now in seeing their photographs—the depth and immediacy of it. As I went upstairs to drop off our bags, I could hear Anjali out on the patio insist it was time for firecrackers.

I returned with my camera to discover a party already in full swing outside. The fluorescent lights in the living room were switched on, flooding the quiet warmth of the diyas. The TV was now blasting at high volume from its corner stand. Diwali or not, Kamala Auntie still wanted to follow her favorite serial, if only by half listening to it from out on the porch. From the other houses up and down the lane, I could hear voices raised in celebration above Hindi pop music that filled the air from unseen speakers and the whizzing, popping, and whooshing of fireworks that lit up the dark lane.

Anjali twirled a sparkler in her hands. Two neighborhood boys, who seemed only a couple of years younger than Anand, had come over, and they stood with arms across each other's shoulders, watching Hemant Uncle sort out firecrackers from a plastic shopping bag stuffed full of them. My mother and Kamala Auntie sat together on the porch swing while Anand stood quiet and aloof in a corner until Anjali gave him a sparkler and Hemant Uncle called him over to pick out firecrackers.

Using the porch light and the flares of the fireworks, I snapped pictures quickly, hoping for a hint of Anjali's and Anand's faces and that the pictures, with their blurred, hectic framing, would carry the laughter and energy of the night. Soon Kamala Auntie brought out bowls of *chavanu* that she'd mixed together herself, along with boxes of meethai fresh from the confectioner's and glasses of chilled, divinely sweet rosewater.

Everyone took turns setting off firecrackers on the small patio. Unlike the kids, who were nervous about lighting the fuses, bolting like rabbits as soon as the first sparks flew, Hemant Uncle stood calmly, a Diwali veteran, striking a match in one hand, lighting the fuse in the other, then waiting, timing the moment when he tossed the bomb sky-high so that it exploded in the air above the lane to the shrieking delight of Anjali and the boys.

Immediately, I was reminded of a Diwali twelve years ago—a Diwali that took place two months after my father had left for America and the year before my mother, Anand, and I left to join him. In preparation for that Diwali, I had sat beside my grandfather on the edge of the cot where he lay weakened from a heart condition. Together we'd made a list of all the firecrackers we wanted for Diwali. On the last day of school before our holiday, Hemant Uncle and I had sped off on his scooter to the fireworks vendor and picked up armfuls of firecrackers, aided by my hand-scrawled list.

"We had a whole basket full of them that one year, didn't we? The year before we left?" I asked Hemant Uncle. He nodded, impressed that I still remembered.

"That was also the year you burned your hand," he reminded me. Of course. How could I forget? When no one was looking, I had tried to imitate Hemant Uncle's daredevil manner of lighting fireworks, only to have a cherry bomb go off in my hand.

"Whatever Hemant Uncle was doing, you used to copy," Kamala Auntie added with a laugh and a flip of her hand.

I laughed too, telling him I must've blocked that part out, but now I could recall the tears, the panic, the trip to the clinic for injections and bandaging. I stared at the palm of my right hand. Healed now, no remnants of the burn peels and blisters.

One of the kids placed the tail end of a rocket inside a Thums Up bottle, lit the fuse, and scrambled out of the way. A few seconds later, the rocket shot out, trailing embers in a whistling hiss before it burst in a sparkling shower high over the house.

"That was our last Diwali," I reminded Hemant Uncle, "before we left for America."

"And it was also your grandfather's last," he said, handing Anjali another sparkler.

My grandfather's last. I remembered now. Two weeks after that Diwali my grandfather had died. I remembered the tiny living room filled with mourners. Many sang *bhajans* while people in white lined up along the cot where my grandfather lay to pay their respects. But my mind, I recalled, was numb, confused. What was happening? Had I stumbled into a terrible dream? Everything was too weird and disturbing to grasp.

As I stood in the midst of this gathering, Hemant Uncle took me by the hand, and we joined the line of mourners. I kept my eyes on my grandfather, familiar but distant, serene, garlanded in white and yellow flowers. I was standing next to the cot, studying him, when Hemant Uncle whispered to me that I should join my hands and say a prayer. I did as I was told, understanding nothing, vaguely wanting to escape, to wake up from this dream, when I felt Hemant Uncle suddenly pull me into his arms and begin to cry. He shook with tears, his face pressed against my shirt. That's when I knew that whatever this was, it represented the end of something. A leaving, a falling away. Hemant Uncle's gesture had made me feel I was not alone, had said to me it was okay, it was safe to drop away the walls of restraint and numbness and to shed my own tears.

In the years since, I'd come to identify what it was I'd felt at that moment of grief—it was gratitude. I was grateful to Hemant Uncle for trusting his grief to a six-year-old boy.

"One second," I said to Hemant Uncle now as he prepared to set light to several firecrackers arranged in a circle on the patio. I stepped beside him, placed an arm around his shoulder. I reversed my hold on the camera, held it out so that it pointed back at us, and snapped a picture.

"Funny way to take snapshot." Hemant Uncle laughed. "Will it come out?"

"It'll be great."

Anjali stood, sparklers in both hands, twirling them fancifully in radiant arcs. "Vikram bhai," she said in Gujarati. "I am so happy you all came for Diwali."

"Me too," I said.

Chapter 13

The next several days felt easy and relaxed, a much-needed break from Xavier's and the daily grind back in Ahmedabad. My world became a cycle of festive meals with the family, roaming the bazaars of Baroda with Anand, Anjali, Kamala Auntie, and my mother; watching cricket games on TV and pirated James Bond movies that Anand and I rented from the local paan shop; and, of course, Diwali fireworks. Anand and I joined in on pickup games of cricket out in the lane with Anjali and the neighborhood kids—they might've been smaller and younger than us, but compared to our stumbling and fumbling, they may as well have been pros. And while I thought of my friends back home all the time, being so removed from my mailbox gave me an excuse not to dwell so much on the distance between us.

Five days into our holiday, my father arrived in Baroda from the conference in Bombay. Anand and I were out in the lane with Anjali and a few neighborhood kids who were teaching us the basics of cricket when we saw Hemant Uncle's car arrive from the station. The car pulled into the drive, and my father got out. He looked drawn, weak, and walked slowly into the house while Hemant Uncle got my father's bags out of the trunk.

"Malaria, I think so," was Hemant Uncle's guess when I asked him about my father. He told me he'd gone straight to bed, right after he had his cup of chai, complaining of fever and chills.

"I knew he was not going to take his pills," my mother remarked as she and Kamala Auntie fixed dinner. "I knew it all along. 'Too bitter, too bitter.' Well, look now what happens." Kamala Auntie calmed her down, saying he would feel better in a few days, that getting malaria was like catching the flu here. Later that night, Hemant Uncle summoned a doctor, someone who lived nearby and ran a neighborhood clinic. He confirmed the malaria, then gave my father an injection and a prescription for chloroquine. For the next three days, my father shook, sweated, kept to the guest bedroom upstairs, emerging only to throw up.

It was true: my father hadn't taken his pills in weeks. Hated the taste, the nausea, and the stomach upset it caused. He also complained that the pills disturbed his sleep. So, in my mother's words, "Look now what happens."

~ ~ ~

Bombay gave my father malaria, but it did not give him back our video camera.

"He went to the customs office," my mother explained one afternoon, a week after my father's return. She sat on the floor of the living room, chopping vegetables into a colander set down on the coffee table. "He spoke with them, spent whole day there." She shook her head despondently. "They apparently lost camera."

"Lost?" I hadn't seen the camera among my father's bags, so my mother's words only confirmed my fears. "They didn't lose it," I said, dropping to the couch with a sigh. I remembered that customs inspector now, a troll of a man, a bureaucrat. Thieving Indians, I thought. "I knew we wouldn't get that camera back," I said. "Can't catch a break in this goddamn country."

The room fell quiet. Hemant Uncle cleared his throat and sipped his tea contemplatively in his chair. I felt a twinge of shame saying those words around Hemant Uncle, a man I knew to take great pride in India, in being Indian. He was like my father that way. But that didn't change the fact of my anger, my despair. The camera was gone, and so were the videotapes. The tapes were a more sentimental loss because they contained the images I wanted close to me—my old room, old friends, parties, wanderings, jokes, conversations, all recorded on tape in the last weeks before we left. Was there some conspiracy, with the loss of my wallet and now the camera, to wipe out all my means of remembering?

We heard my father shuffle downstairs in his slippers. He appeared, tousle-haired, pajamas rumpled, small and hunched from his battle with malaria, and shambled to the dining table. He poured himself a tumbler of water from the steel pitcher and took a gulp before he turned to face us. "Hmm?" he said, taking his glasses off and rubbing at his eyes to wake himself up.

"How do you feel?" my mother asked. "Want something to eat? Chai?"

"So-so," he said groggily, replacing the glasses. He tsked, "Nothing," and shook his head. "Just can't stay in bed any longer."

My mother got up and pressed her palm across my father's forehead. "Fever's down," she said, starting for the kitchen. "I'll fix you something."

"So that's it?" I said. "They get away with losing people's things?"

"I'm sorry," my father said, lowering himself onto the couch. His voice was weak; his eyes looked dimmed. "They did give a check. Equivalent to the camera value. In rupees. So that's something."

Anand perked up. "Maybe we can use that for the Nintendo?" Since arriving in Baroda, he'd modified his fantasy baseball game for cricket. Lying on the floor, propped on one elbow, he'd been engaged for hours with rolling the dice, tallying and jotting down the results in various columns on a piece of paper.

"Or we can get another camera," my father suggested.

"Don't want one." I slouched lower in my seat.

My father went into further detail about his trip to the airport, his voice sounding weak. He told us he'd rushed to the customs office on the last day of the conference, just before heading to the train station. The customs people searched their files and their storage rooms, found our paperwork but couldn't locate the camera. They offered to mail us a compensation check in a few weeks. "But I knew that was just their way of getting rid of me," he said. "No one was sending any check." He demanded they cut the check right there and then. "I didn't budge," he said, "went right up to supervisor and stuck right there in his office and said, 'I'm not leaving till you give me check.' And that's what they did." His voice warmed over, and he seemed pleased with himself.

Hemant Uncle went on to ask details about the visit, the amount of the check, and so on, but I'd stopped listening. Soon Kamala Auntie was commenting on the quality of the okra, the price of oil and onions, and my brother asked if we'd still be celebrating Christmas and for a cricket bat as a present. The subject of the camera had effectively ended. With a check.

But I couldn't see putting monetary value on memories, and I was shocked by how deep the loss felt—the loss of the camera, the tapes, and what they represented: my access to memory. I wanted to rage at that moment. At my father for bringing me here, at India for being such a cruel and despicable place to come back to. But all I mustered was "Unbelievable." I don't think anyone heard me.

~ ~ ~

After dinner, my father went back to bed, Anjali and Anand went over to a neighbor's to set off more firecrackers, and I decided to sit out on the porch swing by myself. I'd closed the front door to muffle the blare of the TV news in the living room. Moths skittered around the single bulb above the door, casting flickering shapes in the grainy light. From up the lane, I could hear the snap and bang of fireworks and the whoops and whistles of children. A greenish-blue cloud from the firecrackers, backlit by streetlights, filled the street, giving the neighborhood a smoky, somewhat apocalyptic look.

I wondered what Shannon was doing that very minute. Maybe she was sitting in a lecture or sitting out on the terrace of the Union between classes. I wondered whom she was with. I pretended I was sitting beside her, breathing in the fresh air off the lake, watching the boats, holding her arm across the table. If I had my video camera right now, I could at least watch images of her, just put in the videotape and watch the playback through the viewfinder. That's what I would've been doing this very minute . . . if I had the camera: watching Shannon's face from that afternoon we spent at Vilas Park or watching scenes of Nate, Karl, and me goofing off in Nate's kitchen the evening of Nate's graduation party.

From an upstairs window, I could hear my father coughing, hacking, and clearing his throat. I heard concerned chatter between him and my mother, too low and muffled to make out. Then silence.

The front door creaked open, letting out a stream of TV noise and fluorescent light before it closed, and Hemant Uncle stepped onto the porch. He smiled at me and shuffled to the edge of the porch, barefoot, his hands in his pants pockets.

"You are enjoying fireworks?" he asked, gazing out at the road.

I told him I was.

"About your Pappa," he said. "He will be all right. Nothing to worry." He spoke softly, yet the deep baritone of his voice filled the air impressively. He began pacing along the edge of the porch, his hands clasped behind his back.

I didn't know what to tell him, but saying I didn't much care at that moment if my father got better didn't seem the best reply. "He's a giant, really," he continued admiringly, shaking his head. "Sacrificed so much. Gave up his whole life here so he could pursue *exactly* what he wished."

"We *all* sacrificed," I said. "We all sacrificed. Mummi sacrificed just as much, maybe even more. She didn't know if Pappa would have a job from one year to the next. Maybe we'd have been better off if we'd never left." That thought was new to me, I realized, and spoken as soon as it had occurred in my mind. "Might've avoided a lot of hardships. I mean, we were coming back here anyway, so . . ."

Hemant Uncle listened closely, his head cocked, eyes squinted, then said, "Without America, your Pappa would not have the job he is having now. It's a quite big position."

"It is." I shrugged. "But what about you at the State Bank? You stayed right where you started and worked your way all the way up. Pappa could've done the same right here in India somewhere, and we'd have avoided the last eleven years."

Hemant Uncle tsked several times and flipped his hand in a dismissive gesture, stopped pacing, and faced me. "You know how I got job at State Bank? They knew I was a cricketer at Xavier's. They hired me so I could join State Bank team only. Otherwise, I was flop as a student. History major, second class." He chuckled to himself. "It is lucky I was a good player, bhai, otherwise I would be just a . . . clerk now, god knows where."

Just then we heard the front gate open on its creaky metal hinges, and Anjali came scampering through in flip-flops, followed by Anand. Anjali was in heady spirits and asked if we could all go to Dairy Den for ice cream. It was her favorite ice cream parlor; we'd gone there soon after arriving in Baroda—a cool, sweet-scented haven where the ice cream, Anand and I had to admit, was better than the local Baskin-Robbins in Madison.

In his mock-weary tone, Hemant Uncle said, "Chalo," and that got Anjali jumping off the steps in delight before she disappeared through the gate, saying she needed a few more minutes at the neighbors' and she'd be ready to go. Anand took a seat next to me on the porch swing.

"School will start soon," he said, "then all this *tamasha* will"—he made a calming gesture with downturned palms—"finally end."

~ ~ ~

"It was hard, no doubt, for you all in States," Hemant Uncle conceded, a few minutes later as Anand, Anjali, he, and I piled into the Fiat. I took the front seat, next to Hemant Uncle. "But ask your Pappa how hard it must have been to lose his parents while being so far away. Not enough money or proper visa to come back for visit."

That was true, I had to admit. Then again, I reasoned, had we stayed in India, my father would never have had to deal with the loss of his parents long distance. We'd all have been better off, I repeated.

"He's thought of all that many times, I am sure. But *his* father, your *dada*, made him promise about that."

I turned to him. "Promise?"

"Ask him about that sometime," Hemant Uncle replied, shifting the car into reverse and backing out of the drive. We pulled into the smoky, darkened lane, haloed with streetlights and the occasional pulse of firecrackers.

Soon we turned onto the road linking us to the city, buzzing with scooters and rickshaws. The road led past the cricket stadium and the train station and into the carnival-like madness of commercial Baroda beyond. Hemant Uncle continued, "Just be happy your father took this job. You do not know it"—his eyes shifted from the road to me—"but he has given you a future."

To my left, we passed a long, dark stretch of land, punctured here and there with the reddish glow of kerosene lamps. Once or twice, our headlights flitted past a goat or a dog in the road or small children in rags or women carrying copper pots. And I realized that beyond the darkness was the shantytown I'd passed so many times before in the daylight, a maze of passageways and low-squatting huts that stretched a half mile before we arrived at the outlying paan shops, tailors, and chai cafés that preceded the cricket stadium and the train station. In the darkness, the shantytown was invisible—a cruel sleight of hand that India could play on you, using the night to pull the wool over the ugly truths that the day made naked. I was going to mention the shantytown to Hemant Uncle, but he was ahead of me: "You may not like your college, you see the streets are dirty, and all the *zopadpattis*." He gestured out at the shantytown, as if the sight of it were obvious to all of us in spite of the darkness. "But we all feel these things too. We wish it were not so." He breathed deeply, his mind turning over these thoughts. "One day, India will change. It will take time. Twenty years, fifty years, hundred years, but it is inevitable. People cannot live like this forever."

We drove on.

"I guess when you can't see your future," I said, "you live in your past."

"What past?" Hemant Uncle said, his tone stern and admonishing. "You're only seventeen, eighteen, Vikram. Your life is in the future, not past."

~ ~ ~

On the train back to Ahmedabad, I watched the sunflower fields and the dust-strewn, cement-built towns that I had passed weeks before. But then they had been shrouded in night, so now it was like passing this country for the first time. I studied the gathering of strange faces whipping by at the railway crossings, the whole circus of Indian traffic waiting for the train to pass. We crossed huge tracts of Gujarat farm country, studded with mud-brick sheds and the enormous fossil remains of disused farm implements. Blackbirds bigger than I'd ever seen scudded low over the fields.

The compartments were packed with families returning home from their holidays. The children on their fathers' laps; the housewives in their saris, veils pulled over their heads against the wind, knees folded on the benches. Strange faces, strange ways, a strange planet, yet the only real stranger was me.

When we stopped at a station, vendors whisked past the windows or through the compartments. "Chocolate—candy—ice cream—cigarette," went the dry, monotonous call as one passed with a tray of wares slung at his waist; another sold bottles of cold, sweetened Amul milk out of a metal basket. The bottles *tink-tinked* in his hands.

The man at the end of the bench got out of his seat and signaled for a cup of water from a passing vendor. Dipping a ladle into a clay pot that he lugged around, the vendor scooped the chilled water into a steel tumbler and handed it through the bars of the window. The man tipped the tumbler over his mouth as he stood in the narrow space between the benches. He gulped heartily, his Adam's apple bobbing up and down his thin neck. He never let the tumbler touch his lips. I felt thirsty, and my father informed me that the water came from the taps at the station. Remembering the dysentery, I shuddered at the thought of drinking it.

Drifting through the compartment, a walking stick clutched in one hand, came a blind beggar, a palm held out while he sang a devotional song about Krishna in his high, reed-thin voice. The beggar's eyes were cloudy orbs floating back and forth in their sockets, and his head and sunken cheeks bristled with a silvery stubble. A small boy walked beside him, skillfully beating a small drum. They passed our compartment, their music receding slowly toward the other end of the car.

"Right here," I heard my father call to the Amul vendor passing by the window. To my surprise, he bought a bottle of the sweetened milk. I couldn't blame him. It had been a hot, stuffy trip in that compartment. He paid the vendor; took the cold, water-beaded glass bottle; peeled the foil cap off the top; and took a slug.

"You were just sick," my mother reasoned with him. "You want to repeat that?"

My father did not answer, just offered the bottle to my mother. She shook her head. He handed it to Anand, who swigged deeply from it. Anand passed it to my mother, who consented to a few sips. I took the bottle from her, tipped it into my mouth, and finished it off. It tasted as delicious and cool as it looked, dysentery be damned. The vendors cleared out, and the train pushed off as evening settled over the countryside. The compartment swayed and rattled across dark farmland, and a row of dim incandescent lights blinked on overhead. The red-orange of the horizon faded, and the lanterns and stars were the only lights to go by.

~ ~ ~

A packet arrived from Karl. Inside was a cassette—a dub of the latest R.E.M. record. The word "Green" was inscribed on the label in Magic Marker, an attempt by Karl at funky, artistic lettering.

November 12, 1988

Vik!

Here it is. R.E.M.'s long-awaited Green. Give it a chance, I think you'll hook into it the more you listen. I've also included some more "Life in Hell" clippings for you from the Isthmus.

Well, my first semester is a month away from wrapping up. Intro to Film has been amazing, and it's got me 100 percent sure I'm majoring in film and about my (our?) decision to launch a film career after college, in whatever form that might take (I'm still holding out for our production company).

Do you remember that girl Bridget I mentioned to you? Well, I'm taking creative writing with her. Her idea. Don't laugh. This past summer, we saw a ton of flicks together at the Union and the Majestic. Then, after the semester began, SHE asked ME if I wanted to get SERIOUS. I'm flabbergasted. So far, so good.

Sorry to hear about you and Shannon. I know it doesn't make it any easier, but you knew it would come to this. If it helps, I ran into her at the Union (she's working now at the Directorate, did you know?), and she was telling me how much she's been thinking about you.

Living at home has one advantage—it lets you save a ton of cash. I've managed to save a good chunk of my WHA paychecks. Why do I bring this up? Well, this to/from campus commute's getting to be a major drag in multiple departments, so next year I'm thinking campus housing.

Anyway, let me know the latest. How's life treating you? How did your exams go? How was your break? Details, Vik. I need details.

Karl

P.S. America got Bushwhacked. (I'm sure you heard already, but there it is.)

I put on my headphones and listened to the R.E.M. tape beginning to end. Then I flipped the cassette over and listened to it all again. This was the pulse of America I was listening to, and all the noise of my life filtered away, leaving only a single wavelength of music. It was as if a dependable friend had reentered my life. The new songs were unfamiliar, but they weren't strangers to me. They were just the spiffy new clothes that my friend came dressed up in. Here was a familiarity I'd craved for months.

Anand demanded to borrow it, but I told him to hold tight. There was something I needed to do first. Gathering up my R.E.M., Police, and U2 tapes, along with assorted selections of the Smiths, Ramones, Elvis Costello, and others from my shoebox, I went to the tape deck we kept in the living room. I switched on the transformer—it hummed as loudly as a beehive. I inserted one of my old R.E.M. cassettes, scanned the track listings for a personal favorite, then reached for a blank tape. Before inserting it into the tape deck, I wrote "Music Mix for Priya" on the label. I put the tape in and pressed "Record," and for the first time since Shannon's exit from my life, my ego felt recharged, this time with thoughts of a different girl.

Chapter 14

I thought the occasion of the mixtape warranted my picking up the phone and calling Priya. She'd given me her phone number, after all. I hesitated making the call at first—boys did not make social calls on girls, unless it was either an overture to an arranged marriage or the sexes were socializing in strictly mixed company. But Priya was surely an exception.

I dialed the number. A woman answered—her mother, I guessed—who seemed cordial but uptight; a stern Gujarati matriarch came to mind. She told me to hold the line. Then a few seconds later, Priya's voice came on. She sounded hesitant, surprised, not entirely comfortable. Our Indian phone, with its rotary dial and dumbbell-heavy handset, made the whole experience feel even more Victorian.

"Priya?" I said. "I didn't mean to catch you at a bad time. I know your birthday's passed, but I made you a gift."

"Really?" she said, "No, this is cool. Thanks. I'm . . ." and she began laughing nervously. "Thanks."

"Well, don't thank me yet. You haven't gotten it. I want to give it to you before classes start. Can we meet up somewhere? Are you free?"

"Um . . . why not in college, tomorrow?"

"Neutral ground," I countered. "Xavier's makes me nervous. You ever get the feeling wolves are watching you?"

"You're talking to a girl. We always feel that way."

I was pondering this feminine insight when Priya suggested we meet up at the Havmor Café that night, near the Navarangpura bus stop. It wasn't far for either of us.

~ ~ ~

The Havmor Café was packed with local families and students. A canopy hung over the rickety tables, and customers thronged the order counter. Filmi tunes blared from scratchy speakers, drowning all the talk-talk to an unintelligible murmur. I had expected to see Manju, Hannah, or any one of Priya's various tagalongs with her that night, but she came alone. She walked up the steps to the café, one hand hooked into the shoulder strap of her canvas-and-leather purse. As I got up to meet her, I noted that the purse looked too sturdy, too finely designed to be from one of Ahmedabad's bazaars. Probably an American purchase.

We did not touch, simply waved hello before hands returned to hip pockets. I sensed looks already from the packs of men and boys at the tables and on the sidewalk out front.

"Here you go," I said, handing her the tape. "Happy birthday."

Priya took the tape, looked perplexed for a half second, then her mouth made a perfect O of recognition. "Oh, right," she said, "you're trying to improve my taste in music."

"I wouldn't say 'improve,'" I said almost apologetically. "Just trying to broaden it a little. Add a little masala, you see."

She glanced over the track listings on the back of the tape cover. "Oh, I know these bands," she said. "I'm not totally out of it. I do have a Police album, you know."

"It's probably *Synchronicity*. Everyone has that one."

She made a face, stuck her tongue out at me, but only briefly; I could tell she was a bit shy among this crowd.

"What I've got there," I said, "you won't have on those Top Forty mixes your cousins are pushing on you."

She smiled to herself, studying the cassette's track list while I searched the menu board—stenciled black letters against white tube-lit paneling—above the order counter. The offerings sounded suspiciously like imitations of American cafeteria and diner food.

"Hot dogs?" I said. "Pepperoni pizza? I doubt they have actual meat, right?"

Priya put the cassette inside her purse. "No, it's all the Gujarati vegetarian version. Edible," she explained, "but not exactly the real thing."

"I'll say." Rather than smoked meats, pizza sauce, and hamburger seasonings, the air was redolent with diced onions, cilantro, *mirch masala*, and *pav bhaji*. The fact that it smelled like the canteen at Xavier's made me a touch queasy.

"You going to order something?" I asked Priya. "Cheeseburger?"

She scrunched her eyes and nose. "Not just yet," she said tactfully.

I laughed, and we moved toward an emptying table. "How was your birthday?"

"Fun," she said as she quickly scanned a group of teenage boys chatting loudly at the neighboring table. She turned to face me and added, "I had a cave party. Do you know what that is?" We sat down, and from her purse, she plucked out some photos. "We had part of our back patio done up to look like caves, see—" The photos showed a lavish party set inside what looked like an imitation cave. The papier-mâché walls were contoured and painted to look like a glistening rocky surface. There was even a miniature waterfall emptying into a small pond lined with plants and flowers.

Diwali lights were strung up along the walls, giving the whole thing a festive air, and a disco ball was suspended in the middle of the "cave." Her friends crowded under the ball, dancing and goofing around, bottles of Limca and Thums Up in their hands. They mingled at small tables abundant with cake and snacks. I noticed Hannah—the half-Indian, half-German girl—cutting loose in one photo, in a T-shirt and jeans—laughing, her pinned-up hair unraveling. Ashok danced beside her, shy and stiff, a half-embarrassed smile on his face, while another shot caught Manju off guard, her mouth full of cake as she gawked at the camera.

Seeing the photos made me relieved I wasn't at that party. I wouldn't have known what to do around these people. But then I saw photos of Priya, pressed up next to her friends, and she looked good, and the relief emptied out and became an ache. "Too bad you couldn't have been there," she said.

Priya suggested we take a walk up the road, past the students—a bunch of rowdy-looking guys hanging out together on their motorbikes—and four or five children off the street milling about in front of the Havmor. Traffic honked and beeped and growled along the road. The dirt fringe of the road bustled with shoppers, strollers, loiterers, and a few beggars, and the evening air was thick with that distinct odor of smoke and exhaust fumes.

"How're you adjusting to life in India?" Priya asked as we maneuvered past a cow nosing through plastic bags.

For a second, I wanted so much to spill my guts, really let loose and tell her how upside down everything had gotten. But I reined myself in and settled for "I'm not." She asked me about my family so I filled her in. I went on and told her about what November was like in Madison and what my friends were up to at school. I hesitated but decided to mention Shannon and the breakup, for no other reason than to impress on her that I had at least some experience in that particular department. Priya asked if we, meaning

Shannon and I, were very close. "I guess so. That's how it goes," I said, but in a casual way so I could show off how tough I could be.

But I don't think Priya bought it. "I'm sure you'll be fine," she said, smiling.

We walked up the road to the corner where she said there was a Vadilal ice cream counter and talked about the difficulties of adjusting to life in India. "The first couple of years were the toughest," she said. "I thought of America all the time. In everything you do, you're reminded of it. From the second you wake up to when you go to sleep."

"How did you do it?" I asked. "You seem to be taking it all in stride."

Priya shrugged. "I don't really have much to complain about. I mean, I'm better off than most of the people at our college, you know."

I nodded. "Not to mention most of the people around us right now."

"For me, India and America always felt interconnected. I've been able to move from one to the other as I've liked, so maybe the transition to living here was easier for me."

The ice cream stand was a burst of candy colors: the Vadilal logo inside a red balloon, the stand painted bright blue with red and pink lettering overhead, and the whole thing bathed in cool white light. A thin, mustached clerk in a paper hat scrambled from order to order, doling out cups of ice cream from tubs set inside the counter. The cold aromas of pistachio, mango, and saffron hovered and mixed with the smells of the street. We pushed toward the counter and ordered two cups of pistachio. I paid for them.

"Belated birthday present number two," I said, handing her the ice cream with a wooden spoon tucked into it.

The ice cream was a sweet jolt to the senses, an expansion of the mind. We turned from the stand and began walking along a line of cars parked irregularly on our side of the road. I told Priya I couldn't help but envy her freedom of movement, her being able to move between India and America as she pleased.

Priya laughed lightly. "I chalk it all up to the American passport," she said, but there was a hint of irony to it, and there was a steady seriousness in her eyes. "I guess you could say the charm of America wore itself out," she said. "Sure, I love it, and it's given my family so much. It's given my dad a great career, for one thing . . . but we didn't feel the most welcome there after a while." Hesitant to say more, she took another spoonful of the ice cream.

"How's that?" I asked.

She kept her gaze lowered. "It's why my father decided to leave." We arrived at her white Maruti—I remembered it now from that first visit to Xavier's when I had seen her driving away in it. Priya leaned back against the hood and propped a heel on the bumper. "It all had to do with this big scandal. The whole community got crazy over it. And let's just say race becomes a target very easily when people stop liking you. Our house was vandalized—graffiti, spray paint, a lot of hateful stuff."

"My god," I said. "What was it all about?"

Priya shook her head, and her mouth formed a half smile as she reflected. "It started with a case my father was defending. He worked for this firm in Boston. The case was a pretty big deal. A real estate developer who'd poured millions into some waterfront property was being sued by the city. Big environmental case. Then before we knew it, my dad was getting charged with harassment."

"*Sexual* harassment?"

Priya nodded, her eyebrow arched as if to say to me, *What other kind is there?*

"She was young," she continued, "just out of college and interning at the firm where my dad worked, a real go-getter, you could say. Then out of the blue, she goes public with these accusations. It came out much later that she'd made it all up."

"Made it up?" I'd never been in proximity to such legal drama. It was worthy of the movies and, for a moment, I took a break from the joy of merely looking at Priya to really take in what she was saying. "Why would she do that?"

"To have something over on my dad. He started to suspect that she was sharing details of the case with someone in the city attorney's office. And before he could confirm it, she one-upped him, knowing that a harassment charge would discredit any accusation he might bring against her.

"And of course the media love a sex scandal. All the local papers and stations portrayed her as one of these hardworking, all-American girls being victimized by her big-shot boss.

"On top of that, the case my dad was defending was controversial enough—I remember people picketing in front of the firm. Anyway, my dad really got disgusted by it all, the scandal, the media circus, the case itself, which was corrupt to begin with, and"—she shook her head—"everything."

"Do your friends here know all this?" I asked.

"Nothing." She looked at me, her eyes vivid with alarm. "Do not tell Manju or anyone, okay?"

I assured her I would not.

She went on: "What hurt was that when people have nothing to go on, they start calling you names. Dotheads, towelheads—where did they get that one? We're not even Sikhs. And 'Go home this and that' graffitied on the garage."

I thought about Priya's father, the trust he must've had in this intern, in his firm, before it all blew up in his face. "Betrayal is the worst thing."

"School sucked that last year." She kept her eyes on her ice cream cup. "I've never felt so alone in my life. All the Indian families stopped coming by. My father realized he could never recover career-wise after that. So when he decided to leave the firm and come back, bring his family back, get a fresh start, I really didn't mind much. It was great to get out of that."

"I'm sorry."

Priya laughed. Her spirits seemed back up again. "It's okay. Like I said, old story. My dad isn't exactly hurting, you know?"

I positioned myself beside her against the car, but gingerly, keeping a half yard of distance between us. "Your nasty experience aside, I still wish I had your choices. I mean, your choices now."

"Don't," she said. "You're a guy, and your choices as an Indian guy are way more than mine as an Indian woman. No matter how rich you are. Or where your passport is from."

Her reasoning was sound, but it rang hollow to me. I may have had the advantage as a male in India, but I didn't exactly see myself as belonging to the club of my fellow Indian males, wandering the streets of C.G. Road or the halls of Xavier's College. I felt nothing like them. Still, I appreciated Priya's words, and I was happy she was with me now.

"Anyway," she went on, "you'll be fine. You'll finish your BA at Xavier's and move on. Probably back to America, and this will all seem like a weird dream."

"What about you?" I asked. "You think you'll get your BA and make your move?"

"Yes and no," she said with a confidential air.

Four young men sauntered by, all giddy in the warm November night. Their intrigued glances in our direction reminded me that I was not a native Ahmedabadi. I did not belong. I wondered if Priya got that feeling too. No matter your skin color, the way you dressed, behaved, the vibe you gave off gave you away. The men passed us slowly, checking us out. Then from one of them came a whistle, and from another a kissing sound. "Abbay-oy! Sweetie!" The third one turned his head toward us and whistled again. Then they laughed among themselves as they drifted into the haze of headlights and mingling human beings.

"We're causing a minor scandal of our own around here," Priya remarked. "We're gonna have to keep our interactions to college, I think."

I felt crushed by her decision. "Really?"

Priya pushed off the hood of the Maruti, licking her fingers. I offered to take the empty ice cream cup from her. "I'll take it home," she said. "You won't find a trash can around here." She turned and opened the driver's-side door and dropped the cup inside. "Thanks for the tape," she said, patting her purse before she took it off her shoulder.

I stood, hand in pocket, at the front of the car. "Okay, well, I'll see you in college then."

She placed a foot inside the car. From her lowered gaze and vague nod, something seemed to be on her mind. "Vik, I know you feel like you've got your hands tied. But . . . remember, it can only get better." The remark made her smile briefly before she disappeared into the Maruti.

She turned on the ignition, flicked on the headlights, and pulled out into the commotion of C.G. Road. I saw her silhouetted against the glare of the road as she waved good-bye before she sped up and was lost in the anonymity of the nighttime traffic.

I began walking back to the Havmor, where my Luna was parked. *It can only get better?* Worse, yes, but I couldn't see how it could get better, especially after her telling me we couldn't hang out together outside of college. A brief encounter it would have to be, a conversation in the cocoon of a shared language. Perhaps here in Ahmedabad, that was more than I had any right to expect.

~ ~ ~

I came back from the holiday to learn I had done well on the midterms. First class across the board. Devasia and Pradeep too. We congratulated each other as we stood before the message board in the college lobby. The board was wallpapered with dot-matrix printouts that listed every student's marks.

We began walking toward our lecture hall. It was almost time for Sridharan's fifty minutes of windbaggery.

"Any word from Vinod," I asked Pradeep, "since his Diwali meltdown? You know—" I imitated the act of toking, but of course, Pradeep couldn't see what I was doing, and Devasia was slow to understand.

"Ah, yes," Devasia said finally, then vigorously shook his head, shut his eyes. "No, I do not know."

"I am worried about him, to tell you the truth," Pradeep said. "He has not been at college this week."

As we entered Sridharan's lecture hall alongside a stream of students, we bumped into Priya and Manju. I said hello, hoping to have a few words with Priya, to ask her if she'd had a chance to listen to the mixtape. But she paused only long enough to smile and say hi, her hands clasping her notebooks close to her chest. Her attitude threw me off, and I chalked it up to the fear of gossip at Xavier's and went off to my seat.

Chapter 15

I got the Diwali photos developed. Six rolls' worth. Most of them were junk. Over- or underexposed, some too blurry. I realized I was making a basic camera work too hard. Except for the focus, everything else on the camera—shutter speed, aperture—was preset and fixed. A few of the photos surprised me, though, especially those from the first night in Baroda, setting off fireworks with Anjali, Anand, and Hemant Uncle, and from the Xavier's Diwali festival with Pradeep and Priya aglow in the golden lights. I made more copies of these and sent them to Karl, an early Christmas present.

It was now a matter of waiting out the month before Christmas break, when we were planning to visit my mother's older brother, Dharmanshu Uncle, in New Delhi. He had lived there twenty-seven years. He worked as a civil engineer for the city, alone since his wife died when I was still a child. His son had grown up now and left India for a new life in London four years ago. All I remembered of Dharmanshu Uncle was his beard, which used to terrify me as a child, and his penetrating eyes, like black marbles set behind his large spectacles. For eleven years, aerograms had been the only mode of communication between my mother and Dharmanshu Uncle; in the weeks before our visit, she talked often of her anxiousness to see him.

I renewed my photography book again and again from the library. I studied the photographs—a Depression-blighted mother surrounded by her children; a skeletal tree dwarfed by the towering Flatiron, shrouded in fog, in turn-of-the-century New York City; anxious faces of immigrants crammed together in the steerage of a transatlantic steamship. The pictures spoke of suffering or loneliness, but to me they were thrilling glimpses of home, as much as the photographs of DiMaggio knocking another one into the stands, of surfers and girls—the most beautiful girls in the world—glistening on Venice Beach in 1959. Lying in bed in the afternoons with my headphones on, I pored over the book, listening to R.E.M.'s "Little America," "Pilgrimage," "Letter Never Sent"; to *Chronic Town* and *Fables of the Reconstruction* over and over; and to *Green*, which I was steadily becoming fond of.

After Anand finished his homework, the bungalow echoed with the electronic cheeps and chimes from the Nintendo in the living room. At the end of Diwali break, my father had bought him the game system. Now and then Anand's friend Jyoti, fat and loud, came by, and they played together till my father came home. The video game drove my mother nuts. She raced from the kitchen into the living room, demanding first that they turn down the volume and eventually turn off the game. "Enough is enough," she proclaimed, the rolling pin in her hand. "Read book." She used to yell the same things at him in America. How little some things changed.

My father hired a pair of gardeners to clean out the weeds and scrub in front of the bungalow. Leaving for classes, I would find them—strips of cloth wrapped around their heads, moving about on bare legs, digging up the undergrowth, piling it into wheelbarrows.

Then they worked the dirt with hoes and arranged the ground into rows for planting. A week later, returning home from Xavier's, I found the first sprouts peeking out of the dirt as the groundskeeper moved along the rows with a watering can. They planted rosebushes, marigolds, vegetables. My mother watched them from the balcony. She loved watching the garden come to life. It soothed her, she said.

Back in the library again between classes one day, safe in the shade and the echoes, I was turning the pages of the *Times of India* when I heard Priya. "You sure like R.E.M."

"Haven't seen you around much," I said. It was true; for weeks, my only interaction with Priya had been brushes before or after our Victorian Lit or French classes. These were short hellos or her asking me to clear up a point in Sridharan's or Varma's lecture. Then she would pull away with Manju and Hannah, usually to the canteen.

"Sorry," she said. "I've been meaning to tell you thanks again for the mix." She nodded nervously and took a deep breath. Priya's kohl-lined eyes looked tired, either from lack of sleep or, I thought, from crying. Her hair fell to either side of her face, strands tucked behind the ears to keep them out of her eyes. She wore a bindi today, a slender red mark on her forehead, and no jeans, but a crumpled black skirt that fell below her knees with some flowery patterns along the hem.

"Are you okay?" I asked, without even thinking. As unkempt as she appeared today, her prettiness still struck me.

Priya chuckled, slightly embarrassed by my question, and said, "Uh . . . y-yeah. Just been dealing with stuff with my dad. I'll tell you about it sometime." Arms folded, she leaned against the stand.

I nodded vaguely and sensed an awkward silence between us. Afraid she'd take that as a sign to walk away, I abruptly asked, "When?" She raised her face to me, somewhat surprised. "You don't talk to me here," I said. "You don't want to see me outside of here. When were you planning to tell me about it?"

She exhaled, then said in a low voice, "Remember that night when we met up for ice cream, and you were telling me about choices? And how you wished you had all the choices I had? Go where I want, when I want?"

"What about it?" I said, a bit on my guard.

"Well," she sighed, "my life's not quite as carefree as you might think. The last couple of weeks reminded me my choices are . . . way more black-and-white than I ever thought." Her eyes fluttered and turned to look out the window. "But you were right about one thing," she added.

"What about?"

"The early Police stuff," she said. "*So* much better than the later stuff," she continued, lightly laughing, mostly to humor me. "I'm meeting Manju here in a few minutes, so I'll catch you later." She pushed away from the reading stand.

"Wait," I pleaded. But she either didn't hear me or pretended not to. I watched as she continued toward the study tables and sat down to her notebooks. She kept her back to me, opening one of the notebooks. She stared at it for a minute or so before I saw her draw back in her chair and hide her face in her hands. Manju hadn't arrived yet, so I took this window of opportunity to approach her.

"You can't be all cryptic with me and walk away," I whispered to her. "What happened the last couple of weeks? All that talk about your dad, what's it about?"

She put on an untroubled air, looked around to be sure we weren't attracting attention, then took out a ballpoint pen and wrote "Downstairs" on a page of her notebook. Then she got up and went casually over to the checkout counter and began searching the rack of magazines behind it, ignoring me altogether. I watched her for a few seconds, her slender figure still discernible through the folds of her blouse and her skirt as she stood with her palms propped on the edge of the counter, the heel of one foot turned over the curve of the other.

I went through the door on one side of the checkout counter, down the now-familiar steps into the dim-lit catacomb of the lower stacks. It was vacant, as usual; few students bothered to come down here. I wondered how long she would be and why she was being so secretive. On the side of one of the shelves, I read "British and American Literature" on a crimped, yellowing label.

I checked the doorway. No sign of Priya yet. So I turned into the aisle, my eyes roving the rows and rows of spines for a literary sign of America. Galsworthy, Eliot, Hopkins, Shaw, Wordsworth—all stodgy British writers we'd covered in class. Then, toward the middle of the row, along the bottom two shelves, I made a discovery—names that echoed like those of my own ancestors: Tennessee Williams, Arthur Miller, O'Neill, Hemingway, Steinbeck—names I'd come across in high school, either in classroom syllabi or in conversations with Shannon, names I'd avoided like mono or stomach flu then but which now warmed me like the summer sun. I had crouched down and begun scanning the books more closely when a shadow fell over the half-light from behind me. I turned and stood to face Priya.

"I'm getting married," she said.

"What?" I said, disbelieving, laughing tentatively. "You're only eighteen. How could you be getting married?"

"My father's arranged the whole thing. It's this guy from New York. He just got his MBA from Columbia. He's twenty-five and going to work for this Manhattan investment . . ." She trailed off as if she were absolutely uninterested in the details, weary of rehashing all of it again.

"How do you know him?" I asked carefully. The words themselves felt icy.

"My dad got us in touch last summer before college started. He came out here so we could meet." She lowered her gaze. "And I told my dad yes."

My mind stumbled around in this maze she'd dropped me in. "Why—? When?"

At least from her appearance, Priya seemed more or less composed, in control. "He's coming here over New Year's, and the wedding will be right after that."

"But how—?" I could only stand there and stare at her blankly. "Do you even know him?"

She arched an eyebrow, one side of her mouth turned down in a sneer. "I suppose." She sighed and looked away. "Anyway, he seems smart, nice enough. Handsome. It's a way out."

I pretended not to hear "handsome" but felt diminished immediately. "I didn't realize you wanted out of India so bad."

"It's not India," she said. "It's just . . . a way out."

"A way out of what?"

She didn't answer. I thought she'd walk away from me again, turn on her heels and go back upstairs. But she stayed, her eyes fixed straight ahead on the spines of books.

"I don't want you to go." It was the most intimate thing I had said to anyone in months.

Priya's eyes looked watery, and holding her gaze upward, she wiped at them.

"You're going right away?" I asked, feeling absurd even asking such a question.

"After April probably. When the school year ends. My father wants me to finish college in the States anyway." She seemed emotionless and there was a resignation to her words, and it was all hard to take.

I stared at the ground, down at emptiness and my future as gray as the floor, and exhaled deeply to get myself breathing again.

"Thought you'd be happy, Vik," Priya said and, laughing, added, "or jealous, 'cause I'll be going back to the States."

I kicked at the underside of the shelf. "Jealous, yes. But not because you're going back." My breath tightened. I soldiered on anyway. "Because of who you're going back to." Even in the dull yellow light, her face glowed; her hair, parted evenly, fell to her shoulders; her black irises gave away nothing. Why was she here now, with me? Why here, in this musty room, to tell me this?

"I hope you'll be happy," I said.

"I should go now," she said.

But she didn't move, lingered instead by the shelves. I took the chance to step toward her, tentatively, pretending to move past her but wanting only to experience a part of her: the scent of her hair, the shoulder bone beneath her shirt, the sway of her dark skirt. Then came a pressing of hands as my body crossed hers, and she turned to me.

Who went for whom, I couldn't tell. Only a flash in the mind, a burst of fire. I was aware only of the warmth of her mouth, kissing her in the secretiveness of that dim room, every second that I could; of the scent of her perfume, whatever it was, entering my senses sweetly faint and mixed with sweat and cardamom; how her body felt smaller and suppler in my hands than I had imagined. She kissed hesitantly, unsure at first; then again, so did I, every capillary in our skin trembling; then she swept in at me, on me, once, and I returned it, hair matting our mouths, not minding because the softness of her mouth against mine made me wish we could keep on and forget whether anyone was there; the thin cotton texture of her shirt below her breasts, only a hint did I get of her skin, her waist, with two nervous fingers. She did return my eagerness—if only for that moment, I sensed that much—but when I wanted more, I heard a gasp. Priya pulled away, the scent of her hair under my nose, before the thudding of feet sounded on the stairs.

Priya, flustered now, leaned her head into the aisle, her eyes on the door. She let go of her breath, her eyes closed, her body caving ever so slightly, as if a fear had been realized.

"Manju," she whispered to me.

"She see us?"

"I don't know."

"I don't care who saw us," I said, reaching for her hand, feeling righteous now. "Forget about her."

She stepped away, exposed in the aisle, then tentatively walked toward me. She did not reach for me but looked at me, a pitying look I did not understand. Then she backed away from me and disappeared. I heard her steps echo up the stairs like the thunder trailing before the sky settles and the storm moves on.

Chapter 16

Fog blanketed the wintry fields as we sped past. It was the last stretch of our overnight journey from Ahmedabad to New Delhi. My father had bought us a full berth, first class, but I had spent much of the ride out in the passageway in my sweater and scarf, leaning against the open entrance to the car with my Walkman and headphones. I thought of Priya and what she was doing just then. Was her home garlanded with marigolds and festive with visitors? I imagined her father dominating a household full of guests in saris and kurtas. Traditional Hindu marriage music snaking the air, sinuous and insinuating. Was she in a crimson wedding sari, her hands decorated with bloodred henna, the color of her lips? I wished for her lips but pushed that thought away, resentfully. She was gone. As distant as America.

America. December now in Madison. Snow powdering the branches, slushing along the edges of Whitney Way, University Avenue, the gray tufts of smoke from the stacks of the power plant near campus. I thought of the decorated shopping centers, the snow-freshened air, the glistening lights strung up on bare trees on State Street and around the perimeter of Capitol Square to make a twinkling wreath of it all, and the white marble dome at its center. I wondered if Nate and Karl were in Madison over Christmas break and who Shannon was spending it with. A new boyfriend? Sooner or later, there would be a new boyfriend. It was inevitable. Here I was, ten thousand miles away, so why was I letting it bother me? Had I stayed, where would the two of us be? I missed her, no question. I missed her graceful, freckled shoulder blade and the swerve of her waist and her mouth that often tasted of Doublemint when we should've been studying. Shannon, you were a prize. Where would the two of us be? Now, all paths diverged, and I was left with a train as it sped farther and farther into the Indian heartland and that feeling of distance between Shannon and me loomed again in the universe of my mind. Everyone blasted into separate ways, fiery flakes scattering in the night.

I had my camera at least. And I snapped photos of the bracing expanse of fields. Farmers crossed the grayness, two by two, wrapped in shawls. It was desolate country, dotted with occasional settlements, these outermost satellites of Delhi. I sighted their signposts at small whitewashed stations, bearing in black letters the undecipherable names of these far-flung places, and the gray-cloaked and narrow lanes that ran in and out of random towns before the view morphed back into farmland, peppered with tumbledown sheds and ancient field implements, all overseen by finches, blackbirds in flight.

I caught as much as I could with the click of the shutter. The frame advance wheezed and locked: end of roll. I lifted the tiny winch and began rolling the film back onto its spool, wondering whether and how any of the shots would turn out.

"Chalo, Vikram." My father poked his head out of our compartment. "Eat something. We'll be there soon."

Anand slept on the upper bunk, his back to the wall.

A steward must have come by already; there was chai steaming from a teapot, ceramic cups on a tray, and a variety of small pastries, sweet and savory, on a square steel plate. My father proceeded to pour the chai into the cups.

"Wake him up," he told my mother, "otherwise, we'll leave him here only." He turned to Anand and, in a show of fatherly authority, commanded, "Anand, get up now! Time to eat. That's it!"

Leisurely, Anand rolled onto his back and propped himself up on his elbows, surveying the food. "We almost there?" he asked groggily.

He climbed down, wearing his striped flannel pajamas, the first time he'd had to wear them since our arrival in India. My mother handed him his toothbrush and toothpaste as he slid open the door and slipped away.

"Like a mule, that boy," my father said. "Never met anyone so stubborn. Reminds me of me." He shook his head, chuckling, and my mother smirked.

I sniffed the pastry and began eating it as my father poured me a cup of chai. "You want anything else?" he asked. "They've got a breakfast menu. *Parathas*, omelet, anything?"

"It's okay, thanks." I sipped the hot, sugary chai.

A wide road with multiple lanes came into view as we passed over a short bridge. Traffic had neatly ordered itself inside the lanes. A redbrick multistory shopping complex girded with yellow railings and colonies of cement bungalows bordered the road.

"See the roads here." He pointed out the window as we passed into New Delhi.

I marveled at the glimpse of orderly traffic. "I had no idea they could have such a thing here," I said. "Ahmedabad is the exact opposite."

The clack-clack of the train slowed down now as we approached the station. A grainy mist covered everything, a kind of fog I'd never seen.

Dharmanshu Uncle met us outside the train. A stout-looking man of medium height, a tad taller than my father, he wore dark spectacles and his hair was a thick, silvery mane. A silvery mustache remained of the beard he'd once had. He greeted us in the same noble baritone I could still hear in my mind from years back. My mother hugged him for a long time, tears gathering in her eyes. He and my father shook hands warmly. Wasn't Dharmanshu Uncle cold? He wore his overcoat unbuttoned, beneath it only a shirt, and a scarf hung uselessly around his neck.

"Anand, good to finally meet you," he said.

Shyly, Anand extended his hand. Dharmanshu Uncle took it and slapped Anand jovially on the back. "Welcome, welcome," he said. "There's much I want to know about your life. How you are getting along here and all. All right?"

Anand nodded and mumbled, "Yeah."

"He's doing quite marvelously," my father said, glancing back at Anand.

"Atcha! Very good," Dharmanshu Uncle declared. "I know India must be challenge." Taking a look at us, he burst into laughter, a powerful boom from his barrel chest, and took the suitcase from my mother's hands.

It was biting cold, far colder than Ahmedabad this time of year. A patina of sunlight, filtering through the glass panes of the roof, cast thin, cold angles across the general grayness. I reached into my backpack and threw on my jacket.

Dharmanshu Uncle turned toward me. "Grown up now," he said, smiling. "How long it's been since you were last here? Ten years?"

"Eleven," my mother replied. "Yes, he looks more and more like you every day." She asked me, "Do you remember him at all?"

I told them I remembered the beard and that he had a son, older than me by a few years.

"Dilip, yes." Dharmanshu Uncle nodded his head. "He just finished his MBA in London. Now he's doing consultancy for one firm there."

"Always a brilliant boy," my father said, more to me than the others. "He was tops in his class right from"—he held out his palm at waist height—"when he was a boy."

"To me, he will always be that boy," my mother said. "I remember babysitting him, when you and Alka used to go out together."

We walked from the platform through the great cement-gray station and out into a crush of traffic. Taxi and rickshaw drivers in knit caps and sweaters, some smoking bidis, waited outside their vehicles, chattering with each other, beckoning travelers now and then as they passed by. We made for Dharmanshu Uncle's black Fiat, loaded our suitcases, and motored away into the roundabout fronting the station.

"Vikram," Dharmanshu Uncle called from the driver's seat, "I can remember you as a baby."

"Mango syrup, mango syrup," my mother said. "Do you remember?" She turned from the front seat to me, seated between Anand and my father, and pointed at Dharmanshu Uncle. "He used to put mango syrup on your cheeks, on your forehead, and we all used to lick it off of your face. You were so cute."

I felt slightly embarrassed, my father sitting there listening to this; I felt no longer myself but another person, a projection of the baby they remembered. "I can only remember the beard," I said.

"It used to scare you," my mother said. "When Dharmanshu Uncle would come near, you'd start screaming."

That got Dharmanshu Uncle laughing again, nodding at the memory.

We drove through a shopping district—sari shops, tea and juice stalls, men's tailoring, the offices of Citibank and British Airways—and into a district of housing colonies, wending around scooters and street children, the occasional congregation of cows. We turned onto a narrow gray lane lined with doorways and cluttered with bicycles and motorbikes. Dharmanshu Uncle pulled over to the side, and we all got out. The shouts of children playing could be heard from one of the flats above us, their voices tinkling like wind chimes in the air.

We lugged our baggage into a narrow room, simple, small, and cold. The paint job seemed only half-finished; a swath of blue covered the upper portion of the living room and the dining area beyond. The rest was whitewashed, smudged hastily with plaster. The bathroom, about as roomy as a phone booth, was of the Indian variety: a pear-shaped pit, a bucket, and a tap. There was a definite air of neglect about the place, and I began to wonder where Dharmanshu Uncle had been putting his civil engineer's salary all these years.

On one wall hung a framed photograph of Alka Auntie, wreathed in garlands as if she were wearing a high collar of marigolds. I knew her only from a small photo, perhaps two by three inches, taken in the late sixties. The photograph showed Alka Auntie and my mother sitting on a bench at the Taj Mahal, both smiling together like the closest of sisters. Between them, in a checked short-sleeved shirt and shorts, was five-year-old Dilip, squinting in the sun, a front tooth missing.

~ ~ ~

As we ate, the cook—a short, grizzled man in a white undershirt, pyjama pants, and flip-flops—shunted in from the kitchen to provide a steady supply of hot rotis. Dharmanshu Uncle gave the cook dinner instructions at one point and joked with him about repeatedly showing up late, at which the cook laughed shyly, nodded, and shuffled away. Mostly Dharmanshu Uncle's attention kept to the conversation as he and my parents talked—about my father's job and about the difficulties of our peripatetic life in America, and, likewise, the difficulties attending the move back to India.

I'd taken a seat next to Dharmanshu Uncle. Though my attention occasionally strayed to a Hindi soap opera that blared from the TV in the living room, I couldn't help but notice how restless he was. As he listened, his knees fidgeted, and he would compulsively brush his sleeve with his hand as if there were crumbs there or pick at his collar or at crumbs near his plate. These actions seemed mostly a way of keeping his mind occupied and distracted while he carried on the conversation. But distracted from what, I wondered. Sometimes he interrupted my father to ask a question with pressing urgency—a point of minor detail—or to make a joke. It wasn't as if he'd disappeared into his own world; Dharmanshu Uncle was very much present, he absorbed everything my parents said, and his observations about our adjusting to Indian life were keen and sensitive. But I sensed a nervous energy at his core, palpable in his every intake of breath.

Dharmanshu Uncle asked Anand and me about our schooling in America, what sorts of classes we took, the subjects we liked. He asked about American TV and cars and shopping malls. He said he wished he could buy a Ford in India and lamented the country's protectionist politics. He said the government was corrupt and useless and succeeded only in making life difficult for everyone, and if you had a shred of ambition, it was best to get out of the country.

Even as a government employee himself, he had no qualms about lambasting the babus. Almost every engineering project he had supervised had gotten whittled to a fraction of its original scale because, he said, "one or another of these bloody bastards—bureaucrat, policeman, some local *goondah*—everyone is taking baksheesh. And, along the way, all my work had to become simpler and smaller. A four-lane highway becomes two-lane after bribes are taken. The quality of concrete to make one bridge becomes degraded. Drainage pipes are poor quality because it's all that can be afforded after payoffs. All kinds of mischief."

"Can't anyone call them on it?" I asked. "This is a free country, isn't it? There's freedom of the press here—"

"Now and then, people do, but it comes to nothing." He wiped at the corner of the table with his thumb and shifted in his chair. "But if you are close to government as I am, there is risk, you see."

"You say something"—my father tsked—"and you're transferred to some backwater."

"You mean like Ghatlodiya?" Anand said.

My father emitted either a quick laugh or a hiccup, I couldn't tell. "Exactly!"

"Or," Dharmanshu Uncle said, "you are dead." The table fell silent. "I do remember a case, long time back, of a colleague who was found murdered. Right there on the railway track."

"Really?" Anand asked, his eyes bugging from his head. "Was he decapitated?"

"Body was found one night in Gurgaon." Dharmanshu Uncle smiled with an ironic wave of his hand. "Police said it was suicide." Then, pithily, he added, "It was not suicide. I don't think so." He sniffed. "In India, corruption is harder to erase than caste. It is not going anywhere. Corruption *is* caste," he added, "and vice versa."

My father nodded thoughtfully, scooping rice and dal together on his plate with his fingers. "Could be," he said, and that was all. His reluctance to sympathize with Dharmanshu Uncle disappointed me. Was he so complacent? So unwilling to admit the baser truths of life in India? It irritated me.

"Sometimes," Dharmanshu Uncle went on, twining his fingers together and looking out over the table, "I've thought it best if India was bombed"—he swiped a palm in a gesture of cancellation—"back to nothing. Get rid of all the politicians and Hindu-Muslim zealots, wipe out all trace of this mess we have made these past thousand years. That's the only hope India has if it's going to have future." He chortled to himself. "Start from scratch. Too hopeless now the way it is." He resumed eating.

My father took up a cup of buttermilk next to his plate and swirled it in his hand. "Maybe," he said. That was all.

What a violent thing to wish for, I thought, and I admired Dharmanshu Uncle for it. Here was an anger I could relate to. Could we start with bombing Xavier's College? I wanted to ask.

~ ~ ~

That week, Dharmanshu Uncle showed us around New Delhi. The government buildings along the stately Rajpath, the embassies, Parliament, Red Fort. The streets were wide, clean, the structures imperial in their symmetry. Predictable, their function preceding the imagination. In Old Delhi, though, came a rush of photographs: the pigeon-crowded terrace of the Jama Masjid, where schoolchildren flitted among worshippers and tourists; the alleyways, snared overhead by telephone wires. I snapped images of college students in maroon sweaters, hoisting backpacks, as they navigated a barricade of scooters, a cow, a telephone stand, and Muslim shopkeepers in their traditional kaftans and skullcaps. Postcard and trinket vendors, beggar children closed in on all sides. We hurried through, but I couldn't help clicking photos of the excited faces, the tangle of hands soliciting, pleading, grasping.

Chapter 17

The morning after Christmas, we waited at a corner along the Rajpath where a coach en route to the Taj Mahal in Agra stopped daily to pick up tourists. Traffic was scant along the Rajpath; Parliament and most businesses were still on holiday. Bundled in scarves and jackets against the chill, we waited along the wide avenue, where the red sand native to this region was raked smooth and flat.

I lifted my camera and, through the viewfinder, found the spectral arch of India Gate on the far end of the road. In the morning fog, it seemed as lost and lonely as the World War I dead it was meant to commemorate. The coach finally arrived, and by then enough tourists—mostly Indian couples and families—had congregated on the corner to fill most of the seats.

Dharmanshu Uncle and I sat together, my parents across the aisle from us. Anand sat in the row ahead of them, his headphones on, listening to R.E.M. tapes. I could see him gently bobbing his head, half-asleep, half listening to the music.

The coach wended through the ghostly avenues of the city. How odd it was to see Indian streets so subdued and silent, almost as if we'd landed in a parallel India. The only people on the streets at this hour were those who lived on them or in the shanties and those at the chai stalls where men sat together, clad in threadbare sweaters, some with knit caps or cloth bound about their heads against the chill.

I wondered how Karl and Nate had spent Christmas. Had Karl gotten the new word processor he'd wanted for writing his screenplays? He probably had, I guessed. Nate usually splurged all his gift money on Pogues and Ramones cassettes and Monty Python, James Bond, and *The Prisoner* videos—they threatened to take over the last inch of shelf space in his room, from what I could recall. I wondered if he would be trolling State Street today, the day after Christmas, hitting every record store from Capitol Square down to Lake Street, the lights still spangling the bare trees and the frosted glass of storefronts.

From the TV monitor installed in front of the coach, a Hindi movie came bursting out at full volume. I tried to keep my attention on the countryside while the movie's concussive soundtrack and noisy characters filled the bus. At one point, I glanced at the monitor to catch Bollywood film stars lip-syncing and gyrating their way through a swoony song-and-dance number, backdropped by some alpine dreamscape of waterfalls, pastures, and mountains. The filmmakers must've shot the footage in the Swiss Alps, a parallel universe unknown to me and, it was safe to say, to anyone else on the bus.

The other passengers stared expressionlessly at the monitor. They seemed neither entertained nor repelled by what they saw; the movie was just a distraction to be consumed, a way to kill time before Agra. I slouched back down, put on my headphones, and popped a Midnight Oil tape into my Walkman. Shannon had bought it for me the night before my leaving.

While the drums thumped and horns screeched like howling outback winds and Peter Garrett lamented our dancing and our

Earth's turning in the face of so much injustice, we found ourselves out in the open Indian country, roaring past an expanse of marigolds, sunflowers, and wheat fields. It was a view of the real India, not the Bollywood India. A lovely India that I imagined sharing with Shannon, Karl, Nate. The music brought them here with me.

~ ~ ~

We stopped for lunch outside Agra at what turned out to be a traditional South Indian restaurant (though here we were in North India). Our group crowded into a plain, low-ceilinged hall patrolled by servers with pots of *sambhar*, coconut chutney, and chilies. We sat shoulder-to-shoulder at long tables—the whole place looked not unlike the mess hall at Xavier's—where we found banana leaves and small copper bowls set out for each of us. Servers ladled sambhar into the bowls, the condiments onto the banana leaves.

The savory redolence of *dosas* and spiced potatoes filled the room, mixing with the pungent sambhar. The dosas, which resembled sleeves as long as a forearm, were stuffed with potatoes and perfectly crispy. I cautiously sipped the sambhar. Never in my life had I tasted anything that hot: one sip was like a stick of dynamite had gone off in my mouth. These guys made the real deal.

Dharmanshu Uncle, sitting next to me, noticed me gulping down my bottled water. He asked me if I'd had any trouble getting used to the Indian food.

"My mother's right," I said. "It tastes better here than it does there." I set the water bottle down, nearly empty now. "But I won't lie. I do miss hamburgers. *Real* hamburgers."

He laughed. "You're in the wrong country for that."

Anand sipped the last of the Limca from the bottle he'd ordered and asked my father for another. As my father tried to hail down one of the servers, I turned to Dharmanshu Uncle and asked if he'd ever wanted to travel to the States.

"Once upon a time," he said. "In the sixties. I loved America. Lots of idealism back then, you could say." He straightened in his seat. "Especially in college. I wanted to go for my engineering degree or begin my career there. I used to study schematics, the city layouts, you see," he said with a flourish of his hand, "of New York, London, to see from ground up how these cities were functioning. Sewer systems, subways. I studied these cities, and then I would make up designs of my own cities. Built from scratch. Cities I wanted to build for India."

I told him I would love to see those designs.

He waved his hand from side to side. "Those are all gone now." After a pause, he went on, his voice lowered, more thoughtful. "When Dilip was nine, well after my degree, and I was working for Delhi municipality, I was offered a position there, one urban planning firm in New York." He then turned his attention back to his meal laid out on the banana leaf and began nimbly tearing pieces of the dosa and dipping it into the sambhar.

"But you didn't go," I said.

"Things change," he said, "when you least expect." He stared off, pondering his words. After a moment, he cleared his throat and turned to Anand, who sipped from a new chilled Limca bottle. He joked with Anand about not being able to handle the spiciness of the food and asked him what his favorite American foods were. Soon they fell into conversation about baseball versus cricket and Coca-Cola versus Thums Up.

As before, Dharmanshu Uncle was lively and talkative but disengaged somehow, restless, as if this wasn't so much a conversation as a means of distraction. He wasn't here in the moment but racing in his mind, still running to stay ahead of . . . whatever it was.

~ ~ ~

Agra, home to the Taj Mahal, was a smaller city than Ahmedabad but just as noisy and disarrayed: traffic spilled in from everywhere, weaving in and out past cows, carts, and pedestrians. It was a tumbledown city, a far cry from the Mughal principality it used to be. I wondered what Dharmanshu Uncle must've thought of it.

"Story here is the same as everywhere in India," he told me. "Too much population, too many are moving into cities."

"So the government just can't keep up, huh?"

Dharmanshu Uncle fixed his stare out the bus window. "Not that it *can't*. It's just indifference, you see. We have the money, materials, know-how to keep pace with roads, drainage, bridges, so forth. But these politicians—my bosses—simply don't care. They let things turn to this." He gestured to the chaos outside the windows. "Sometimes, whole neighborhoods go up without any planning."

"Must get frustrating for you," I said.

"Not so much now," he said. "Not anymore."

The murmuring among the other tourists on the coach became livelier, and the monitor switched off (to my relief). My mother kept her eyes shut, and my father sipped chai from the thermos he'd brought along. Anand, by now, was intently watching the scenery, fascinated by the frenzy all around us.

We pulled into a roundabout, some distance from the road, where we parked and began filing off the bus. Everyone chattered excitedly, relieved and glad to have arrived. I had never seen the Taj Mahal, and beyond the pictures of it on postcards and in movies, I had no idea what to expect.

The moment we got off the coach, we found ourselves in the line of fire of an army of hawkers: young boys and men peddling postcards, miniature photo albums, trinkets of the Taj. We passed a wrought-iron gate and walked through a tree-lined paved pathway that offered some shade from the sharp late-afternoon sun. We joined a procession of tourists filing through the gate with an air of solemn expectation, as if we were all pilgrims on our way to some holy spring.

I snapped a picture of gray, surly-looking macaques that had taken over an entire bench. A few ate morsels of food dropped by passersby; others stared out at us haughtily, perched on the bench or the trees above.

A boy about my age, hawking postcards, trotted up next to me. "Postcards, sir, postcards, very nice." He held up a clutch of them, all of them dull and shabby. I bought a couple of them for five rupees. Before he took off, I told him, "One minute," and raised the camera, clicked off a photo. I did it quickly, before he knew what was happening and started posing. He smiled—"Thank you, sir"—and went away.

Anand scanned above the line of trees as we walked on. "I don't see it. How far away is it?"

The moment he said it was when we saw it. The finial, topped by the Islamic crescent, appeared like a secret above a high crenellated wall.

I got my camera ready as we passed through a gate into a stone-paved courtyard fringed by rosebushes and other garden flowers. We stopped at a massive gateway, all stone and marble, with two small decorative arches on each side and an enormous one in the center. Guards—army soldiers with guns—stationed within the archway frisked everybody and directed us to metal lockers set up to one side, where we stashed bags and purses.

That's when I turned and caught my first glimpse, through the archway, into a celestial otherworld.

The sun hit the Taj's marble dome full force, setting the whole structure and the minarets at each corner of the white plinth on fire.

Whatever this was, I thought, it did not belong among us. A shimmering ark brought down to Earth. For an instant, I floated away, above myself, and thought I was looking at an exquisitely carved mountain of moon rock.

It was more than the mind could take in at once. More than any camera could take in, for sure. Postcards and movies did not do this place justice; no photograph could.

We descended the steps on the other side of the gateway and entered a sprawling space. Visitors thronged the pathways that flanked the long clear pool that stretched from where we stood to the Taj in the far distance. Stands of low cypresses bordered the pool. There were pathways fringed with zigzag ornamentation, dividing evenly an enormous expanse of lawns and bursts of trees. Families sat on the grass, strolled the lawns and the pathways. On the plinth, hundreds of people as tiny as ants crawled about the base of the Taj and the minarets.

"Guide? You all need guide?" inquired a stocky, bossy man with a beard, wearing a knit cap and a sweater over his kurta pyjama. He chucked his bidi away as he descended the steps of the gateway toward us. "I am tour guide here." He spread his arms as if to encompass the whole place. "Happy to show you 'round. Not much fee."

In Hindi, Dharmanshu Uncle told him we didn't need him, at which the man, unfazed, turned to offer his services to other visitors stepping in from the gateway.

Turned out Dharmanshu Uncle knew a fair amount about the Taj Mahal. He told us that in the Taj's seventeenth-century heyday, the gardens covered ten times the present area, that they were once lush with fruit trees, towering palms, and cypresses, as thick as a forest. But then after the fall of the Mughals, it all fell into disrepair and the Victorians razed the forest and built gardens to resemble their own manicured English lawns, totally incongruous with the surrounding landscape, culture, architecture. He took a deep breath and scanned the Taj grounds. "This place was really something before that. Three hundred years back."

"It still is," I offered, "wouldn't you say?"

Nodding, he replied, "It puts many of our own civic projects to shame. That's true."

We stopped at the marble water tank at the center of the grounds, where the north-south and east-west pathways bisected, and Dharmanshu Uncle pointed out the symmetries all around us. He pointed to the gateway and how its alcoves and massive archways were built to mirror perfectly those on the facade of the Taj. "And see there," he said, holding out both arms toward red sandstone structures with domed roofs and arched entrances on either side of the Taj, "on west you'll find a mosque and on east you'll see an identical structure."

"Another mosque?" I asked.

"No one knows what that structure was for. It's a mystery," he said, "but it gives perfect counterpoint to the mosque." He swept his hand across the panorama. He was right: the mosque, the Taj, the mystery structure—harmony on a scale I'd never witnessed. He turned around and pointed out how the gardens were divided into quadrants and these quadrants subdivided into four perfectly sectioned lawns. Visitors lounged there now or strolled among them with children. I imagined when the lawns were full of peacocks, parakeets flitted between the trees, and noblemen, priests, and scholars enjoyed the mango- and jasmine-scented air. "It all follows the Mughal aesthetic," he said. "Finely developed over centuries and centuries."

"And what were the Indians—I mean, the Hindus doing all this time?" I asked.

"This is not just an Islamic structure," Dharmanshu Uncle said. "Many think so, but you'll find many Hindu elements. The spire on the dome"—he pointed to the peak of the Taj—"was designed to resemble Shiva's trident. And the carvings of the *chhatris*"—he indicated the ornate kiosks that stood like smaller siblings on four sides of the great dome—"are very much like what you see on medieval Hindu temples and the Rajput palaces in Rajasthan. The Taj is really a pan-Indian structure. Pan-*Asian* structure, in fact. Materials are here from all over India, China, Persia, Sri Lanka, even Caspian Sea."

"Who knew India produced such an international building," I said as we moved from the water tank and made our way toward the plinth.

"The *great* international building," Dharmanshu Uncle replied, "before there was such a thing."

The light on the Taj shifted, mellowed, the dome glowing like a desert flower in bloom. I could see the marblework clearly, the tiling of the dome evidence of the involvement of human hands. The alcoves resembled half-closed eyes as the shadows within them lengthened, and the whole facade gradually felt more mysterious, more romantic as the sun began to set.

Anand and I walked on ahead, past the lingering tourists—I heard German, Japanese, and English, along with the polyglot of Indian languages. I trained my camera on the Taj. Took pictures like everybody else—framing the dome and the minarets on either side. *Click. Click. Click.* It felt pointless, though; there was just too much in the frame, too many intricacies to be captured; it was like trying to snare the moon with a butterfly net.

Following a train of tourists, we handed in our shoes to a kindly clerk in exchange for a claim ticket and mounted the steps to the plinth with its great veined marble floor. We walked all around the soaring perimeter of the Taj. Our necks got sore from staring upward at the vaulted archway and the calligraphy engraved along the ornate framework.

We took in as much as our eyes could, and it wasn't long before I had to load a new roll of film into the camera. A guard reprimanded

Anand for trying to clamber onto the low ledge of one of the alcoves for a look through a window.

The wide angles weren't doing it; the minarets, the archways, the spandrels and kiosks—all that loomed off each side of the great dome seemed territory already covered in millions of generic picture postcards. I wanted something different, what didn't occur immediately, the drama of the minute, the unexpected.

I drew in close and got at the sinews of the Persian engravings, the delicate herringbone of the minaret that divided the sun-touched marble from the steel blue of the sky, the play of light and dark in the high hollows of the archways.

Behind the Taj is where I found the gold-pink ribbon of the Yamuna River unspooling into the far distance of farmland. Across the Yamuna, villagers walked along the riverbank—women with pots on their heads, vibrant saris trailing behind them. I snapped pictures of them and of Anand looking out over the plinth against the stark earth in the far country and the line of trees along the riverbank.

For perhaps the first time since coming to India, I felt a flush of privilege at being here, a discovery of heritage that I felt proud to share with everyone in the world, with all who were here, all whom I'd left behind and held close to my heart. What a strange feeling.

"You know," I said, "if we had a boat, we could get out there. This camera is no good this far out."

Anand nodded vaguely, humming a tune, something else on his mind. "Definitely," he said. "You think from here to the far side of the river is about the distance from home plate to the center-field bleachers at County Stadium?"

I eyeballed the distance. "I'd say so," I said.

"So, Mr. Photographer," Dharmanshu Uncle called from behind us. "Did you take any good snaps?"

"We'll see," I said, "soon enough."

"You wish to become photographer, is it?"

I looked at the old Minolta in my hands. "I've shot some Super Eight and video," I said, "but never really shot still pictures before I came here." I described to him the photos I'd taken over Diwali, the ones I'd taken so far on this trip.

"If you enjoy it," he said, "go as far as you can with it."

He stared out over the riverfront. I sensed he was negotiating a difficult thought.

"At first, Alka was against going to America," he said, half to himself. "'This is our country,' she would say. 'Why leave it and raise Dilip where there is no family?' She had a point, but finally I convinced her to go. The firm in New York was ready to sponsor my green card. We had visa, passport. We were only a week away from leaving." He sighed. "Then came Alka's accident."

I remembered my mother's recollections of the telegram she'd received from Dharmanshu Uncle. There had been a road accident. Dharmanshu Uncle and Alka Auntie had been riding his scooter when a bus collided with them. He was okay save for a few injuries, but she had died instantly. We boarded the next train from Ahmedabad to Delhi. Being three years old when it happened, I had no memory of the event nor had I personally felt the shock and grief. But my heart had felt their echoes many times over the years as my mother recalled the story, and now it was as if the memory were my own.

"After she left us," he said, "I told myself I would do my best to make good on Alka's wishes to stay on here. Honestly, America, India . . . it made no difference to me then."

"But don't you think Alka Auntie would've wanted you to go?"

He sniffed, pondering my question, and stared straight ahead. "Yes. But you realize only after you have lost someone how much that person truly meant. Without Alka and to raise Dilip in America without her, no, it didn't feel right to me."

I weighed in my mind whether to ask him my next question. "Did you ever regret not going?"

He nodded, then added, "Thankfully, the toughest years are behind me, when the thought of leaving India was most strong. And now Dilip is a success, so there is satisfaction in that too."

Dharmanshu Uncle hadn't spoken much of Dilip during our visit. "When was the last time you saw him?" I asked.

"Before he left," he said. "Diwali eighty-four, just before London."

"You haven't seen him since?" I blurted out, instantly feeling I'd breached a boundary.

Dharmanshu Uncle smiled, keeping his stare straight ahead. "Maybe one day."

I heard Anand making whooshing sounds, imitating crowd noises, and muttering in his monotonous sports-announcer's voice. He stood in a batter's stance at the edge of the plinth, swinging an imaginary baseball bat, knocking home run shots over the Yamuna River. "Pretend baseball again?"

"Molitor just hit a grand slam, bottom of the ninth." He beamed, both arms raised exultantly.

"And the Brewers just won their ninety-fifth World Series," I said.

My parents approached. Taking the jacket draped over her arm, my mother slipped it on over her salwaar kameez. They walked close together, and my mother took my father's arm.

Dharmanshu Uncle touched my shoulder and leaned toward me. "To you I would only say go as far as you can with what you love. And start quick, hmm? Youth is brief."

~ ~ ~

The five of us stood on the plinth side by side for a while, quietly watching the villagers across the river. Small children scampered, shouting and playing among the women who washed clothes at the riverbank, dipping their pots into the water. It seemed serene, ancient, a world apart.

"You got so quiet," my mother said. "What you men were discussing?"

"Man talk," Dharmanshu Uncle joked. "That's all."

"He was telling me more about the Taj Mahal," I said, then asked Dharmanshu Uncle, "How do you know so much about this place?"

"What I know, I picked up from her." He jerked a thumb toward my mother. "Only she forgets, but I remember." He tapped his index finger against his temple.

"From Mummi?" I asked, surprised, and turned to her. "Were you so interested in the Taj Mahal?"

"That was long time ago," she said, casting a reflective glance at Dharmanshu Uncle. "I was here with you and Alka, I think so. Twenty years back."

"Is that when that picture was taken?" I asked. "The one of you, Alka Auntie, and Dilip?"

Her eyes widened as if the memory had blinked like a flashbulb in her mind. "Final year of college, yes," she said. "I came here to do research." She explained it was to gather data for a research paper on Mughal architecture. "I spent that day drawing sketches, taking pictures. All different details of the Taj."

"What was all that research for?" I asked.

"They were giving architecture scholarship to the two top papers," Dharmanshu Uncle said.

"Wait," Anand said, interrupting his own daydream. "You were an architect?"

"I was *almost* an architecture *student*," my mother said. "I got the scholarship but didn't take."

"Oh, no," I heard myself say.

"I told her we can wait to get married," my father said. "The school was in Delhi, so we would have been apart for a while, but I didn't mind . . ."

"Water under the bridge," she said.

"Our father," explained Dharmanshu Uncle, turning to me, "he was a man of different generation, different time, let us say." One side of his mouth turned up in a wry smile. "Neera, your mother, had already turned down two marriage offers, and both our parents were very upset."

"Not so," my mother cut in. "If Father were so conservative, he would have insisted on that arranged match. But he didn't make any fuss."

My father began to say something, but my mother interrupted, a tad vehemently. "And it was not a good time under that roof. No one will know but me the home I came back to after that Delhi trip. Mother was on her last breath, and Father . . . his spirit was gone."

Dharmanshu Uncle nodded contemplatively.

"Did you feel guilty?" I asked. "I mean for turning down the match?"

"More than guilty." My mother cast a glance at my father, her arm locked in his. "I remember feeling I had disappointed both of them. And mostly angry at myself for that. It was not a good time."

"That I remember," my father said. "But . . . did you want to get married out of guilt or because you really wanted to?"

My mother considered that, an eyebrow arched for a moment. "Guilt," she said.

"Hmm." My father considered this solemnly.

"But marrying *you* out of love," my mother added, pressing herself against my father, smiling warmly.

"But those sketches you did that day," Dharmanshu Uncle said, punctuating his point with a wave of his hand, "they were beautiful."

"She's always been that artistic type," my father said. "Always sketching and designing in those early days."

"I had no idea," I said. "Couldn't you have gone back to it after you got married?"

"My heart was not in it then, I don't think." She shook her head. "Then I had you, and everything changed. I cannot even remember now. So long ago." She withdrew her arm from my father's and pulled her jacket around her shoulders, gazing across the river.

That moment, I sensed a desert in her heart. A desert years and years from end to end, spanning between this moment and that day, twenty years ago, when she last visited the Taj Mahal.

Far upriver, a lone fisherman hauled up a length of line into his small boat. His movements were barely perceptible from that distance, and the boat on the glassy river was still as a heron eyeing its prey.

Dharmanshu Uncle's words echoed in my mind. *Youth is brief.* "I would've taken that scholarship," I said.

~ ~ ~

On New Year's Eve, on the crowded platform of the train station, Dharmanshu Uncle kissed my mother on the cheek, gave her a warm hug. The Rajdhani Express waited on the tracks as passengers boarded.

Anand and I bent down and touched Dharmanshu Uncle's feet, and he gave us his blessing.

My mother wiped her eyes dry. "Only we missed Alka," she said, half to herself.

"She was here," Dharmanshu Uncle said. "By remembering her, she is here." He spun around to face us and, in his generous baritone, addressed us: "So, boys, come by on your summer vacation.

We'll go on grand tour of Sikkim, Darjeeling. You just write me if you're coming, hmm? Rahul bhai, don't hesitate."

"Of course, of course," my father said. They slapped each other on the shoulders, and my father thanked him.

Anand nodded, smiling. "You sure?"

"Why not?" Dharmanshu Uncle said. "I take holiday every March-April. I can give you driving tour of some of the roadworks and bridges on which I have worked."

From the loudspeakers came the station announcer's litany of garble about incoming trains, arrivals times, distant destinations. My father said we'd better get on board.

"I'm only sorry Dilip could not be here to share," my mother said and proceeded (I sensed) delicately, "You should visit him in London. He would like to see you, I'm sure."

"Perhaps," Dharmanshu Uncle said, a note of skepticism in his voice. "He's only begun his job there. He may not have time for an old man visiting."

We gathered our luggage together. "It's been a real pleasure, Dharmanshu bhai, after so many years," my father said, hoisting up a shoulder bag.

"Happy New Year," I said to Dharmanshu Uncle, and, taking up my suitcase, moved toward the train.

"One minute," I heard him say. "Here you go." From his coat pocket, he pulled out two envelopes and gave one to Anand and one to me. There was a hundred-rupee note and a one-rupee coin in each of them. Dharmanshu Uncle clapped our shoulders. "New Year gift," he said.

We said our good-byes and stepped onto the train. As I boarded, I was surprised by the feeling that Dharmanshu Uncle was a kind of cautionary tale. In him, there had been joy and ambition and dreams—that was clear from our conversations. But he spoke of his dreams in the past tense, and that made me anxious as I considered my own future. Could that one day be me?

In two days, I would be back to Xavier's. Back to the doldrums of its lectures, the essay-cribbing from tattered textbooks, the anxious waiting for word—any word—from home, the need to determine what I must do. A new year would soon begin. But already, somehow, it felt old.

We arranged our things in our compartment and took our seats. Dharmanshu Uncle and my mother spoke together at the window. He joked with her, recalling something from when they were kids; advised my father about how best to file his income tax; and told me he enjoyed our company. We waved good-bye to Dharmanshu Uncle as the train heaved forward, clack-clacking along the station platform. He watched us depart, keeping his hand raised, waving good-bye as the train put distance between us. He dropped his hand finally as we receded. But he did not move, only stared at a spot of ground at his feet.

Chapter 18

We got back to Ahmedabad on midmorning of New Year's Day. Before I even unpacked or went downstairs to check the mailbox, I opened the top drawer of my desk and took out the Wisconsin admissions booklet.

From behind the half-closed door to my parents' bedroom across the hallway, I heard them unpacking their suitcases, the clanking of clothes hangers, the opening and closing of the metal cabinet. I heard their muffled voices over the filmi music on the radio—a frolicsome number probably from an early-sixties movie that made me imagine Dev Anand and his heroine in a swishing sari romping across a Himalayan pasture.

"What's he sitting on all his savings for?" I heard my father ask. "His house is bare-bones. Lives like he's making a clerk's salary."

"If it bothered you so much, we won't go there again, okay?"

"Did I say it bothered me?"

"Maybe he's saving his earnings for retirement, I don't know. He won't tell me anything. Never has." More unpacking. "Saving for retirement. Something I wish we could have started long ago—"

"Stop that *bakwas*. Things are not the same now. How many times must I say it?"

"Sorry," my mother sighed. "I don't know. To be honest, how he and Dilip are relating these last four years, I have my doubts. Hardly any contact with his own son except a few lines in postcards. Really since Alka died, they're like this. Never close."

"Gotten worse it seems," my father said. "All that angry talk about India, doesn't mix with anyone anymore. His life is in standstill."

"He's given up. Is that what you think?"

"That's the feeling I get," my father answered. "Don't think I don't remember the way he used to be. That's what struck me this time. That feeling he's in limbo."

I strained to hear more, but all I got were the needling violins and pattering tablas and then the crooner's high voice coming from the radio. "What is he waiting for?" I heard my father say. "Future doesn't make itself."

Their voices fell quiet after that. I took a deep breath, and turning my attention to the booklet in my hands, I detached the application from its spine. Before I knew it, I'd begun filling out the form. It felt absurd, silly—I didn't have the grades, I didn't have the money—but I knew I had to do this. I had to get back to America. I couldn't languish here forever. And the future didn't make itself.

~ ~ ~

December 28, 1988

Dear Vik,

Happy New Year. On cue, Madison's in its post-Christmas deep freeze. I've spent a lot of the break so far watching a ton of films—Fellini, Godard, Polanski mostly. Otherwise, I've been tooling around campus with Nate, at the Union mostly where it's warm while the students are all gone and the place is still deserted.

So, here's the scoop. Before break, Bridget told me she was having doubts about us. Says she's not ready for a serious relationship. Go figure. And she's the one who got us started down this road in the first place. I didn't know what to tell her except that she should use the break to figure out her feelings. But I still care for her, and I'm not sure how I'd handle it if she killed the relationship. So I've been slumming a bit. How's the woman situation at your end? You've mentioned a girl you liked but no details—any progress in that department? (Nate and I think we know who it is from the pics you sent a couple of months ago and, if we're right, we agree: She's hot.)

Hope you enjoyed your trip out to Delhi. Can't wait to see more pics. I loved what you sent of your Diwali celebrations. You say it's not much of a camera, but if that's true, I think your eye more than makes up for it. Keep 'em coming.

Your last couple of letters have sounded a bit, I don't know, aloof. I do think there's a lot for you here if you do decide to come back. Though I know there are hurdles to jump through, right? Admissions, finances, etc. Let me know what I can do, and I'll do it. I'm sending a mix of Warren Zevon, Kate Bush, and Camper Van Beethoven. You'll dig it.

Write soon,
Karl

~ ~ ~

It took me a week to finish filling out the Wisconsin application—getting a copy of my midterm grade report alone took three days. But finally, after dusting off and refurbishing one of my old college-entrance essays, I gathered it all up into an envelope and breathed a sigh of relief. At the very least, applying might give me fleeting hope, something to break the dismal routine of the next few months. I figured I could seal the application up and mail it out quietly, and no one would be the wiser. It was a long shot, so why bring my parents into it? But as I signed it, I noticed in fine print a note below the dotted line reminding me of an application fee: fifteen dollars. *Shit.*

I found my parents in the living room, watching episodes that they had recorded of *The Mahabharata* TV serial. Me, I couldn't stand the show, all that loud acting and in-your-face theatrics. I groaned and considered backing out of the room, but my purpose held. The application in my hand, I took a seat.

On TV, armies in chariots massed on a chroma-keyed battlefield, the orange banners snapping in the studio's fan-driven wind. Foot soldiers stamped their spears on the sand-strewn studio floor, and the blowing of conch shells rang across the sound track.

"I need to borrow some money," I began. "Er, would you mind if . . . ?"

"Not now, Vikram." My father fixed his gaze on the TV screen.

I left the application on the coffee table and walked back to my room. Leaving it like that was a risky move; I'd just laid down a landmine in front of him. But, if I was going to do this, I needed to face the brunt of his reaction ASAP. I didn't have time to dance around the topic and miss the application deadline.

My father had frowned on the idea of my staying behind in Wisconsin and attending whatever college would take me. He couldn't afford it then and probably couldn't afford it now. I would find the money myself (if I even got in, that is). Still, I feared his reaction could be worse this time. The gathering storm of words formed in my mind: *"You just refuse to give this a chance, Vikram. We live here now; get used to it . . . I will not have you going back to the place that ruined you . . . Your behavior in America was despicable . . . The answer is no."*

That's when I would throw his own words back at him: *The future doesn't make itself.* I was trying to carve out a future with this, and he had to respect that. I wasn't the same kid anymore. Wasn't that obvious to him? How could he continue to hold a grudge? To mistrust a son who'd more than proven his worth?

Why should anyone else have such a say in my future? I didn't ask to be born any more than I'd asked to go to America or to come back here. Any more than Priya had asked to marry a man she barely knew.

Was making your own future such a freedom struggle?

I began to wonder about Priya. I'd said nothing about her to anyone since that moment in the deep dark of the library. But all through Christmas break, I couldn't escape her. I looked out my room's open doors to the balcony as the afternoon light mellowed to evening. Priya was probably married by now. Maybe she and her new husband were honeymooning somewhere. She was not in my world anymore. At least I would see her in college. Hearing her voice might even be enough—that lovely accent that brought me home.

Shannon too. Not a word from her in months. We were out of each other's orbits completely. And I realized I'd have to settle for the memory of lying together on her bed, the memory of what we did but now regretting what we did *not* do. She had wanted to do it, but I couldn't. Fine work, Vik. What are you, a monk? Why don't you go join a monastery like your friend Devasia? You would be a perfect little monk. Couldn't bring yourself to have sex with Shannon when you knew, she told you, she wanted it. What's the matter with you?

Shame, wasn't it? The thought of your parents so devastated, bottomed out, at the police station to pick up their delinquent son. I was spared jail time that night, but wasn't shame another kind of jail time? Jail time you imposed on yourself? Nothing to be done about it now. Eleven more weeks of college lay ahead, eleven weeks of rote and drift. Then the finals. Then the goddamn April-May-June of summer before the monsoon again. Then another year of Xavier's. And another.

I went out to the balcony. The air gritty and the breeze cool. On University Road, traffic droned and clattered. A bus roared past, a rusting obscenity, its horn sounding like geese gone berserk. The tailpipe of a putt-putting rickshaw backfired. Streetlights blinked on along the road and above the dusty shopping plaza. Bollywood pop music blared from speakers mounted on a truck plastered with Hindi movie posters, parked in the plaza directly below a streetlight. A man set up a canopy attached to the side of the truck and began piling music cassettes on a table. The evening crowds arrived.

"Here you go."

I started. My father had appeared behind me on the balcony. He held out the check for fifteen dollars and the application to me. "Just let me know what you need, and we'll take this one step at a time." Then he walked away, back through the door and to his *Mahabharata* program.

I stood there, stunned, aware only of a sudden peace in place of what I fully expected would be a tense confrontation. *Let me know what you need*, he'd said. *We'll take this one step at a time.*

What would I need? He'd given me everything by just saying those words.

I stared at the check, grateful, and noticed it was drawn on the University of Wisconsin Credit Union. I guessed we hadn't cut our ties to America completely.

~ ~ ~

Back at college, I came across no sign of Priya. Each day I expected her to show up, to catch sight of her in Varma's or Sridharan's lectures or, if not there, then in the library. But she was gone and stayed gone.

I would see Manju and Hannah regularly, but something held me back from approaching either of them. I did notice that they stared at me coldly or made marked attempts to avoid me. I didn't really care—Manju and Hannah didn't matter much to me. I figured they knew what had happened between Priya and me; maybe Manju had seen us together that afternoon under the library. So I didn't find their aloofness toward me surprising. What held me back was my fear that if I asked them about Priya, their sure-to-be-snide replies would only confirm what I suspected—that she was never coming back.

One day, sitting in my customary spot in French class (a bench toward the back), I noticed Harish Rajkumar—old Ferret Face himself—saunter in with a slip of paper, dressed in the clerk's garb of a short-sleeved shirt with a ballpoint pen tucked into the breast pocket. Madame Varma took the paper from him, set down her textbook, put on her half-glasses dangling from a chain. She inspected the note.

"Vikram Mistry," she said, taking off her glasses. "Principal wanting to see you."

What could the principal want with me? I braced myself, shoved my books inside my bag, and went out, following Rajkumar.

We walked along the veranda, Rajkumar keeping a brisk pace. "You are Rahul bhai's son, no?" He grinned at me, punishing me with the sight of his nubby brown teeth, his eyes becoming slits behind his enormous glasses. Whether his manner was malicious or ingratiating I could not tell.

I told him I was.

"How your father is doing?"

"Fine. Very busy."

"Hmm . . . sure, sure."

The air buzzed with the murmurs of students in the quad and the slap of Rajkumar's heels against his sandals as he walked.

Rajkumar continued, "Rahul bhai was very studious, always like that. Are you like that also?" There was a petty, ironic tone to his question.

"No," I said, "I'm the exact opposite."

We arrived at the foyer to the principal's office. I had started to walk on through when Rajkumar's voice stopped me.

"At Xavier's, boys and girls must behave themselves," he said. "Otherwise you are out." He nodded, closing his eyes sagely, and continued back to the rat's maze of the college office.

I didn't bother pondering Rajkumar's words. He wasn't worth it. I knocked on the crackled-glass paneling on the door. A plate below the panel read "Father D'Souza, Principal."

"Yes?" a muddy voice answered. I walked in.

"You wanted to see me?" I said. "Vikram Mistry, FYBA?"

Seated at his desk, Father D'Souza looked exactly like the picture in the college office. His head was a fireplug with a pair of black spectacles and thick, silvery hair parted with military precision.

"Oh yes, oh yes." He sounded as if his mouth were stuffed full of cotton. For a moment D'Souza stared about his desk with an absentminded air before he folded his hands, assuming a solemn expression. His bulldog cheeks hung gloomily on either side of his tight, downturned mouth.

Just as I sat down, D'Souza stood up. I debated in my mind whether to stand back up but decided to stay put and play it cool. Folding his hands behind his back, D'Souza turned his round-shouldered bulk around to the barred window that looked out on the trees and shrubbery fronting the college. The bleached-out afternoon light angled sharply into the room, directly into my face.

"Mr. Mistry," he said, "I've received complaints about you from a fellow student."

"Complaint? Who complained—?"

"Name is not important, Mr. Mistry. What is important is that you understand that you are not in America now, you are in different culture, and you must respect the customs of our culture." The syllables spilled from his mouth like marbles. "So when I hear that you and a certain female here are not conducting yourselves in a decent manner, I am forced to take action."

"I am sorry" was all I could muster.

D'Souza pivoted toward me. "Mr. Mistry, at Xavier's"—he raised his downturned palms side by side—"we want to discourage boy-girl pairing." The palms slid away from each other. "It is okay for boys and girls to mingle in groups, but when they pair up, it tends to interrupt the flow of college life and academic progress. I am not just saying this to reprimand you, Mr. Mistry. We have proof of this." I wondered what proof. "This rule we enforce for the social and emotional health of Xavierites. It is also consistent with our Indian culture. You seem not to understand that."

Just then Rajkumar strode in through a side door, from the college office.

"Just needing your stamp, sir," he said obsequiously, laying a sheet of paper on the desk. He took a step back and waited, eyes lowered.

D'Souza grunted, reached for his inkpad, and began thumping the document with the stamp. Then he picked up a fountain pen and signed in several places. As he did this, Rajkumar shot a quick glance at me, closed his eyes, and shook his head.

Rajkumar took the document from D'Souza and spun around with a "Thank you kindly, sir." He threw me another look, and faintly, so I could hear it, tsked a few times as he trotted out the side door.

D'Souza sat back down, hatched his meaty fingers together, and trained his pig eyes at me. "So where does this leave us? Suspension. Probation. What choice do I have?"

Suspension, did he say? Probation? I sensed my life, my Wisconsin college application, vanishing into the black depths. "Father D'Souza," I began, my brain reeling, "I apologize for my conduct, and whatever distress my actions with another student may have caused a fellow Xavierite. My action was stupid, insensitive, thoughtless. I request humbly that you take into account that this has been a jarring shift for me and make an exception. You are right. This is not America. And for a brief moment, I lost sight of that. But I promise from here on in to keep the reputation of Xavier's in mind and to be respectful"—I grasped for the words, felt I was losing steam—"of our cultural . . . of our culture. I would be grateful if you would do that." Did I just use the word "Xavierite"? I felt like a cheap, spineless whore, but it had to be done.

D'Souza studied his thumbs. "Your records show you are doing well thus far." Then, with a sigh, he looked at me. "If I find you are back in this office again, for any reason, you will find your standing in grave jeopardy. The complaint lodged against you has put you in the dock. Is that understood, Mr. Mistry?"

"Absolutely, sir."

"You may go."

I got up, gripped my book bag in my hand. "Thank you, sir."

I walked out, my shoulders hunched contritely, keeping my gaze on the ground. As I returned to French class, I felt numb, in shock, like I'd escaped the firing squad.

~ ~ ~

After my French lecture, I followed Manju across the quad. She swayed along in her lime-green salwaar kameez, chattering with Hannah, taller than Manju with her European skin and her chestnut hair cut short. They talked closely, chuckled together. Before they entered the canteen, I called out, "Manju."

She turned and the grin dropped from her face. I stepped up to her, faced her. "Did you go to the principal and say something about me?"

Manju's eyes flared up for an instant, her mouth parted in shock. "I did not say anything to the principal." But something in how she darted her eyes away added to my suspicion.

"If you want to ruin people's lives, I wish you'd pick someone other than me."

She sneered. "And look who ruined Priya's life! Her future was all set, she liked the boy she was going to marry, and you had to start toying with her."

Hannah stood to the side, glowering at me, an implacable statue.

"I wasn't toying with anyone," I said, lowering my voice. "Priya's her own person. She does what she wants with her own damn life. Or is that too crazy an idea?" I wanted to get away from the stares I was drawing from the canteen, but the implications of Manju's words struck me. *The boy she was going to marry.* "Wait," I tried, "did Priya not get married?"

"Let's go, Manju," Hannah said, touching Manju's elbow, but Manju swiped her arm away and glared at me.

"No, she did not. Her fiancé found out about her running around with other boys and called off the wedding."

This was turning into one of those overblown Doordarshan soap operas my mother watched in the evenings. I was stunned. "Who told him?" I gave Manju an accusing glance.

"Priya did so herself," she said brusquely. "She wanted to be honest with him." She took a step toward me. "And if you don't like our culture, why don't you get out of here? We don't want any of you Indians here thinking you're so superior because you lived in America. Just get out of here." She turned away and disappeared into the rabble of the canteen, talking heatedly with Hannah.

~ ~ ~

I finished recording lecture notes into Pradeep's tape recorder—Sridharan's lecture that day concerned "the major characteristics and practitioners of Pre-Raphaelite poetry."

The lecture had been a grueling exercise in staying awake. But I managed, driven by my determination to take thorough notes for Pradeep. I hit "Stop" and seeing the tape was full, ejected it from the recorder.

"Thank you, Vikram bhai," Pradeep said, taking the cassette from me. "Very helpful, yaar, very helpful." He sat at the edge of his dorm room cot, his shades covering his eyes, his ever-genial smile on his face. I said no problem, put my notebook back in my bag. After my run-in with Manju, I felt the urge to get the hell off campus.

"So you had fine time in Delhi?" Pradeep asked.

He had asked me that question before, and as before, I said I did and that I'd taken a lot of pictures.

"I spent my Christmas break performing in one function after another," Pradeep said, rising from the cot. He took up his walking stick and followed after me as I started for the door.

"That's really awesome, Pradeep. Your future's taking off," I said.

"But I'm so much busy nowadays," he said.

I stopped and touched Pradeep's shoulder. "Well, I guess I'll leave you to it."

"I'm so busy nowadays I really must take care not to get too lost in my engagements"—he shook the tape in his hand—"and study all these notes you and Devasia are providing." I got the feeling Pradeep was trying to stall me. As I stood at the door, I saw him reach an arm out for me. I took the cue.

"What is it?" I stepped toward him.

"Vikram"—his voice became a half whisper—"did something happen between you and Priya? I do not mean to intrude, you see, but I don't like gossip. Especially concerning my own friends."

I told him Priya and I had "gotten close," left it at that, and said nothing about my chat with D'Souza.

Pradeep nodded thoughtfully. "I did not know she was planning on marriage, bhai," he said.

"She wasn't," I said. "But her father was."

"She is only eighteen, I think so. Why now?" He swung his stick around and made for the metal cabinet that stood on the wall opposite his cot.

"Not sure," I said. "Either she really did fall for this guy, or her father put her up to it. Anyway, I guess she didn't go through with it. Hence all the gossip."

"Atch-cha," Pradeep muttered. Then, his head tilting slightly away from me, he beckoned me over to him with a swing of his stick. Pradeep leaned sideways toward me and asked confidentially, "You think she is . . . in love . . . with you?"

I laughed, shaking my head, stepping away. I couldn't help it—the question made me laugh nervously. I was glad Pradeep couldn't see because he would've seen me flush, get fidgety and embarrassed. "Maybe . . . maybe she felt like we had something in common. I don't know. I mean, I don't think so."

Pradeep turned the handle of the cabinet and jerked open the metal doors. He placed the cassette on a stack of them on a shelf at shoulder level. Then his hand switched over to a stack of brand-new cassettes, still in their wrappers, sitting beside the used ones. He grabbed the top one. "For months," he said, "I felt something was not right. Priya *sounded* happy, but it was obvious she was not. I am surprised that her friends didn't see it."

"She didn't talk much about it," I said. "She always seemed so sure of herself."

Pradeep considered my words for a second, smiled. "Then you were not listening."

A knock sounded at the door, and Devasia appeared, his notebook and a pocket-sized Macmillan edition of *The Way of the World* in hand. He strode in, sharp-featured and shiny-haired in his kurta and slippers. "Happy New Year." He smiled, shaking my hand. Pradeep held out to him the new cassette, telling Devasia to use it for his dictation, when I noticed what looked like a box upholstered in red velvet with a worn gold clasp sitting on the floor of the cabinet. A sturdy padlock hung from the clasp.

"What's with the treasure chest?" I asked.

"Treasure chest?" Pradeep pondered my words and turned toward me. "Oh-ho! You mean—" He tapped the box with his stick and lowered his voice. "For winning that Diwali contest, I got trophy, of course, but on top of that, they gave me cash prize. Three thousand rupees."

Devasia and I replied with cries of "Fantastic" and "Wonderful."

Pradeep clanged shut the cabinet door. "But we must be, how do you say, discreet." He tapped his nose with his index finger and held out his palm in a gesture for us to keep things under wraps.

Devasia asked why Pradeep didn't just deposit the money. "There's a Bank of Baroda here." He waved his hand toward the college building where the Bank of Baroda did indeed have a tiny branch on the second floor.

"This is only temporary, yaar," Pradeep assured us. He said his cousin would be visiting in the next couple of weeks, and he planned to hand the money over to him as soon as he arrived.

"Why your cousin?" I asked.

"He is living in Bombay, you see," Pradeep explained, "and this coming summer, he's planning to book one recording session for me in studio there. He knows few friends in music business, so I am hoping . . . we will see now."

"Nothing to see," Devasia said, beaming. "You will be most popular singer in India."

"A Bollywood recording star right here," I said.

Pradeep chuckled, a bit shyly and incredulously. Devasia went over to the desk at the far end of the room to get started on the dictation. He and I waved good-bye as I walked for the door, and Pradeep followed close behind.

"Priya is a smart girl," he said to me privately. "Independent. Whatever she has done, wherever she has gone, she is happy. I feel that." I stepped out the door, onto the veranda. "She was not happy here," he added. "Even *I* could see that." He laughed softly.

"I just wonder how she's doing, that's all."

Pradeep lingered at the doorway. He tapped his stick a few times against the floor. "I think," he said, "you will hear from her again." And though his eyes were masked by his shades, I could tell there was a coy twinkle in them.

I told Pradeep congratulations on his success and hurried off campus.

Chapter 19

My father bought an off-white Premier, an upgraded version of the classic Fiats that Hemant Uncle and Dharmanshu Uncle owned. He drove it home from a showroom in Paldi one Sunday afternoon. We went downstairs, stood around it, and I had to admit it looked stylish, like one of those boxy European sedans I'd seen in German or Italian movies.

"So what do you think?" He beamed. "You like it? Now we can drive to Baroda whenever we want and visit Hemant Uncle. I'll teach you and your mother how to drive, and you can go wherever."

The exterior shone like a trophy; the light-brown leather interior had that factory-direct smell; the dashboard, the gearshift—everything was glossy, untouched. "It's really something," I said. I thought of Ahmedabad's traffic—a stock car rally, a zoo, and an open-air market all mashed together—and knew the Premier wouldn't stay so pristine for long.

"What do you think?" my father asked as Anand peeked inside.

"Does it have AC?"

"It's got everything," my father said, snapping his fingers. "Get in, everyone. We'll go for a drive."

My mother brought out a tiny canister of vermilion powder, mixed it with water in a silver tray so it turned into a dab of paste, then dipped her finger into it and inscribed a swastika on the hood of the Premier. She had done the same thing in America when my father had bought our Ford Escort hatchback. But within a couple of days, as surreptitiously as I could, I had wiped the swastika off the hood of that Ford. I had hoped my mother would think it was the wind that rubbed off the symbol.

"Here," my mother now told me, "you will not need to rub off *swasteek*."

"I didn't rub it off—" I began, then switched gears. "Okay. I did. I'm sorry. I just didn't want our neighbors to think we were Nazis."

"It is a holy symbol actually," my father said solemnly. "Chalo, let's go." He unlocked the passenger-side door and Anand promptly jumped into the front seat.

"Backseat, backseat," my father reprimanded, laughing.

Anand moved over to the backseat, making room for my mother. I watched her in the car, chatting with my father. She had not protested the car purchase, how costly it was and all that. She had blessed it instead.

"Vikram, get in!" my father shouted.

I was happy for her, completely happy that her holy symbol could remain without qualification on the hood of our new car and guide us forward.

~ ~ ~

While the mornings were still cool, I decided to get some exercise. Before classes, I went out jogging. I'd jog east from the bungalow along University Road while the traffic was still light and there were fewer vendors out wheeling their wooden carts around. I jogged past the Indian Oil station and the shantytown, where I observed the women washing clothes in buckets, dusting the narrow lanes between mud homes while half-dressed kids scampered with stray dogs and men lay on charpoys smoking bidis. I circled the perimeter of the shantytown and took a back road that led me home past a line of shacks and produce stands.

After jogging, I went out to the balcony and did my sit-ups and push-ups on the stone tiles still cool from the night. I sat out there, flipping through the *Times of India*, reading stories about Rajiv Gandhi involved in the Bofors scandal, the Pamela Bordes–British Parliament sex scandal, and any news from America I could scrounge up before I went inside to eat breakfast. That's when I began to notice my mother skipping her meals or taking unusually small portions. "I'm not having much appetite these days," she would say.

One by one, I checked out books by the American writers from the narrow shelf space they occupied in the lower stacks. A couple of times a week, I'd sneak down there and find something new to read. Steinbeck at first, his stories about Cannery Row and the migrants and itinerants of Northern California, and Hemingway's determined Cuban fisherman rowing farther out than he ever had. I switched to the plays—a volume of Arthur Miller, another of Eugene O'Neill, and an anthology of Tennessee Williams, Shannon's favorite. They were windows opening to America—every line hummed with the energy of American life—and they comforted me when I could take the time to read them. I felt a kinship with every soul in these pages, and they became my companions in the long, heat-blinded slog from one Ahmedabad afternoon to the next.

One evening after dinner, I started reading *A Streetcar Named Desire*, and I got so drawn in by the romance of New

Orleans—delicious with jazz, alive with the strife of lower-class American immigrant life, with loud men at poker tables, couples in love in cluttered rooms divided only by beaded curtains, the air sweetened with mint juleps and cigar smoke and New Orleans sweat—that I read it all through in one sitting. I thought I'd discovered America's beating heart, and strangely enough, I felt turned on by the deluded yet wildly erotic Blanche DuBois, so fragile and dangerous. Lies and dementia and all, I still fell in love with her. And when I finished, I flipped back and reread the passages that had struck me. It was past midnight when I put the book away, turned over, and gave in to sleep, hoping I would dream the scenes.

In the middle of that night, my father woke me up. I saw his figure stark against the hallway light as he leaned into the room.

"Vikram, I'm taking your mother to the clinic," came his words.

"What happened?"

"She's having some pains. We're going to check it out."

Anand lay on the cot on the other side of the room, still sleeping.

"Look after things till I get back," he said.

"All right."

I heard my parents' voices muffled in the deep night.

I heard nothing from my father the next morning, and I went to my lectures as usual. Afterward, I picked up Anand at his school. On our way home, I stopped by the photomat at the shopping plaza for my pictures from Delhi, and to buy a couple more rolls of film.

As we pulled into our bungalow driveway, the groundskeeper was working his way along the rosebushes with a watering can. Inside the bungalow, we could hear the bathroom cleaner, his bottles of solvents clinking and his brushes scrubbing behind the bathroom door. The cleaning girl was gone, her work done for the day; clothes and sheets swayed on the line on the balcony. But there was no sign of my father, no message. I heated up leftovers for my brother and me, and as we ate, the phone rang—the shrill double-ring: *trrrnngg-trrrnng!*

"Hello?" I said into the receiver.

"Vikram? It's Pappa. I'm calling from clinic."

"Where?"

"In Navarangpura. Okay, so, your ma needs to have surgery. It's her appendix, doctor says. Needs to come out."

I breathed a sigh of relief. "And that's all it was?"

"Well, it got septic. And apparently, last night it burst."

Septic . . . burst. The words invited feelings of disaster.

"And they need to go in and take care of it."

"When?"

"They're taking her in now."

"Where are you? Can we come there?"

"Hang out there. I'll drop by at home later on. Just do your studies, carry on as usual."

"Fine," I said. "We'll see you later."

I hung up. The handset clunked back on the console, as heavy as deadweight.

"What'd he say?" Anand asked from the dining table.

"We wait."

Do your studies. Carry on as usual. How was this consolation?

All afternoon I tried to study but couldn't concentrate. I switched back to the Tennessee Williams plays. I noticed now how the paperback was water-stained and a tad warped. I moved to *The Glass Menagerie*, the play in which I'd seen Shannon in the fall of our senior year. But still I felt restless. I thumbed through the photography book again, studying in particular the Stieglitz photograph of the immigrants on the ship, my eyes searching the faces. I wondered what became of each of these people. What were their separate fates upon reaching the far shore?

It wasn't until the sky had darkened and the streetlights flickered on that Anand and I heard the Premier roll into the driveway, crunching across the gravel, and the engine silenced. The sound of fidgeting with the downstairs door echoed up the stairwell, followed by the padding of a lone pair of footsteps. I went to the front doors, unbolted them, and let my father in.

"Did the cook show up?" he asked, entering. He seemed a bit dazed. His sleeves were rolled up and his shirt was half-untucked.

"Who?"

"I had asked for the cook. He should have been here by now." He peeked through the dining room into the kitchen. Shaking his head, he returned. "Okay. Guess we go out for dinner."

"I can get some chai going if you like," I offered.

"That would be good," he said. "I'll take a quick bath."

"What's going on?" Anand asked, standing in the doorway to our room.

He exhaled. "Surgery went fine. She's in recovery right now." He paused, turning something over in his mind. "I'll explain later."

I added milk to water, sprinkled in chai masala and spoons of sugar, and let the concoction steep on the small stove. You let it boil, the froth rising to the rim, took it off the burner, stirred the browning liquid so it settled, and set it back to steep again. You did this several times so that the flavor of the chai could concentrate. I strained the chai into three cups and set them on the dining room table, along with the package of Parle-G biscuits.

My father sipped the chai quietly, his mind distant. He never even touched the biscuits. I was about to press him for information when he spoke up: "The appendix had burst so there was"—he made vague circular movements with his hand—"a lot of cleanup to do. But while they were in there, they found one thing."

My mind froze. Time stopped.

"An abnormality," he said. "On the uterus. They removed it, sent it to the lab."

"What do you mean?"

He took off his glasses, his elbows against the edge of the table, fingers pressed against the bridge of his nose. He shut his eyes.

"Doctor will tell me more tomorrow," he said. He put his glasses back on. "Nothing to worry about yet."

I knew I was going to get nothing more out of him. I let my breathing even out. Let time flow again.

"Can we see her?" Anand asked.

"Not today. She's sleeping mostly. Tomorrow we'll go."

The chair scraped loudly as I pushed away from the table. I stood, taking up the cup of chai, and left the room. I suddenly needed to be out on the balcony, out amid the pulse of traffic, the thrum of music, signs of life.

"We'll have dinner at Havmor or something, Vikram," my father said behind me. "Be ready."

"Okay." I didn't want to tell him I had no appetite.

~ ~ ~

It was a private clinic not far from our bungalow. The fluorescent tube lights cast an insufficient glow that gave the clinic a mortuary pall. Everything underlit: the gray walls of the tiny lobby, the wicker chairs, the cement floor. My father led us past the doctors skulking around in their white coats, their necks noosed with stethoscopes.

The tube light glowing above my mother's bed only accentuated the shadows and made her room look somehow darker. The light hardly reached across the room to the half-closed door of the bathroom. From beyond the shuttered window came the bellow of rickshaw horns, the trill of bicycle bells, the roar of a passing bus—Ahmedabad's evening madness infiltrating even here.

My mother lay very still under her sheets, eyes closed. I walked up to her. An IV coiled from a stand next to her bed into her forearm. I studied the drip-drip of a clear solution from a bag hooked atop the stand into the tube. Somehow, it made me glad to know it was there, either nourishing her or sedating her.

"How are you?"

She nodded her head weakly, drowsily. I had never seen my mother in such a state before. I bent down and kissed her on the forehead. Never in my life had I done that, but at that moment, the four of us in that gloom, it seemed the right thing. The only thing. I took a seat on a plastic chair by the door, next to Anand, who sat rigidly with his arms crossed, chewing at his fingernails.

My father leaned over my mother's bed as if she were trying to tell him something. A moment later, the door handle turned, and the doctor, a woman, entered. She looked to be in her midfifties and wore owlish glasses, a red bindi, and a sari under her white coat. She looked overworked, worn out now at the end of the day.

"*Kem cho?*" she asked gently, though I wasn't sure to whom.

"She is doing okay," my father said, straightening up, "but she wanted to tell the staff there is a rat in this room."

The doctor looked unfazed, nodded. "We have had such a problem in past. I will tell the attendant."

My mother's face scrunched up momentarily, then relaxed.

"Do you need more painkiller?" my father asked.

"This is normal," the doctor said with a confident toss of her head. "There will be some periodic pain, but it will go away by tomorrow. Best not to overmedicate." She checked my mother's pulse against her watch and noted it on a chart. She checked her pupils. A nurse, just a young girl in a salwaar kameez with frazzled ponytailed hair who could have been a Xavier's undergrad, walked in on brisk feet. She took my mother's temperature.

"Ninety-eight-two," she whispered to the doctor, somewhat shyly.

A knock sounded at the door, and a thin man loped in on flip-flops. I couldn't tell if he worked here or had just wandered in from the vegetable stand across the road.

"There is a rat here," the doctor informed him. "See to it."

The attendant acknowledged her by bobbing his head from side to side and went back out.

"Pulse, temperature, recovery is all fine," the doctor said. There was a pleasing forthrightness that comforted me. She could easily have been a housewife in any Gujarati home were it not for the fact that she had ambition, that she challenged the norm and had risen to become a surgeon. I wanted her to care well for my mother. I wanted to be proud of her.

"So let us talk," she said to my father and slowly closed the door.

~ ~ ~

It was the size of a child's fist, what they had removed. A growth on the uterus. They had also drawn a lot of blood for tests. Tests and more tests. I thought of my mother at the clinic, gaining her strength either to resume her future or to gear up for another battle. Did she know as much?

The cook my father had arranged for finally showed up. For the next few days, he'd arrive late in the afternoon and throw dinner together. He cooked us rotis, dal, mixed vegetables, rice. It was strange to eat food prepared in your own kitchen by a complete stranger—by someone who made his living cooking for strangers. It was digestible, I thought. Too oily, my father said, but it would have to do. The cleaning girl still came in the mornings, washed and hung our laundry, cleaned the floors. In the evenings, she returned to wash our dinner dishes. And each morning as I left for classes, I passed the groundskeeper watering and clipping, his duties unaffected, his thoughts untouched.

I could hardly keep my focus in class. There, as the ceiling fans whirred, students yawned, and lecturers droned, I kept my eyes on my notebook, and I wrote pages and pages of driveling notes, if only to keep my pen busy, my mind distracted. Other than Devasia and Pradeep, I kept my own company. I found consolation in the library, browsing the *Time* magazines or picking through the shelf of Hemingway, Steinbeck, and the other signals from America, still beaming faint voices from the shelves underground.

Anand and I got home one afternoon to find Kamala Auntie emerging from a rickshaw with luggage. She paid the driver as Anand and I each took up a suitcase.

As we hauled the bags through the front doors, I noticed out of the corner of my eye an envelope in the mailbox. I undid the hasp, took out a small postcard—the standard-issue kind from the Indian postal service, cream-colored, scribbled in Hindi, addressed to my mother—along with an envelope. The envelope was to me, from the University of Wisconsin.

"I'm glad you're here," I told Kamala Auntie in Gujarati. Her being here, it felt like a reunion with an old ally. A sign that our numbers were not diminished.

She smiled. "Everything will be all right. When I found out your pappa hired a cook, I said, 'No way. I am going right now. I won't have them eating food cooked by some stranger's hands.'"

We jostled with the suitcases through the narrow entry doors and up the stairs.

"How is your mummi?" Her voice echoed off the stairwell. "Any news?"

"Pappa hasn't told us anything yet," I said.

Anand and I set the suitcases in the hallway. I handed Anand the postcard. "What does this say?" I asked him.

He scanned it front and back, eyes intent. "It's from Dharmanshu Uncle." His lips formed the words as he read. "Just asking how Ma is doing and to keep him posted."

In the dining room, Kamala Auntie spoke on the phone with Hemant Uncle in Baroda. She briefed him on the food she'd left in the fridge for him to heat up for dinner and issued stern warnings that Anjali had better stick to her studies; she wasn't so happy with her marks lately. "I don't care," she said into the phone, "let her think of that the next time she decides to lie to me, then I find out she failed the exam." The Gujarati words were like nails driven into the phone. "That girl," I heard her shout, "she should have been a boy. All the time, cricket, cricket, cricket. And she doesn't study."

I went to my room with the envelope from Wisconsin. It felt thick. If they were just writing to reject you, I thought, why bother with such a thick letter? Maybe it was something else, totally unrelated to admissions, a brochure about housing or something equally irritating and irrelevant.

I fanned myself with the envelope, pacing between my desk and the bed. Finally, I tore open the seal inch by inch with a finger. Blocking out the noises of doubt in my mind, I fished out the papers inside and began shuffling through them. My eyes scanned what looked like a student visa application. What was that doing in here? Then I reshuffled the papers, turned it all right side up, and braced myself as I began to read the first words of a letter telling me I'd gotten in.

Elated! Disbelieving! I got up. I sat down. I got the urge to rush out into the hallway to cry out at the top of my lungs that I'd gotten in. I had won.

It did feel like I had won something. That day I won a bet I had made with myself. A bet I'd made with all my inner self-doubt.

But no sooner had the celebration welled up in my heart than it was all smothered out. Something wasn't right. This victory felt strange, wrong. A false celebration. The letter I held in my hand was the golden key, and it had opened a golden new path for me. The path I wanted and that was now mine to take. I thought of my mother at the clinic that very moment.

Could I go down that path now? Did I even want to? I stood there for a moment, aware of anger simmering and rising inside. I stuffed the letter back into the envelope and slammed it against the side of my desk, letting it fall to the floor. The best of things at the worst of times. The universe had to be rigged.

Chapter 20

My father returned after sundown, straight from the clinic. Kamala Auntie had prepared food for us. We all sat at the table, our plates before us, and listened. The news was not good. The cells in the mass indicated cancer. More results were pending. We would know more as they came in. The doctor could then determine a strategy, my father said. His tone was even, almost matter-of-fact. He finished his dinner quickly, and we all cleared the table so that we could go to the clinic. Whether she was sleeping or awake didn't matter. We wanted to see her.

"Does she know?" I asked.

My father nodded. "The doctor suggested we wait till we knew the full results. But I didn't want her to be in the dark. It's not right." He shook his head. "She knows what's going on. If she didn't, she could well guess, I am sure."

"How did she take it?" I asked.

"Better than I thought," he said. "Your mother's a strong woman."

"I know she is," I said.

"Always been that way. All those years of uncertainty till now," he said, shaking his head, half admiringly, half regretfully.

"Is she going to die?" I heard Anand ask hesitatingly.

My father didn't answer for a few seconds. "Let's not worry about that right now."

At the clinic, none of us brought up the tumor. It hovered in the space above us, a toxic cloud, weighing down our minds.

My mother did say the pain was less, and they had removed the rat from the room. Still, her voice was weak, and she spoke little. It sapped her strength to speak. From where I sat by the door, her voice sounded gossamer-frail.

Kamala Auntie stood at the foot of the bed, told her there was nothing to worry about. She could take care of things back home till my mother was feeling better.

"Has the doctor come around?" my father asked. He clutched the metal railing at the foot of the bed. "How've you been eating here?"

She said the doctor had come by a couple of times. "Said temperature was normal, BP normal. They gave me dal-rice, yogurt." She stopped to catch her breath. She winced.

"Still the pain?"

"Thodu thodu," she replied, sounding muffled, as if she were speaking from the other side of a wall. "But you know . . . ?" She paused and shifted in her bed. Kamala Auntie stepped around and adjusted the pillows under her head. "She says not much," my mother said. "The doctor. Always looks at chart. And when she asks questions, she doesn't look in the eyes."

My father told her not to speak too much. Told her be good, get her rest, and she would be going home very soon. My mother asked if the doctor had given him any more information, asked if he knew about the lab report results.

Anand stood opposite my father. He mumbled a question, and my father said something in reply. Kamala Auntie added something to it, and Anand nodded. Words and voices floated unintelligibly in the grainy half-light.

Then my mother spoke. "Whatever the results, I'm not staying here."

"Soon." My father nodded. "It'll be soon. Don't worry."

They stood there, and their images began to warp together in my eyes. When I saw my mother turn her head, deciding to fall back asleep, alone in her weariness, something broke inside me. I began to cry. Not sobbing, but a steady stuttering in my chest, a tripping of breaths and tears. Something about the lack of answers did it, the lack of any alternative to this horrible thing and her surrendering herself to sleep.

~ ~ ~

Lights came on one by one after we returned home. I realized I'd been standing in the dark when Anand turned on the light switch in our room, and the tube light above my desk flickered on. How long I'd been standing there thinking, I wasn't sure. On the floor lay the envelope from Wisconsin, with its contents stuffed back inside. It was where I'd left it, before my father had come home and given us the news.

"What's that?" Anand asked.

I picked up the envelope. "Oh, it's nothing," I said, and put the thing in a drawer.

~ ~ ~

Awoke early morning. Try not to think, I told myself.

Kamala Auntie was already in the kitchen, chai steaming on the burner.

I put on my sneakers. Nikes I had bought at West Towne Mall last summer. I went out and jogged my regular route. Read the *Times of India* on the balcony. Ate breakfast—a small bowl of cornflakes, a cup of milk, toast, a boiled egg. Filled the bucket in the bathroom with hot water from the mini water heater. Bathed and got dressed.

I could hear the radio from my parents' bedroom: Hindi-language morning news, the shrill jingle of detergent commercials. My father sat at the dining table alone, sipping chai, eating pastry picked from a large steel canister. As usual, the Ambassador arrived to pick him up. He poked his head into our room, told Anand and me he'd make a half day of it at the office. Then on to the clinic.

Anand, in his school uniform, went out to meet his rickshaw. The rickshaw puttered away. Kamala Auntie left too, her purse in hand, saying she was off to the market and would make arrangements for flour, oil, milk.

The door clanged shut.

I opened the desk drawer, dug out the envelope. Read the admissions letter again. The words were pearls to my mind. There was a visa form to fill out and bring with me to the consulate in Bombay. I tucked the envelope back in the drawer. The cleaning girl came, the hem of her skirt brushing against the floor, the bangles chiming at her ankles as she glided through the hallway and into the bathroom.

Before leaving for college, I knocked on the bathroom door and gently pushed it open. She squatted on a low stool, her back to me, pins holding her bun in place behind her head. She'd already turned on the tap. The water whooshed and splatted on the tile floor, and she thwacked the sopping clothes with a short paddle. I watched her, mesmerized for a few seconds, as she wrung out my Clash T-shirt—thanks to Indian soap, it had faded to a pale yellow from its former neon splendor—and dropped it into a bucket.

"No one is home," I told her. She started as if I'd barged in on her naked, and understanding me, she closed her mouth and tipped her head sideways, a gesture that meant "okay." "Didn't mean to scare you," I added in my pidgin Gujarati. (No response.) "Be back later. Let yourself out. Okay?" She tipped her head to the side again, half uttering, "Okay."

The next few days passed by in a numbing haze. A cloud of lectures and note-taking. Victorian Literature. French. Psychology. Economics. I sat with Devasia in the mess while he ate and went to Pradeep's hostel room to record lecture notes. I filled them in on the situation with my mother till there was really nothing more to add. I felt wrung out. My thoughts leaned toward the evenings, to the visits to the clinic where we waited with restless patience on the hard wicker chairs, in the pale shadows. My mother was recovering, at least; the IV was out, and she could sit up, take steps, carry on conversations.

Two weeks into my mother's stay at the clinic, while we were visiting, the doctor knocked on the door and entered. She was dressed in her white coat and sari, diminutive in her oversize glasses. She crossed to the bed with a folder in her hand. "Okay, now we have something," she said.

Long pause. It was like any folder, but this one, it was an oracle. And everyone in the room, every atom, gravitated now to whatever it contained.

"Atch-cha," my father said. He adjusted his glasses and ran his fingers through the thinning hair on his scalp. "Go on." He focused on the doctor as if she were a colleague about to run a mathematical problem by him.

Kamala Auntie stood up and went over to the bed. "Do you wish to speak in private?" she asked.

"No." My father shook his head. "This is fine."

The doctor pivoted toward Anand and me, surprised at first, then a smile appeared on her face, and she said, "Okay." She opened the folder, turning to my mother. "As you know, we found malignancy." I hated that word. It was a dragon in the night sky. "But the numbers I got back today show normal white cell count. Your liver function, your lymph nodes also, those tests are normal. All healthy. So"—she closed the folder—"we had scare. But this is good news. Growth contained malignancy. But those cells stayed inside it." Her palms closed together.

Not a word from anyone for several seconds, just a deep sigh of relief that might've come from me. My father cleared his throat, but my mind was filled with this sensation of profound clearance. A renewal. As if all the funk of the past weeks had been aired out, cleaned out of the room through its tiny barred windows.

"That appendix was a painful experience," the doctor remarked, "but it was a blessing." She rested one hand on the bed, stood next to my mother, and said to her, "Because who knows how much longer before that growth would have caused you to see doctor. By then, cancer may have spread."

My father went on to ask a slew of questions. His tone was direct, and he wanted to hit every angle: How many more tests? What sort? Any dietary changes? The doctor answered calmly, her answers brief but sure. She said we had crossed the most critical hurdle, but she still wanted my mother to see a specialist in Bombay for a more rigorous round of tests when she felt up to it.

"I will ring him up," she said, "and tell him you'll be calling. Make an appointment to see him, earlier the better."

She took out a prescription pad from her coat pocket and wrote down the name of the specialist.

"And how long must I be here?" my mother asked.

"You can check out tomorrow," she said, tearing the sheet from the pad, "and call this number. He is in Breach Candy Hospital—"

"He's good?" I was startled to hear my own voice. I stood up. "This specialist in Bombay, he's good?"

The doctor turned to me, surprised to hear from me. "He's the best that I know," she said, turning back to my father. She handed him the paper. "You can trust him."

Trust. Such a lonely and fragile word, as uncertain as a sheet of ice on a frozen lake. I hoped it would hold.

~ ~ ~

Kamala Auntie stayed several more days after my mother's return home. She cooked and made sure the house was tended to while my mother rested and my father returned to work. The mood slowly lifted, normalized, and we began to go about our lives as before. Anand and I came home in the afternoons to find my mother chatting casually with Kamala Auntie as if nothing had happened. We lingered in that momentary suspension, when normality could roam about the home, an eager dog set free of its leash; a season of peace, as when the artillery between opposing sides ceases and a lovely calm settles over the field. I loaded a new roll into the Minolta, a more light-sensitive stock than I'd yet used, sat with my mother and Kamala Auntie at the dining table—the shutters open to let in the light filtering through the peepal trees—and snapped off shot after shot. Close-ups and group shots of Anand, intent on his Hindi homework, and the women in conversation, sifting mung beans or snapping peas out of their pods onto large steel plates.

The glint in my mother's eyes had mellowed now, as if the steel within them had cooled and hardened. I tried to capture it and thought I did once, on the first evening she stepped outside since coming home. The groundskeeper was surprised and happy to see her. My mother remarked how nicely the flowers were doing, and she stooped down to take a closer look at the marigolds. The sun was flush with the tile roofs of the neighboring bungalow, slanting orange against the purple tint of the evening as I bent down on my knees, level with my mother's gaze, and took the picture.

Later, when I saw the picture, it took me a second to recognize her. Sure, her face was a touch thinner, the creases around her eyes and mouth were deeper. But what got me were the eyes: they seemed defeated yet undefeated at the same time.

She'd been fighting a continuous battle, not just with her illness but these past twelve years against displacements—first, from one country to another, then from town to town across America—while being as steady a supporter to my father and nurturer to my brother and me as she could be. She'd made sure we were clothed, schooled, fed, that our bills were paid and we still had money in the bank, no matter where we ended up from one year to the next. I knew that America hadn't gone the way of her dreams, not even halfway, not with our yearly uncertainties and upheavals. Yet here she was in this picture, on the other side of all those years, a steady, solitary figure. And that's what that picture said to me—that we steadily endure our lives and ultimately we are alone in our endurance. In this aloneness, we find our strength.

As we walked along the rows of jasmine and marigolds that evening, she stopped in the path, looked up from admiring the flowers, and told me that at that moment she felt happiness for the first time since . . . And here she trailed off. "Since?" I asked. "Since coming back to India?"

After a pause, she shook her head and said, "Since we *left* India."

And I wished that what she felt at that moment would set the new standard of happiness in her life from then on, for all the years to come.

I've kept that picture of my mother ever since.

~ ~ ~

Almost March. Six weeks to go till another round of wretched exams. The finals. Six weeks holed up inside the barracks of rote learning. I had to comb through sheaves of notes, memorize dates and definitions, and throw together another set of practice essays. An essay a day—that was the goal.

At my desk, poring through my Macmillan textbook and my Sridharan lecture notes, I felt slow-burning despair. I decided I could not do this anymore, not two more years of this. But at the same time, I no longer felt right about leaving for Wisconsin after everything my mother had been through—and would continue to go through. It wasn't about feeling guilty; I just couldn't consider leaving her now, not like this.

But if I was going to stay in India, I had to consider alternatives to Xavier's. I had to find another school I might actually find relevant and meaningful to me, even semi-enjoyable.

There was a step I'd yet to take—a stone yet unturned, an option my father had once mentioned, worth investigating.

I began going through the last several rolls' worth of photos, going back to the past Diwali and the trip to Delhi. There were a few I was actually impressed with. I considered these photos, then shoved them inside an envelope and set out on the Luna for NID, the National Institute of Design.

It was a dust-strewn haul along my side of the Sabarmati, south past the Alliance Française. I rode past the Alliance's redbrick complex, and I thought of my teacher. I wondered where she was now, if she'd made good on her plans and left for Paris to begin a new life. I sped on farther south, into Paldi, a neighborhood raucous with traffic, both hoofed and wheeled, and found the massive, tree-lined enclosure that I knew had to be the NID.

I stood the Luna on its stand. Clutching the envelope, I stepped through narrow iron gates and into a plot of spacious green.

Eucalyptus and bougainvillea flowered here; rows of them jutted off on either side of the gate, muting out the city noise. On the far side stood the cement buildings housing classrooms and the hostel. These buildings were modern, not like stodgy Xavier's colonial loggias overrun with Hindu-Catholic moralists and the Old World commingling of paan, sandalwood, and coconut oil. I passed large, polished windows with steel-black sashes, and structures built like interconnected redbrick rectangles, and squares set high over landscaped greenery on tall, stemlike pillars. This campus was some modernist art project, and I was pleased that it existed in Ahmedabad.

On the far side of the green, an entrance led into a hallway. I noticed a lounge off to one side and, around the corner, males and females together at work in video editing suites. They conferred confidentially, partners in a secret creative endeavor, with their headphones on, hands adjusting control knobs. Images played on monitors, stopped and started as they worked the editing decks. I turned the other way and saw an office, its door shut. On it a nameplate read, "Prof. Sheshank Menon, Director."

I knocked on the door.

"Yes? Come on in."

I turned the handle and peeked in. It seemed a tornado had just blown through, shaking and reshuffling the whole room. Tottering piles of paperwork and videotapes lay on the desk, smaller piles were strewn like coral around the cramped floor, and the bookshelves too were stocked full but in disarray. Menon was graying and straggle-haired, lanky, in a checked short-sleeved shirt and dark slacks. He leaned against the desk and looked up from a thick volume in his hands. Seeing me, he bunched his brows together. "Oh"—he shut the book—"I thought you'd be one of my students." There was a tone of disappointment in his voice.

I took a step inside, introduced myself, shook his hand. I asked if he would mind if I talked to him for a moment. "Or I could come back if you're waiting for someone."

"No, no, what is it?" he said, unable to mask his irritation, and set the book on a stack of videos on his desk. I noticed it was an Eames volume on industrial design. Menon raised himself to his feet and looked around with an expression of mild despair. "Why don't we step outside?"

We walked together as students passed by or lounged on chairs in the hallway. I told Menon I'd arrived from the States recently, that I'd heard about the NID and wanted to see about enrolling myself. I told him about my photography, about the short videos I'd made in high school. I knew the school had programs in all those things, I said. "And it's what I really want to do"—it was the first time I'd heard myself say those words—"and I've brought some samples here for you to take a look." I held out the envelope to him. But his attention was on a student rolling out of one of the chairs nearby, hoisting up his backpack and preparing to take off down the hallway.

"Mr. Bose," he commanded. The student froze, turned toward us, eyes wide with surprise. "Were you not aware of our meeting?"

The student—Mr. Bose—chuckled nervously. "Oh, Professor Menon," he said. "I was, in fact, on my way to see you. I just remembered the letter you wanted, from the judge in Bhopal, and I was on my way to get—"

"I won't have you putting my program in legal troubles."

"Yes, sir," Mr. Bose said. "No, sir. If only they had warned me before I conducted my interviews with the victims' lawyers, whatnot—"

"Tomorrow be in my office at noon. I want all transcripts from your interviews, all video footage, and this cease-and-desist order in my hands, understand, Mr. Bose?"

"Tomorrow, yes, sir. Of course."

"Good day."

The student turned on his heels through the entryway, out onto the lawn. Menon exhaled heavily and, almost as an afterthought, turned to face me. "Yes?"

I felt sort of absurd now, taking up the director's time with this envelope in my hand. "I've brought some photographs," I pressed on, "if you'd like to take a look—"

"Mr. . . . Mistry, is it?" Menon sighed. "There's nothing I, nor anyone here, can do for you. We run a highly structured program, and we don't accept transfers. Why don't you finish your BA and then apply for our postgraduate program? Just now, I'm afraid you're wasting your time." *Finish your BA*? The words sucked all the oxygen out of the air.

"But I wouldn't need to transfer," I said. "I'd be happy to apply as a first-year. I think NID would be perfect for me. If you'd consider these"—I held out the envelope in my hands—"I'd appreciate it."

Menon inhaled impatiently. "Quite impossible. We have an exhaustive selection process. All our students are the best of the best." He began to chuckle lightly to himself. "You can't just—" Then, assuming a serious expression, he pointed to my envelope and added, "See, leave your things just there by my door. If I find they have merit, you can apply for our postgraduate course once you're done with your BA. Just now I'm running late."

I wasn't going to leave my "things" by his door. I knew he'd shove them under a pile of junk in his office and forget about them. I didn't want to leave my pictures to suffer the fate of my video camera.

"Well . . . thank you," I said. He offered his hand. I shook it. Menon told me good luck, then shuffled away to the editing suites. I watched him standing at the door to the suites, his back to me, greeting his students and discussing their work. A vague feeling of disappointment and embarrassment began to overflow inside me. I felt suddenly anxious to leave.

Out on the lawn, students gathered in groups. A boy went around with cups of chai on a tray, handing them out to takers. On the lawn's far side, a groundskeeper went along trimming the shrubbery. I followed the pathway back toward the gate.

In just the little I'd seen, I sensed that NID was everything Xavier's wasn't, a place where I could change things around for myself. Finish your BA, he'd said. Good lord! That was two years from now. And then what? I wasn't guaranteed acceptance to this school. What was I *guaranteed*? The only guarantee I had was my admissions letter to Wisconsin. There, in the drawer of my desk. But it was just a letter. It was not a future. A future you made on your own. And good luck with that.

Just ahead, I noticed the student, the one named Mr. Bose, short, floppy-haired, in a T-shirt and jeans, on the grass smoking a cigarette alongside a group of friends. There were four of them together, two guys and two girls. As I passed, Bose nodded hello to me, and I waved back.

"Good luck with your meeting tomorrow," I told him, slowing as I passed. "He seems tough."

Bose chuckled. "You don't know half of it, yaar. I just don't want a bounty on my head from those Union Carbide bastards."

"Like Salman Rushdie. He's like Hindu Salman Rushdie," the guy sitting opposite Bose said to him, chuckling. He had close-cropped hair, a scruffy beard, and round-rimmed glasses, giving the impression of an Ahmedabadi chai-café intellectual or an adolescent trying on the guise of an arty-farty bohemian. "Corporate fatwah. You're finished, *butchu*!"

"Don't even say that," Bose said, shaking his head, drawing on his cigarette, and staring out drowsily into the middle distance.

"Sounds exciting," I said. "Hope you don't run into more trouble."

I recalled Union Carbide now. Images on American TV of dejected, impoverished factory workers, all victims of a poison gas leak from the plant, huddled like concentration-camp inmates against the grim walls of their shanties. I recalled feeling sorry for them, but also resenting them, their emaciated and hopeless faces signaling to Americans the sorry plight of the place I was from.

"You a student here?" Bose asked. Before I could answer, he pointed to the envelope in my hand, and added, "Those drawings or what?"

"Photographs," I said. "I wanted to show them to the director, thought it might help my case. I was thinking about transferring here."

"Sit down, dost," Bose said cordially. "You smoke?"

I shook my head and sat on my haunches.

"Sunil. Sunil Bose." He extended his hand. I shook it and waved at the others. I was amazed: Sunil was into video production; so was Scruffy Beard. He and Sunil were making a documentary together on the Bhopal disaster. Of the two girls, the one with short, stylish black hair—what Kamala Auntie would call a "boy cut"—was an animation student, while the other—more aloof, but with a ready, pretty smile—was studying furniture design. I couldn't believe such things could be studied here, in the midst of Ahmedabad. The tea boy came around. Scruffy Beard and Short-Haired Girl took a cup before the boy moved off to another group on the lawn.

Sunil and I got to talking about American movies. He told me about how, after a screening of *Jaws* at the Calcutta Film Festival (he was from Calcutta), he snuck into the projectionist's booth, found a foot or so of discarded film—too damaged to run through the projector—and pocketed it. "It's the shot where Quint is half eaten and blood is pouring from his mouth. Too good."

"Solid movie, yaar," Scruffy Beard chimed in, pulling a cigarette from the packet Sunil held out to him. Scruffy Beard poked the cigarette into his mouth, then dug into the deep side pocket of his kurta to fish out a matchbook.

"That's fantastic," I said.

"I've got it on display in my hostel room," Sunil said, nodding his head with an assured, indolent air. "In a box frame that I myself made. I put one bulb behind the film that I can turn on so people can see the frames."

"It doesn't work," Short-Haired Girl said, sneering playfully at Sunil, before she took a sip of chai.

Sunil laughed and tugged at her hair. She swatted his hand away, laughing.

"Where you studying now?" Sunil asked, flicking ash from his cigarette.

I gave them my whole story. America. India. That I was at Xavier's now, an English major.

Aloof Girl groaned disdainfully. "God, my condolences, huh?" Hers was a low, velvety voice, surprisingly seductive.

Scruffy Beard and Short-Haired Girl glanced at Aloof Girl, and they all shared a laugh. I wondered if it was at my expense. Sunil only nodded, smiling thoughtfully. "Well, you've got to get BA somewhere, right?" he said. "What's Xavier's like?"

I was weighing a reply in my head when Short-Haired Girl said, "Wah-re-wah, that good, huh?"

Sunil tsked. "Leave him alone, huh?" He lay back, one elbow on the grass. "They allow transfers here or what?"

I opened my mouth to respond when Short-Haired Girl, lowering the teacup from her face, said, "Either you're here from the start or not at all."

Sunil nodded thoughtfully.

Here from the start or not at all. One of us or one of them. I felt one of neither.

By now, Aloof Girl seemed to have lost interest in our conversation. She lowered herself onto her elbows and gazed around the lawn.

Short-Haired Girl took the cigarette from Sunil's hand. Clutching it in her fingers, she pointed at me. "Don't turn into one of the cogs. The system can turn the best of us into one of them." She punctuated "them" with a wave of her arm in the general direction of the outside world. "Stay strong, huh?" She made a fist out of one hand and put on a mock-defiant expression for a second.

"Stop messing with him," Sunil said to Short-Haired Girl, giving her a light shove and taking his cigarette back. They laughed together as if there were a rare and secret compact between them.

Scruffy Beard tossed out the rest of his chai onto the grass. "Lousy shit, man. They've got proper chai in Delhi. Chandni Chowk. You get world's greatest chai there. Here, it's like sewer water with sugar."

An awkward silence followed during which I was aware of the hum of cicadas, the distant barking of a dog, and the exchanges of polite stares. I raised myself to my feet. "Thanks for the chat."

"Come 'round again," Sunil said. "You want to talk movies, smoke, whatever. I'm usually in my room."

"Or in hers," Scruffy Beard broke in, chuckling. Short-Haired Girl cleared her throat and glared at Scruffy Beard, who shrugged his shoulders, grinning, as if to say, *What'd I do?* The air felt stifling all of a sudden. "Okay," Scruffy Beard said, drawing from his cigarette, "I'm going to go get those Bhopal tapes." He lifted himself onto his feet.

"Yeah, best you go now," Sunil said sternly, then turned to me. "So why don't you bring 'round your pics next time. Are they cool? What do you take pics of?"

"I can show them to you now if you want," I said, turning the envelope over in my hands.

Sunil's tone became guarded. "Right now, yaar, I've got to get back to editing. A lot of tamasha going on. But I promise next time . . ."

"Sure," I said. "So long."

I got about twenty steps toward the gate when I heard Sunil's raised voice: "Good luck!"

I waved back, smiling, and saw Scruffy Beard walking in the opposite direction, back to the main building. Sunil was stroking Short-Haired Girl's ankle, laid across his lap. He didn't seem in a hurry anymore to "get back to editing."

Chapter 21

Something about that experience at NID did it.

It actually made me grateful for Xavier's. Sure, I stuck out like a sore thumb, but strangely I felt like I (almost) belonged there, like the oddball loner in the far corner of the happy family picture.

Menon and Bose and those beautiful girls were all members of the cultural elite, but why did they have to be so snotty about it? Xavier's had its own snotty crowd, but it wasn't cruel. See, the kids at the Xavier's canteen had money but no ambition. Not even any pretense to ambition; they would've been laughed at by the NID crowd. And that's what endeared the Xavier's kids to me, made them more down-to-earth in my eyes.

Still, my relief in retreating to Xavier's was not the reaction I expected or wanted, nor did I find it very comforting. Xavier's was still Xavier's, a place of boundaries, dead ends, and boredom. I switched to plan B.

Sorting through the stacks of photos from over the past few months, I picked out a couple dozen that might make an impression. I found the matching negatives, went to the photomat, and made copies—blowing them up and flattening the finish. I also did something new: I had the photo wallah (his name was Ajay) test a few out with over- and underexposures.

Some of the tests flopped: Anjali was completely bled out in one of the Diwali shots, replaced by an orange blob with ghostly eyes. In another, a minaret of the Taj looked so faded, the marble edging so blurred, that you'd think the camera had cataracts. But the others . . . interesting. Sharp. Surprising. Diwali rendered as an expressionist fever dream, an India processed by alien retinas: it was what I'd been after all along. With the pictures blown up, it was like seeing the photos for the first time, as if they were taken by someone else.

The glass counter in Ajay's shop was stocked nominally with photo supplies, mostly photo albums of various sizes and a meager selection of Kodak film rolls. But Ajay did have a black vinyl portfolio with a zippered seam. It was modest, looked like it'd been stitched together in a hut by small, nimble hands back in Ajay's native village. Nothing fancy, but it would do the trick.

Over the next couple of nights, I arranged the photos inside the portfolio. Then I opened the application booklet for Wisconsin and looked up the director of the art department. It gave no name. Just an address. I wrote up a letter introducing myself, then made a request for the director to consider the pictures. I wrote that while technically I was an international student, I'd gone to high school in Wisconsin; that I was driven and dedicated to my art and, given my circumstances, any financial help the department could provide would greatly ease things up, etc. etc. . . . It was a long shot, a Hail Mary, but it was all I had left.

My mother would need long-term treatment and medicines—that wouldn't be cheap. If I wanted to go to the States, it had to be with as little damage to my parents' bank account as possible. I didn't want it raising a whisper of distress in this house. No. My leaving and the costs of my leaving had to pass through here with no more effect than the wind blowing through the balcony, ruffling the sheets on the line and the pages of one of the notebooks on my desk. No. This America thing was my idea, and I didn't want my parents feeling the burden of it.

But you know what was weird about the letter? The stuff in it that I wrote—about my dedication and so forth—it all felt genuine, and it felt good to write it all out. It was like my heart was speaking. Not one word of it set off my personal bullshit detector.

Stashed in a corner of the pantry, I found a box, last used during our pack-up from Wisconsin and stuffed full with Ziploc bags of turmeric, coriander, and *dhana jeeru.* I removed it all, put my portfolio inside along with the letter, and rushed it over to the post office the next morning. I sent it registered SpeedPost. I wasn't taking any chances.

Later on, sitting in Sridharan's lecture, it occurred to me how sharply pungent with Indian spices that box had been. The delivery could cause the entire art department to smell like an Indian spice shop. You can leave India, I thought, but India never leaves you.

~ ~ ~

During this time, my mother was able to resume something of her normal routine—handing in a list for the grocer to fill and deliver; running shirts, slacks, and saris for pressing; overseeing the garden; chopping vegetables in the mornings—okra, potatoes, eggplant—that Kamala Auntie would use to cook our dinner. It pleased me to come home and hear her voice in conversation with Kamala Auntie or Anand, but these interactions were short-lived. Once she'd seen to putting lunch on the table, she would retire to bed.

In the evenings, after dinner had been cleared, Kamala Auntie would phone Hemant Uncle at his State Bank office in Baroda. She would then watch the Gujarati serials that played over the local Doordarshan feed, about two hours' worth. These tended to be crude productions, broad, loud, and peppered with laugh tracks. In terms of production values, I imagined, they were probably equivalent to the public access TV shows that Karl worked on at WHA. Anand complained to me that we needed a second TV while Kamala Auntie was here so he could play his Nintendo.

My father returned to reporting the goings-on at work. The institute had landed a government-funded astrophysics project ahead of the launch of an ISRO weather satellite scheduled for that fall. He relished the details: how they were computing the satellite's launch trajectory, correcting for the effects of the sun's gamma rays once it was in orbit and calculating the velocity at which they needed the satellite to travel so it would stay above the Earth. Anand found it intriguing too, his attention drifting from his plate to ask questions that eventually veered into more exotic topics: Was life possible on Venus? "No." Mars? "No." Neptune? "Impossible." Could moon dust kill you if you ate it? "That . . . yes."

I asked my father if he'd had any luck contacting the specialist in Bombay, the one the doctor had spoken to us about.

"We go Monday, next week," he said, wrapping his fingers gently around my mother's hand.

"And let's put it behind us," my mother said with a sigh, "and move on. I've been away from you all too long."

"How long are you two going?" I asked.

"We're all going," my father said. He pushed his plate away. "How else will you apply for your student visa?"

"Student visa?" I feigned utter ignorance.

"You will need to go to the consulate yourself. Present your application in person, like I did once upon a time." My father emptied the last of his dal from the steel bowl and cleared his throat. "How else will you get to Wisconsin?"

I blinked. "How did you know I got in?" I turned my gaze to Anand.

"I told him," Anand confessed with a mix of guilt and pride.

"You went into my desk and read the letter?"

"You told me it was nothing," he said. "I just wanted to know. For sure."

After dinner, I stood with my father on the balcony as the University Road traffic passed back and forth, fretted with honking, the clashing of gears from buses, the puttering of the rickshaws. Headlights blinked on as the sky's bands of pink and purple began to fade. Shadows darkened over the balcony. The wind shifted and, for a moment, carried the scent from the rosebushes below.

From the living room, I could hear *Die Hard* pounding from the TV. Anand had rented it again, a dubbed copy, from the corner paan shop. I heard Kamala Auntie speaking above the noise of machine guns, asking Anand who was shooting at whom and what was all that racket about. Anand's voice rose above the TV as he explained the plot to her point by point, and it stunned me how fluent Anand's command of Gujarati had become. Eight months ago, he was like me—we understood it well enough when spoken to us. But no chance in hell could we speak it, not more than a few phrases here and there. We were hopeless. But listening to him now, I thought, this kid's a genius.

"I knew you boys would one day go back to the States," said my father, leaning against the parapet. "But I thought perhaps after college, for graduate school or something. I didn't think it would be so soon."

We stared out at the cricket grounds of the H.L. College of Commerce across University Road, thronged now with children, strolling families, and students playing pickup games of cricket.

"I didn't think it would come up this soon either," I said. "But"—I fumbled for the words—"for who I am . . . what I want to do, I feel I'm wasting my time here." I told him about my recent visit to the NID, the general feeling that I was spinning my wheels, that I didn't think I could hold out another two years before I had any say in my future. "It's just not my world," I said, adding that I'd made a couple of friends at college, good friends, but this was about so much more. "I can't help feeling . . . that I'm letting something slip away."

My father turned to me, arms folded, nodding. I felt the need to explain somehow, to rationalize this feeling. "At first," I said, "applying to the school was just something to kill the monotony. To see if I could even get in. It kept me going."

"But now that you're in," my father replied, "you need to do all you can to see it through, no?"

"I don't know," I said. "With Mummi's health the way it is . . . I feel like . . ." A valve turned, shutting off the words. I couldn't bring myself to say them.

Across the road, a Hindi pop tune blasted from the speakers of the truck parked in the shopping complex. The noise aggravated the senses—a chirrupy voice bouncing above a crazy arabesque of tablas, trumpets, a flamenco guitar. One by one, the streetlights blinked on.

"I don't want to not be here," I tried, "if something happens to her."

"Your mother's health should not be an issue. You can't let what is unknown run your life, can you?" He was obscured now in the lengthening dark, the skittering of headlights. He shifted his weight from one foot to the other. "When I myself left for America, my father said to me one thing: 'Do not come back until you've accomplished what you've set out to do. No matter what happens.'"

"Was that the promise?" I asked him, remembering Hemant Uncle's words.

"Hmm?" He gave me a quick, curious look. "Yes." He nodded pensively. "He made me promise. He knew, of course. He knew he was not going to live much longer. He was already in poor health by then. Deep down, I think we both knew. But he made me promise. And as difficult as it was for me, especially after I got the telegram that he was gone, I stuck it out. I knew no one. I was just a new student up there in New York. And you, Anand, your mother hadn't left for America yet. I had maybe a hundred dollars. Yet somehow I got through."

I thought about that, my father alone, a student just beginning his studies at Cornell. Feeling cut off. And I thought more about my conversation with Hemant Uncle that past Diwali, how angry and bitter I'd then felt toward my father, and Hemant Uncle's words to me. "He thinks you're a brave man," I told my father now. "Hemant Uncle. He really admires you."

My father smiled. "It's not a question of brave or not. It's just . . . see . . ." He held out his palms. "Every opportunity is a dividing line. Here, you have things as they are." He raised one palm, then the other. "And here, things as they can be." His palms were but vaguely discernible shapes. "You choose if you want to commit to stepping over the line, easy as that, really."

I filled him in on the visa form I'd received and about my gambit with the art department.

"Can't hurt to try to get some money out of them," he said with the skepticism of a jaded gambler. He told me he had money back in the States, at our bank in Madison. Over the past few years, he had begun saving, whatever he could put aside, for the possibility that Anand and I might one day need it. But at this point, it wouldn't cover more than a year of tuition, so he had put in for a loan. Enough, he told me, to see me through undergrad studies (and paying out-of-state tuition at that). That had to be a monster of a loan, I thought.

This was sounding outlandish to me again, a selfish scheme on my part that would set my parents back way too much. I told him I was sorry. I'd see my way through another two years, but this was all getting out of hand. As I said it, though, I felt a wrenching, a resistance from deep within. I couldn't go back now, not against myself.

"Money or time, it's going to cost one or the other," my father said. "Which is more precious to you—money or time?"

I said all right, fine. "But I *will* pay back the loan, whatever it is, down the road. You need to let me do that."

My father laughed, but it was the laugh of a father. "Don't worry about that. We'll cross that bridge when we get to it."

The Hindi song from the speakers across the road rose in a smash of tablas and trumpets, the whooping of singers, then a narrow bridge of silence before the next track.

"When will you know?" I asked. "About the loan?"

"Before Bombay, I should think."

The living room doors opened, and my mother's silhouette appeared, edged against the wash of interior light, the blaze of guns from the TV. She stepped onto the balcony and slipped out toward us. Leaning over the parapet, she peered down at the garden.

"Nice how you can smell the roses from up here, no?" She turned to me, reached up, tucked a strand of hair behind her ear, and touched my shoulder. "So, you're leaving us?"

I put my arm around her. I could think of no gesture, no words that could express the inner breaking I felt, that contradiction of loss and optimism. And I realized that there is a gratitude that cannot be articulated. No words I knew, and no picture I could ever make could be equal to it. It was a gratitude you spent your whole life trying to live up to—you tried in the choices you made, the paths you took. You tried in the sum total of your actions. This, I sensed, was a rare kind of gratitude. It made me feel like a small child.

It reminded me that, above and beyond everything, I was their son. The feeling infiltrated the nerves and the blood and got me a bit jittery as I let it sink in. And as scary and overwhelming as the feeling was, I welcomed it and wanted to be equal to it.

~ ~ ~

We heard nothing more from Wisconsin before we left for Bombay. My father did hear from the bank. They had approved half the amount he had applied for. Anyway, we put together my visa application, along with my admissions letter, my passport, my father's bank statements, and the loan letter. We figured we had enough ammo to forge ahead.

In Bombay, I felt the presence of a metropolis that owed nothing to the rest of India. It lay sprawled on the Arabian, a massive, glittering sea creature made out of soot, steel, asphalt, and sweat, stretching its tentacles of train tracks and roadways into the Indian coastline. The city sent out energy waves in all directions, from every Victorian cupola and modern-day high-rise that studded Marine Drive. We walked along the drive, and I could feel Bombay's warm breath in the sea air. The hotels and office buildings were its organs, coursing with white light, electrical currents in its veins. Its neurons and pulsations registered in the call of vendors and revelers on Chowpatty Beach, the roaring of the beaten-in red double-deckers, the drone of the hornetlike taxis, the clip-clop of horse-drawn buggies, the flower sellers who worked and slept on the street corner. In the evenings, we maneuvered past the bodies of migrants camped on the pavement, wrapped in and surrounded by everything they owned, as we headed back to our hotel on Marine Drive. It was a cramped room for the four of us, but it was clean. The leaky bathtub pooled water all over the bathroom floor, but at least we weren't sleeping on the pavement under the shadow of high-rises and storefronts like the many we'd just seen outside. Plus we were near both the hospital and the consulate, the twin purposes of our visit.

We spent our first couple of days in the lobby of the Breach Candy Hospital while my mother underwent the tests that the specialist had ordered. I saw this specialist briefly when we went up to meet him at his office on one of the hospital's upper floors. He was a small, genial man with eyes as gentle as the tone in which he addressed us. I supposed he knew how to put his patients at ease, and that gave me comfort. Soon after we introduced ourselves, though, my father asked Anand and me to wait down in the lobby.

We sat through the afternoon on cushioned black chairs along-side an anxious mother—a Muslim woman, I guessed, with a sheer veil pulled over her head, who tried to keep her bored child from getting crabby. The lobby sweeper swept, the orderlies in their shirt-sleeves sauntered past, and now and then the intercom itched with a gravelly voice paging one doctor or another. The unsettling smell of sweat and pharmaceuticals hung in the air.

We kept our attention on our books. Anand's finals and mine were coming up in a few weeks, and the only way to see our way through this—all of this—was to be like those explorers hacking through the African jungle with machetes toward signs of daylight on the far side.

It was late in the afternoon when our parents appeared. My mother looked tired, but at least she was in good spirits. She told us it was more of the same—a sonogram, biopsy, blood tests—along with an abdominal CT scan "just to be safe," the specialist had said. She said it would be a couple of days before the results came back, and she had to see the specialist again.

"Crap," I said, "not more waiting."

"He's a good man, though," my father said. "At least there's that."

My father took us around his old stomping grounds—the restaurant where he used to eat lunch when he was an IIT student back in the late sixties. It was a low-ceilinged hall, strictly working class, much like the mess hall at Xavier's. Servers rushed around with rotis, vegetables, and dal in tin pots, making sure everyone's plates were full. We hired a driver who took us around winding

Malabar Hill, lined thick with trees, past shady colonial bungalows, the addresses of the moneyed, a stark contrast to the city's teeming open-air markets, all jostling warrens of trade and traffic, where I couldn't take pictures fast enough of flower stalls, fabric shops, hole-in-the-wall record shops, anything that flitted past the window of my camera. The Gateway of India seemed to me a gorgeous monstrosity of volcanic rock, a sea god's throne lifted straight out of the Arabian Sea. It had none of the subtlety of the Taj, but it was impressive still in all its blunt, imperial features—thick-shouldered, with muscular columns on either side of a Mughal-style archway, topped by turrets that decorated the Gateway like epaulets on an admiral's shoulders. From the jetty along the sea-facing side of the Gateway, we boarded a boat along with a handful of Indian tourists for a ride far out into the bay.

Anand and I stood on the top deck. Not a sound out there in the still and heavy air but the boat's ripsawing motor as we plied the dense gray-blue water. I saw warships anchored farther out past Bombay's promontory, and out where the water became glassy white, merchant marine freighters floated like phantoms against the horizon. I wondered where they were headed and about the lives of all the people aboard all those ships. People I would never know. People whose futures, out there in the shimmering silvery expanse, along all the shipping lanes of the world, seemed the most exotic and adventurous of escapes.

~ ~ ~

On the morning before our appointment at the consulate, I was anxious, couldn't relax. After a couple of hours of attempting to study, I finally put away my books and got dressed. My father and I got our papers together, and we walked to the consulate, past the

Breach Candy Hospital, past a glimpse of the sea. We didn't say much. There was nothing left to do now but to see this through.

The consulate was a high-security fortress. Marines stood guard at the front gate, flanked by palm trees, while the American flag hung from its rooftop pole in the breezeless air. Metal detectors scanned us as we passed through the entrance.

While it all gave an intimidating impression, I tried to think of it as a brief return home. I filed in with a steady stream of visa hopefuls through the security area. To the Americans dressed in navy-blue blazers, walkie-talkies clipped to their belts, I was no more and no less than anyone else in that crowd of would-be immigrants.

We took numbers that told us our place in the queue, and we were ushered into a gray-carpeted waiting room filled with rows of chairs where everyone gathered: families with infants, the newly married, old women who could scarcely speak a word of English, and students like me applying for their own visas. Artificial plants in decorative pots stood in the corners of this strangely antiseptic space, and a portrait of President George Bush, in his square metal glasses, stared back at us from the wall.

Seated behind thick glass windows along the far side of the room, like tellers at a bank, were the consulate's staffers, calling up and interviewing the applicants one by one. The applicants being interviewed leaned toward narrow slots at the base of the windows—the only channel of communication—through which they spoke in low, anxious tones and pushed files back and forth. The air hummed with nervous anticipation punctuated now and again by a tinny, two-note chime that summoned the next applicant in the queue. My father and I waited for our queue number to flash up on one of the displays above the windows.

I don't know how long we waited—an hour, two hours—before we heard the chime and saw our number come up. We got up and approached our window, where a youthful-looking American man who could've passed for a high-school guidance counselor greeted us with an officious smile. Hunched forward, his fingers intertwined, the interviewer began asking for our passports, case number, and the "nature of our visit." The doors of the landing boat had finally dropped, and I felt myself charging from the boat and up the choppy strand under a hail of interrogation.

To be fair, the interviewer was friendly and welcoming. He spoke admiringly of Wisconsin and of the university. He looked over my visa application, the admission letter, and the loan papers—everything we had in our small arsenal. Then he told me that he was placing my file on hold, saying he wasn't convinced that the loan amount, plus whatever money my parents would be putting up, would be enough to meet my board and tuition costs. My father countered by showing him proof of his employment as director at the institute and his balance at the State Bank. With his income, he assured him, he could easily supplement the loan and the money already in our Wisconsin account. But the interviewer held fast and told us the consulate would communicate with the university about my case. "Sorry," he said, "but that's the best I can do." He smiled, his mouth a thin comma, and sat with his shoulders hunched, his hands clasped, as if he'd just finished reprimanding a student about poor grades. "Good luck," he said as we gathered up our things.

Chapter 22

March 18, 1989

Dear Vik,

Sorry to hear that the news from Bombay is so mixed. I'm glad to hear your mother's doing much better. But on the "coming back" front, we're still in the dark, I guess.

Nate and I were kicking around ideas for a bunch of ten- or fifteen-minute shorts we could shoot this summer. We're thinking a James Bond–meets–Woody Allen spy spoof, like we tried in the fall of senior year, remember? But with real dialogue and editing this time. What do you think? Over spring break, we're going to start roughing out ideas. Feel free to jump in.

By the way, when you see Nate again, if you ever do, you won't recognize him: his hair's down to his shoulders, and he's grown a goatee. The man thinks it makes him look sexy. But I don't see the girls exactly flocking to his dorm room.

Let me say, though, that it's not his hairdo that bothered me recently but his attitude. After winter break, Nate called up and invited me over to his dorm to hang out. We hadn't seen each other in a couple of months because of classes and work and so on, but I was eager to see him. Then I get to his room and realize he's throwing a kegger with all his floormates. He's halfway to hammered when I show up, and after an hour, it's like I'm not even there. I tried to catch up with him, find out how his semester went, but the whole night he pretty much blew me off. It was very strange. All he's doing is getting shitfaced with all his smarmy dorm friends, passing the bong around. After a couple of hours, I just left. Something felt very wrong. He didn't seem like the same Nate.

The next day, I called him up and confronted him about his dick attitude, and he, of course, got defensive and called me a priss. The whole thing got ugly. Anyway, we didn't talk again till last week. I ran into him at the Union after class, and we actually sat and talked. Really talked this time. He apologized and said he had cut down on the partying—guess the day after his kegger, he got into some major trouble with his RA. We talked about our spring semesters, about working on some creative projects again, and little by little, it began to feel strangely like old times again. Minus you of course.

Speaking of the spring semester, I'm a busy bee these days. The job at WHA is going great—I'm actually running the switcher during the Badger basketball games now, and they got me working a couple more shifts. It gets pretty intense over there. In fact, I may be able to get you work at the station if you're interested. You know, work-study or something.

Vik, if you want my two cents—not that it matters—I would say to let things take their course and don't let them bum you out just yet. Let's see how this visa thing shakes down, take it from there. Write as soon as you can.

Karl

P.S. So we were right in guessing who Priya was in those Diwali pics. All I can say is well done.

~ ~ ~

No information came from the consulate for weeks following our Bombay trip. My afternoons were abandoned caves in which I hunkered and studied while outside the late-March heat reared its angry head. By midafternoon, the streets were blinding white.

Anand spent more time with his new tutor, cramming for his own finals in Sanskrit, Hindi, Gujarati. He grumbled because the Nintendo was off limits for the time being.

I continued to wonder about Priya: where she was and whether, as Manju alleged, I had anything to do with whatever had become of her.

One day after French lecture, Madame Varma asked if I'd had any news of Priya. I told her no, I hadn't, but perhaps Manju or Hannah might have. Madame Varma shook her head, bundling her notes and textbook in her arm. "They say they haven't heard anything," she said in a tone both concerned and disappointed. "Her family simply says she's gone away on holiday or some such." A corner of her mouth turned down, and she shrugged. "Wherever she is, I do hope she keeps up with her studies. She would do well to continue in her French." I was still mulling over Madame Varma's mysterious bit of information—or lack thereof—when she stopped at the door to say, "Tell me, will you, Vikram, if you find out anything?" I told her of course I would.

As I crossed the college courtyard, I wondered why Madame Varma thought to ask me about Priya. How could she have known that Priya and I knew each other? Had we been so obvious? Ah, well, I thought, what does it matter now anyway? She was gone. Safely away from this place.

I arrived in Pradeep's room to find Devasia seated at the desk, recording his notes into the tape recorder. Pradeep sat at the edge of his cot, his back straight, head bowed, listening attentively. After a few more minutes of dictation, Devasia hit "Stop" on the recorder. That was it, he said, that was everything he had. Between Devasia and me, Pradeep now had on cassette all the notes he would need ahead of the exams.

The three of us spent the rest of the afternoon going over notes, quizzing each other, making sure every last scrap of information was stuffed into our heads. When I couldn't take it anymore, I shut my notebook and lay back on Pradeep's cot. I had a headache. I realized I hadn't eaten since breakfast. A sour feeling found its way into my stomach.

Pradeep said he had medicines that might help. "I always keep stomach pills handy here," he announced, feeling his way from the cot to the metal cabinet on the opposite wall.

"Is the hostel food that bad?" I joked.

Devasia chuckled knowingly, patting his stomach. "You need guts of steel here."

"Not only that," Pradeep said, "but the tension over these exams too can give indigestion or like that." Pradeep ran his hands along the bottles and packets of toiletries on one of the cabinet shelves, feeling for the stomach pills. On the floor of the cabinet, I noticed Pradeep's padlocked red velvet box in which he kept his Diwali money.

"You still have that money, Pradeep?" I asked. "I thought your cousin was taking it."

Pradeep slapped his palms together. "*Hut-teriki!* You know, my cousin's visit was postponed so now he is coming after finals only. But about studio and all, he has arranged. He has spoken to his music contacts, and they are even interested to hear my recording, so it's good news, I think so."

"Next stop Bollywood?" Devasia smiled, turning in the chair toward us.

Pradeep shut the cabinet door, and I took from him the antacids encased in a sheet of plastic and foil.

"What Bollywood?" Pradeep countered with mock outrage, a satisfied grin on his face, and he leaned on cupped hands on his walking stick, cutting the figure of an impresario. "I am aiming for Ravi Shankar, bhai, Zakir Hussain. Not Bollywood songs."

"Wah! *Ustad* Pradeep Prabhakar," Devasia said jovially, with a playful flourish of his hand. "Very good!" He rose from the chair, stretched, and yawned. "I'm going to take nap," he said, "then I can continue."

I stubbed out two pills from the sheet, turned them over in my mouth, letting the metallic grit dissolve. "No matter what, you guys are all set and on your way," I said, lying back and staring up at the ceiling.

"But you are also, Vikram bhai," Pradeep said. "You are also on your way."

I swallowed the last gritty bits of the antacids.

"Because—" Pradeep tapped his stick on the floor, his head turning from side to side, searching for the words. "Because . . . where there is intention, there is action, and action means change."

"Please," I said, sitting up. "Intention means zilch. Now and then, you need a lot of luck." I shook my head and got to my feet. "That action and change stuff," I continued, "I've tried it. It doesn't work. You need luck, and I'm always, always short." I shook my head, sat back down, and stared at my shoes. "It's like an anaconda." I looked up at Pradeep and Devasia. "Life. The more you fight it, the tighter it gets its grip on you."

Pradeep and Devasia said not a word. What could they say, anyway? What could they do for me?

"I admire you guys, I really do," I said. "Pradeep, you'll do great, and Devasia, you're going to be an awesome priest." I couldn't think of anything more to say.

"But luck is the result of our actions, don't you think so?" Pradeep offered.

"No," I said and made for the door.

I didn't want to drag them down with me, and I didn't want empty words to cheer me up either. All I could think to do was walk out of there. There was nothing to say. I needed to get home, eat something, and crash. And no, I wasn't going to even look at the mailbox.

~ ~ ~

Classes let out at the end of March to make way for study week, after which the finals kicked off. I felt ill much of that time. Life itself felt in suspension, a source of churning pain. I studied till my eyes were bleary and my mind fogged. I slept. Awoke. Ate little. And I studied with Pradeep and Devasia at the hostel in the afternoons.

One day, coming back from a study session, I discovered our cleaning girl in close conversation with a young man I had never seen before. They lingered downstairs as I dragged my Luna into the entrance hall to stand it up under the staircase. The man stood almost touching her, his elbow propped casually against the wall. He spoke in intimate murmurs to the girl, her back to the wall, her hands crossed behind her. They smiled surreptitiously at me. I got the feeling I'd interrupted something, smiled hello, and hurried up the two flights to our place.

"What's going on down there?" I asked my mother.

"She is meeting her fiancé, that's all," she replied, serving Anand and me our rotis and vegetables. "She asked if they could meet downstairs."

"Hmm," I intoned suggestively. I was glad someone was having fun around here.

~ ~ ~

The finals lasted through the second week of April. Seven exams, one or two each day. All I knew was I needed the marks. Without the marks, the future receded, like a mountain climber losing his grip and sliding helplessly. Climb. Just keep climbing.

For the finals, every student in the state university system—and St. Xavier's was one of dozens of colleges that made up Gujarat University—got assigned a seat number at one of various sites around Ahmedabad. Your seat number could be at any random college in the city, regardless of which college you actually attended.

My seat assignment took me across Nehru Bridge into a huddle of low-slung office blocks and tea stalls, to C.U. Arts College, a whitewashed, moldering structure of many floors. Scooters lined up along an unpaved alley where students, none of whom I recognized, lingered aimlessly, looking dazed, their notebooks and ballpoint pens in hand. I made my way through, climbed up several flights of stairs in a dusty stairwell, joined in with the drift of other test takers.

It was like a mental asylum here: wide, murky hallways shrieking with echoes. The walls were stained; the corners needed sweeping. Stray dogs could have been wandering here, and I wouldn't have been surprised. I found my lecture hall—a cruel white room where sullen-faced students filled the rows of benches beneath a cloud of tense whispers. A hot wind blew through the windows, which looked out on a cement wall opposite the alleyway, a drainage pipe, and a shard of daylight.

The proctor was a stern-faced woman, fiftyish, with a frump of black-dyed hair, protruding teeth, and a squat, sari-clad torso. Her watchful eyes, seeped of all love, scanned the lot of us as she passed out exam booklets and the question papers. She snapped at a girl, telling her to shut her notebook, then at a boy for talking. I did not recognize her, knew nothing of her but that she was a university bureaucrat.

The finals were administered by the university's central testing bureaucracy. No matter which college you went to, you took the same set of exams as every other student in your major throughout the state. These exams were created, enforced, and graded not by your own professors but by a committee of pitiless strangers—Orwellian bureaucrats—and that made everything that much more stressful.

I wondered where Pradeep and Devasia were assigned to take their exams, how they were doing today, when I would see them next. That's when I realized I missed them. I missed being at Xavier's, even pined for the familiar faces and the shady lecture halls, the teachers who knew my work. I took a deep breath, turned my attention to the question paper, and got ready to write. A deluge of writing lay ahead. A glance at the questions would hint at my fate.

~ ~ ~

When it was over, I felt like I'd survived a week of artillery fire. I came home, sank in my bed, groaned with exhaustion. My mother asked me how I thought the exams went. I shrugged and shook my head. Something felt off. I felt relief, of course, that it was over, but little sense of accomplishment. You want that feeling of connection between the ball and the sweet spot on the bat. The batter knows, just knows that very instant, even before he drops the bat to take the bases. Knows he's knocked it out of the park. I closed my eyes. I knew I had *not* knocked this out of the park.

One morning three weeks later, there was an announcement in the newspaper that Gujarat University's exam results would be posted that afternoon. With trepidation, I got on the Luna and made for the university's main administration building, an enormous, utilitarian cement block in a barren field. Students had already gathered at a kiosk just outside the building, looking up their marks. I managed to wedge myself in and found my seat number on the list.

I ran my finger from my number to the cumulative score next to it. I did it again, to double-check. No doubt about it. I'd scored two points below the first class cutoff. Just as I suspected: second class.

I turned away and, in a daze, returned to my Luna. I revved the motor and started back for Navarangpura. I felt numb. Questions swirled around my head. Could I have done better? I didn't know how. Did I study hard enough? I thought I had, just short of going blind and frying my brain. Yet a wave of self-loathing came over me, and I tried to figure it out. There was finesse to these things that Pradeep and Devasia had mastered after a lifetime of Indian schooling. They knew how to decode the questions, dance with them, phrase their answers in the way the graders wanted them phrased. It was more exhausting than it was worth. It didn't seem fair to me, but there was no budging from the sheer and naked fact: I was second class.

The marks weren't high enough for me to continue pressing my case with the consulate because Wisconsin would surely reject them. I imagined the pall of disappointment that would cling to me like a foul odor once everyone knew. Because they would ask how the exams had gone, and I would tell them, "Second class." May as well brand it onto my forehead. It wasn't good enough. No better than my grades in high school. Mr. Second Class. A spade is a spade.

I arrived back at the bungalow. As I got off the Luna, I heard soft voices behind the entrance doors. The doors opened, and the cleaning girl appeared, giggling. Seeing me, she covered her mouth, embarrassed, and swished away on bare feet and jingling anklets. Her boyfriend—fiancé, lover, whatever—followed close behind, swinging open the doors. He almost ran into me.

"Sorry," he uttered, then, laughing, called to the girl to come back. He ran after her, disappearing around the corner.

I hoisted the Luna through the doors and pulled it up onto its stand under the staircase. From behind me, I heard the trilling of a bicycle bell. It was the postman, who made his rounds on his bicycle with his canvas sack of mail slung at his shoulder. He came to a stop and riffled through the contents of the mail sack. Finally, he pulled out a large envelope and a clipboard. Glancing at it, he called out, "Vikram Mistry?"

"What is it?" I asked him in Gujarati.

"Sign, please."

I signed a sheet on the clipboard, and he handed the envelope to me. Replacing the clipboard inside the sack, the postman pedaled away as hushed as the wind.

The envelope was from the US Consulate.

Chapter 23

My heart pounded—a stampede of hooves in my chest—all the way up the stairs and back into my room. It pounded as I pulled a tab that opened a seam along the long side of the envelope. My passport dropped out, fell to the floor. Inside the envelope: a letter.

I scanned the opening words: They had contacted the university, made mention of a scholarship. I knew of no scholarship. I was baffled. They said after reviewing all my information, they determined that I showed "sufficient proof of financial support" and were granting me a student visa. I flipped through my passport. No lie. There it was. The visa stamp. Bearing the insignia of the United States government.

Euphoria. A lightness. A floating feeling. I flung the letter and passport into the air, didn't know whether to laugh or cry, and slumped into my chair. I pounded my fist on my desk.

My mother rushed to the door. "My god! Why all that noise?"

I showed her the letter. She read it over; her eyes went wide. "Wow," she said, and immediately she went to the phone in the dining room and dialed up my father at the institute. Her tone on the phone with him was businesslike, low-key—I knew she was trying to contain her excitement. She told him I had news for him and handed me the phone.

It still seemed unreal to me. Things like this were only supposed to happen in movies or to other people. And that bit in the letter about the scholarship? "What was that about?" I asked my father.

"Maybe your department tried to contact you about it, but the letter never arrived," he said. "That portfolio you sent might have done the job."

I laughed to myself: the one windfall to come out of this whole scenario never actually arrived. My father suggested sending a telegram to Wisconsin's admissions office to verify the scholarship, and I told him I'd head over to the post office right away.

"Get on it," he said. "And congratulations."

I hung up and sat in a daze on a dining room chair as Anand and my mother set up the table for lunch. As we ate, I was aware of the others asking me questions, pressing me for details. When would I go? Where would I stay? What would I study?

"Can I come?" Anand asked.

"How are you going? In suitcase?" my mother asked. She turned to me, began laughing, "Yeah, do that. Put Anand in suitcase." She continued laughing. "House will be nice and quiet."

Anand didn't laugh, though, and his face grew sullen. He poured some of the *kadhi* from his steel bowl over the rice on his plate, keeping his eyes lowered.

"Did you find out," my mother turned to me, "about your marks?"

"Hmm?" I said. "What marks? Oh." I remembered. "Yeah, they were all up," and the thought was an anchor weighing me down.

My mother must've noticed the sudden drop in my tone. "But you are not happy with them."

"Let's just say," I said, "this couldn't have come at a better time."

~ ~ ~

Pradeep, you nailed it. That's what I wanted to tell him when I saw him. *What you said about intention, action, and change. Action creating the possibilities for luck.* I knew he was still at the hostel, along with Devasia, and that he wouldn't be leaving for Bombay for another week.

The next day, I decided to drop by and pay him and Devasia a visit, so I slung my camera across my shoulder and rode down on the Luna. I had to go to Xavier's anyway, to pick up a leaving certificate from Rajkumar.

I wondered if, after today, I would ever see Pradeep or Devasia again. Devasia would soon be leaving, back to Madras for summer break. Thinking about it, I began to feel the first stirrings of the sadness that leaving brings. It was like that moment when, taking my finals in that grimy college across the bridge, I began to miss Xavier's. In spite of ourselves, we put down roots. When we're least aware of it, we form kinships.

The college grounds were quiet except for the cawing of crows. The shed under which all the scooters were usually parked was largely empty. I parked the Luna inside the gate, next to a couple of scooters, and headed up the gravel walk that led to the front entryway. The lobby was airy and vacant; the bulletins posted inside the glass cases looked neglected. They seemed like relics from another life, a long-turned chapter. I went up the stairway to the second floor and into the college office.

As always, the table fans oscillated, and the sashes on the far wall, thrown open, gave on the eucalyptus and neem trees that fronted the college. They hung there, barely swaying in the hot afternoon, reluctant to move at all. A clerk at the other end of the room muttered something, and I heard the clink of a chai cup behind a stack of folders. Stacks of files fluttered in the drafts of oscillating air. Rajkumar sat at the counter, eyes closed behind his glasses, chin resting in one hand. His other hand, holding a ballpoint pen, rested on the table. Gradually, as I stood there, his head began to tilt in his hand. He began snoring. I cleared my throat. Rajkumar shot awake, grumbling to himself, and adjusted his glasses on his ferret nose.

"Sorry," I said, "didn't mean to wake you."

"No one is sleeping." Rajkumar darted quick glances behind him and to the side. He took a look at me and blinked, his beady eyes popping out at me behind his glasses, and he said, "Oh-ho, you are Mistry's boy, no?"

"I came here about a leaving certificate."

Rajkumar's mouth became an O and he tsked a few times, shaking his small ferret head. "Where are you leaving? No troubles here, I hope?" There was a false tone of alarm in his voice, then he smiled in the way you would imagine a snake smiling.

I explained there were no "troubles." I was transferring to a school in the States. I asked if he could make up a certificate for me. I could come back that afternoon, pay whatever fee the college charged.

"But it is not enough you get leaving certificate. You must also see Father, he must approve, then sign it."

"Fine," I said. "Is he in?"

Rajkumar bobbed his head, that bell-like signal for yes. "Summer vacation for students only, not for staff." He wagged his index finger. "We keep on here."

Rajkumar's self-righteousness was entertaining, but I wanted to hurry things up. I told him I'd stop by later, pick up the certificate and get Father's signature.

But Rajkumar held out his palm in a gesture for me to settle down. "It will take some time to prepare certificate, bhai."

Time? If there was one thing in abundance in the college office, it was time.

In the back, a clerk hocked up phlegm, then leaned over and spat out the window. Rajkumar dug around in a drawer, finally came up with a pen and paper, asked for my name and student number.

"You know m— Sorry. Vikram Mistry. Student number one-eighty-four."

Rajkumar scratched it out with his pen.

"So I can pick it up this afternoon?"

Rajkumar twisted in his chair, peered up at the clock. "Now it is too late," he announced. "Come back tomorrow noon."

I sighed. "Do I need to make an appointment with the principal to get his signature?" I wanted to be sure he wasn't hiding another bureaucratic loophole from me. But he said no, I ought to be able to go in and see him. He lifted his head and squinted at me. "You could not adjust to Xavier's, is it?" He sneered. "This is tough college. Not everyone can handle."

"You're right about that," I said. "See you tomorrow."

Only a few students were still in residence at the hostels. Most had taken off for the summer—from the end of exams in April, through May, until classes reconvened in late June. I walked down to the library, but the doors were locked. I peered inside: everything still and hidden in half-light. No librarian behind the counter. And there was the table where I always sat, browsing the *Time* magazines, and the stand where we read the papers. I pointed my camera up to the library shingle, took a snap. I walked out through the empty quad, past the bare canteen, feeling, in that brief lapse of time, like the place was mine. I took a few pictures, then stood still, listened. Birds cheeping somewhere. A rickshaw whined along the road. Then a voice raised in song, rising and falling in classical ghazal style, effortlessly. It came from one of the upper windows of the hostel. It sounded like Pradeep.

I hurried toward the hostel, hoping to catch him in midperformance so I could take pictures. I guessed he was rehearsing for his

Bombay recording session, up in the meeting hall on the second floor. From the sound of it, he was more than ready: his voice lifted and turned with the melody as nimbly as I'd ever heard it. But as I began climbing the steps, I noticed that the door to his first-floor room was open.

"Pradeep?" I called, and peered into the room. No one there. From the far wall, daylight from the barred window cast hard angles and silhouettes around the room. "Pradeep?" I called again, though by now I was sure it was Pradeep's voice coming from upstairs.

I was about to shut the door when I noticed signs that someone had just been here and left. In a hurry. The bedsheets were upturned, the desk looked rummaged through, and the cabinet doors hung half-open. I walked over to the cabinet to see if all was in order.

Clothes lay strewn on the floor of the cabinet, shucked from their hangers; toilet articles were scattered all over the top shelves. On the bottom of the cabinet, I saw the upholstered box—the one in which Pradeep kept his prize money. But the lock was missing, and the clasp turned open. I found the lock on the floor, to the side of the cabinet, and picked it up. It looked like it had been smashed open, with a rock maybe. I laid my camera on the cot, then brought the box from the shelf over to the desk and checked inside.

The money was gone.

Chapter 24

I heard a scooter rev up and went over to the window. From between the clump of trees that bordered the college building and the hostel, I sighted Vinod in his Harley-Davidson T-shirt, pushing his Bajaj scooter out onto the drive. He zipped closed a satchel, unlocked the bin below the scooter's handlebars, and stowed the satchel away. He glanced around, as if to make sure he was unnoticed, then climbed onto the scooter.

"Vinod," I shouted out the window.

He started and jerked his head in my direction. His eyes squinted to get a better look through the trees. Then I saw his mouth part in a quick smile, and from his shirt pocket, he took out a pair of sunglasses and put them on.

"Bye-bye, boss." He waved his hand, then pulled out toward the gate.

I rushed out of the room, along the veranda, jumped the ledge on the far side, and ran through the trees. By that time, Vinod was already at the gate, about to pull into traffic. For a split second, I thought to go back to the hostel, find Pradeep and tell him he'd been robbed. Or else to find Devasia. But if I lost track of Vinod,

I got the feeling we'd never see him—or Pradeep's money—again. My mind jumped back and forth, and even before I knew what I was doing, my legs were pumping hard toward the gate where my Luna was parked.

Vinod zipped onto the road as I jerked the Luna off its stand and cranked the pedal to power up the motor. I revved up the accelerator and pulled into traffic as a rickshaw sped past me, leaving a trail of honking in its wake. Vinod was at the end of the road, past the chai café. I saw him and managed to close some of the distance between us before he sped on past the university bus stand.

I kept my sights on his baggy black Harley T-shirt. It billowed out from his back so that it looked like a parachute as he rode. He slouched low in his seat and kept a hard pace past the bicycles and rickshaws and scooters before he rounded a sharp left at the Vijay Cross Roads. I rode the Luna as hard as it could go, swerved along past a camel cart and a crowd of laborers taking a break from digging a trench along the side of the road.

Vijay rode much farther and longer than I expected, and I began to wonder if I had enough fuel in the moped to keep going. I didn't think he was aware I was behind him; I'd kept a good distance and plenty of intervening traffic between us. Once he did glance back in my direction, but I managed to duck out of sight. By now we were past the buildings and scrubby fields that marked Gujarat University's main campus and the adjoining Expo grounds, and we'd entered a new subdivision of housing blocks and teeming bazaars and shantytowns. Children in rags ran alongside the traffic; women filled buckets or washed clothes at roadside taps. Scooters bunched close together in the plots of dirt that became makeshift parking lots at the foot of mildewed and soot-stained apartment high-rises. Cows slouched in the gutter, their ears flicking off flies; more cows huddled in the middle of the intersections.

The neighborhoods began to look familiar now. Strangely familiar. I realized that I was heading back into dreary Ghatlodiya, on its outer edge. The road narrowed, became more potholed, with shop fronts jammed against each other on both sides. Past this narrow stretch, a large field opened up on one side, separating the road from a row of apartment blocks ranged like gray and dismal bluffs. This was the site of my long-ago monsoon-logged rickshaw-bicycle accident, when I'd gotten a mouthful of rainwater and dysentery as a result. For a flash, I wondered if the woman we almost trampled that day was all right; she probably lived in one of these apartments. Dogs and street children scavenged here, and the locals crisscrossed the field on scooters, bicycles, and rickshaws in an all-day migration. Up ahead, past a knot of traffic, I noticed Vinod veering into the field. I followed. Now that we were in the open, with less traffic to hide me, I needed to be extra cautious.

Vinod reached the other side of the field and disappeared in the spaces between the apartment buildings. The buildings loomed up sooty and gray on all sides, forming a labyrinth of alleys and lanes overhung by a webwork of telephone wires. These were not the surroundings I had associated with Vinod—they just didn't mesh with all that talk about America and studying in Florida, San Diego, and New York.

A rooster pecked at the earth; an infant sat in an open doorway from which I could hear a blaring television. I saw no sign of Vinod, and his tracks were lost in the palimpsest of tire marks in the dirt. The tire trails from motorcycles and scooters had left deep grooves in the lanes, hardened now like dinosaur prints. I heard voices echoing from the upper floors—the clamor of children playing, Hindi music from a radio. Revving up the motor, I turned a corner and rode up a wider lane. I reached the junction at the end and took a look around. Nothing.

Then, in the narrow space between buildings, I saw a dark shape dart past on a scooter. I took off again, threading between the buildings, skidded left, and sighted Vinod directly in front of me, pulling farther away. Dust from the scooter clouded the view, but I could see his billowing T-shirt, his shoulders hunched and head low over the handlebars.

I tried to keep up with him, but that was when the Luna began to alternate between a smooth whine and a series of sputtering coughs. I checked the fuel gauge: the needle had settled under the *E*. Shit. Out of gas. *Goddammit!* The Luna hiccuped and managed to sputter along till the end of the block before the motor simply petered out, and I glided noiselessly for a few yards. I scrambled off, leaned the moped against the side of an apartment building. Vinod couldn't be far off. I ran as hard as I could up the next lane.

"Vinod," I yelled at the upper stories. It was all I could think to do, now that I'd lost sight of him. "Vinod!"

I wiped at my eyes and shielded them. The sun hit me hard from its perch just above the rooftops. Then against the glare, not far away, I could make out a figure standing in the opening to a ground-floor apartment patio. A few steps closer, I could see it was Vinod. He stepped off the patio, his shoulders squared, and moved toward me. As he did, I noticed the satchel in one hand. It bulged with the money. "What the hell you doing here?" he demanded, stopping a few yards in front of his patio, next to his gray, dirt-smeared Bajaj scooter.

I could see his face now as I approached. Flushed, shiny with sweat, eyes wide.

"Thought I'd lost you," I said, trying to catch my breath. "Why did you take it, Vinod?"

Vinod's eyes narrowed. "Hmm?" He bunched his shoulders together, spread out his arms in a gesture of outraged confusion. "I took nothing."

"That." I pointed to the satchel in his hand.

"Vinod bhaiya?" a boy's voice called out. Against the sun, I could make out nothing but his eyes leering down at us from an upstairs balcony. "Some trouble?"

Vinod waved him away. "It's okay, Raju. Go on." But the boy stayed where he was, leaned forward on the parapet.

From inside the apartment, a woman in her forties in a yellow sari emerged, agitated, patting her hair as if she'd just finished pinning it. She wore her hair long and braided, the way my mother used to wear hers before we left for America. She took a step onto the patio and stood there, one hand at her hip. "What's happening, Vinod?" she snapped in Gujarati, thrusting a flat, upturned palm toward him. "What did you do now?"

"You took his money," I said. "What'd you do it for?"

The woman shot me a glance. "What money?" And she turned to Vinod. "If I find you stole money—"

"Ma, get inside, I'm just talking to my friend here. Everything is fine." But Vinod's tone was too agitated to convince her.

Still, she relented and withdrew into the apartment. I heard her muttering, shaking her head dismally, "I've really had it with that boy."

"Give Pradeep back his money," I said, "and no one will ever hear about this."

Vinod thought for a moment, then let out a short, disdainful laugh. "Tell whatever you want to whoever. Go on. Go on, tell the people at college Vinod is a thief."

"How's this going to fly?" I said. "You know Pradeep'll be looking for his money. Sooner or later, you'll have to go back and answer for it."

"Go back?" he looked at me as if I'd just said the most ridiculous thing. "Why would I go back?" He held up the satchel. "This is so I never need to go back. By the time you fools start up in college again, I will be long gone."

"With Pradeep's money. Come on, man, he's your friend."

"*Pradeep's* money?" Vinod huffed. "*My* money." He stepped back onto the patio. I followed a couple of steps behind and stopped at the opening to the patio. "I'm no thief, American. I took only my fee. My manager's fee."

A motorcycle, or I should say *most* of a motorcycle, leaned against the wall in the far corner of the patio. On the maroon-colored fuel tank, I could make out the words "Harley-Davidson." Chunks of the seat padding were missing, and spare parts—springs, an exhaust pipe, a gearbox—lay scattered on grease-stained rags alongside assorted tools. A few potted plants were lined up along the floor and against the parapet, trying to hide areas of crumbled plaster, and a pair of neglected-looking lawn chairs sat haphazardly in the patio's center.

Vinod spun around to face me. "Pradeep has got more than one way to get to Bombay," he said. "He has his talent. See how many bookings he is now getting. Why? Thanks to me." He tapped the satchel against his chest. "You know that I am the one who told him to take part in Diwali festival? Otherwise, he would not have done it. He would not have this"—his shook the satchel at me—"without me anyway." He stepped toward me till we were face to face. "Pradeep does not need this where he is going." His voice was calmer now, as if he was shifting strategies. "For you and for Pradeep, come on, this is nothing." He lowered his voice to a hoarse whisper. "But for me, everything."

"You can't get to America on three thousand rupees, Vinod. You can get an awful lot of pot with it, though—"

At that, Vinod shot a glance back at his apartment, then grabbed me by the collar. "You make jokes. But I'm being so honest with you. I am like a friend to you." His eyes locked in on me, unblinking.

I sensed that we had an audience now: children and housewives across the lane all stopped to stare at us. He must've sensed it too and took a step away from me. "You all are gone. On your way," he said. "But myself . . . first year fail, start from scratch—no way! Not for me, dost." He spun one of the lawn chairs around so that it faced me and dropped himself into it, letting out a deep, weary breath. He kept a hand on the satchel.

"You might actually make it out, Vinod, if you gave yourself half a chance."

"Here is some real news from the real world, American." Vinod stared at me, his tone thick with condescension. "When all the assholes are against you, there is no getting out, no winning. No matter how hard you try. Sridharan, D'Souza, your own family"—with each word, he thumped the satchel against his knee—"there is no winning." He flipped his hand at me dismissively. "You think you're some superior bloke. You can come here, talk to me like I'm some naïve villager." He leaned forward in his chair, eyes fixed on me. There was something in them so unflinching that it was beginning to worry me. "For me, Xavier's is finished chapter. And you, Pradeep, and all you fools, you are also finished chapter."

"Have it your way," I told him, "but not with Pradeep's money. Look, I can go to D'Souza with this, you want that?"

"So you are that principal's servant now?" he huffed. "Look, Pradeep does not need this money." He held up the satchel. "His outcome is already known. So why make bigger issue out of this, bhaiya?"

Vinod stared at me through the long silence that followed. Then a smile slanted one side of his mouth, and he lowered the satchel, clasping it in both hands. "I see," he said. "You want some, huh?" He nodded at me. "Sure, of course. I understand, dost. You've gone through so much trouble to follow me here. Why involve anyone else? I will give . . ." He raised his chin, eyes narrowed, contemplating a bargain. "Five hundred. Five hundred for you." He unzipped the satchel, clutched the bills inside, and drew them out partway for me to see. "You can enjoy with five hundred." He zipped the satchel back up. "And you will not see me again. All this is past."

I could see that no matter how much more I pleaded, Vinod wasn't going to budge. I turned around and made to leave. "This isn't over," I said as I neared the edge of the patio.

"You want trouble?" Vinod said, swiftly rising from his chair, stepping toward me. He nodded, turning something over in his mind, and then he got very still for a moment. Neither of us said a word. That's when two things happened: I made a lunge for the satchel, and Vinod pulled out a knife. I stopped and drew back. He'd produced it just like that, in a single movement from the back pocket of his pants. It was a Swiss Army knife. Vinod held up the handle for me to see as he reached in and pulled out the blade. "This is trouble," he said, nostrils flared. "Got this one from America. Can't get such good knives here." Then he waved it back and forth, brandishing it the way I'd seen guys do in knife-fight scenes in the movies. "Eh?" He jutted the blade in my direction. I knew it was for show, but it made me flinch anyway. "Eh?" He did it again. I backed to the opening of the patio. Vinod smirked and came closer till he was within arm's length—stabbing distance, I thought. He kept the arm gripping the satchel behind his back, out of sight.

"Just give it back, man," I said. "We'll figure something else out."

"Vinod, what is all this tamasha—?" It was his mother again, appearing in the doorway. She gasped when she saw the drama unfolding, and that instant, Vinod drew away the knife. "Oh *bhagwan*, what is happening?" Flailing her arms, she screamed, "I'm calling your brother. I cannot handle you anymore!" She turned and retreated into the apartment.

"It's nothing, Ma, calm down," he shouted back. It was now or never, I figured, so I lunged forward and grabbed the satchel out of his hand and began backing off the patio. As I did, Vinod made a leap for me, then stumbled as his foot caught on the leg of one of the lawn chairs.

I was away and a half dozen steps up the lane when I heard him shout, "Hey! Bhai, where you are going with my *rupiya*?" In Gujarati, he went on, "Hey, he's got my rupiya!" and I saw he was trying to appeal to the group of onlookers opposite the lane.

Vinod stared at me, stunned, on his knees. Then, pointing at me, he called to the onlookers again, "Hey, he took my cash. Take hold of him!"

I turned and began walking up the lane, back toward where I had left my Luna. The onlookers simply stared at me as Vinod pleaded. No one made any effort to intervene.

"Hey, American! You want trouble?" That wasn't Vinod's voice. I looked up to see the boy on the balcony, the one whom I'd seen earlier watching us. I shielded my eyes to get a look at him, eclipsed by a jag of light. For a flash, I saw him sneer. Then something like an asteroid collided against my forehead, above my right eye. A thud shattered in my ears, the slap of rock against skull, and I staggered.

I heard a woman scream, a man call out, saw the boy duck out of view no sooner than I hit the earth on my knees. The balconied sky got blocked from view by my own blood-webbed fingers, the thump and stagger of feet, the occlusion of the blood and my own dirt-smudged hands. Faces hovered over me, expressions of horror. In seconds, though, the clamor faded. I felt my back against the stony earth. My vision went out of sync, and I entered blackness.

Chapter 25

The tug of thread, the itch of skin pulled taut as thread glided through the suture. I opened my eyes. My head on a pillow, my body flat on a cot.

How'd I get in here? Where was I? What day was it?

A man's face—plump, with a flat nose and tiny eyes—came into view. He smiled pleasantly as his hands worked the thread back and forth over the right side of my head.

"It is okay now," he said. "You were needing seven, eight stitches. Very deep. But don't worry. It's all fine now." His tone was businesslike, as if he were giving me the price of produce at the market. He smelled of Ahmedabad: of dust and sweat, of paan masala mixed with a trace of cologne.

I heard concerned voices in the small blue-painted room. A ceiling fan whirred above me. Pictures of Krishna and a Ganesh figurine in a niche in the wall. A Hindu devotional calendar hung next to it. Above the niche, high on the wall, hung a picture of a middle-aged man, garlanded. Some dead relative, no doubt.

"Do not move too much." He cut the thread, dabbed iodine—cool to the forehead—and taped on the gauze.

Incense burning. The redolence of Gujarati cooking, the clank of kitchen utensils.

"Where am I?" I groaned. No sooner had I asked than Vinod came into view. His eyes were bleary, bloodshot. He carried a tray with a steel cup of water. He put the tray down and slumped into a chair.

The man rose from the cot, scooping up a metal pan with scissors, thread, gauze, and dark bottles.

From the corner of my eye, I saw Vinod in his chair, head bowed, hands covering his face.

"Quite a deep cut," the man said. He wore a dark-green safari shirt with a pen in the breast pocket. He extended his hand; I shook it. "I am Dr. Arvind Deshpande. You are in our flat. I am . . . I am his older brother." He gestured at Vinod and sighed. He said I had no sign of a concussion and asked if I had a headache.

"Just where the rock hit me," I said, sitting up. "I'm glad you're a doctor. Don't know what I'd have done." I touched the gauzed-up wound. It felt tender. The wound bit at my nerves where I touched.

"Dentist, actually," Dr. Deshpande said. "In two weeks, you go to clinic and get the stitches removed, hmm?" He cocked his head at me, waited for my reply.

"Two weeks," I said. "Okay."

The older woman in the yellow sari—Vinod's mother—entered the room. In Gujarati, she asked if I needed anything.

"Just water," I said and took the cup that Vinod had set down on a small square stand beside the cot. I sipped it.

"Okay?" Dr. Deshpande asked, palms upraised.

"Yes, thank you."

He tipped his head once to the side, smiled. "Okay." He turned and spoke to his mother. "Chalo, to the kitchen."

They went away. Vinod did not look up, his face buried in his hands. He began to shake his head and wouldn't stop. When he raised his face, his eyes looked worn out from tears. "I am sorry, Vikram. So sorry. I did not know that boy would do that."

"You with your knife and him with his rocks. What is he? Your personal hit man or something?"

Vinod turned away, smirked. "That knife, that was only to scare you, I would never—I am so sorry." He broke off, choking back tears, then continued, "And that boy Raju is thinking I am some hero. So he comes to defend me. He ran away. Scared, I think so." He sniffed. "I am no hero."

He hung his head. His breath came in sniffs and gasps. "I am sorry, truly sorry, Vikram bhai."

"It'll heal," I said.

My eyes turned to the picture on the wall, a black-and-white portrait wreathed in a marigold garland. The man's expression had a military sternness. He wore a tie and a starched white shirt, clasped his hands in front of him, and looked off at an angle from the camera. I asked who he was.

"My father," Vinod answered. "Died two years back." He turned his eyes away, gazed off through the kitchen onto the patio at the gathering evening. Nervously, he rubbed his palms together. "Ever since," he said, "I am feeling a bit . . . stuck."

"I know the feeling."

Vinod kept his face in the direction of the kitchen, but his eyes shifted toward me. I noticed a tentative smile on his face. "You are stuck also, huh?"

"Yes," I said. "I was. For a long time. It's a rotten feeling. But"—I thought about my photography and the college application, the constant studying and the scholarship—"it's possible to get ourselves unstuck. I'm still working on it, but it's possible."

"I don't think so I will get to such a point. In jail perhaps, but . . ." he trailed off, and the bitterness in his eyes finished his words for him.

"You'll get it together, Vinod. And it won't be in jail," I said, smiling. I got off the cot unsteadily, keeping my hand over the bandaging. "We get to a point where we just want to cut out all the bullshit, you know? Fix things so we can at least live with ourselves. Even be a little proud of ourselves sometimes."

"Proud of myself." He considered those words for a moment, then got to his feet. From his pocket, he produced Pradeep's money—three thousand rupees—folded and paper-clipped, and handed it to me.

"Why don't *you* give it back to him?" I suggested.

He lowered his eyes, staring down at the pebbled tiles of the floor. Gradually, he drew back his hand and nodded. "I only hope he will forgive."

"He will," I said, "or I don't know Pradeep."

~ ~ ~

I picked up my leaving certificate from Rajkumar the following day. He asked about the bandage on my head, and I told him I'd gotten mixed up in a riot at a BJP election rally. He tsked a few times and riffled through the final-exam mark sheets stacked beside him on the counter. He finally found mine and pulled it from the stack. He glanced at it, scrunching his nose, and handed it to me. "But your father was so bright," he said, his face putting on a look of mock pity. "Such a shame."

"It *is* a shame," I said. "With marks like these, I may end up like you. See you around."

Father D'Souza stamped the certificate with the college seal and signed it. He just sat hunched at his desk and passed it back to me with a quickly worded "Good luck." He then took up a sheaf of papers lying to one side and began stamping away some more.

I wondered if he was happy to be getting rid of me, the American interloper. I wanted to bow my head and tell him, "I'm sorry I made out with a girl in your library. But, boy, it was the most fun I had all year," and see what he would do. But I settled for "Thank you, Father," and made my exit.

~ ~ ~

Pradeep was in his room, all smiles, and greeted me. He wasn't wearing his customary sunglasses today, and it was strange seeing him without them. His eyes weren't clouded over the way I'd imagined, but were dark and clear. His irises roved slightly back and forth, tucked up into the upper rims of his eye sockets. Pradeep told me Vinod had indeed stopped by that morning and returned the money. Vinod had told him everything that had happened, right down to the rock-to-the-head finale.

"How is it looking?" he asked.

"Check it out yourself." I leaned forward, and he felt around the gauze bandaging.

I flinched. "Ouch."

"Sorry, bhai," Pradeep gasped.

"Just kidding."

"And, Vikram, you must have forgot this."

He went across the room, his arms feeling for the edge of his desk under the window. From the desk, he picked up my camera.

"There it is," I said, taking the camera from him. In all the commotion of finding Pradeep's room broken into, I'd left it here and forgotten about it. I thought of the events of the previous day and my conversation with Vinod. "In all this," I said, "I guess I feel worst for Vinod."

"I do as well," Pradeep said. He opened a desk drawer and began running his fingers over the contents. "I am having trouble finding my glasses today. Ah, here." His fingers fished out his glasses, and he put them on. This was the Pradeep familiar to me, and it struck me how until I had seen him without his glasses, I hardly ever noticed his blindness. He lived beyond the handicap, above it; he had defeated it, and he welcomed the rest of us, while we were in his company, to share in that victory with him. It was a courageous fight that he had won.

"When he returned the money, I was angry," Pradeep said. "But not at him. Angry that it had gotten so bad that he felt he needed to steal it." He grabbed his stick leaning against his cot, thoughtfully tapping the stick on the floor.

I lined Pradeep up in the viewfinder of the camera and snapped a photo.

"You said so yourself, no? The system is not kind to you if you function outside its rules."

"If I did, you just said it better," I said. "One question, though. I take it Vinod also lied about studying at all those schools in America?"

"He is having an uncle in New York," Pradeep answered, his tone now solemn, almost secretive, "who he visited once after his father passed. Uncle paid for his ticket and all. But I think Vinod tried to stay longer there, illegally you see. His uncle could not find him. Then Vinod called from Florida after six weeks. It was a big tamasha, yaar. He got kicked out, his uncle paid fine or some such to immigration people, and I don't think so he gets on well with his family."

A knock sounded at the door, and Devasia craned his head in.

"Pradeep," he began, "you have spoken with Vikram—" Then seeing I was there, bandaging and all, his eyes went wide. "My god!"

"It's okay," I told Devasia. "Glad you're both here now," and that's when I caught them up on my American news.

"So it is official. You will not be with us." Devasia sighed. "I had no idea you had even applied."

"It was a lark and a long shot till only recently," I said.

"Not lark," Devasia countered. "Faith. It took faith to do it, no?"

For old times' sake, I wanted to contradict him, tell him faith had nothing to do with it. But then I wondered what it was that had gotten me this far, if not faith—faith in myself. "Damn it, you holy men are always right. How do you do it?"

"We get our information from above," he said with a laugh. Devasia said he'd be returning to Madras in a couple of days until college started up again. He jotted down, in his florid hand, his address at the hostel and in Madras where I could write to him.

"Come to South," he said as he left. "It's much more beautiful than this Ahmedabad."

I told him I would. "But don't knock Ahmedabad. It's my town, you know."

~ ~ ~

An express letter came from Wisconsin two days later. It explained about the scholarship. The art department liked the portfolio enough to offer to cover half my tuition. Along with the loan and whatever on-campus work I could get, my father and I figured we had things in hand.

"I'm proud of both of you," my father told Anand and me after he finished reading the letter. We stood out on the balcony, watching the evening sun swell over the shopping complex and the endless and expanding tracts of cement housing colonies beyond. Anand swatted at pigeons roosting in the eaves just above us, trying to distract them, and the traffic honked and rattled around the crossroads. From the dusty lot of the shopping complex, the "music truck" blared its repertoire of Bollywood show tunes while shoppers browsed the tables of music cassettes under its awning.

"And Anand, I know this has not been the easiest transition—" my father said. "Anand? Stop that, listen to me." Anand turned his attention from the pigeons. "I know this has not been the easiest transition. But in spite of that, you're doing better in Hindi and Sanskrit than even I was doing at your age." He patted Anand on the back and told him how proud he was.

I agreed with him and asked Anand how he did it. His answer was matter-of-fact: "Once you figure out one language—say, Gujarati—it's not too big a jump to figuring out Hindi and from there to Sanskrit. They're all related, so . . ." He shrugged. There was a strangely dismissive tone to his answer, as if he couldn't be bothered with our baffled admiration and didn't want to spend much time explaining his own genius. He turned his attention to the traffic, leaning his thin frame against his elbows on the parapet. "I still want to go back to America."

"But so long as you're in India," my father said with a smile, "I want you to love it." He turned around to address both of us. "I'm thinking of building a house in Gandhinagar. I've been looking at land there, and it's much quieter and cleaner than the city. Close to the institute. Your mother will like it." He waved his hand at the plot of ground in front of our bungalow. "She'll be able to garden properly there. Lots more land."

"Am I going to have to switch schools again?" Anand asked.

"Not for another year, and only if you want to." He clasped his hands behind his back and rocked on his heels, plans for the home taking shape in his mind. My mother and he were going out for a walk, he told us, and he handed me back my letter. "Take care of that. That'll be a souvenir one day."

Anand and I stayed out on the balcony watching it grow dark, the flash and pulse of traffic. Swallows made graceful arcs in the open sky.

"So I guess you're gone, huh?" Anand said. "You think you'll ever come back?"

"Of course I'll come back."

"To visit?"

"To visit, but after college, who knows? I could come back or stay . . . don't know."

After a long pause, Anand said, "Yeah, but what about me?"

"What do you mean?"

"You're leaving, and that leaves me here." He turned his head toward me. I sensed him staring at me. "No one here knows what we know."

"Anand, I'm not leaving you. I'm just going away to school."

Anand nodded, leaning his back against the parapet, and nervously fidgeted with his fingers.

"Look," I said, "you'll be in ninth grade. In four years, you'll be out of there too."

"I don't mean four years from now. I'm talking about right now."

I didn't know what to say. I hadn't given much thought to how Anand might react to my leaving. He always seemed so engrossed in one thing or another—his studies, video games, movies, baseball (or cricket, depending on his mood), and his friends. "It's not terrible, is it, Anand?" I asked. "You seem to be getting along well here."

"But they don't know our life, what it used to be, how much it's changed," he said, the words rushing out. "Only you and I do. My friends are all right, but they think America is some big Disneyland. You know, like what they see in the movies. They don't know America or what this has been like for me. And Pappa, he just wants this all to work out for Mummi and him, and that means America's pretty much forgotten about here. Only you and I went through what we did."

"You're not forgotten about," I said. "One thing I found out: what you want is what Pappa wants, even though it may not always seem like it." I stepped up next to him, propped my arms against the parapet. "It's going to be fine. You're going to have a great next four years. And after that, you can go wherever, do whatever you like."

"Maybe I won't even want to go to America anymore in four years."

"You might not," I said, "but that would mean something even better came along and took its place, right?"

Down at the gate, we noticed a rickshaw pull up. The driver got out to unlatch and open the gate, then proceeded in the rickshaw down the gravel drive, puttering round the bend to the downstairs doors. It couldn't be Hemant Uncle; he'd have driven up from Baroda in his own car. Maybe Kamala Auntie was paying us another visit.

I unbolted the front doors and switched on the stairwell lights. As I descended the steps, I could hear the rickshaw motor idling and voices talking outside, near the front entrance. I threw on the outside light and opened the doors to see Devasia lifting a wooden box, about twice the size of a tackle box, from the rickshaw. Its brown veneer was flaked and chipped.

"Devasia?" I called. "Aren't you supposed to be on a train?"

Devasia turned around, beamed his perfect teeth at me. "I am on my way."

I stepped out, and we shook hands. "What're you doing here?" I noticed suitcases filling every square inch of the rickshaw's backseat except for the far corner, where Devasia could perch. The driver, meanwhile, slumped in his seat, staring ahead idly, smoking his bidi.

"On my way to station," Devasia said. "But before that, Pradeep wanted me to give you this." He held out the brown case. I took it by the handle. The thing was heavy and looked like it had been dragged around for years, through mud, up and down mountains. "And here is a note from him," he said, producing a folded slip of paper from the front pocket of his kurta.

"Thanks," I said, asking if he had time to come upstairs, chat, meet my family.

"I would like that," he said, "but I should be going. My train leaves in one hour." He placed one foot inside the rickshaw. "Hold on to my Madras address," he said. "You are always welcome there. Also, send me some photos."

"Will do," I said, wishing him a safe journey. "I expect to see them framed and on display when I visit."

"Promise." He smiled, and in Hindi instructed the rickshaw driver to proceed. I watched the rickshaw putter away, its tiny headlamp bobbing like a giant firefly.

~ ~ ~

Back upstairs, I unfolded Pradeep's note:

> Dearest Vikram,
>
> I think you will get better use out of this than I am able. Please accept it as a token of my appreciation for your help settling difficulties with Vinod. I hope it is still in working order. It has not been used in many years.

I unlatched the top of the case. Anand stood beside me, as curious as I was. A whiff of mustiness spiced with cumin and turmeric hit us as soon as I opened the lid to find a movie camera inside.

It was a bulky camera, industrial brown, molded out of thick plates of steel, with the words "Bell & Howell" on a tiny metal plate. I imagined you could crack a skull with it. It seemed indestructible. In front was a turret with three lenses, fixed, of different sizes—like those eye-testing gizmos in the optometrist's office. The turret turned on gears that connected it to a smaller turret—a miniature of the first and with tinier lenses. This smaller turret was attached to a tube that ran the length of the camera's body, ending at a tiny eyepiece. On the side of the camera I found a metallic windup key edged with rust and nearly as wide as my palm. What a strange and fabulous machine, I thought, ancient and intimidatingly blunt yet gorgeous and delicately precise. I returned to the note:

> My father arrived this morning to take me back to our home in Bharuch for one week then I am off for Bombay for the remainder of vacation. After your visit two days ago, I remembered that we had this stored in a trunk for many years, and I asked my father to bring it with him. My father or sister is not using it so I hope it has found a home with you.
>
> This film camera used to belong to my late uncle who was a cameraman in Indian Army during 1960s. There are also a few old film rolls which, who knows, may still be usable. If not, I'm sure you can find more in States. I am sending it with Devasia to pass on to you.
>
> I shall send you copy of my Bombay recordings when all is complete. Wishing you much success in your future, Vikram bhai. Please write at your earliest.
>
> Best wishes,
> Pradeep

"Check it out," Anand said. He pulled out three cases of square black plastic. Masking tape sealed their lids shut. I peeled off the tape and pried open one of the cases. Inside, a film roll—the acetate shone in the room's white light—within a black metal spool. Quickly, I snapped shut the lid.

"What was that?" Anand asked. "Is it old?"

"Film," I said. "Probably."

From the bottom of the brown case, Anand pulled out a booklet, stained and dusty. "Man, this looks ancient," he said. "Like museum ancient."

I blew a film of dust off the booklet and wiped it clean before I leafed through it. It was the camera's instruction manual. "It might have a bit of kick left before it's time for the museum," I said.

I needed to be frugal with the film rolls. The next day, I managed to get one of them threaded inside the magazine, using the diagram in the booklet. I didn't dare press the button till I knew what all the dials and levers and the settings and the different lenses did. Anand lost patience with me after a while and went over to his friend Mayank's house to play Nintendo.

Finally, I just couldn't resist. I had to shoot some footage and listen to the film whir inside the camera. Through the eyepiece, I framed my mother, her hands, actually, as she sifted through grains of rice out on the balcony. The film glided smoothly for several seconds, then stuttered angrily as it jammed in the gate. I went back to my room and tried rethreading it till the film whirred softly through the magazine again. That sounded right.

As inconspicuously as I could, I got at something I'd been framing in my mind for months: the cleaning girl's copper-dark hands against the shimmer of her bangles, her sun-scorched face upturned as she hung the wash on the line, the swirl of her skirt as she moved across the balcony.

I went down to the garden, ran off close-ups of the flowering shrubs, the textures and elliptical designs left by the tire tracks in the drive. I roamed the H.L. College cricket grounds—got off shots of the wickets, the sunburned pitch, the shady neems that lined the field's far side. Then I went out under the peepal at the center of the crossroads. I'd looked out at this spot of ground every day from our balcony and had never till now stepped inside it. Farmers in white turbans and tunics took shelter from the heat here, sitting or lying on the floors of their wooden carts. Their bullocks dozed against the great tree roots. The farmers smiled as I framed them in my lens, then went back to sleep as I bopped from angle to angle, aiming the camera lens up at the gnarled, sun-flickering tree branches, at the Fellini-esque circus of scooters and rickshaws, and at flies diving like Japanese Zeroes at the bulls' ears.

Dharmanshu Uncle sent us a postcard, asking after us and apologizing for our summer tour of the northeast not panning out—the one he'd proposed during our Christmas visit. He said a roadworks project had stalled, and he had to postpone taking time off for his vacation till June. He'd been thinking about my mother's suggestion, though, to visit Dilip in London finally. I wrote him back immediately to tell him my plans to return to the States, but more than that, to express to him how glad I was he'd decided to visit Dilip, to see a bit of the world after meaning to for so long. I was sorry our excursion to Sikkim and Darjeeling had to be put off, I said. Still, I couldn't pass up the photographs a trip like that could inspire, so let's put it on our agenda. Let's make it soon, I said, because time has a way of getting away from us.

At the end of May, the cleaning girl suddenly went away. My mother said she'd gone back to her village in northwestern Gujarat. I asked if she'd gotten married, maybe to that man I'd seen her with in the stairwell.

"No, he was a drunk, they found out," my mother said, shaking her head. "I knew he wasn't right for her."

The girl had been vague about her going away. A match had been found, was all she would say, and she needed to leave the city. We never saw her again.

~ ~ ~

I got the stitches from my forehead removed at a clinic just across Nehru Bridge, not too far from that lunatic asylum of a college where I took my final exams. In the side mirror of a parked scooter, I checked the scar the rock had left: an inch-long seam up the side of my forehead, with small dots where the thread had pulled through. Quite the war wound, I thought.

Near the clinic was an Air India office where we bought my ticket—Bombay to Chicago, via London. To buy the ticket, I insisted we use the money from the compensation check issued by the Bombay airport customs office for the lost video camera. It seemed fitting somehow.

~ ~ ~

At my usual photomat, I asked Ajay where I could get film rolls for the Bell & Howell. He scratched his head and ponderously swung it side to side. "No such film in Ahmedabad for such old camera. Bombay maybe or Delhi, but here no."

Still, I trolled around Ahmedabad's camera and antique shops in the old sections of the city—in the hive of bazaars, alive with bartering and music and the fantail sparks from welding torches. Bicycle and moped parts, motorcycle and scooter parts, radio and cassette parts, TV and VCR parts. Men pushed past each other, past the cows and over the dogs that had retreated from the scorch of the open streets. I asked around for where or how I could get my hands on more film rolls, but everyone stared at the camera as if it were a prehistoric turd and shook their heads. By the end of that afternoon, Ajay had proved himself right.

As I rode west on my Luna over the Sabarmati, the grit buffeting my face, I thought of how the monsoon would soon be here again. The winds would cool off the asphalt and concrete, and the thunderheads would roll in like an armada from the Arabian Sea over the Gujarat plains. In the hours before the first storm, the city, like a muscle that had for months kept itself contracted under the weight of summer, would relax. The streets would feel deserted, their noises muted, and everyone would feel a quiet kinship in having survived together long enough to enjoy that very moment. I looked forward to it. It would only be a few weeks now. But I realized that no sooner would the rains arrive than I would be gone.

Chapter 26

I was stingy with the second film roll. I wanted it to last the whole week we spent at Hemant Uncle's place in Baroda. He and Kamala Auntie seemed happy for me when I told them the news of my leaving for the States, but not Anjali.

"But you just got here," she said, "and now you want to go away again?"

I told her this was only for school, and that I'd be sure to visit. She didn't look at me, though. Only shrugged and dangled her feet from the chair where she sat, eyes on the TV screen.

"I promise," I said. She tipped her head sideways once—an indifferent "okay."

From the half-open front door, over the cartoon playing on TV, I could hear Hemant Uncle coaching Anand and a couple of neighbor kids on batting techniques. The cricket bat smacked against the ball; Hemant Uncle shouted instructions and encouragements. "Keep the bat closer," I heard. "With the wrist like this, then turn away." Another smack. Laughing from Hemant Uncle and yelling from the kids.

I turned to Anjali. "Want to get a Cadbury? My treat."

She said nothing at first. "You must really not like here with us." Her eyes kept straight ahead.

"I never said I didn't like it here."

"You don't need to say," she said flatly. "But I know it. From the first day we saw you at airport. You were not so happy to be with us." She slid off the chair and went out to the porch. "So go then."

~ ~ ~

Kamala Auntie made my favorite dessert that evening—*doodh pakh*, rice pudding served cold, scented with cardamom and laced with slivers of pistachios. I went through three helpings. "Who knows in America who will make this for you?" she joked.

"Could be," my mother teased, "he will find some good Gujarati girl there." Then she gasped with delight, "Maybe we should put ad in *India Abroad*."

Kamala Auntie began giggling.

I looked at the food laid out on the table. I wondered how long it would be till I ate Indian food this good again after I set foot on that plane for America.

As we ate, my father asked Hemant Uncle what it would take to build a home in Gandhinagar, just outside Ahmedabad. My father already had ideas for acreage and square feet and how many rooms and floors, even building materials and landscaping. I had no idea he had already given the subject so much thought, and I sensed that this was the culmination of something, the peak after a long climb.

"You've thought this all through, my god," Hemant Uncle remarked.

"It was her," my father admitted, pointing a thumb toward my mother. "Home layout is all her idea and landscaping also."

"I managed," my mother said, tossing her head in a whimsical gesture, "to remember few things from my school days."

Hemant Uncle said he could help with loan arrangements at the State Bank and spoke of his own experience building his home. "But first you will need land itself."

"We have already begun that process," my father said.

Anand and I looked at each other.

"We have?" I asked.

My father turned to us. "By end of the year, we should have it finalized and start building."

I was stunned. "So everything will be different next time I see you."

"Hmm." My father finished his doodh pakh, cleared his throat. "You won't be coming back to that bungalow in Navarangpura. But a brand-new house. All ours."

"Congratulations," Kamala Auntie said to me. "On scholarship and admission." In Gujarati, she added, "That's a big achievement."

"Hmm," Hemant Uncle concurred, nodding, watching me with a bemused smile.

Kamala Auntie got up, stepped around the table, her plate in one hand, and tousled my hair. "Make us all proud, huh?"

~ ~ ~

The day we left Baroda was the day the monsoon clouds appeared. Throughout the morning it grew darker, and the world looked as if all color were drained from a photograph, leaving only shades of gray. Anand, Anjali, and I went up to the rooftop terrace, where I ran off my last roll of 16mm film: figures silhouetted against the pregnant sky, the anxious earth, the branches stirring in the first cool breezes of the season. The rain fell in tentative drops at first, then began smothering the city in a lovely and luxurious torrent. It sizzled against the asphalt, pattered like mad against the city's rooftops. In seconds, we were drenched. I ducked into the door-way, covering my camera with a towel I'd brought upstairs with me.

Anand followed me into the doorway, but Anjali stayed out on the terrace, mouth open to catch the rain, jumping up and down, arms flailing. Hers was the last image I framed—a laughing, capering girl, gesturing for us to join her—before I heard the roll empty, and the camera wheezed with nothing left.

~ ~ ~

When the train arrived at the station platform, Kamala Auntie was sniffing back tears. Hemant Uncle stood, his hands in his pockets, composed enough for both of them. I touched his feet, then Kamala Auntie's, hugged them both.

"Vikram bhai," Anjali said, pushing in between Kamala Auntie and Hemant Uncle, "send me all pictures, okay?" Her tone was as direct and authoritative as ever. "I am curious to see how you're doing."

"You got it," I said.

"And what else?" Kamala Auntie said, as if prodding her.

Anjali turned away, her eyes on the floor. In a hushed voice, she muttered something, stopped, tried again. Finally, she gave up, came forward, and threw her arms around me. No one had ever hugged me like that before—doing away with words because the act of embracing meant so much more.

I pressed her close and told her we would see each other again soon. She nodded and wiped at her eyes.

"And I don't hate it here at all," I told her. "How else would I have met you?"

Chapter 27

Letters from Karl arrived, ecstatic about my return. He offered the spare bedroom at his parents' place on the west side of town till he and I found a place on campus later that summer. I promptly accepted. Nate wrote too, a rambling and profane recap of his past year. He said he needed to buckle down sophomore year and really hit the books. With the letter, he sent along two short comedy scripts that he and Karl had managed to crank out for shooting that summer, and said he was glad I'd be home soon to join their collaborations. Nate also mentioned he'd begun fooling around with his roommate's girlfriend, Debra, and couldn't decide what to do about it. He felt awful, just awful, but Debra was too cute to turn down. It seemed an appropriate predicament for Nate.

That week, through a colleague at work, my father tracked down a lab in Bombay that could process the 16mm film rolls. We booked a train ticket for two days in advance of my flight so I could get them processed and avoid the risk of the airport's X-ray scanners ruining undeveloped film.

~ ~ ~

Dear Vikram,

I got your address in Ahmedabad from Pradeep. He tells me you're heading for the States soon, so I wanted to be sure to get this to you before you left. As you can tell from my address on the envelope, I'm far away from you right now but apparently not for long.

As you probably know, things didn't go quite as planned last New Year's with the proposed wedding and all. My father wasn't happy, of course, and I don't think he's a hundred percent over it. A part of him, I'm sure, still thinks I'll "wise up" and marry this glorified stockbroker he arranged for me. Apparently, he talked the guy into holding out a bit longer.

Also, rest assured it wasn't because of you, or what happened between us, that I broke my engagement. I know my father just wanted the best for me, and it's true it would've been a perfectly comfortable life with this man who was smart, successful, and, okay, even handsome. But two nights before the wedding, I guess I snapped! I couldn't go through with it and ditched the engagement dinner. It wasn't easy, not easy to run out on everyone like that, especially after all the expense and the trouble my whole family had made to be there (yeah, even my cousins in Boston). But I think, finally, I was more afraid of what my life would become if I did let this happen. How long do you let other people, no matter who they are or how much they love you, live your life? I was afraid it would start being one regret piled on top of another. Anyway, it was really difficult for a few weeks, and I just couldn't be there anymore, in that house.

I left India, and it hasn't been easy being so far from my sister, my mom, and, yeah, even my dad (who thinks this is just an extended holiday for me, before I come to my senses . . . He'll come around. He'll have to). So, Vik, I've made good on my American passport—as you hinted I should all along—and I'm staying at my cousins' place outside Boston for now. So it was a rough last few months, but

I'm glad to put it behind me and make plans for myself. I'm moving to NYC in August. I start up at Hunter College in the fall.

I am so, so excited for you. Pradeep wrote that you even got a scholarship and everything. Congratulations! Write me and give me your new address after you land.

Can't wait to hear from you. Here's hoping our paths cross again . . .

Priya

~ ~ ~

The driver of my father's company Ambassador insisted on loading the suitcases into the car himself. As thin as he was, he handled the bags so adroitly, it amazed me. He shut the trunk, took his seat again behind the wheel, and waited. Anand came downstairs, carrying a gold plate that held two small copper bowls. In the center of the plate was a tiny copper diya in which a cotton wick daubed with ghee produced a flickering flame.

"Okay," my mother said, coming forward in a crisp blue sari. With a tiny spoon, she scooped out a dollop of yogurt from the first bowl, emptied it into my palm, and from the second bowl took a spoonful of sugar grains. She sprinkled the sugar over the yogurt, and I tipped the confection into my mouth.

She took the plate from Anand. In front of the glowing diya, I noticed a tiny gold Ganesh and, at its feet, a coin-sized mound of vermilion powder and a scattering of rice grains. Looking closer, I saw engravings along the rim of the plate, interwoven strands with figurative leaves. She must've sensed my curiosity about it.

"This was marriage gift," she told me. "From my mother."

She took a pinch of vermilion from the plate and daubed my forehead with it to make a thin streak between my eyebrows. She picked up a few rice grains from the plate and sprinkled them over my head. Then she held the plate before me and made three circles with it, chanting a few Sanskrit words under her breath. "Okay," she said, "you are free to go."

I touched her feet and hugged her. Tears appeared in her eyes, and she wiped her cheek with the back of her hand. I knew that if I thought too much about what was happening, I would break down myself. It was important now to stay on task. Get in the car, I thought to myself, get on the train, and you'll be all right.

"I will see you in two days," my father told my mother. They spoke together closely, and I walked over to Anand, standing against the doorframe.

"You going to be okay?" I asked.

"I'll see you . . ." he began. "I don't know . . ."

"Soon," I said. "Before that, you'll be in a new house. And a whole new life."

Anand took a deep breath. "I thought we'd all go back together," he said. "That's not going to happen."

I didn't know what to say. Neither of us spoke for a few seconds before Anand added, "We're all breaking apart."

Breaking apart? For a moment, I felt horrible. Horrible for making Anand feel that way. Since I was seven and Anand was two, the world had pulled us in every direction, year after year. Yet we'd stayed together as a family. And even here in India, our mother's illness had threatened to break us apart too, and we'd remained whole. But now was it finally happening? Were we breaking apart?

I looked at my parents, still in conversation.

"You know what's weird?" I said, turning to Anand. "All that time we were moving around, different schools every year, I felt alone. Like it was me against the world. You remember."

Anand nodded thoughtfully and took a deep breath.

"But this doesn't feel the same. I'm leaving, and I'll be thousands of miles away. But I feel closer to this family than ever."

Anand turned his eyes toward me. "You sure I'll be okay?"

I told him I would make sure of it and hugged him.

My mother approached with the plate in her hands. I asked her if she had a Ganesh I could take with me. Her jaw fell open. "You want to take Ganesh with you? I never would have thought."

"Are you kidding? The Remover of Obstacles. I can use all the help I can get."

She gave me the Ganesh idol from the plate. It was about as big as my thumb, its gold enameling scuffed here and there over the years. "Keep Ganapati close to you at all times," she said, "and say your Gayatri Mantra every day."

"Promise," I said. The Ganesh and the Gayatri Mantra were the assurances I needed, the tethering to my history, to who I was and to the people who would keep me strong.

~ ~ ~

When you leave, you leave everything. Not just your brother, your mother, your father, uncle, aunt, and cousin—you leave everything. You leave the light in your room; you leave the tiles of the floor you walked on from your desk to the balcony. You leave the sound of running water as the cleaning girl washed your clothes. You leave peacocks in the courtyard cawing under the trees, the sandalwood and jasmine and oils anointing the air of the college corridors, the play of wind from summer to monsoon to winter and back to summer. You leave arguments and conversation, notes recorded into a tape recorder. You leave Vinod to his choices, Pradeep to his songs, and Devasia to his sureness of purpose. You leave the hallways of students you avoided out of shyness. You leave the aromas of snacks at a vendor's stall on C.G. Road, the route you walked to and from the dairy counter or the barbershop while the afternoon sun silenced everything but the call of crows by the roadside. You leave the scent of the wash hanging on the line, the sun creating lemony trapezoids through the saris, and the squares of the balusters. You leave the bed where you slept and the desk where you read and wrote letters, listening to your music in retreat from the alien rhythms of an alien world.

How could it ever be that way again? By what trick could I bring all that back? If I could have it back, it wouldn't be the same anyway. Because the discoveries would already have been made. What you left behind had its time and its purpose, and all became memory, a sentiment, a lesson learned, and history. I told myself you had to leave; it could never be again.

Epilogue

June 30, 1989

I can't sleep. The silence in this house is deeper than I'm used to. This room, the spare bedroom at Karl's parents' place, smells faintly of paint and fresh linen. There's a scratched-up walnut dresser in which I've put my things, a small color TV (with cable) on a chrome stand, a closet where winter coats and blankets are piled, and this twin bed. This mattress is so soft it gives under my weight, like I'm on a cloud, and I remember now how soft the beds in America are. My old mattress in India was like an army cot compared to this, and even this is just a modest, old mattress by American standards. Still, I can't sleep.

I miss the nighttime roar and buzz of Navarangpura traffic out past our balcony doors. I get out of bed and step across the hardwood floor to the window. A streetlamp up on Midvale Boulevard pools light over an empty section of road. So quiet, still, vacant. I can't believe I'm back. It's been two days. Already tomorrow afternoon in Ahmedabad: Anand's back from school, doing his homework now or playing his video games. My mother, what must she be doing? Cooking? The rotis on the *tava* and vegetables in the wok. I can smell the food. The pillowy rotis on which my mother pours the ghee with quick, delicate turns of a spoon. Is my father finishing out his day at work? Chatting with a colleague in the corridor about particle theory or the price of land in Gandhinagar?

From O'Hare, I took the Van Galder bus back to Madison, a three-hour drive through farm country scoured clean by early summer rains. I kept my headphones on, listening to an R.E.M. mix—the music back on its home ground now—and felt relieved to see the fields thriving again. This summer is being spared last summer's drought. Karl picked me up at the Memorial Union, and we drove here to his parents' house. His parents welcomed me heartily, with the courtesy and generosity of Old World Wisconsin settlers, and asked how I was, what it was all like, and told me to make myself at home.

When Karl offered me a glass of water, I noticed how he filled it from the tap—the water flowing clean and clear from the faucet. No boiling, filtering, refrigeration needed. When I drank the water, I felt guilty somehow, and I realized how much I missed India. It was like I'd rejected a poor lover in favor of a wealthier one. I felt sick about it as I drank.

Karl and I sat around the first afternoon drinking Coca-Colas and watching TV—so many channels, it left me shaking my head, stunned—and we caught up on everything. He made us grilled cheese sandwiches, which I tried to eat, but after twenty-four hours of airline travel I had no appetite. My gut felt like a cinder block. After a while, I did ask him about Shannon, but Karl said he hadn't seen her since running into her on campus the previous fall. He heard she transferred to an acting program out east. But he wasn't sure. I left it at that. He did tell me that the offer of a part-time job at WHA was still on the table if I wanted it, and he handed me an application.

Now, I stand here in the deep quiet, staring out at Midvale Boulevard, watching the occasional car whoosh by. I have a meeting with the director of the art department tomorrow. This afternoon, I called the department to let them know I was here and to see about setting up my fall schedule, get details about the scholarship and all that. They told me they'd been waiting to hear from me and patched me through to the director. Talking to him made me nervous—the image of that haughty, imposing Professor Menon at NID kept running through my mind. But the director sounded warm and cordial, said to drop by the next day after lunch and to bring the rest of my portfolio of photographs and anything else I'd been working on. I said sure.

But that's tomorrow. How do I get through tonight?

I return to the bed, take up the remote control on the nightstand, and switch on the small TV. The room fills with a sickly cathode glow, and I resign myself to cycling through the channels, round and round, with the volume turned way down, just watching the miniature spectacle of sitcoms, sports wrap-ups, and late, late talk shows till my eyes droop from fatigue and my brain shuts down, if only for a few hours. I doubt I'll dream.

~ ~ ~

I put the job application that Karl gave me into my backpack, along with a manila envelope of photographs—a few from Delhi, from the old quarters of Ahmedabad, and from Bombay. I also bring the three tin cans of film, each developed back in Bombay, each as big around as my hand, none of which I've looked at yet. Before meeting the director, I'm having lunch with Nate at the Memorial Union.

I get off the Madison Metro on Lake Street near the university bookstore and walk through Library Mall to the Union. The lake is startling: as clear and smooth as glass. And the air is sweeter and mellower than I reckoned, so used have I gotten to the acrid tang of Ahmedabad, Baroda, Bombay, Delhi. I walk through a promenade bordered by flowering trees, the Union before me.

The Union is a stately and unblemished structure, with wide stone steps that lead up past a columned archway to the entrance. Inside, I walk into a cool wash of air, scented with Babcock ice cream and French fries from the Rathskeller. When I see Nate in his T-shirt, shorts, and sandals, with a book bag slung across his shoulder, I hardly recognize him: he's grown a beard, and his hair is tied back in a ponytail. I laugh at first and tell him I'll get used to it. We shake hands, and he says I've lost weight and let's put some greasy American food in that belly.

"India will do that to a guy," I say as we make our way to the Rathskeller counter where we get burgers—I've hankered for one since the evening I met Priya at the Havmor, last November, and we talked about American food. That night feels like ages ago.

We sit out on the terrace and watch girls sunning themselves and sailboats on Lake Mendota. The terrace is packed with students and university staffers on their break, but their voices hardly rise above the breeze off the lake stirring the trees and the commotion of birds.

After lunch, Nate's got a shift at Four Star Fiction and Video. It's walkable from here, up off State Street about twenty minutes away. He needs the job, he says, to save up for a house he's going to be sharing with a few dorm buddies that fall. He confesses to me that the startup work involved in housepainting—making flyers, canvassing neighborhoods, doing up estimates—got to be too much of a hassle.

"I just needed a ready-to-go job, know what I mean? Where I could clock in and start making some dough," he says. He asks if

I'm going to start working too, and I mention the possible gig at the TV studio.

"So you're going into photography?" Nate asks me, settling back in his chair. "Congrats on the scholarship, man. That's great news."

"Thanks," I say. "And, yeah, looks like it. Or anything where they let me use a camera."

"Speaking of which," Nate says, "you think you'll be up for shooting these scripts Karl and I wrote up?"

"Wouldn't miss it."

We eat our burgers in silence, and I can see Nate's eyes narrowing as he stares past the far shore of Lake Mendota, in sight of a distant dream.

"You know what would be cool," Nate says, wiping his mouth with a napkin and sitting up in his chair, "is if the three of us started up a production company."

"Oh god," I laugh. "You mean the one in LA? I've heard that idea before, Nate." I remind him of that stoned and drunken night two years ago, wandering up Monroe Street after Emily Price's party. Nate responds only with scrunched eyes, a puckered mouth as he tries to remember. "That night we got busted by the police!" I say. "How could you—?"

"Oh, man!" Nate slaps his forehead. "Okay, so you *have* heard this before." He shakes his head, his mind still zeroing in on this new vision for the future. "No, no, that was my *LA* studio idea, which we could still do down the road if we wanted to. I'm talking about a production company right here in Madison." He picks out a French fry and, tapping it on the table for emphasis, adds, "We could write, direct, shoot, produce, edit, whatever. We know our way around a production, do we not? We've shot a ton of movies, haven't we?" He shoves the fry into his mouth and grasps at more.

"Not a huge leap from short films to commercials, PSAs, industrials, whatever . . . and down the road, I'm thinking features. Who knows?"

"Sure," I say. "Who're you going to get to run this company? It's not exactly a part-time gig."

"Karl will do it," Nate says, smiling, balling up the emptied burger wrapper. "I'm the idea man."

I laugh, glad to be in Nate's company again. Listening to him, I realize I've opened up a future for myself with possibilities that weren't there a year ago, even three months ago, as shimmering and palpable as Lake Mendota in the sun, so vibrant right now with the play of sailboats and windsurfers.

Getting here, to this chair on the terrace in Madison, Wisconsin, USA, was an operation as wild as any of Nate's ideas, but I made it happen. It's hard to believe. And for the first time I'm thankful to myself, thankful for making this moment, in this place, happen.

Nate says he'd better get going if he wants to make his shift on time. We make plans to get together later tonight, and he shuffles off in his sandals and ponytailed hair. I've got some time before my meeting with the director, so I pull out paper and pen from my backpack. My first letter is to my parents and Anand, to let them know I've arrived safely, and I write a second one to Pradeep, each letter a page or so. Then I start a third letter, the one I've been putting off, the one most difficult to get started on. There's so much I want to tell Priya. I want to tell her how much I've thought of her these past six months, how much I want to see her and to hear her voice again—No, no, I don't say that. I keep things cool, very composed, not too long, just as Priya's letter to me had been. It takes me three tries and three sheets of clean paper before I get into the flow. But by then it's getting late. I fold up the letter, put it away to finish afterward.

I leave the Union and head over to the Humanities Building a couple of blocks south on Park Street. It's got the size, scale, and subtlety of an aircraft carrier—a monstrosity of cement bulwarks and parapets in which a crosswork of rectangular windows lie encased. Aesthetically, it's the exact opposite of the Taj Mahal, and I imagine my mother's disapproval of it if she were here with me.

The art department is up a few flights. I walk along a hallway lined with student photographs and paintings. I pause to take a look; they are landscape shots taken upstate, black-and-white, stark in their borderlines between earth and sky, man and matter, really impressive, and I wonder if I'll ever meet the artist who made them.

The art director's office is at the end of the hall. I walk into a room cramped with office miscellany: there are high shelves packed with files and correspondence, a bulletin board crowded with announcements of gallery showings, a few armchairs, and a rickety coffee table littered with art and photography magazines. A small secretary dressed in a powder-blue jacket and skirt, a ruffled blouse, and pearls sits behind a tidy desk, peering at a computer screen. She has a puff of white hair and a lined but pleasant face. I tell her who I am, that I have an appointment that afternoon. She says the director is running a half hour late, but he's looking forward to meeting me and hopes I won't mind the wait.

I sit for a few minutes but get fidgety, get up and walk out into the hall again. About halfway down, I happen past a room, a studio, where chairs lie cluttered every which way, and a film projector stands in the back, a white screen—the kind you roll down over a chalkboard—in front. I walk inside, over to the projector, unzip my backpack, and take out the film cans.

I find a laminated diagram on the corrugated rubber pad on which the projector sits and use it to thread the first roll of film into the projector. I'm anxious. I wonder if anything even turned out. The film stock Pradeep provided was old and so haphazardly stored, I might get nothing but fog and flare. My fingers tremble as I wind the film onto the take-up reel. I check the threading again against the instruction card and flip the switch to activate the projector. A bulb throws a square of white light onto the screen. Then a flurry of slashes and dashes as the leader races through the gate. I hold my breath, hope for something, anything from the camera. Then there it is: my mother's hands, in crisp focus, sifting through rice grains. Then her face as she looks up at the camera. And there's our balcony—sure, a little more shadowy than I hoped, but there it is, clear as day. Anand appears, looking so serious before he moves to the railing. There he goes pestering pigeons again before he's distorted momentarily in a flare of hard sunlight.

I switch rolls—I can't help myself—thread it as carefully as I can, as nervous as I am, and flip the switch. Baroda. Hemant Uncle. Kamala Auntie. My father. The unpaved dirt lane outside Hemant Uncle's home. It all comes back to me as if I'm standing on the porch next to the swing, watching the clouds arriving with messages of monsoon. In a burst of pans and panoramas, the messages arrive: the gorgeous gray rain pelting the rooftop, veiling the train station; the swaying canopy of the silhouetted trees fronting the university grounds, just visible above the line of bungalows; men with newspapers over their heads and a woman obscured by her black umbrella, a hand to lift the hem of her sari; all running to who knows where, I'll never know. In the next shot, I see Anand dashing out of the rain, beside me under the doorway, soaked in his Brewers T-shirt. What's he doing now, I wonder. Sleeping, I guess. But here, awake and thrilled and soaked, he mouths something at the camera, shivering, and points at something off-screen. I pan the

Glossary of Gujarati Terms and Phrases

Abbay-oy—an expression of alarm

Atch-cha—an expression of acknowledgment; "I understand" or "I see"

Aavjo—"Good-bye"

Babu—an old-school government bureaucrat, often perceived as lazy and corruptible

Bakwas—nonsense

Beh-bhaan—unconscious

Beta—"child" or "son"

Bhabhi—sister-in-law

Bhagwan—lord

Bhai/Bhaiya—literally "brother," but it can mean a male friend or companion; depending on the situation, it can be used either affectionately or ironically

Bhajan—devotional Hindu song

Bhelpuri—a popular Indian snack consisting of a mix of seasoned puffed rice, crispy thin noodles, crunchy pieces of fried bread, potatoes, onions, and sweet-and-sour chutney

Bidi—low-cost, hand-rolled unfiltered cigarette

Bindi—the cosmetic dot or mark between the eyebrows that South Asian women wear for fashion or religious reasons, or to signify their marital status

Bolo—literally "Speak up"; an informal way of asking someone, "What do you want?"

Butchu—infant or small child

Chalo—"Let's go"

Chavanu—a sweet-and-savory Gujarati snack mix with a potpourri of ingredients including fried chickpeas, lentils, whole black pepper, peanuts, raisins, and various seasonings

Chok-kus—"Certainly" or "Surely"

Dada—an affectionate term for "grandfather"

Dada-giri—hassle; bullying behavior

Dal—a lentil soup, a staple of the traditional Gujarati meal

Dahi vada—deep-fried lentil dumplings smothered in a savory yogurt sauce

Dandiya—wooden sticks struck together by dancers in time to the rhythm of a garba, a Gujarati folk dance

Dhana jeeru—a blend of coriander and cumin powder used in a variety of Indian foods

Dhoti—loincloth

Diya—an oil lamp, usually made from clay and used on special occasions

Dosa—a savory crepe made of lentils and rice, a staple of South India

Dost—friend (though the term can be applied sarcastically too)

Garba—a Gujarati folk dance

Ghazal—classical Indian lyric poems set to music

Goondah—a crook

Haah-haah—"Yeah-yeah"

Hutt—"Move aside"

Hut-teriki—a good-natured exclamation of frustration or surprise

Jao—"Go" or "Get lost"

Kachurputti—trashy or low-rate

Kadhi—a seasoned, buttermilk-based Gujarati soup

Kem cho?—"How are you?"

Kurta pyjama—traditional South Asian male formal dress, consisting of a long-sleeved tunic and leggings—either baggy or slim—tied at the waist with laces

Lathi—a truncheon

Masala—mixed spice

Meethai—sweetmeats

Mirch masala—chili powder

Mushkari—mischief

Paan—traditional Indian chew made from the paan leaf, stuffed with various aromatic ingredients and sometimes tobacco, known for its mild narcotic effects

Pandit—a supremely gifted teacher, artist, or scholar

Paratha—potato and whole-wheat flatbread

Pav bhaji—popular Indian fast food consisting of fried bread and a variety of mixed curried vegetables, and sometimes cheese or dried fruits

Pav vada—popular Indian street food consisting of fried battered mashed potatoes served inside sandwich buns with chutney and chilies

Phadda-phut—an onomatopoeic expression of the sound of slapping someone, or a slang term for "rapidly"

Puri—a deep-fried puffed bread, small and round

Roti—traditional Indian flatbread

Rupiya—rupees

Salwaar kameez—the female version of the kurta pyjama (see above); usually worn with a long sash around the neck as a scarf or over the head as a veil

Sambhar—a spicy lentil-based South Indian soup or dal, a staple of the South Indian diet

Tamasha—ruckus, a scene

Tava—a griddle

Thodu—"A little bit"

Ustad—a Persian honorific for well-regarded artists, teachers, and musicians

Wah-re-wah—an expression of wonderment, amazement, or delight

Yaar—equivalent to the American slang "dude" or "man," used as informal address

Zopadpatti—slum

Acknowledgments

I'd like to thank all those who helped in creating this book. Among them are my teachers Rita Williams, Gina Nahai, and Shelly Lowenkopf at the University of Southern California; senior acquisitions editor Jodi Warshaw for her belief in this book, and the entire team at Amazon Publishing; my excellent editors David Downing, Laura Cherkas, and Annlee Ellingson; my wife and no-nonsense critic Susan Antani; novelist Kashmira Sheth for her generosity and insight; readers Melinda Warren, Lois Schmidt, Paul Morrissey, Kent Hayward, and Elizabeth Hurchalla for their longstanding support and keen feedback; and Pappa and Bhabhi, without whom there is no story.